T0132444

The Saladin Affair

A Robbie Cutler Diplomatic Mystery

WILLIAM S. SHEPARD

iUniverse, Inc.
New York   Bloomington

The Saladin Affair
A Robbie Cutler Diplomatic Mystery

Copyright © 2009 William S. Shepard

This is a work of fiction. All of the characters, names, incidents,
organizations, and dialogue in this novel are either the products
of the author's imagination or are used fictitiously.

iUniverse books may be ordered through booksellers or by contacting:

iUniverse
1663 Liberty Drive
Bloomington, IN 47403
www.iuniverse.com
1-800-Authors (1-800-288-4677)

ISBN: 978-1-4401-8752-0 (pbk)
ISBN: 978-1-4401-8753-7 (ebk)

Printed in the United States of America

iUniverse rev. date: 11/10/2009

For those who upheld the rule of law.

"Military necessity does not admit of cruelty - that is, the infliction of suffering for the sake of suffering or for revenge, nor of maiming or wounding except in fight, nor of torture to extort confessions." Article 16, General Orders No. 100, "Instructions for the Government of Armies of the United States in the Field" (The Lieber Code): Approved by President Abraham Lincoln, and issued by order of the Secretary of War, April 24, 1863.

"It is good, I think, that we should have to bestir ourselves from time to time to protect our liberties, as our ancestors did on many occasions in the past. If we take these rights for granted, if we accept them as a matter of course, we may simply fritter them away, and end by losing them, and possibly deserving to lose them. And so I would suggest to you that you not be discouraged, nor even be unduly concerned if basic human rights are under attack. These are rights which thrive in vindication, and each generation better understands them and their significance if it has to think them through for itself. We are given a great opportunity today, to which I think we will measure up, if the past is any guide. Like the barons at Runnymede, like Coke and Locke and Otis and Adams and Madison and many others whose names are lost to fame, we may be able to make our own contribution to that ancient concept which has rallied the spirits of free Englishmen and Americans for many centuries - the law of the land."

Dean Erwin N. Griswold, *The Fifth Amendment Today* 51-52,
Harvard University Press, Cambridge, 1962.

ACKNOWLEDGEMENTS

I owe a considerable debt of gratitude to Mrs. Astra Pavlovskis for her encouragement to write in the Riga setting, and then for her patience in supplying the background for that setting. My particular thanks go to Ambassador James Holmes, who was the American Ambassador to Latvia 1998-2001, for his detailed help, particularly regarding the presentation of credentials in Riga. It is his ceremony that I describe here - minus the reflections on murder, of course!

All wine lovers are indebted to Christian Moueix of Château Petrus and other fine properties in France and California, Decanter Magazine's "Man Of The Year" for 2008. I recall his kindness in giving me a private glimpse of the vineyards of Pomerol when I lived in Bordeaux. I also particularly value the morning when he showed me around Château Magdelaine in St. Emilion, sharing insights into the estates of the region as we strolled through the vineyards. My gratitude is increased by his kind permission to use a label from his Dominus Winery in California's Napa Valley for the front cover of this book.

It is tempting to assign an active role to Shakespeare in the events described in the Prologues, but that is a temptation best resisted. The Bard of Avon should continue to rest in the shadows, his bones and spirit undisturbed, as he directed. The memory of Edward Alleyn, however, suggests no such restriction. I am glad to assign a new role to Marlowe's main actor, one that bridges the gap between Marlowe and Donne, as Alleyn did during his lifetime.

There are several new sources of information dealing with the literary age of Tudor and Stuart England. I have found Asquith's *Shadowplay: The Hidden Beliefs and Coded Politics of William Shakespeare*, Public Affairs, New York 2005, to be particularly useful. I am grateful to the author for her suggestion that Shakespeare might have taken Robert Cecil as his actual model for *Richard III*. Similarly, Stubbs's *John Donne, The Reformed Soul*, W.W. Norton, New York 2007, is a thorough and helpful consideration of the life and times of Dr. Donne. Park Honan's *Christopher Marlowe, Poet & Spy*, Oxford University Press, New York 2005, does not attempt the impossible task of explaining all of Marlowe's life and death, but it casts much illumination along the way, particularly on the shadowy world of Walsingham's spies.

CHARACTERS

Prologues:
Christopher Marlowe
Edward Alleyn
Dr. John Donne

American Officials on Air Force Two:
Secretary of State Ronald Adams. Pamela Adams
Missy Bronson, secretary to the Secretary of State
Assistant Secretary for European Affairs Donna Palmer
Sam Jardine, Diplomatic Security
Charley Sherburne, Department of State Press Spokesman
Robbie Cutler, Special Assistant. Sylvie Marceau Cutler
Ron Jackson, Team Leader, Executive Secretariat.

Dublin:
Ambassador to Ireland Mary McGowan
Embassy Dublin DCM George Smiley
Embassy Dublin Political Counselor Frank Sulivan
Embassy Dublin Administrative Officer Bob Starett
Prime Minister of Ireland (*Taoiseach*) Thomas O'Bryan
Robert Dillman, Irish Intelligence Officer
Kelly Martin, Trinity College, Lecturer in Celtic Studies

Moscow:
Dmitri Sergeivitch Popolov, Russian Intelligence Officer

Riga:
Ambassador to Latvia Rudolphe Carlisle
Embassy Riga First Secretary Roger Saunders
Embassy Riga Consul Stan Bartlett
Inspector Juris Jurovits, Latvian State Security

London:
Embassy London Political Counselor Joshua Running Deer
Audrey Turner, British Foreign Service

Waziristan and Paris/Moscow:
Osama bin Laden
Ayman al-Zawahiri
Hassan al-Massoud

Cape Ann, Massachusetts:
"Uncle Seth" Cutler

Contents

PROLOGUE

THE PURCHASER WORE A GREEN doublet with ruffled sleeves, an outer leather jerkin to fend off the cold, breeches, and hose fastened by ribbons that matched his doublet. Fastidious, carefully shaven, perfumed and fashionable, he dressed for comfort and for show. The new silks of his doublet announced a measure of prosperity; his worn woolen undergarments would have shown that prosperity to be recent indeed.

He was an educated man who commanded interest, not noble, but surely accomplished. His wit was a ready weapon. His bearing commanded respectful attention in any gathering where merit was measured for its own sake. That there were few such gatherings in the reign of Her Majesty Queen Elizabeth was unfortunate. That such men existed at all in Tudor England despite the tides of religious controversy that equated religion with treason or loyalty, would astonish the world for generations. But the uncertain times did create opportunities.

His reputation was growing. He was a prodigy, not anchored to class, for he had come a very long way from his start as a shoemaker's son in Canterbury. An ornament at The King's School there, he had won a rare scholarship at Corpus Christi College, Cambridge, where his writing had begun in earnest, despite the tavern temptations of Trumpington Street. Not for him the religious fervor that would soon flourish there, at Corpus Christi and Emmanuel Colleges. For now, Shakespeare aside, Kit Marlowe

1

was regarded by many as the ornament of the age. His *Tamburlaine, Jew of Malta, Edward the Second,* and *The Tragical History of Doctor Faustus* had electrified London and helped create the theater, a real theater, rising far beyond the bloody stage spectacles of recent times, and the beloved miracle plays of the church period.

Soon he hoped to give all of his attention to his writing, and give up the hazardous work that he had begun under Sir Francis Walsingham. Truth to tell, he was no longer entirely comfortable in his own conscience with the results of his trips to France and Flushing in the low countries, the lists of Corpus Christi and other Cambridge men that had been compiled who were secret supporters of the old religion. Well, treason was treason. But religion was religion, and his doubts were growing.

The Year of Our Lord 1592 was a time for discretion. He was now 28 years of age. There had been too many warnings and close calls already. Marlowe shivered as he recalled the rumors that had been current at Cambridge during his absences while enrolled there, and the suspicion that he intended to attend the English Catholic college in Reims, France. It had taken an unprecedented intervention by the Privy Council itself attesting to his work "in the Queen's service," for that suspicion to be allayed, so that Marlowe could be awarded his M.A. in 1587.

But more recently, there had been other dangerously close calls. He had been called in and questioned closely more than once. Were the times changing again? For it was all against the background of the times and the succession. Guess wrong, and it was your neck. Not to mention, your immortal soul.

Marlowe looked long and carefully at the oak desk. He measured its details, the sloping front for writing, with pigeon holes on the sides of the lid for ink bottles and quills. Substantial but not too heavy, the legless desk was designed for travel, not for standing in a room. It would fit easily on a table, and would then be just high enough so that he could write upon it with comfort, without leaning over unduly. He could settle back on his bench and reflect between times, and then as inspiration served resume his writing with comfort on the sloping surface. He stroked his chin and nodded appreciatively. The desk suited him. Practical, solid and well made, it would not attract undue attention.

The carved decoration on the front lid was simple and mannerly: a dragon *couchant* facing a lion. Nothing quite suggested royal arms. The placement and attitudes were wrong for that. The choice of motifs, particularly the Tudor dragon, should if challenged be seen as a flattering compliment to power, not an attempt to appropriate the royal arms.

Marlowe opened the front lid, which opened backwards. There was a single deep drawer, with space for files for sharpening the quills, and for paper, and wax for seals. Carved motifs on the back shelf of the drawer showed five songbirds. Beneath them was a crescent moon, its concave shape angled upwards so that its tips pointed towards the first two carved birds.

He placed the desk back on the table and smiled. "Your design, of course, Master Sparrow?"

"Yes. We were five brothers that started out. Jonathan, William, Charles, Seth, and myself, Peter. Now I'm the last. It goes on all my work."

The purchaser fell silent for a moment. It would be almost rude to pry. So many lost members of their families that death was commonplace. It certainly had been for him.

"Primus, tertius, quintus. So, Peter Quintus."

Peter Sparrow smiled and was silent. Let these playwrights have their folly. As long as they paid good money for his work.

"Now, Master Sparrow, once again show me how the wooden spring works. Or rather, the springs." He had sketched for Sparrow the basic design, based on desks he had seen in France. The French court, and then the moneyed classes who favored the new religion, had been fascinated by the secret compartments that a Medici queen had introduced in her personal furniture. At first merely fashionable, secret compartments had been necessary at least since the St. Bartholomew's Day Massacre twenty years before. The civil war that followed required French carpenters to adapt their work to the requirements for secrecy of the times. The mechanisms became more and more ingenious. It was said that sometimes the clients themselves could not find all of the hidden drawers in their own furniture. In that case a later generation might suffer or profit from the revelation of a long forgotten secret drawer.

Peter Sparrow opened the desk lid carefully. "It is as you wished, Master Marlowe, with hidden drawers. The crescent moon holds the spring in place," he said. "In turn, the hidden section is held in place by a slot of wood. By pushing the crescent moon, the wooden spring is released and descends, pushing aside the slot of wood that holds the hidden section in place. You see, like this." He pressed the carved moon lightly, and with a slight click the wooden spring descended, dislodging the hidden slot of wood below. A lower second drawer rose up within the desk from beneath the drawer space. Facing the front at an angle, it would secure objects the same length and width as the desk drawer itself.

Peter Sparrow smiled in satisfaction. It was natural to worry at the last moment that it might not work. But it had, perfectly. Then he closed the front lid.

"Now as to the second hidden drawer," he said. "It only works when the first hidden drawer is open. With that open, the hook beneath that drawer which holds the second hidden drawer in place is disengaged. It then can be opened, like this." He pressed the carved dragon figure on the front lid directly, and a second hidden drawer slid open, this time from the bottom of the desk directly backwards. "You see, now the second spring can be activated."

The carpenter slid the second drawer back into the desk, where with a slight click it stayed. Then he opened the front lid and lowered the first hidden drawer until, with another click, the wooden slot securing the drawer and its false lower drawer slid into place.

He closed the front lid and pressed the carved dragon figure. Nothing happened. "You see?"

His customer nodded. "Yes. Ingenious. You have followed my instruction perfectly. But won't the second hidden drawer be noticed?" The first drawer and its mechanism were based on a desk that Marlowe had seen in France. The second hidden drawer was Sparrow's own design.

"It can't be, even if anyone had the wit to look, which isn't very likely. It is carved into the hollow of the bottom of the desk. It is not really a separate drawer at all. It is the bottom of the desk itself that is sliding out. So that when the first hidden drawer is revealed, what lies under it seems to be only the desk bottom."

"Did you create the desk by yourself, or do others know its secrets?"

"My joiner, Carrington, helped with the final assembly. It was only with the spring for the first hidden drawer. After I had finished with the deeper second one in the false bottom, I called him from the other room. One man's reach is just sufficient to install either spring, of course, although it proved rather awkward setting the first one. I used a few oaths myself while trying, before I called him in. And Carrington is curious by nature. All matters considered, I thought it best to involve him in the project. There is no reason for him to suppose that a second hidden drawer exists. In fact, it occurred to me that having a witness for the first false drawer might be prudent, proof that there was just one such hidden drawer. The second hidden spring I had of course already placed by myself."

"Are there other desks that you have made like this one?"

"No. However, the basic desk design is not uncommon, and the way times are, I'm sure that others will outfit them with a secret drawer. Perhaps some have done so already. But as you ordered, the design for the second drawer is unique."

"Well done indeed, Master Sparrow. That will serve nicely." He opened his purse and took out coins to pay for the purchase. He thought for a moment, fingering and then dropping a shilling back into the purse, and then added a new glistening half crown for good measure. He looked Sparrow straight in the eyes.

"Remember our bargain. No more like this one will be made." He was too much the realist to suppose that Sparrow would not profit from the basic idea and make more desks with single hidden drawers. The times would surely create a greater demand. But the second hidden drawer must at all costs remain their secret.

The carpenter smiled broadly in appreciation, and nodded in agreement. The second hidden drawer would never be made again. Returning the compliment, he scooped the coins into his own purse without biting them.

"Would you like to me summon Carrington, to carry this for you?"

"No, thank you." He already seemed elsewhere. He picked up the desk and walked out into the teeming street, both highway and sewer, his body lurching from time to time to avoid the contents of chamber pots being emptied from upper windows.

CHAPTER ONE -
Changes In The Wind

IT WAS GOING TO BE another stormy session before the Senate Appropriations Committee. The past committee chairmen whose portraits hung on the walls of the United States Capitol Appropriations Committee hearing room seemed in worse temper than usual. Was it the lighting, or were the frown lines on their foreheads somewhat deeper today? They certainly seemed more dispeptic, setting an unpleasant example for their twenty-eight living colleagues, who were filing into the room purposefully. Their young, earnest aides carried folders, each struggling to get his Senator's attention for one last moment for the acute observation, the killer question, something, anything that might be the lead in tomorrow's Washington *Post* account of this hearing. It was hard to seize attention in the largest Senate Committee, but they tried.

For this was the realm of budgets, policies, and priorities, all from the proxy Secretaries of State who sat on this committee and its dozen subcommittees, now once again fashionable assignments both for their powerful budgetary focus, and in the parent committee because an unpopular war had shown Senators the advantages of clear thinking in international affairs. Not that lucidity was often on display in this Congressional session, the actual Secretary wryly mused, as he looked around the room before taking his seat in the witness chair.

At least, reform on the organization of the Senate Appropriations

Committee had made sense. He had to give them that. For years, the State Department budget had been considered by a subcommittee along with those of Justice, Commerce, and the Judiciary. But finally, with the 109th Congress which convened in January, 2005, a new subcommittee had been established for State, Foreign Operations and Related Programs. State's budget would now be taken up in a subcommittee with a subtext of international relations rather than line item expenditures. The Secretary hoped that the reorganization would insulate the Department more from the absurdities of spending cuts when funding State wasn't fashionable. It certainly might now help her secure adequate funding for the Foreign Service, which the previous administration had neglected for years, to the nation's cost. The Secretary was prepared to make that case right now, at this hearing. She looked forward to it, silently rehearsing her arguments.

The Secretary of State glared at her law school classmate and moot court adversary from forty years ago, Senator Alvin Maxwell, now Chairman of the Senate Appropriations Committee. Oddly, each still remembered that competition vividly, but each also distinctly remembered having won it. Senator Maxwell glared back, and then, realizing that photographers were present, altered his expression while sweeping off his glasses and, with a practiced smile, half rose from his chair, extending his hand. Taking the cue, the Secretary quickly left her chair, circled the witness table and strode towards the raised semicircular bar which separated the Senators from the mortals involved in the hearing.

She got about halfway across the room. A dull, unremitting heaviness in her upper arms and shoulders, followed by a crushing chest pain, disabled her and made her unsteady and witless. She reached for a chair to steady herself, but pulled the chair over as she fell heavily onto the floor. She saw a beautiful young girl, in a silk dress, coming to meet her. It was her granddaughter Nancy, lost in the second Gulf War, and this was a birthday party at home in Charleston. She smiled and extended her hand. Now garbed in dazzling white, Nancy took it.

— — — — — — — —

Robbie Cutler glanced at his fellow passengers in the half empty State Department shuttle bus. He smiled as he recalled the telephone call that had snatched him away from language training at the Foreign Service Institute in Arlington, Virginia, just across the Potomac River from Washington.

This was his very first month of Greek language training - his and his wife Sylvie's, that is - and they had been seated around a long rectangular table with other students, straining to hear the instructor's insistent pronunciation of an everyday phrase. "It's what the Greek people say when they are having a drink together. Like your English, 'To Your Health' or 'Bottoms Up.'

"Now try it again. 'Stin-Hee YA Sas!' No, Mr. Cutler. It is not 'Stinny YA Sas,' all at the back of the throat. Now listen well. You have a drink with a friend and this is what you say, 'Stin-Hee.' Expel some breath there, THEN 'Ya Sas ...'"

Robbie tried hard to hear what Mr. Petropoulos was saying, and he was mispronouncing, but the grins on the faces of several fellow students hadn't helped. He stared, not for the first time, at the wall behind the instructor's head. It was decorated with pictures of Greece cut from magazines and newspaper travel supplements. Colorful windmills, beach scenes and overhead pictures of the Acropolis and the Temple at Sounion inspired the students. Well, if that was the purpose, Robbie thought, they succeeded. The pictures made it easier to picture yourself not struggling over pronunciation or grammar here in northern Virginia, but actually using a memorized or, increasingly as time went on, an improvised phrase in Greek, to the delight of your companions and the astonishment of the local waiter, who had you pegged as a clueless American. Mr. Petropoulos cleared his voice. It was but one step removed from the dreaded last stage of impatience, finger rapping on the desk.

Then Robbie was rescued. The rap had come, not on the instructor's desk, but on the classroom door. It was a rather perfunctory and insistent rap, at that, most unusual at the Foreign Service Institute, where language training created its own reality of time and space, in order to encourage the student's total immersion into another culture.

In Robbie's case, assigned to Embassy Athens as Political Officer via language training, it was a wonderful opportunity to enhance the Greek slang he had picked up somehow during his father's tour as Consul General in Istanbul, when Robbie had spent a summer touring the Greek islands, and learn modern Greek properly in congenial surroundings. At least, that earlier experience had given him some practice, and some understanding of the way that the language was supposed to sound, good assets for the formal training he was now receiving.

Besides the Cutlers, there were six students who were learning Greek prior to their assignment to diplomatic missions in Greece or Cyprus. That meant the Embassy in Athens or the Consulate in Thessaloniki, Greece, or the Embassy in Nicosia, Cyprus. There were two lieutenant colonels assigned as Assistant Defense Attaches, a somber political analyst leaving Washington - or was it Langley? - for some overseas seasoning, the just assigned Commercial Officer for Athens and his wife, and a newly minted Vice Consul for Nicosia.

It was a senior secretary with a worried look who peered through the door and said to the instructor, "Sorry to disturb you, Mr. Petropoulos. It's a call for Mister Cutler. Ambassador Adams!" She emphasized the name, but didn't have to. At the very word "Ambassador," everyone in the room sat up just a bit straighter. The instructor coughed, and nodded towards the door. Sylvie looked perplexed. Robbie shrugged his shoulders and raised his eyebrows a bit. The last thing on his mind, as he struggled with Greek, was a call from the former Ambassador in Paris during his Bordeaux assignment. He got up and left the room, following the briskly pacing secretary to a private office to take the call.

"Hello, Robbie. It's Ronald Adams here. Sorry to have called out of the blue."

"Yes, sir. Good to hear from you."

"Robbie, I've got something I'd rather not discuss over the phone. Can you meet me at the Department in an hour, no, make that two hours, say at 1:15. I'll be in the courtesy office of the European Assistant Secretary, on the sixth floor."

"Of course, Mr. Ambassador. I'll be there."

"Fine. Sorry to be cryptic. Oh, and my very best wishes to your bride, Sylvie. Pamela and I remember her so well. Your gain is French television's loss."

It was not an empty courtesy. When Ambassador Ronald Adams was in Paris, he knew that Sylvie Marceau was one of the best French national television news reporters. He and his wife Pamela Adams had watched her television news reports frequently then. Although Robbie and Sylvie were now newlyweds, they didn't fit the template of a diplomatic couple - if a template could be said to exist, in these days of dual diplomatic careers and tandem assignments. It used to be that women were not fully accepted into the Foreign Service. Then, when they were admitted, marriage involved resignation. Now, a few class action lawsuits and several generations later, women followed their own careers, and if both husband and wife were Foreign Service Officers, attempts were made to place both officers at the same Embassy. Sylvie was not a Foreign Service Officer, but she fully intended to continue her television news career, as circumstances permitted.

Ambassador Adams rang off. Robbie returned to the language class, now in total disarray, and made his excuses to the instructor. He had unexpectedly been called to a meeting at the Department. Sylvie saw Robbie to the door, and agreed that she should finish the day's language instruction. Robbie would take the shuttle bus back from Main State when his meeting was over. Probably nothing much to it, but Robbie liked Ambassador Adams, and was glad to help him for the short run. He hoped that nothing had come up that would force him to lose an extended part of his Greek language training. Up to a certain point, but not beyond, you could do double duty with the language books and CDs that were provided with the course. A few weeks lost, and with real application, you could just get yourself back to snuff. Beyond that, it would be a year - no, an assignment too - wasted. Then you'd be back on the assignment roster with nothing in prospect, and the best jobs already taken. Well, no sense worrying. He'd find out soon enough.

When was the last time he had seen Ambassador Adams? It was a few years previously, when the Adamses had hosted a dinner party at their official residence in Paris. It was during the good early days of his assignment to the Consulate General in Bordeaux. He had just met Sylvie Marceau, then a journalist for the regional French newspaper *Sud-Ouest*. Robbie had hosted one of the tables at that Paris dinner. It had been a meeting of consular offices from posts around France and the Caribbean. But shortly afterwards, the Basque terrorist ETA group had tried to assassinate Robbie in Bordeaux where he served as Acting Consul General.

Robbie remembered that with a shudder, and the fact that his sister Evalyn had very nearly been the unintended target of a bomb planted in his car. It was after that episode that Robbie had been reassigned to the Embassy in Budapest, for his own safety, it had been said. That was a coveted assignment, and one that had recalled the diplomatic past of his father, a retired career Foreign Service Officer who had been assigned to the American Legation there during the hectic, heroic days of the 1956 Hungarian Revolution.

He had joined Sylvie for a short vacation, during a trip she made to Prague to cover the state visit to the Czech Republic of then French President Jacques Chirac. The reunion was more than romantic. When he returned to Budapest, Robbie and Sylvie were engaged to be married.

And then - some idyllic honeymoon! They were in the scenic Dordogne region of France when family history from the Second World War came alive once again. Cave searchers in that famous region, honeycombed by cave etchings and paintings, had found the remains of a person long dead. Forensic evidence confirmed that the body was female. But it was an inscribed silver disc that identified the dead woman for Robbie. His Great Uncle Seth, as a young intelligence officer in London during the Second World War, had given the silver disc to his *fiancee* before her last mission, parachuting into Occupied France. Solving her murder - and stopping a determined killer from silencing Robbie permanently - had made theirs no ordinary honeymoon.

And so, after a welcome visit home to New England, Robbie and Sylvie had looked forward to their assignment to Embassy Athens, and to their reinsertion into the regular diplomatic world, following so many murderous detours. And it had seemed to be going smoothly according to plan. As the shuttle bus neared the employee entrance of Main State on 23rd and D Streets in Washington's Foggy Bottom, the driver carefully noting each lowered traffic barrier and nodding to the security guards, Robbie hoped that it still would be going according to plan, a plan that included a family. But why jump at conclusions? After all, he did look forward to seeing Ambassador Adams.

Robbie stepped off the shuttle bus and walked briskly to the entrance of the State Department. He was in good time. It was exactly twelve thirty, perfect for a quick luncheon in the downstairs State Department cafeteria before keeping his appointment with Ambassador Adams. He checked through security, emptying his pockets, and then turned left, to take the escalator down to the cafeteria.

"Hi, Robbie! How are things?" It was Stan Bartlett, who had served with him as Vice Consul at the Consulate General in Bordeaux. A very good man, take charge guy, Robbie remembered.

"Couldn't be better, Stan. Have you had lunch? No? Good, please join me. I'm on a break from language training."

"So you came over here for lunch? Not likely. Better food over in Virginia, isn't there?"

Robbie nodded. "Used to be, when FSI was in Rosslyn. Then there was a choice of places for lunch. Anyway, you're right. I'm here for a meeting." He let it drop. They checked through the hamburger line, helped themselves to soft drinks, and found a table.

Along the way, Robbie saw several persons he knew, from his A-100 entering Foreign Service Class a few years previously. He nodded back, juggling his tray. And over there at a full table for six was Arnold Johnson, who had been second man, Deputy Chief of Mission, at the Embassy in Budapest during Robbie's tour as Political Officer there. He was talking with his neighbor earnestly, and was smiling. Maybe that meant that he had gotten his own embassy.

At Johnson's stage in life, Robbie had observed, senior officers either turned ingrown and bureaucratic, which meant they had seen the handwriting on the wall and were making their retirement calculations, or they were still hopeful of getting an ambassadorship. Newer shirts and a fine fitted suit, as Arnold Johnson was now wearing, were evidence of the latter. The broad grin on his face meant that he had heard good news. Ah yes. The man he was talking with was a midgrade officer that Robbie knew slightly from the H Bureau, Congressional Relations, who had once visited Budapest with a Congressional Delegation. That might mean that he and Johnson were planning Johnson's Senate confirmation hearings. No wonder it was invigorating to come over to Main State from time to time. It kept the juices and ambition flowing.

Robbie and Stan took an empty table near the courtyard window. "Haven't seen you since Bordeaux, Robbie. How did you like Budapest?"

"Just fine, when the Russian Mafia wasn't trying to do me in. I guess you know that Sylvie and I are married."

"No surprise there. A wonderful girl. Much too good for the likes of you."

"Guess I wrote your personnel report too soon! But you're right. We were in the Dordogne for our honeymoon. Do you remember George Nivins, the British Consul General in Bordeaux when we were there? He was helpful to me in getting some background to solve a murder case when we were in the Dordogne."

Stan whistled. "So even on your honeymoon you attract trouble! Yes, I remember George. A good, solid man. It was idiotic that we ever closed the Consulate General in Bordeaux. More false economy. That used to be the best listening post for tracking Basque terrorism." Robbie nodded in agreement.

"Where did you serve after Bordeaux, Stan?"

"Back in the European Bureau. Now I'm getting itchy to get out of Washington. I've finished my language training, and I'm just doing some reading in on the desk. Then it's off to Latvia, to be Consul at our Embassy in Riga."

"Terrific news. We'll both be in Europe at the same time. Maybe we can swap holidays I'd love to see the Baltic region, and you could check into Athens to see us. When my Greek language training is over next year, I mean."

"That would be great. Well, sorry to rush. I'm also doing a bit of handholding on the desk. They've got enough to do with a state visit coming up, so I'm babysitting the ambassador-designate through his meetings around town prior to his confirmation hearings."

"Not bad duty. At least you'll get some insights into what Washington has in store for Riga. No weapons of mass destruction there, I hope?"

"No, none at all, except possibly for Ambassador-designate Carlisle. Rudolphe Carlisle. I'd never heard of him, but then I don't track politics. He was a big contributor in the last election."

"Where did he make his money? Or did he inherit it?"

"That's the interesting part. He made it, at Osborne's. From stock clerk to appraiser to auctioneer to self-taught authority on European paintings, early Renaissance, I think. He did well enough to open his own New York firm, and then a few discoveries and sales later ... well, he won't have to rely on a government salary, let's put it that way."

"How will he be to work for."

"Well, hard to say exactly. He only arrived a few days ago. I just met him yesterday. To me, the first impression is that he is tough. Very tough. Demanding. Insistent, rapid fire. Maybe he's just trying to set the stage, establish some ground rules while he feels his way in a profession that he doesn't understand. New appointees are sometimes like that. Meanwhile, I keep looking for a human side, beyond the surface polish. But he seems to be a flashlight that only shines upward. If he ranks you, you hardly exist. I expect he'll turn on the charm, though, with those he considers his equals, if anybody fits that term."

"Well, you'll survive, I'm sure. Probably even prosper. How did he get Riga?"

"Luck of the draw. It was open and offered. I don't think he is Baltic."

"How about your own assignment there?"

"Sheer good fortune. And I mean it. I researched the place before bidding on the Consul's job there. Even read the post reports in the Foreign Service Lounge. Friendly, tough people. Rich history, and well disposed towards the United States, particularly since we never recognized their forced incorporation into the Soviet Union. And now they have a new start. Independent once again, and Russia's neighbor. Potential for trouble there, of course. The recent Soviet police state past still floats about the country like Caesar's ghost. But they are trying to modernize, and join the twenty-first century. The recession, though, has really set them back."

"Yes, all around the EUR portfolio, but it has hit the Eastern Europeans and the Baltic states particularly hard."

"Yes. By the way, I saw our old boss getting onto an elevator an hour ago. Ronald Adams. He looked great. He saw me and waved in my direction. Well, he had a long run in Paris. The Adamses were well liked. It was a tough assignment in some ways, but if we and the French are pretty much back on an even keel, they should get a lot of credit. Good people. Anyway, the scuttlebutt around EUR hallways is that he may be back for good."

"His assignment over?"

"Changing jobs. He may be moving up. With the death of the Secretary, who knows? So when you see him - don't act surprised, Robbie - I saw that expression on your face when I mentioned his name - remember the old Bordeaux gang."

"Will do."

Stan got up and carried his tray over to the cleaning station. Robbie smiled. It really was true that you could pick up confidential information here readily. It was just a matter of knowing where to look, whom to talk to, and picking up the clues that casual visitors would miss. He finished his soft drink and the last few French fries, and wondered just exactly what his meeting with Ambassador Adams would involve. But first, he strolled over to the State Department Credit Union office and cashed a check. That had been his New Year's Resolution: don't use the credit cards for living expenses. He'd need the cash for grocery shopping on the way home. Now, would that wine store near the Safeway count as living expenses, or could he use the card for the Bordeaux wine specials he'd seen advertised in the *Post*?

— — — — — — — —

Rudolphe Carlisle glanced up, and smiled as Stan Bartlett entered the room, several minutes early. Time to ease up a bit, after all, this young fellow would be a colleague in Riga, probably handle a fair amount of chores. Carlisle wasn't too sure what a Consul did, exactly. Surely the Ambassadorial course at the Foreign Service Institute would get into those mechanics. It sounded rather pedestrian, but probably necessary. It would be just as well, having given him a dose or two of what former employees at Osborne's used to call "the treatment," nothing quite right, demanding, but not to the extent that any complaint would be justified, this side of misery with a sardonic smile attached. Come to think of it, when they got to Riga, Bartlett would certainly pass on to other career people his first impressions of the new Ambassador Carlisle. So there was no point in alienating the new Consul. It was time to ease up a bit, and get his loyalty.

"Who are we seeing this afternoon, Stan?"

"Well, first, we'll go upstairs for a bureau overview, at one o'clock. Then, fifth floor briefings. I've scheduled a briefing by the desk officer and country director. Basic stuff, on the state of our bilateral relations with Latvia, and then the regional picture, how Latvia and her Baltic neighbors are getting along with Russia, mainly, some unfinished business from their days inside the Soviet Union."

"Whom are we meeting with first, on the sixth floor?"

"The Assistant Secretary for European Affairs, Donna Palmer. She was in Riga as Ambassador for the President's visit a year ago. Top career officer. She's really pressed for time today, so it's just a short meet and greet. I thought you would want to do that right away. Then, next week, after your briefings, there will be time for a longer meeting with her on substantive matters."

"Good idea. We won't expose my inexperience too soon! Where else has she served?" Carlisle knew. He was just checking to see if Bartlett had done his homework.

"Largely in EUR territory. She was Consul in Istanbul, Political Officer in Bonn, switching to Berlin when we moved the Embassy, Political Counselor in Warsaw, DCM in Helsinki, then Ambassador in Riga. Of course, she had several tours back in Washington during her career, including one at the Pentagon. Something to do with NATO expansion planning. And she was a DAS, sorry, Deputy Assistant Secretary, for the Congressional Relations Bureau, or 'H' as we call it. She handled the Senate, briefings and confirmations mostly."

"So 'H' is Congressional Relations, and 'EUR' is the European Affairs Bureau."

"Yes, sir, All bureaus and offices have acronyms. It saves time. For what, I'm not sure."

Carlisle shared an ingratiating grin. "That's true in the auction world, too. Where time should be savored, not saved. Lead on, MacDuff!"

— — — — — — — —

Sylvie wished that she were with Robbie. She was dying to know, to be a fly on the wall during his talk with Ambassador Adams. No, that was too undignified. What she would really prefer doing was interviewing Adams on his next assignment, if there was to be one, and scooping everyone else in town! It was obvious from Robbie's whisper to her on leaving FSI that Ambassador Adams had been friendly in his brief telephone call. No, it was more than that. He had been cordial.

Then, thinking things one step further, Robbie had called her cell phone from the State Department and sounded her out on the possibility that Ambassador Adams might have a new job offer in mind. Maybe, all things considered, Adams was moving up in the Department. If so, signing on as a member of his personal staff would be a lifetime career break, one just too good to miss. Sylvie had said, "As your sister Evalyn would say, 'Go for it!'"

She thought of it first as a breaking news story. After all, Ambassador

Adams had still been in Paris last week. So he had come home, and shortly afterwards, had been in touch. It sounded like someone who was assembling a team. And she knew that assembling a team was a favorite Washington pastime. This time, possibly they would be part of it.

What was Adams's background? Money, certainly. Politics, of course. Yes, that was it. A Senator, and a member of the Senate Foreign Relations Committee at that. His wife, Pamela Adams, had been a leading Georgetown hostess. No, probably the leading hostess, when this town still valued them. For years it had been rumored that Adams was headed for a cabinet appointment. Quite possibly the death last week of Secretary of State Chalmers Johnson had opened that possibility. Or maybe, he was moving up, but not all the way. To Deputy Secretary perhaps? How did he stand with the President? Very well indeed, she had heard.

Sylvie let her mind wander for a moment, to all the embassies that might need a changing of ambassadors. It was fun to speculate where he might go, and if he would take Robbie with him. Just as long as it was not to one of the increasingly long list of unaccompanied assignments! She had not left her television career to be a stay at home wife. Far from it.

Well, no use stewing about what she didn't know. Robbie would find out this afternoon what Adams had in mind, and they would have plenty to talk about this evening. If there was anything to talk about. She'd serve a special wine with dinner. "Stin-Hee YA Sas!"

— — — — — — — —

Ambassador Adams rose from his borrowed desk chair and with a smile walked over to the office's open inner door, the one that connected with the Assistant Secretary's waiting room. He had left the door open on purpose, and now had just spotted Assistant Secretary Donna Palmer entering her reception area from her private office. She was seeing to the outside door two visitors whose appointment was just ending.

A determined and focussed career officer in her fifties, Donna Palmer had benefitted from the past sins of the State Department in not giving women a fair share of promotions and the assignments that might have led to them. But if anyone made her own breaks, it was Donna Palmer. She would have bristled at any suggestion of favoritism. When the Secretary's call had come to then Ambassador Palmer, picking her for the senior diplomatic post in the Department dealing with Europe and its manifold diplomatic issues, it was assumed that she would pick a female FSO to be her aide. She had not done so. Competence alone got you an assignment with her. And so she had been annoyed when Robbie Cutler had declined the EUR staff aide position.

"Good to see you, Madam Secretary. I appreciate the loan of an office."

"Not at all, Mr. Ambassador. It's good to see you again. You and Mrs. Adams certainly helped ease our relations with the French. Things haven't gone so smoothly in years."

"Well, I spent summers there, as you know."

"Yes, indeed. Your French is bilingual, and your art discoveries and contributions made you something of an icon."

"Well, we were lucky. When we bought that property and its furnishings in Charentes-Maritimes, I couldn't help but see that some of the pictures were covered with centuries of grime. Heating by wood fires will do that. And then, a century or so of industrial pollution, which nobody seemed to notice in the days before tourism, didn't help. Having them cleaned was a natural impulse. And the experts knew what they were doing. They consulted with me every step of the way. Finding what we did below the grime, though, was a piece of luck."

"Inspired luck, if it was luck. It isn't every day that a Da Vinci is rediscovered."

"Well, I was glad that it was saved. And it belonged in the Louvre, after all."

"No film prospects?"

"Hardly," Ambassador Adams smiled broadly. "Not a blasphemous theme in sight. It's just a brilliant portrait of a young matron and her daughter. A Florentine matron, that is."

"A thoroughly generous thing to do, giving it to the French nation."

"Well, perhaps, thank you," the wealthy man's dismissiveness kicked in, closing the door on a personal conversation that threatened to become embarrassing. "But, you know, the French have tax breaks too."

Assistant Secretary Palmer turned towards the well dressed man on her left. "By the way, have you met Rudolphe Carlisle? He is our Ambassador-designate to Riga."

"Your former post. I've heard of you in art and auction circles of course, Mr. Carlisle. Your knowledge of your field is something of a legend. By the way, you have a good man here in Stan Bartlett," Adams graciously added. The junior officer blushed, a beguiling reaction for a burly, muscular young man who had made the Associated Press second team All American as a sophomore halfback for Baylor. "He was of great help in Bordeaux in a rough period. A coming man, that's for sure."

Bartlett nodded and stammered an appreciative and embarrassed greeting to Ambassador Adams. Who knew you was important at State, where word of mouth reputation was all-important. The comment would be worth something to Bartlett as Carlisle made his future calculations in this unknown diplomatic labyrinth. Beyond that, it was a nice gesture from a nice guy.

"That's for sure. Now, he has me scheduled to meet with the fifth floor experts. I'd better get up to snuff before I come back up here and try to talk intelligently with you about Riga!"

She smiled. "You'll do just fine. Is there any word yet on your confirmation hearings?"

Carlisle shrugged. "They tell me in Congressional Relations that the Foreign Relations Committee has finished its backlog of policy hearings, so the decks are cleared. Sooner rather than later, I hope."

There was a moment's silence, as Stan Bartlett later remembered, which was clearly understood by Adams, Carlisle, and Assistant Secretary Palmer. It was on the tip of Carlisle's tongue to ask Adams whether confirmation hearings might be in the offing for him as well. But he dismissed the idea, to the almost visible relief of Assistant Secretary Palmer.

Carlisle and Bartlett left. Turning to the Assistant Secretary, Ambassador Adams very softly asked if she were free for a few minutes, received a muttered assent, and with a graceful wave of her arm, they entered her private office.

— — — — — — — —

Robbie Cutler entered the Assistant Secretary's outer office and went to the appointments secretary's desk. "Hello. I'm Robbie Cutler. Ambassador Adams called, and asked me to meet him here. I believe the Assistant Secretary gave him a courtesy office?" A little stilted, as were most conversations in State. Oh well, at least it didn't have to be in Greek. Not yet, anyway! Robbie shuddered at the thought of translating for a visiting dignitary in Athens. He'd better get serious and start memorizing those language lessons.

"Yes indeed, Mr. Cutler. His office is over there, past that desk. Perhaps you'd care to wait for him in his office? I'm sure it would be all right. He is just meeting with the Assistant Secretary. Shouldn't be too long."

Robbie stepped inside that office, took a seat, and found there was nothing to read. There was not a magazine in sight, and the morning's papers were already in the wastepaper basket, scanned and discarded. It certainly was a temporary office. Well, there were some of Assistant Secretary Palmer's watercolors on the wall. He went over and had a look. They were actually pretty good, and quite colorful. She had a good eye for detail. Robbie guessed that they were scenes from her previous diplomatic assignments. That medieval city scene could be old town Riga. Behind the desk he also recognized the Brandenburg Gate from Berlin. They were nice touches, an attempt to humanize the tired bookcases and elderly leather chairs and sofa that were standard government issue, even at this fairly senior level. Robbie saw that Ambassador Adams had left his monogrammed briefcase on the desk. Well, no need for it to be secured. There wouldn't be anything classified in it anyway.

There was a flurry of activity behind him, towards the Assistant Secretary's outer office. Robbie turned, and saw Ambassador Adams taking his leave of the Assistant Secretary. They seemed to be cordial. Robbie sensed that they were sealing a deal of some sort. Then Ambassador Adams entered his temporary office, and shut the door carefully before walking, hand extended, over to Robbie.

"Good to see you again, Robbie. And thank you for coming over at such short notice."

"Good to see you again, sir."

They shook hands and sat down facing each other on the leather couch.

"I suppose you have some idea why I called?"

"It would be presumptuous of me to guess, Mr. Ambassador."

"How is your Uncle, Seth Cutler?"

"Fine thank you, sir. We saw him when we returned from the Dordogne. I believe you know about that episode."

Ambassador Adams nodded. "Yes, continuing your skills in crime solving even during your honeymoon. Really quite remarkable. I hope what you found out brought some peace of mind to Seth Cutler."

Robbie nodded. "Thank you, sir. It seems to have done so."

It intrigued Robbie that the one person most people knew of his family was his Great Uncle, Seth Cutler. Well, the entire nation knew about him. Starting as a young intelligence officer in London during the Second World War, Seth Cutler had made a national reputation as an educator in New England. He had stressed at his preparatory school, St. Mark's, equality of education for young women and for black students and other minorities, setting a standard that the nation followed in later decades. Uncle Seth had been *Time Magazine's* "Man Of The Year" and he still, although retired, kept in touch with his former students and retained his keen interest in national intelligence matters. Robbie consulted with Great Uncle Seth from time to time on the cases that fate and his detecting aptitude seemed to throw his way. And during their honeymoon in the Dordogne, Robbie had even been able to unravel the long unsolved mystery of the disappearance and murder of Seth Cutler's *fiancée* during the last phase of the Second World War in Occupied France. His Great Uncle had remained a lifelong bachelor.

"Your Father was also in the Foreign Service, isn't that right? Something of a family tradition?"

Robbie nodded.

"So now you have served in Singapore, Bordeaux, and Budapest?"

"Yes, and now Sylvie and I are in Greek language training, as you know."

"That is what I wanted to talk with you about, Robbie. First, as you may have guessed, I have some news. It is not public and will not be until the White House chooses to make it so. That will be sooner rather than later, I'm sure, given the way that this town fails to keep secrets."

Robbie nodded again. He knew better than to interrupt a monologue at this level.

"The nation has just lost a fine statesman. You know, nobody even knew that she was ill, much less that she had a heart problem. Actually, I don't think that she did. Anyway, she was a fine statesman. She could have been one of the great ones, I think."

Robbie waited.

"The next day, National Security Advisor Goldman called me. All hush hush certainly, but he wanted me to know that the White House had a short list for Secretary of State. Her husband was not on the list, but I was. He wanted me to come back to Washington immediately, for a meeting with the President. There were, he said, three other persons under consideration. Well, I met with the President and Mr. Goldman last night. I got the call first thing this morning. The President has asked me to be the next Secretary of State, and I have accepted."

"Congratulations, sir. That's wonderful news."

"That means that I will need a first-rate staff here. I've taken a very preliminary look at the Secretary of State's office staffing pattern. I have a clear hand, of course. Clearly, there would be a prominent place for you, Robbie. We would give it a month or two until we both see how it works, and then you could carve out that part of office staffing that most interests you.

"I'm sorry about your language training and Athens assignment, but after a stint working in S - another acronym I'm afraid - you'll be able to get any job you want. I'm sure that you will want to talk things over with Sylvie."

"We already have, sir. I'm glad to accept."

"That's wonderful news. Now, this is under wraps until the president's announcement. What I want you to do immediately is to get out the briefing books that were used for the last confirmation hearings. We won't use them, of course, but it will give you a good idea, working through the Executive Secretariat, of what to ask the bureaus to assemble in preparation for my own hearings."

"I'm on it, sir." Good thing he was used to State Department cafeteria food, Robbie thought. It sounded like he would be having a steady diet of it in the months to come.

— — — — — — —

For Osama bin Laden, the appointment of a new American Secretary of State furnished the perfect opportunity for action. No, it was more than that. It was a necessity. This Adams was extremely dangerous precisely because he seemed reasonable. He was a new American face. He was the sort of man who might even recommend closing the prison at Guantanamo. Such a gesture would damage Al Qaeda recruiting. The people needed to be enraged in order to volunteer, and Guantanamo and Abu Ghraib had fed that indignation, the Abu Ghraib pictures being endlessly recycled over thousands of websites throughout the Moslem world. No, Adams must be eliminated, and quickly. The people must clearly see the real, brutal face of the Crusaders.

And so in the mountain fastnesses of Waziristan, the no man's land in Pakistan on the sparsely inhabited Afghanistan frontier, the leaders of Al Qaeda met. The call for the gathering had gone forth the week that the President had announced the Adams appointment as Secretary of State. Osama bin Laden thought it wise to exert his leadership personally from time to tme. His deputy, Ayman al-Zawahiri, had agreed. Now was the opportunity.

Osama bin Laden's wounds had long since healed, and his state of health had stabilized. There was no worry that those meeting him now would conclude that his leadership should in any way be challenged, not here, at least. But there were now several Al Qaeda groups swarming, and unlike the original, their loyalty was increasingly to their own groups. Certainly that had been initially true of Al Qaeda in Mesopotamia. Perhaps, given the need for immediate action and the difficulties of coordination, they had earned a margin of discretion. But a major initiative coming from Al Qaeda's undoubted leaders would reinforce the central authority.

And so, the messengers had gone forth. Bin Laden had long ago learned not to trust any communications except personal messages. The paraphenalia of computer websites, email, telephones, satellite and cell phones, all could be tracked and had been, now with reaction times so quick that their initial use brought great risk. He could no longer even rely on American reluctance to target an area where civilians might be present.

He did not underestimate the enemy, but even bin Laden had been surprised at the extent to which American intelligence resorces had been consolidated since the successful attacks on Washington and New York, "9/11" as the enemy called them. The Americans were well organized, he would give them that. It was necessary to make them waste those resources. And what better way to accomplish that than to strike once again? Confuse the infidel hive and make them swarm in wrong directions while we pursue the goal of purification of our homelands.

He met the visitors in small groups. That way his personality could be brought to bear more forcefully, forging individual loyalties more strongly. It also lessened the security problem, for a few visitors at a time could be thoroughly searched. The danger of someone slipping into a large meeting at the last minute had been eliminated.

There was a further incentive for good security, for it was understood that any incident would involve the immediate punishment of everyone in the group. That had already happened a year or so previously. Al-Zawahiri had not been amused when the Pakistani authorities, finding the small group of dead Al Qaeda operatives after that event, had trumpeted to the Americans that it had been their vigilance that had led to the killings. Well, in an odd sort of way, they had been right. It had after all been their operative who had been detected at the last moment, prompting the killings.

The meetings were emotional. Bin Laden had a word for each visitor, most of whom he had long known and trusted, to the extent anyone was worthy of trust. He spoke as usual in riddles. Anyone who did not understand the rich literature and fables of their heritage would be mystified by their conversations. But they all understood that there would soon be a new initiative, this time once again aimed directly at the Americans. Everyone would then understand that Al Qaeda's silence had been merely tactical, a time for further planning, an interval between spectacular missions. Their preparations had been carefully made. With everything in place, they could choose when to strike.

Bin Laden saw no need to inform his visitors that assets were already in place for a strike against the American leadership. Let everyone think that orders were just now being given. Given the difficulties of their hand to hand communications, if there were any leaks, the Americans would assume that it would take weeks for plans to be underway.

It was time to launch Operation Salah al-Din.

CHAPTER TWO -
Three To Get Ready

ROBBIE WAS LEAVING THE OFFICE early. They were getting a very early start from Andrews Air Force Base the next morning in any event, and he had doublechecked with the Executive Secretariat, both Ron Jackson, the team leader who was accompanying them on the first trip by Secretary Adams, and the assigned duty officer who would pull whatever cables came in overnight into a special folder for Robbie's attention. If anything urgent came up, Robbie would be called and then would stop by the State Department to pick up the message. But for now the diplomatic landscape seemed fairly serene, or as serene as it ever got.

The idea was to arrive in Dublin early evening local time, in time for drinks with key Embassy personnel, and the Ambassador's informal welcoming dinner. They would have a full working day aboard Air Force Two, get their land legs and briefings over by the end of the day, and retire for the night. Then the official visit would begin the next day. Fewer mistakes would be made when the principals were fresh. That, at least, was what was said. The real story was that Secretary Adams hated sleeping on airplanes, which upset his metabolism for days. He wanted to try a daytime flight instead. The early departure, plus the late informal dinner, should ensure a good night's sleep in Dublin. Not a bad idea, Robbie thought. It was worth a try. But what it probably would actually ensure was a grumpier and more rumpled than usual press corps, a dozen of whom would accompany the Secretary on the trip.

Robbie looked carefully around his office, a small afterthought on the seventh floor, part of the Secretary's suite of offices. He had, however two unusual perks. One was a side door that led directly into the Secretary's private office. The second was nearly as rare nowadays, an actual window looking down towards leafy Constitution and Independence Avenues. It was too far to spot the Mall, and the Lincoln Memorial was usually blocked by tree canopies, but the idea was restful anyway. He swept all of the files on his desk into his arm and placed them in the top drawer of his safe. He kept nothing classified inside his desk, but from force of habit, he checked every drawer anyway. Nothing there to worry about.

He made sure that his computer was turned off. Then he had a few words with the Secretary's Executive Assistant, Clark Framsen, in theory Robbie's boss, and the man who wrote his annual efficiency report. The Executive Assistant, a street smart Philadelphian and a senior career officer, was heading for his own ambassadorial post before the end of the year. That is what happened to good Executive Assistants at this rarified level. Clark Framsen was a holdover from the previous Secretary, and his departure for language training had been gracefully configured so that Secretary Adams could bring his own man over from the Embassy in Paris.

Robbie compared notes with the secretary he shared with the Executive Assistant. She was a career secretary, unflappable, and had served several decades on the seventh floor. The Secretary of State's own secretary, Missy Bronson, was already on board. She had followed him over from the Paris Embassy immediately. Indeed, she and Robbie had pretty much functioned as a transition team unto themselves during the early hectic weeks of the Secretary's confirmation hearings, when they were all feeling their way. Now they felt less like an occupying force, and more that the offices they occupied were rightly theirs. Robbie thought this was something of a dangerous feeling, when the holding of office felt entirely natural, and could with a stretch be considered an entitlement. "Well, we'll never do that," he had thought, and immediately wondered how many other politically blessed Washingtonians had made precisely the same promise.

As he always did before leaving for the day, Robbie lightly rapped on the door that led to the Secretary's office. There was no reply. Since Robbie's copy of the Secretary's schedule, not an infallible but a usually reliable guide to the Secretary's day, had not shown any further appointments at that hour, that was no surprise. On an impulse, Robbie opened the door and stepped inside the Secretary's office. Desk lights and the floor lamp by the Secretary's favorite chair were still on. He had probably left not twenty minutes previously.

Robbie gave the room a searching glance. This was the office that Secretaries of State had used for decades. Negotiations, diplomatic initiatives, and high strategy had been hammered out here, some of it remembered with a sense of national pride, some of it not. Robbie wondered what the difference was, in the long run. One thing seemed obvious to him. A Secretary of State needed political smarts, an ability to size up a situation. She had certainly had that. Diplomacy had that in common with politics. Timing was everything. But there was something else, something about being the world's last superpower, that seemed to change the dynamic.

American diplomacy, it seemed to him, now often lacked continuity. Someone won the national election, and everything seemed to change. There was a temptation on assuming office to believe that you had an anointed purpose, a reforming agenda, that would play irresistibly on the international stage. That created fierce resentments. Some other nations tried to bide their time while the latest enthusiasm cooled. The Brits had over the years developed a nuanced tactic. They would try to smoke out severe policy changes and modify them before they became public. They knew that diplomatic fashions in the United States changed with political fortunes.

"Quite a sight, isn't it?" It was Clark Framsen, at his elbow. "Sure, when I had your job, Robbie, I used to have some great thoughts about this room, this office. One of them was that what we need are fewer diplomatic messiahs who want to change the world, like Woodrow Wilson, and more stubborn pragmatists like Benjamin Franklin. Keep in mind the best interests of your country and don't go around trying to reform the world. Well, my boss had a good head on her shoulders and so, by the looks of it, has Secretary Adams."

Well, Robbie thought, we agree on that. It was like the Oath of Hippocrates: first, do no harm. There must be a diplomatic equivalent, when even more lives could be at stake. At least that would cut down on the number of people in other countries who ultimately suffered for our enthusiasms. Why didn't American proponents of change for some other society understand those other nations, their culture and history? And why couldn't they also understand that their own backgrounds in America, while inspirational, were largely irrelevant overseas? If they changed the way things worked here, that didn't mean they could do so overseas. Far from it. Amateur diplomacy could make things far worse. Then there was a national election, and they moved on. And had their memoirs ghostwritten. While somebody else had to pick up the pieces.

Well, enough gloomy reflections. Secretary Adams was a sound man, and that was a blessing. If he tried to wreak some good around the world, it would be in a measured way, with the cooperation of other good people. If he assented to the use of America's awesome military force, it would be because there really was no rational choice, and because our national interests were actually at risk. Also, he not only listened to people - he actually heard what they said.

"You should have a good run here," Framsen added. "Particularly after the President's promise. I guess we owe that to Secretary Adams." He turned and went back to his office.

Robbie nodded. Perhaps it had been a back stiffener for the White House, for when the last Secretary of State died, Congress had seen an opening and had rebelled at the closing of Guantanamo. Adams said when he met with the President that if the prison at Guantanamo remained open, he would not serve as Secretary of State. And he had meant every word of it. He had seen the erosion of our national standing, and he wanted none of it. America must regain her rightful place. It really was time, as Brezezinski had said, for the national symbol of the United States once more to be the Statue of Liberty, not Guantanamo.

Adams argued that American traditions and laws going back to the Lieber Code, issued by Abraham Lincoln in 1863 before the Geneva Conventions even existed, mandated the humane treatment of captives. Was the nation in more danger now than we were before the Battle of Gettysburg? Traditional American courts martial could deal with captured terrorists, and the federal courts had also dealt with habeas corpus petitions. Surely for those whom it was too dangerous to release a prison could be found in the United States.

It was time to close Guantanamo and move on. And it was time to comb through legislation and restore the balance on civil liberties. Fighting terrorists was one thing, but weakening what the United States stood for was something else altogether. And as we regained our moral compass, the terrorists lost. They probably had gained too much stature as it was. Go after them hard as a police matter, strengthen our border defenses, mend our alliances, but for God's sake, do it right.

The President had agreed. Robbie was sure that that had been the White House opinion in the first place. Could raising the issue, for the President had done so during the initial interview, actually have been a sort of test for the new Secretary of State? If so, it was a rather comforting thought. The President was wilier than he seemed. "You'll get the allies on board, Ronald. Have them take some prisoners off our hands. It will make things easier here. Then we'll move with the Congress."

It was against that recent background that Adams had decided to make his first trip overseas, as Secretary of State. He would visit allies and potential adversaries alike. They must all be part of the fight against terrorism, for they all had a stake. With a shudder he thought of the comparison with World War One. Terrorists then could not possibly have done on their own what governments had done in overreacting to their threat, with millions dead.

Robbie stood in the doorway, and wondered about his own career prospects. He had done well, and now had this fine springboard. He could look forward to an interesting and honorable diplomatic career, and that was just fine. Better not get ahead of himself. There was a huge chasm between this office and his own next door. One or two career diplomats could dream of making it this far, but they were very rare exceptions. The first thing for him to bear in mind, he suspected, was that he was not the Secretary. Any attempt to "wear the stars," as the military put it, would be remembered for a very long time after he left this office and Secretary Adams had retired. His job was not without its risks. Robbie shuddered, and returned to his own office.

He had another perk. The Secretary let him share the private elevator that took him directly to the Department's parking garage. Just open the door, turn the key, and no waiting for crowded elevators. It was particularly handy when the Secretary was running late from a meeting and had to get up to Capitol Hill quickly. Just a quick call or two to alert the chauffeur and the security detail, step into the elevator, turn the key, and they would be met at the garage level by the official car and driver. Then, out the door and they were on their way to the Hill.

He left the elevator and walked rapidly over to his car. He was pleased just to be able to park there in the building, a real bonus in bad weather. It wasn't much of a time saver, a few minutes perhaps. The parking arrangement didn't make the difference in his being comfortably on time for work, or having to race to the office. Robbie was not a late arriver in any event. He would have been at least half an hour early to work wherever he worked. Force of habit. But it was a relief not to have to fight the crowds and the weather. And it did, let's face it, nurture his growing sense of entitlement.

He drove down Virginia Avenue and then cut up Rock Creek Parkway, switching over to Massachusetts Avenue, for the drive past the Naval Observatory, now the Vice President's official residence.

He looked forward to the trip. When the Vice President was aboard the plane they would be taking, it was called Air Force Two. As a matter of fact, when the Veep was aboard the President's plane, that plane was also called Air Force Two. As far as Robbie was aware, there was no designated nickname for the aircraft when the chief passenger was the Secretary of State. Perhaps that was as it should be. Maybe he and Sylvie would make one up. Why not?

He turned right onto Wisconsin Avenue, and drove past the National Cathedral, slowing down as he drove past the Chevy Chase shopping area, now one expensive designer shop after another. Then the residential area began, and Robbie turned into the Dorset area off Kenwood Park. That area was pricey enough, without hitting the full fledged millions that still were the going rate now for estates in neighboring Kenwood. Quite a price to pay for those magnificent blooming cherry and dogwood trees each spring, he thought, but some day, who knows?

Meanwhile, he and Sylvie had been fortunate to have enough pooled savings to place a down payment on their home. They had done so, cutting some corners elsewhere. That was all thanks to some remembered financial folk wisdom from Sylvie's great grandmother, that neither of them had ever met. And so, they hadn't been tempted by those alluring ARM refinancing arrangements, and when the housing boom had begun to go sour and the toll of repossessions climbed steadily upward, he had been glad of her advice.

Sylvie was waiting for him with a hug and kiss. He knew she wasn't delicate, really, but still, the idea of hugging Sylvie and a child at the same time made him extra careful. It had always been his notion that women were especially lovely during their pregnancies, and his wife certainly proved that. They had decided to start their family when they learned they would not be going abroad. Instead of a year of language training and then going out to Athens, it seemed that the young couple would be in Washington for several years. And so, the decision to start their family had seemed a natural one. So had their idea of buying a house. Fortunately they had been living in a temporary apartment when the career change came, and had not settled into an apartment with a long lease that would have had to be broken. It had all happened so quickly. Just a few months had passed, but everything had changed.

They shared a glass of wine while Robbie went over the essentials of his day, the meetings attended, celebrities met, a few anecdotes from the front office. Sylvie was amused to note that her husband quite naturally had fallen into the habit of censoring what he told her about the office. And as a fomer television news reporter, she knew when he was hiding something. His censoring seemed to follow a pattern. If the information was classified or confidential and rather dull, she had noticed, it stayed with him. But if it was juicy and mildly scandalous, he couldn't wait to tell her!

"You'll have just time to pack while I watch the television news," she said, dispatching him upstairs, and refilling his glass, up he went..

Robbie ran over the checklist of things to bring for the trip. Suits, shirts, several pair of shoes, underwear, socks, an assortment of ties. He placed his Dopps kit carefully on the bathroom counter to be added to tomorrow morning, shaving and contact lens necessaries and toothpaste, and then zipped into his suitcase. He was glad that he didn't have to worry about tiny jars of fluids, as he might have for a commercial flight. The prospect of substituting super glue for contact lens rinsing solution by mistake was horrifying. He would carry his laptop separately. There would be an early departure from Andrews Air Force Base on the far side of the beltway, but Robbie and Sylvie were too keyed up to go to bed early.

His parents called as he was packing in the upstairs bedroom. Robbie could hear Sylvie answer the phone, and she had a nice chat in French with

Robbie's mother Lucille, who was Belgian. The cadences of the talk, from this side, were clearly pleasant. Then Sylvie called. "Robbie, your parents are on the phone."

He picked up the upstairs extension. His parents lived in Concord, Massachusetts. His father Samuel Lawrence "Trip" Cutler was a retired Foreign Service Officer, and so his parents had been thrilled by his designation as Special Assistant to the Secretary of State. It seemed to mean that Robbie was destined for a fine career. Robbie called them from time to time, and also kept in touch by email.

He spoke first with his mother. She was excited about the trip, and wished him well, switching into English after saying goodbye to Sylvie. "Please let us know how it goes. Now I'll put your father on. He's been reliving his own trips with Secretaries Rusk and Rogers all day!"

Trip Cutler got on the phone. "Hi Robbie. I'm sure you'll have a great trip. Don't let anything bother you. Just remember, it's the Secretariat that does all the work. You're just along for the ride!" There was something to that, possibly, but it would be from him, not an unknown member of the Executive Secretariat team, that Secretary Adams would demand answers if some briefing paper was missing or worse, not anticipated. But mostly, Trip Cutler was reminding his son, and himself, of the travels with two earlier Secretaries of State that he had taken as a staff officer. Working in the Executive Secretariat was a choice if exhausting assignment - now rewarded with a salary differential - and clearly Trip Cutler relished the memories.

"Remind me of your trips, Dad. You never talked much about them."

"Well, there was the Fall NATO trip to Brussels in, let's see, 1967. My last trip there, come to think of it. I did get to see the Grande Place, great *moules pommes frites*, but I didn't get to see Waterloo after all. It's not far at all from Brussels, and we had laid on a drive over there with a member of our NATO team, an Army major who had taught military history at West Point."

"What happened?"

"You know, the usual. A flap came up. Secretary Dean Rusk needed some more briefing papers, so I had to take care of that, and missed the trip." His voice sounded a note of real regret. It dawned on Robbie that it would not have occurred to his father to carve out the time and money to take a trip to Waterloo on his own later. He was a man who lived with his regrets. He always pictured the capitals of his diplomatic assignments as unchanging since the family had lived there, often decades previously, settings that awaited the family's return. When Robbie would tell him about a city that he knew well, his father was invariably surprised at the changes that Robbie detailed.

"But there was a bonus. In those days we flew down to Madrid and Lisbon to keep our friends who were not part of NATO then informed. It paid off in the long run. That sort of courtesy usually does. Do more than what you have to do. Since we are the most powerful nation by far, that sort of gesture to the less powerful doesn't go unnoticed. Not by a long shot."

Robbie suspected that the point was made for a purpose. Well, fair enough. It was a very good one.

"What about that trip with Secretary Rogers?"

That trip was favorably stored in Trip Cutler's memory. "Lord, yes. That was an eighteen day extravaganza. We literally flew around the world on Air Force Two. Let's see. That was during the Viet-Nam War, of course. We flew to Saigon, stopping first at Honolulu so that Secretary Rogers could confer with CINCPAC. I forget which Admiral that was at the time. Possibly Senator John McCain's father, I'm not sure. It's the only time I ever saw Honolulu. Come to think of it, we ought to take a cruise there. Maybe we will for our anniversary."

The hint was filed away.

"In Saigon, Secretary Rogers got the full briefing treatment from Ambassador Bunker and MACV. The war wasn't going well, and the Nixon Administration was probably looking for a way out, even then. We were there for a couple of days. I remember the Embassy treated us very well. I even had a wooden plaque with my name painted on it, to mark my office. That told me something else, that the Embassy was too anxious to please. Which meant that the disagreements between Saigon and Washngton were widening. That turned out to be right."

He paused, and chuckled. "Then off to Bangkok."

He was in full memory flight. "I suppose you've heard that episode before, Robbie. I flew to Bangkok ahead of the Secretary's party, in order to set up his office and procedures at Embassy Bangkok. Actually, I flew commercial. I took a diplomatic bag with me, and got courier letters that designated me as a diplomatic courier for that flight. We've still got them somewhere. That was fun. Thank God the bottle of scotch I had with me in the bag didn't open!

"Then, after Bangkok, the fun really began It was Secretary Rogers's introduction to the subcontinent. He went to India to talk with Prime Minister Gandhi. Indira, of course. We landed in May, the hottest season, and when I got off Air Force Two, it was 122 degrees, and no shade! It felt like a moving wall of hot bone dry air, one that was forcing me almost back step by step into the plane again. It was a real effort to go down the steps instead. So I really don't recommend your having Secretary Adams visit India in May!"

"I'll bear that in mind."

"Then we flew to Lahore, Pakistan. I still remember seeing the Red Fort, you know, where *Kim* begins, the tale by Kipling. Wonderful story. The Great Game, of course. That's where I started my collection of British medals, in a little shop in Lahore." Trip spent hours over his collection, each medal recalling service in a little remembered nineteenth century campaign or battle, for valor in the service of Queen Victoria. The way stations of empire: India, Omdurman, Khartoum, Lahore, Kabul, two Afghan campaigns, the Boer War. Robbie sometimes thought about that collection and its meaning. Was there going to be an American equivalent?

"Finally it was off to Afghanistan. I had some fun then, got the Captain to announce when we were flying over the Khyber Pass. Nobody had ever heard of it then. The Hindu *Kush*. That was great fun. We were only there for a few hours. It was while it was still safe, long before the series of wars and terrorism hit Kabul. It was the time of King Mohammed Zahir Shah. We had just time for a state meal, and exhibits of those marvelous works of art, recalling the time of Alexander the Great."

He warmed to his memories. "I've read in the newspapers that many of those works of art were saved. It was an act of great bravery by the Kabul Museum guards. When the Russian *coup* took place, and the fighting, and the Taliban takeover, they hid hundreds of priceless treasures. Many of them were saved. You remember Kipling's tale, *The Man Who Would Be King?* That recalls the conquest by Alexander. These works of art, many statues, are the living proof. They show human faces, and the inspiration is obviously Hellenistic, not Asian. Perfectly amazing collection. It was a miracle that they were saved. The Taliban, of course, would have smashed them all.

"But that wasn't the only memory I had of those few hours in Kabul. The Embassy had brought several Afghan hounds owned by staff to the Embassy lawn, so that we could see them. They were just magnificent. We were told, then, that Zahir Shah personally had to approve each hound that left Afghanistan, and the royal permission was rarely given. If I'd ever seen the like in the United States, Robbie, you would have grown up with an Afghan hound for a pet rather than cats."

"Was that the last stop, Dad?"

"No, the alphabet soup continued. It was SEATO in Bangkok and CENTO in Tehran. By the time we got to Iran on a Sunday night, we had ripped through five countries in one weekend - Thailand, India, Pakistan, Afghanistan and Iran! Really, one has to wonder. Particularly for the Foreign Service, when years are spent getting to know a country and a people. What do you make of a series of visits, just a day or two long at most? Sometimes all it amounts to is a motorcade and a joint press conference. How does that help our diplomacy? What do the local people you visit think? Not to mention, when the Secretary of State changes plans and doesn't stay overnight, just to show her temper. We've had too much of that. junior high school stuff!"

"Wasn't Tehran where you had the caviar, Dad?"

"Yes. Well, I was below the caviar line. Everyone else got some. I had a free day, so went to a restaurant and bought some. It was surprisingly good and fresh, Caspian Sea stuff, the real thing. And it didn't taste oily at all, like what you get in little cans or jars. I could see for the first time why people liked it. And I also got to see the Shah's Peacock Throne, which was in a sort of museum with precious gems, so many that they just kept them in sacks. Literally innumerable.

"But my main memory of Tehran - this was in the time of the Shah, remember - was wandering through the streets during that free day. The people looked miserable, and I stopped at a mosque, where a service could be heard. Clearly the emotion was running very high. I took off my shoes and peeped inside. Nobody saw me. They were enraptured by the speaker, who was devastated by emotion. I never saw anything like it. After a while the audience started wailing and tearing out their hair as well. It was very moving, and rather scary. And it was a complete contrast to what officials heard during their government contacts, the all was serene routine.

"I often wished I spoke Farsi, to know what was really going on. But we found out soon enough, when the Shah was overthrown. After all, the CIA had overthrown Mossadegh, paving the way to install 'our type Shah,' as Kennedy called him. No wonder all of that is still with us."

"Then you flew back to Washington?"

"Not directly. Tehran was the last official stop. But Secretary Rogers was a golfer, so we ended up for a day or two in Scotland, near Gleneagles. I remember the cables being couriered up from London. There was no classified place to keep them, so I ended up burning some in the hotel courtyard! Anyway, it was good having some down time. Secretary Rogers did try to look after the troops, unlike most who have held that office. It wasn't all work. And we needed that relaxation, after an eighteen day trip.

"By the way, I've been nattering away. What's your itinerary?"

"Not as overwhelming as the caravan you've been remembering, Dad. Just six stops. We're doing Dublin, Paris, Vienna, Moscow, Riga and London. Yes, that's the right order. Ten days, which is a very long time to be away from Washington."

"Why are you going to London last, rather than after Dublin? Why not first, for that matter? Isn't that the tradition for a new Secretary of State?"

"You may be right. It has something to do with the Prime Minister's schedule. The London stop was scheduled and then rescheduled, at least once. But Secretary Adams really wanted to fit in London during his first trip, as you say, so it got tacked on."

Trip shook his head knowingly. It was quite a start. He could just picture the Paris stop. It would suit French vanity, and go a long ways towards restoring our traditional friendship. They would make sure that it was a memorable visit for the former American Ambassador in Paris, all ruffles and flourishes. Trip sometimes wondered which nation, France or Great Britain, was the monarchy, and which really the republic.

"Are they all bilaterals? No multilateral alphabet soup, like the CENTO and SEATO of our trip?"

"Well, some of that will come up. The Irish and the Latvians are key nowadays in the G-20, representing the European Union. But it is mainly bilateral. And we will be dropping off a new ambassador in Riga."

"Wish I could be with you in Riga. I've always wanted to go there, particularly since my days on the Baltic desk."

"I'll have a good look around, and fill you in on what is new. Still prickly relations with the Russians, I'm sure."

"Well, Robbie, do try to get off by yourself for a look around. Enjoy the trip. Believe me, forty years from now you won't recall the flaps you had to deal with, or the meetings that ran late, or the briefing papers that you handled. But you will recall a free afternoon if you can get one, and your own discoveries. That's what will stay with you."

The talk petered out. They rang off, and Robbie went downstairs to dinner. His packing and then, the conversation with his parents had eaten up the television news broadcast that Sylvie had watched. "Come to the table," she said, "but put on some music first. Some nice music. No commercials."

It was a special occasion, and Sylvie had prepared a festive meal for their six months' anniversary, with Oysters Rockefeller, trout *meunière* and green beans with almonds, a salad with fresh *croutons* and then a cheese course, before the chocolate cake and ice cream, her husband's favorite dessert. He produced a chilled bottle of dry white French wine from the *Entre Deux Mers* region near Bordeaux.

He punched on the Washington classical music radio station out of habit, but sensing rather than seeing Sylvie's pained expression at the endless commercial that followed, quickly turned the radio off in favor of an elegant CD by Charles Trenet. Trenet started to sing his signature creation, "La Mer." Hummable if you didn't know the words, the singing was not regretful like Edith Piaf or full of anger like Juliette Greco. It had a wondrous grace to it, like a fancied perfect childhood that you wished you had really had. Trenet's smooth and genuine delivery made Maurice Chevalier sound almost awkward. Perfect for an intimate dinner.

"That's better. Your parents were pleased to talk about your trip, I'm sure."

"Yes. It recalled for Dad his own trips flying with the Secretary. He once flew around the world, an eighteen day extravaganza with Secretary Rogers, back in the Nixon Administration. And he was intrigued by our stop in Riga. He was Baltic Desk Officer, you know."

"Why are you going there after Moscow, rather than the other way around?"

"It seemed more convenient. The Latvians didn't seem to mind."

"You know what I think, darling?"

"What, Sylvie?"

"I think this is a really odd conversation for two honeymooners to be having."

—   —   —   —   —   —   —   —

The telephone rang at two o'clock in the morning. "I'm really sorry, Mr. Cutler, but there is a NODIS cable in from Embassy Tripoli. FLASH precedence."

Embassy Tripoli? Robbie had to think for a moment. Then he remembered. After years of diplomatic standoff, following the December, 1988 downing of Pan American Flight 103 over Lockerbie, Scotland, there had been a gradual restoration of diplomatic relations. Libya had promised to renounce terrorism. That was small consolation to the families of 180 murdered Americans, many thought. The first American Ambassador to Libya was accredited as the Bush Administration ended, and the first Libyan Ambassador arrived in Washington in January, 2009. That's another problem with reestablishing diplomatic relations with some countries, Robbie yawned and grumbled - we send people out who can't tell day from night.

"Who else is seeing it?" he asked.

"Well, we are calling in the Assistant Secretary. Or rather, his staffer. Should be in within a few minutes." That would be Clarice Evans, a sound midgrade officer whom Robbie knew fairly well, and whose judgment he trusted.

"And we're starting a new series."

"Good idea. Please put a copy in the Secretary's reading file to go out to the plane. Which should be in 90 minutes or so."

"It's already done, Mr. Cutler."

Robbie turned off the light and tried to get back to sleep. After twenty minutes or so, he did so. The next sound he heard was the alarm clock at four o'clock. Guess it hadn't been such a big flap after all, he thought.

—   —   —   —   —   —   —   —

Sylvie drove Robbie to the airport. There was little traffic at that early predawn hour, and so they made good time. They decided to skip the hazards of driving through downtown Washington, even though that was a shorter route and there should be no traffic. One never knew. Instead, Sylvie made her practiced way over to Massachusetts Avenue, then turned onto River Road, which led shortly to the Washington beltway. They were in luck. Traffic was medium, and there were no accidents.

They watched the beltway exits go by one by one, and finally, in good time, saw the exit leading to Andrews Air Force Base, Maryland, home to the 89th Airlift Wing, and Air Force One and Two. The Secretary would be taking the C-32A known as Air Force Two when the Vice President was aboard, a modified Boeing 757.

The Secretary's party and newsmen had started to arrive. The newsmen were not there to cover the departure. There was nothing newsworthy in that. They were the ones actually going on the plane, and they would file stories throughout the trip. There were several officials whom Robbie did not recognize. They were perhaps from Commerce and Treasury, and involved in some of the bilateral talks that the Secretary would be having. There was an Air Force major general, but whether he was there as an official passenger, or was from the 89th Airlift Wing, just showing up to make sure that all went smoothly this morning, Robbie could not tell.

Robbie saw Assistant Secretary Donna Palmer, who was talking with Charley Sherburne, the Department Press Spokesman. He tried to remember who else was on the manifest, but it didn't come to mind. Oh yes, there were the two Executive Secretariat officers, checking their document bags. The Secretary was not here yet. He would probably arrive last, and just in time. And there was the Ambassador-designate for Latvia, his confirmation hearings a successful memory. He waved at Robbie, who tried in the early morning fatigue to remember his name. Oh yes, it was Rudolphe Carlisle. He looked friendly enough.

The Secretary's secretary, Missy Bronson, was here already. He couldn't see Clark Framsen. But there were the Country Directors for Ireland, France, Austria, Russia, Baltic Affairs, and Great Britain. They were sort of walking encyclopedias for their countries of responsibility. They had written and rewritten the briefing papers in the bulging briefing book that Robbie would shortly give to the Secretary.

And they would be on tap, along with Assistant Secretary Palmer, for personal briefings with the Secretary, to supplement what had been written. Robbie remembered his father's story about an Air Force Two trip that he remembered during the Ford Administration. It hadn't been generally realized, but Vice President Nelson Rockefeller was dyslexic. He couldn't make out the briefing papers that had been laboriously written for him. No problem. One by one, the drafters were called into his private Air Force Two cabin to summarize their presentations orally. It had worked just fine.

Robbie gave Sylvie a hug and peck on the cheek, and added an unnecessary warning to drive very carefully back around the beltway, for traffic would be starting to build shortly. "And don't forget to pick me up again when we return!" he added.

She smiled and walked towards the car, then turned and waved and blew him a kiss. More than one newsman wished that he had had a similar sendoff. Notebooks and bottles were very poor substitutes for the real thing.

Robbie went through security and boarded the plane. The Secretary had asked to meet him in the private cabin, so Robbie would wait for him there. First, this was his opportunity to take a look around the plane. It did seem like a natural film set. But this plane didn't seem to resemble the flying wonder that he had admired in the film *Air Force One*, the Harrison Ford epic. But then, this was not Air Force One. Robbie recalled that Vice President Cheney had used Air Force One several times. The President wasn't using it then. Possibly that was because of Cheney's heart problems? After all, Air Force One had emergency medical facilities. One never knew for sure.

He couldn't remember any movies about Air Force Two. Wait a second, there was that Mariel Hemingway film *In The Line Of Fire*, but he hadn't seen it. He could get it from Netflix when he returned from this trip, and then compare the film version to the real thing. He'd have fun talking with Sylvie about that. He wondered what sort of plane Secretary Rusk and Secretary Rogers had used when his father had flown with them. Probably an earlier Boeing. He'd have to ask his father.

Come to think of it, the modified Boeing 747 that was the actual Air Force One probably didn't look much like the film version either. The differences between Air Force One and Two, he had heard, were primarily of scale. Air Force One had even more extensive communications and defensive hardware, as well as medical equipment, and it could cruise much farther than Air Force Two's 5,500 nautical miles without refueling.

On the other hand, if you had fairly short runways to contend with, Air Force Two was a better choice. It could land on a runway as short as 5,000 feet. From what he had heard from his father about the scary runway at Baguio, The Philippines, which seemed to drop off a cliff, neither plane could land there. He wasn't sure about the Hong Kong Airport either. That was another very difficult landing strip, hemmed in, with no room for second thoughts. Well, they weren't going to either Baguio or Hong Kong, thank heavens.

Robbie wanted to get a feel for the plane's layout. After all, he would probably be doing some back and forth, as the Secretary asked to see people. He kicked himself for not having asked for a schematic floor plan of the cabin. Well, no matter, he'd figure it out now. He had flown on a commercial 757 once, so there was some similarity to this plane, but the differences were immediately obvious. It was as though the interior had been stripped and reconfigured. Come to think of it, that was probably exactly what had happened. He walked back and forth, and could see that there were several main sections of the passenger cabin.

An Air Force steward, Tech Sergeant Sullivan, looked at him with an appraising eye. Well, might as well get the details from an expert, Robbie thought. He stuck out his hand and introduced himself. As always, "Special Assistant to the Secretary" brought immediate attention. The steward's voice changed to an even keener pitch of polite deference, and he said he'd be more than glad to give Robbie a quick tour of the flight deck and the cabin. No, Robbie had assured him, he wasn't interested in the flight deck, not right now. Maybe he'd join the Secretary if he asked for a tour later. No problem, sir.

Robbie was developing a finely honed sense of what he could ask for, and what would be considered a reach. They would have shown him the flight deck, but it would have been presumptuous on his part, and he wasn't sure the Secretary would have appreciated it. Besides, if Secretary Adams was interested, he could surely join along, and get a far better tour at a higher level.

"First, of course, down from the flight deck, is the forward galley. I usually work there." Robbie sensed some pride in his voice. That probably meant that he served the flight captain and top passengers. "Between the flight deck and that galley are crew seating and the communications systems operator station."

They walked through the forward galley. "This is an area you've probably seen in news photos." It was the conference/staff area, with two worktables and eight business class seats. "News photos or videos showing the Secretary of State or Defense - who also uses this plane - often will be taken here.

"You'll be mainly interested in this area, I suppose, Mr. Cutler," the steward said. He designated a door off the conference/staff area. "This leads into what we call the distinguished visitor stateroom. It's got a bed and bathroom area, changing room and a worktable. It's probably not as luxurious as the movies show it, but it serves the purpose."

"Sure beats trying to sleep in economy class, if there were an economy class."

"That's for sure, yes, sir."

Their walk continued. "Past the stateroom is the general seating area. You'll see that the front portion is partitioned, and is reserved for security personnel. Then there is the general seating area, set further back. No sense in taking any chances. The press and other passengers are seated there. Further aft is the aft galley."

"For meal preparation for passengers."

"Precisely."

"How many passengers can you take?"

"Well, it varies. Surely three or four dozen, plus crew."

"Many thanks for the tour. I appreciate it."

"Any time, sir."

The team from the Executive Secretariat was on board, two young officers and their secretary. He recognized the team chief, Ron Jackson. "Anything new?" Robbie asked.

"No. Just the usual mix. Flap in Georgia again over oil deliveries from Russia. Attempted coup in Pakistan, that seems to have been put down fairly readily. And brutally. The usual Zimbabwe mess, getting even messier. As you know, the Senate Foreign Relations Committee is continuing its investigation into human rights issues in China."

Robbie nodded. He recalled that in the recent past, a Deputy Secretary of State had tried to raise precisely those issues with the Chinese leadership in Beijing, only to be told that the American human rights record wasn't pristine by a long shot. They cited testimony and newspaper accounts in the Western press about secret prisons and torture. It would take a very long time to repair that damage. Well, this Secretary of State and President had already made a fine start. He recalled an unjustly accused Reagan Administration cabinet officer asking, "Where do I go to get my reputation back?" Did that apply to nations too?

"Any schedule changes that you have heard about?" The staffer nodded, no. "Neither have I. Not yet." They would confer dozens of times each day to make sure the paper trail was absolutely up to date. Although Robbie and this officer had only met briefly once or twice, they already had established their shorthand working relationship.

"How about new papers?"

"Yes, I have an updated briefing paper for Dublin. Northern Ireland issues, for background. It should be substituted for the one in the book."

"Thanks. I'll give it to Missy. How about cables?"

"Here they are."

Robbie sat down at a conference table and quickly read the Secretary's cable file. His routine was to mark those cables that the Secretary should read, and then those that might furnish background, interesting but not essential. Then he would make a third, larger file of cables that weren't worth the Secretary's attention.

There it was, the NODIS cable from Tripoli. That is why he had been called in the middle of the night. It passed along a new rumor from what was said to be a reliable source, under deep cover. Al Qaeda was planning something big. The source only knew the codename, Operation Salah al-Din. The Operations Center officer who first read the cable had served in the Middle East. He had called the new series NODIS SALADIN.

Robbie took the cable file and the briefing paper, then went back to the Secretary's stateroom and knocked on the door. Secretary Adams had just arrived, and told him to come in.

"Good morning, sir. Good morning, Missy." She was seated at the worktable, bringing up the day's schedule on her computer screen. He handed her the Secretary's cables, which she accepted with a nod. She would handle them in her practiced way shortly. Woe to any aide who thought it was his business to bypass Missy Bronson! She would riffle through the cables, taking Robbie's order of precedence. When the Secretary asked for cables, he always got the first batch. When he looked as though he might want more reading, or asked for more, she would have the second batch ready, plus any new ones. The third batch she would save for a special request if he was bored and out of material. That didn't happen very often. Anyway, today there was the briefing book, which would probably be his primary focus, after a negotiation or two that he was following in the cable traffic.

"Just one briefing paper to switch with the one in the book, Missy. A backgrounder on Northern Ireland issues." She wordlessly stopped her computer work, took the paper, inserted it into its proper place, removed the earlier paper and consigned it to an already bulging burn bag at her feet. This morning routine would ordinarily have taken place in her office area, which adjoined Robbie's office and lay just outside the Secretary's office.

The Secretary seemed somewhat amused by the morning paper drill, seeing it for the first time. "So that's how you two manage me," he grinned. "Well, have a seat Robbie. Let's talk about the day, and the trip. Oh, Missy, would you ask Charley Sherburne to step in? Say, in ten minutes? I'd like to go over the press interviews with him."

"Yes, Mr. Secretary." She walked out the door in search of Sherburne.

—   —   —   —   —   —   —   —

"You've had quite a time, these first few months, Robbie. We haven't had much time for a talk. I am grateful that you changed your plans, and you've been excellent at this job. I hope you still get home from time to time?"

"Yes, sir. I'm developing a taste for leftovers" He couldn't resist that. The Secretary laughed. "Happens to all of us from time to time."

He leaned forward. "We had some bad news about Clark. I suppose you haven't heard?"

"No," Robbie said in surprise. "I just saw him yesterday, in your office. He and I were talking, and I know he was looking forward to this trip."

"Well, his wife Sandra called. It looks like it was a heart attack. They aren't quite sure. He was rushed to the hospital, the one near the Department, where Ronald Reagan was taken after that shooting. I stopped there before coming here. That's why I was a bit late. He wasn't seeing visitors just yet. He couldn't. In any event, the doctors were still treating him in the emergency room. But I was able to talk with Sandra."

"How is she holding up?"

"All right, but that is the odd part. She said that Clark seemed very worried and preoccupied. Almost a different person. The attack happened at home, late evening, just as he was about to go to bed. It may be nothing. I've known people - too many, now - who have some sort of premonition before they get a heart attack. They seem to feel it's coming on. It doesn't necessarily mean anything. Probably doesn't. By the way, he did mention my name, Sandra said. Nothing else. Just 'tell the Secretary.' Then he clutched his heart and collapsed."

"Good God! I hope he's going to be all right."

Secretary Adams paused silently, shaking his head in dismay.

"Well, sir, I doubt he meant anything in particular. Clark was probably out of his head, and what he said doesn't indicate anything. He is the hardest worker I know. I'm sure that what he was referring to was this trip, and the fact that he was going to miss it. Something like 'Tell the Secretary I'm sorry to let him down' would be totally in character for Clark." The Secretary nodded in agreement. "Perhaps the best thing to do would be for me to call Sandra, and see how things are going. That's a logical thing to do anyway, and not upsetting for her. If he were conscious and had anything to add, she would then tell me."

"You certainly haven't lost your touch, Robbie, and not just with murder investigations."

The Secretary was referring to Robbie's talent for solving murders across international lines. There had been that series of ETA attempted assassinations in Bordeaux when he was Consul, then the Russian Mafia hired thugs in Budapest. And perhaps one might add the murder that he and Sylvie had solved last summer, during their honeymoon in the Dordogne. He was developing a bit of a reputation along those lines, it seemed.

Robbie acknowledged the compliment with a smile.

"By the way, sir, was Clark working on anything special that he might have been referring to in particular? Something that he was going to report on to you directly, and very soon?"

"Several things, actually. But nothing that was not in the normal run of diplomatic business. Oh, and Robbie?"

"Yes, sir?"

"With Clark in the hospital, that leaves his job for the time being. By the time somebody else could read in, we'd be back already, so a substitute here and now would serve no earthly purpose. So would you mind taking on his chores for this trip?"

"Of course, sir. What would you have me do?"

"Well, Clark knows my priorities. Generally, he sits in on all of my meetings with people in the Department, including Charley Sherburne. That helps with follow-through. Not, though, with the press, although he helps set up meetings and priorities. Then in mid-afternoon we block out the substance for the following day, and on Fridays, for the following week. What we want to get done, if that is possible. It's so I don't get so utterly lost in daily meetings that I lose sight of the larger priorities.

"And from time to time, when I want a record, he sits in on meetings with ranking foreign officials. No notetaking, so our local Embassy people don't get their noses out of joint. That's their function, of course, and for good reason. They have to stay in the loop. Clark just records salient points in that agile mind of his and sets them down after the meeting for our record and again, possible follow-through. I find that very useful. So you'll have to pass the word, and get yourself on the list of participants on our side for any bilateral meetings that we'll be having on this trip where Clark was mentioned."

"With pleasure, sir."

"Oh yes, and don't forget to save some time for shopping. I'm sure that Sylvie would appreciate that!"

"I'm sure she would."

"And please give my very best, and our prayers, to Sandra when you call her."

A knock came at the door. It was Missy Bronson with Press Spokesman Charley Sherburne."

"Come on in, Charley. You know Robbie Cutler, of course. It looks like poor Clark Framsen has suffered a heart attack. So Robbie will be sitting in with us. Now, I know how touchy the press is. Who wants to see me first, and in what order?"

CHAPTER THREE -
A Dublin Welcome

SECRETARY ADAMS'S PLAN FOR A low key arrival seemed to have worked. Air Force Two was met at the official section of the Dublin International Airport with a minimum of fuss and protocol. The unavoidable arrival statement was brief and to the point, and questions from the press had been waived by mutual agreement, greased by some soft soap about later one on one meetings with the Secretary from Press Spokesman Charley Sherburne. Even the motorcade which escorted the party to the American Embassy on Elgin Road in the Ballsbridge district of Dublin was expected to be fairly unobtrusive. But that was where unobtrusiveness dissolved into something like controlled frenzy.

What had not been expected was the crowd of Dubliners lining the road, holding pro-American signs of welcome, for miles along the way. Many signs referred to the closing of Guantanamo.

"I've never seen anything like it, even on St. Patrick's Day" blurted out the Irish Chief of Protocol, James O'Malley, who accompanied Secretary Adams in the official car to the Embassy. "Really, we Irish have always had a soft spot for America, but this is truly exceptional. It's like the Pope's visit."

And indeed it was. Homemade signs seemed to have sprouted up all along the route, with hundreds, then thousands, of people holding them up, then waving them as the cars passed, with cheers of welcome. "America Is Back!" read a typical sign.

"Well, Ambassador O'Malley, I wish the President could see this. It was all his doing, you know, one of his very first actions on becoming President. Clearly, it is important to him, and we all believe that it will make our pursuit of terrorists more vigorous and united than ever.

"Tell me, I know our peoples have a special kinship. But what explains this outpouring?"

"Well, Mr. Secretary, several main ingredients, I suspect. First, our country is loaded down with the past, so many prisons, and so much suffering. On many sides, I suspect. If you have a few hours, I'll take you around. I'm not claiming that right was always on our side. But oppression there was, and no mistake. And suffering there was, too. They really did 'hang men and women for the wearing of the green,' you know. So seeing your great country voluntarily close down what we - harumph, most Irish - see was a symbol of oppression just is wonderful news. It's a victory for everyone, all of us. We know what oppression is like.

"And then, Mr. Secretary, if you've seen America mostly from afar, you see it in terms of hope and opportunity. That's why it's been so hard to recognize your country. We wanted our vision of it back. Now we do have that hope back, and it is our own hope as it was the hope of our great grandparents in the starving time. So if I wasn't here in the car with you, Mr. Secretary, I'd surely be waving a sign of welcome out there!"

It was good to start the trip on friendly soil, and the Republic of Ireland was clearly that. Secretary Adams shared with Ambassador O'Malley the stories he had heard of American fighting men and women transferring to planes to the Middle East during Operation Iraqi Freedom. Despite the unpopularity of the Iraq War even here, American soldiers had been cheered as they made their way in full uniform through Shannon Airport. It had been spontaneous and stirring.

The Embassy was white, new and imposing, a fairly recent addition to Dublin's Embassy district. It fit well on its triangular site, with a rounded exterior that was said to incorporate traditional Irish designs. Benches and shrubbery leading to the building softened the inevitable security features. It seemed to Robbie's eye, in the setting sun, to be attractive and probably functional as well. He entered the building and was pleased to see that it seemed like a rotunda. Casting eyes upward, the visitor could see walls of glass near the top of the structure, which surely flooded the interior with daylight. And the immediate interior space was bright and spacious enough for public receptions.

Robbie checked with the Marine Guard on duty and found his way to his own office for their Dublin stay. Up the elevator, down the corridor, virtually next door to the Ambassador's suite, now of course commandered for the Secretary's use. Nearby were offices for the Executive Secretariat team, and for Assistant Secretary Palmer. He was sure the secure conference area would be close by.

The organization for their arrival had been well thought through. Secretary Adams, Assistant Secretary Palmer, and Press Spokesman Charley Sherburne would be staying at the Ambassador's official residence in Phoenix Park. The Ireland Country Director would stay with the Embassy Political Counselor, and most of the other travellers, many of whom were not directly involved in this stopover, were ferried by cabs from the Embassy to their hotels across the Liffey River in downtown Dublin. Meanwhile, the press corps on the trip were already filing their stories from the Embassy's press room. All emphasized the tumultuous Irish welcome.

Robbie Cutler was pleased to note that he had been upgraded to take Clark Framsen's place as a guest of the Ambassador at her official residence. But first, he checked into the office he would be using at the Embassy, next to the team from the Executive Secretariat. He secured his classified material, checking the incoming cables for the Secretary that had already been assembled. There was nothing that couldn't wait. He memorized sufficient details from the cables to give Secretary Adams a short briefing.

Robbie closed the door and placed a call to Sandra Framsen. There had been no answer when he had earlier tried to call her several times from the airplane. Either she had been at the hospital and had shut her cell phone off, or she was trying to sleep. This time, she answered her home phone. "Oh hello, Robbie, I'm just getting some things together for Clark."

"Secretary Adams wanted to send you his very best wishes, and prayers for Clark. I'll add mine too. How is he doing - and how are you bearing up?"

"Well, it was serious, but they got him in time. He'll be in bypass surgery when he is a little stronger. Meanwhile, he's being monitored all the time."

"Anything we can do for you? I know that Sylvie would be glad to help. Unfortunately, I won't be back for ten days or so."

"Thanks, Robbie. It would be good to see Sylvie. This waiting is the worst."

"Has he been conscious?"

"Yes, most of the time. He said something about how you must really be earning your money now. Just don't stop his."

"Sounds like he's got his sense of humor back."

"I hope it's not whistling in the dark."

"The Secretary said that you had told him that Clark had started to say something, 'Tell the Secretary...,' when he collapsed. Did he add anything to that?"

"No. I'm sure he just meant for me to call and let you know what happened."

"Well, give Clark our love and prayers. I'll try to screw everything up so he's really missed."

"Thanks, Robbie."

He thought for a minute and then called home. Sylvie was awaiting his call, and wondered why it had been delayed.

"Oh, that's terrible. I'll get right over to the hospital. She must be going through hell. How is the trip going?"

"Well, I've got some of Clark's brief now, and it seems to be going all right. Fortunately, the team from the Executive Secretariat are real pros. Dad would be pleased. From their standpoint, I'm almost being spoon fed the right material, briefing papers and cables. And it looks like I'll be in on a meeting or two that I might otherwise have missed."

"Sounds like fun. But your Dad was absolutely right. Take some time off if you can. After all, you are scouting out our future vacations! I know that somehow you'll manage to see the Book of Kells. Well, don't forget the shopping too. I hear Grafton Street is world class."

"That's what Secretary Adams told me. G'bye for now. Love and kisses."

Robbie left his office and walked towards the Ambassador's suite. It was time to meet with senior Embassy staff for drinks and an informal briefing. Robbie supposed that it was being held in the Ambassador's office to preclude any embarrassment for staffers who were not invited to dinner. If so, it was a thoughtful move on her part.

The Secretary was in the Ambassador's office. He called Robbie over, and introduced him to the Ambassador to Ireland, Mary McGowan. She smiled, said a few welcoming pleasantries and left them to confer for a moment, while she attended to the lineup for their briefing. Robbie gave the Secretary a summary of incoming cable traffic. He then went over the schedule for the following day, and to his delight, found that the Secretary was going to play a round or two of golf in the afternoon, following luncheon with the American business community. That meant that Robbie would be able to get in some shopping and sightseeing after all. He found himself already looking forward to it.

Robbie asked and got answers to a point or two for the Executive Secretariat briefing team. Then he told the Secretary about his telephone call with Sandra Framsen. Things looked fairly good, he guessed, and Clark was certainly in a fine hospital facility. The surgery would be serious, and of course Sandra was very upset and concerned. But she sounded like she was hoping for the best. There hadn't been any particular message for the Secretary from Clark, as far as he could tell. Certainly there was nothing special that Sandra had been asked to pass on to them. Secretary Adams nodded. "Tell Missy to send some flowers to the hospital," he said, and then walked over to meet the Embassy officers.

To Robbie's surprise, Rudolphe Carlisle joined the group for drinks. What was he doing here? But his presence was soon explained. It turned out that Ambassador McGowan was an old acquaintance of Carlisle. Robbie hadn't met her before today, but like everyone else, he knew of the legendary McGowan Fellowships. Whether her money was new or old, it was certainly well used. Then he remembered that she was very well known in New York's rarified artistic circles as well, as a determined and single-minded collector of fine art. She was introducing her staff to Carlisle just before Secretary Adams arrived. From what Robbie could gather, he had given her opinions and vouched for the authenticity of several works of art that she later had been delighted to purchase, and just at the right time, in the volatile art market. Even more to the point, he had steered her away from a fraud or two, saving not only money but, perhaps more important, embarrassment at having been gulled..

So that is what Carlisle was doing here. He was going to stay for a few days after they left, then fly directly to Riga, and greet the group on their arrival near the end of the Secretary's trip. Well, now at least his presence in Dublin made a kind of sense, Robbie thought. He gave his drink order, "Bushmills and ice, splash of water," to a steward. There was time to be introduced to the Deputy Chief of Mission, a career man named George Smiley ("No jokes, please, it really is my name"), and the Political Counselor, Frank Sullivan ("Where else would they send me, I ask you?").

Ambassador McGowan greeted all of her guests as they entered, and then, as the waiters left the room, rose to say a few words of welcome, standing behind a small, portable podium. She gave a brief overview of American bilateral relations with Ireland, and then turned to Frank Sullivan for an overview of the political situation.

"Don't worry," he began, "nobody is going to use Power Point!"

"What a shame," Charley Sherburne grunted, "I could have used the nap!"

Sullivan's presentation was helpful and upbeat. He started with an overview of the domestic political scene, the last elections, the curent economic woes, and the nation's political dynamic. Who were the next generation of political leaders, and what was their attitude towards the United States? He then added a grace note for the visitors. "For those of you whose families come from Ireland, I'd be glad to talk about the region of the nation that they came from after this meeting, if that would be of interest." That was a nice thing to do, Robbie thought. More than one visitor would love to go home and give his family an update on how things really were in County Cork or County Kerry. A very nice touch.

Sullivan continued, more broadly. "More than at any other time in the existence of the Republic of Ireland, we see great promise here. In some measure, that is because of expectations in Northern Ireland that the violence has finally ended. People in the Republic of Ireland won't have half an eye cocked towards that violent situation in the future. I hope and pray that it will continue to evolve peacefully there. It's a tragedy that has to finish. How it will finally work out is anybody's guess. And from the Dublin point of view, on the positive side of the ledger, hopes are strong that the Republic of Ireland will once again be the Celtic Tiger. The economy had been taking off since Ireland became part of the European Economic Union. No reason that can't resume." His colleague from the Economic Section provided details.

The informal briefing session ended, and it was time to go to the Ambassador's Residence in Phoenix Park. Robbie remembered some of the background reading about the region and its rich history. Said to be the largest municipal park in the world within a city's limits, Phoenix Park served as the city's family strolling area for good weather relaxation. It was also the location of some prime real estate, including the residence of Ireland's President, the *Aras an Uachtarain*. Both that imposing state residence and the American Ambassador's residence nearby were from the eighteenth century.

The Ambassador's residence was as magnificent as the reading had stated. Located on sixty two acres, it was completed in 1776 as the residence of the Chief Secretary of the British Government, who had also served as Bailiff of Phoenix Park. It was purchased by the British Government and became the Chief Secretary's official residence shortly thereafter, serving sixty nine Chief Secretaries until 1922, when Ireland's independence was gained.

Sir Arthur Wellington, later the Duke of Marlborough, had lived here. So had Sir Robert Peel and Castlereagh. There was a great deal of history about the residence itself and the treasures it was said to contain. Robbie smiled at the guidebook mention that Randolph Churchill had lived here as a private secretary, while his young son Winston was said to have enjoyed the grounds in his donkey cart.

"Stunning, isn't it," Frank Sullivan said. He was riding over to the dinner with Robbie. "We've been the official tenants since 1927, and for a number of years, the mission's offices were located here as well. As you'll see, there is plenty of room."

There certainly was. Robbie went to the upper floor with his bag to freshen up. He was directed to his suite, one of six on the upper floor, and with a barely audible whistle he entered his spacious quarters. "Guess I really owe you one, Clark." He put his clothes away, prepared for a quick shave - five o'clock shadow is no respecter of time zone changes - and glanced around the bedroom briefly. He was intrigued to note what seemed to be superb furniture throughout the room, clearly never issued by a parsimonious government.

It was the real stuff, and he tried to remember what he had occasionally viewed on PBS and the *Antiques Road Show*. Yes, that cabinet seemed to be mahogany and well styled. And there was a secretary, with fold down desk, the upper portion containing a selection of reading material. Really very nice indeed. Whether the pieces were Irish or English, he really had no idea.

Robbie went downstairs. He paused on the upper landing, and took in the vast dimensions of the mansion. There was, in addition to the library and offices, which the Secretary would probably be using, a reception room and formal dining room, and even a ballroom. It was on a magnificent scale. Perhaps it was time to start thinking about the future, and how one could actually get to live in this magnificent residence. Well, Robbie doubted that a career Foreign Service Officer's salary and allowances would cover the upkeep for this residence, no indeed. You'd have to have made some real money to afford that.

It seemed that pieces of expensive furniture could be found throughout the mansion. There in the hallway was another fine piece, a highboy if he remembered correctly. And over there, on the ground floor in the hallway leading towards the reception area, was a rather large and imposing secretary. It looked early Victorian probably, and was not very stylish. The wood, possibly oak, was darkened by time. At the foot of the stairs, Administrative officer Bob Starett was telling several of the travellers about the furnishings. He stopped abruptly.

"I can't go on, with an expert like Ambassador Carlisle here. Would you care to say a few words about this secretary, Mr. Ambassador?"

Robbie looked around. He saw Rudolphe Carlisle coming down the stairs behind him.

"Before I stick my neck out, whose is it? Does the Government own it, or does it belong to Ambassador McGowan?"

"Like the other period pieces, we sort of inherited it. I don't know the full *provenance*, but clearly it was brought over from England at some point by a previous Chief Secretary. I seem to recall that we, that is the USG, bought this piece, along with some of the other period furniture. So it is not her personal property."

"That lets me off the hook. Quite a surprise, seeing that here, with all of the fine pieces throughout this residence. Actually, that isn't early at all, although it is supposed to look like it." He paused and took a searching look at the secretary. Then he nodded, his mind made up. "It's Gothic Revival, 1840s to 1850s I would gather. The early Victorians had a thing for Gothic architecture and furniture. And that is when Sir Walter Scott was writing his immensely popular novels about medieval times. So anything remotely Gothic or Tudor looking became quite the vogue for the sentimental Victorians. This secretary is worth a hard look, but it doesn't really fit in here at all. It's an interesting piece for all that, particularly if you like Victorian furniture." Since nobody would admit to that taste, the conversation ended.

They entered the dining room. Dinner was pleasant, well served and relaxed. Under portraits of previous Ambassadors who had lived here, the party enjoyed the Irish salmon and fine white Bordeaux wine. Robbie sat next to Nancy Starett, wife of the Administrative Officer. They had been assigned to Dublin for several years, and liked it so much that they were trying for a second tour. This was unlikely to be granted, as they well knew. A plum assignment like Administrative Officer at Embassy Dublin would attract a lot of interest from bidders at the annual job sweepstakes in the Department of State held by the Bureau of Personnel. Fair was fair, and somebody now in a hardship post would surely get Dublin. He asked her about the residence.

"It's really magnificent. One of the finest. I'm told that the Ambassador's residence in Prague is also quite something, but I've never seen it."

Robbie, who had seen that residence during a visit to Prague that he had made while assigned as Political Officer at Embassy Budapest, confirmed her impression. It was a fine town residence, virtually a palace. The Ambassador there had given a reception for visiting diplomatic firemen that he had attended during a conference of political officers from the region.

"By the way, your husband was showing a few people around, talking about some of the furnishings. They must be quite valuable. I suppose that he has an inventory?"

"Oh yes, Bob worries about that a great deal. Most of it is permanent, but some of the pieces do belong to Ambassador McGowan."

"Does he like antiques? I suppose that just goes with the job."

"If you mean does he have any special training, the answer is no. But as Administrative Officer, he kind of feels that they are somehow his responsibility. He's very responsible. And he has read up some."

"Well, I'm sorry to have missed his tour. Perhaps he'll favor us again sometime during the stay here in Dublin."

"I'm sure he would be glad to do so."

Although it was an informal dinner, still, the temptation to give and receive toasts couldn't be resisted. Ambassador McGowan ran through the list of Irish-American Presidents of the United States, and wondered whether Secretary Adams, whose mother was Irish, might some day add his name to the list. Secretary Adams responded in kind, noting that Dublin was such a pleasant assignment that he was thinking of applying for it himself one of these days. That is, in the highly unlikely event that Ambassador McGowan's lease on these premises ever ran out.

It was an early night, as planned, after such a long day. Robbie looked forward to a good night's sleep and then to the chance to see Dublin. Drat, he'd forgotten to exchange some dollars for euros. Well, surely he could take care of that at the Embassy in the morning. He went to sleep with a number of dream sequences vying for attention from Washington to Dublin.

— — — — — — — —

Robbie took a second cup of coffee and some muffins from the counter at the Embassy cafeteria, paid for them, and went upstairs to his office. Along the way, he stopped off at the Budget and Fiscal Office, and cashed a check on his Chevy Chase Bank account for euros, introducing himself to the cashier, who seemed pleasant and anxious to please. Surely the DCM had given them all the usual pep talk, Robbie guessed.

He had had a fine early breakfast at the Ambassador's residence, but was now just stoking the fires for the morning's work. He had awakened and gotten up far too early, after a disappointed glance at his travel alarm clock showed him that it was two hours too soon to get up. Oh well, it was still the middle of the night Washington time. How long did it take to make up the difference, and get your inner clock adjusted? Well, he was halfway there. And downstairs in the dining room, the staff had been told to prepare for an early breakfast.

Robbie had a free twenty minutes to stroll around the grounds. He was pleased to see that security men tracked him every step of the way. Whether they were always here, or extra hires for the Secretary's visit, he couldn't say.

But the lawns were freshly mowed and rolled, and all looked pristine and smelled wonderfully of fresh country. The birds were up early and fluttering about in pairs. Bird watching, come to think of it, was a hobby that might be interesting, when he got more time on his hands. Maybe it would even interest his father. Didn't seem to cost anything, and it was a healthy hobby that got you out into the fresh air. Certainly here, in this beautiful park and property, it could even change him into a morning person!

He had killed time until the Embassy would be opening, and then had taken an Embassy car to the office. Entering his office, he looked over towards the next office and saw that the Executive Secretariat team was already in business. Great. He poked his head in through their door, and was rewarded with the Secretary's morning take of cables and wireless files. There was also a courtesy assortment of Embassy Dublin traffic, and a sprinkling of newspaper articles on the Secretary's arrival.

Robbie sat down and went through the traffic, marking the cables in the usual three piles for Missy. He checked the schedule once again. No changes. There would be a meeting with the Irish Foreign Minister at 10:30, followed by a joint press conference at noon. The Secretary and Ambassador McGowan would be having luncheon with the leaders of the American business community at one o'clock, followed by the Secretary's golf date.

Then protocol took over. Late afternoon would feature a courtesy call on the Prime Minister, the *Taoiseach*, at his office in Upper Merrion Street. Nothing substantive was expected. They would hold a business meeting the following morning, followed by a press conference. After today's courtesy call, a reception hosted by Ambassador McGowan at her residence would introduce the Irish A List to Secretary Adams. Breaking precedent, since the visitor was not a Head of State, the Irish President would then host the formal dinner that was the social highlight of the visit. Robbie supposed that that was perhaps because the Irish President's House, *Aras an Uachtarain*, was located so near Ambassador McGowan's residence in Phoenix Park.

Robbie gave the cables and newspapers to Missy Bronson, all business now that she had a real office within which to function. "No changes, I suppose?" What she conveyed was that Secretary Adams was very organized, and expected others to be. Some changes were always to be expected. They went with the job. But keep them for essential things, please, so that everything we've already been through doesn't have to get recalibrated.

Secretary Adams waved to Robbie from the inner office, to come in and join him.. The only detail that he wanted to be absolutely sure of was that the ceremonial gifts that he was bringing for the Irish President and Prime Minister were being handled. He didn't want to carry them himself, or have to worry that they wouldn't be there at the right time. "No, sir. Your security detail has both. How about the Foreign Minister?"

"Oh, he's a fly fisherman. I met him in Paris at a G-8 meeting two years ago. I've brought him a box of some really fine, hand-tied flies. I've got them with me."

"I'll be sitting in on your meeting with the Foreign Minister, along with Assistant Secretary Palmer and Ambassador McGowan. I saw that Clark Framsen had been scheduled for that. How about your courtesy call?"

"No, don't bother. That's all it is. Just take the afternoon off when we leave the Foreign Ministry, and I'll see you back at Phoenix Park. You'll be right near one end of Grafton Street. I see that their Foreign Ministry, Iveagh House, is on St. Stephen's Green. Grafton Street runs right into that park. Nice area."

He turned and concentrated on the morning's cables that Missy had just brought in. Robbie saw that in Missy's office, which guarded the Secretary's inner sanctuary, Press Spokesman Charley Sherburne was already waiting, with his perennially uptight expression. Is that the way he is, or the way he's become from dealing with the Fourth Estate, Robbie wondered.

— — — — — — — —

Leaving the Foreign Ministry was a bit like playing hookey. Robbie felt let out from school while it was still in session. The meeting at Iveagh House had gone well, and the joint press conference stressed the Guantanamo prison closure, cooperation in fighting terrorism, and the welcome that the party had experienced. "This is what President Kennedy must have seen when he came home to Ireland," was Secretary Adams's delighted comment. It was also the headline that led the television news that evening, and the next day's press throughout Ireland.

As a bonus, the Foreign Minister had been genuinely delighted with

Secretary Adams's gift. "How thoughtful! I was worried that it might be another paperweight with the State Department on top. I've got three of them already! This is something I really like and will use. When you come back, I'll show you some real trout streams. They don't come any better than those in County Wicklow."

County Wicklow. That sounded very familiar, but Robbie just missed placing it. It couldn't be a personal memory. He'd never been to Ireland before. But it did sound familiar. He wondered why. He'd better ask his sister Evalyn. She was the walking family scrapbook, and remembered just about everything.

Robbie found Grafton Street, a broad, long walking street that stretched all the way from St. Stephen's Green to College Green, south to north. At that further end was the famous Molly Malone statue, a busty female with her cart selling cockles and mussels, as the song demanded. A photograph there with her statue was an absolute must, and if you didn't have one taken, some doubt surely arose whether you had really been in Dublin at all.

And the buskers! He'd never seen them before, street performers that played in pantomime, dressed as musicians or figures from the past. Sometimes they just stood silent as passersby first halted, then came to a full stop, then went up to them, living statues, to have their pictures taken. Others offered mime performances, or sometimes, silent dances. Several had makeup, white faces with clown markings that delighted the children, and made some passing adults think for a moment. A cap on the ground in front of each street performer collected the tips. It was great fun watching, so much so that you could forget other surroundings.

The weather was perfect, and so was the shopping. There were the familiar favorites, department stores and modish clothing stores galore. It was always fun to wander the aisles at Marks and Spencer and see what was new, and what would do for a souvenir that really didn't look like one. Genuine stuff, not airport trinkets, that was the key. But there were also expensive specialty stores, jewelry shops, displays of fine Waterford crystal, Irish woolen goods, crafts and works of art. Most of the expensive specialty shops that you would find in other European capitals were represented here.

He remembered when the euro was worth just 80 cents! Those were the good old days! Multiply the euro price by about one and a half to get the real dollar prices now! Well, the dollar was beginning to gain strength as the United States started to pay its bills. It had been foolishness indeed, the richest country on earth living beyond its means, and that had been going on for decades! On the other hand, frugal Norway was becoming for its size an economic powerhouse.

Robbie went into the Waterford shop. He wished there would be an opportunity to visit the showroom itself, but there just wasn't time during their too short stay to permit stops around the countryside. All of the items for sale in the shop were beautiful, but most were too large for him to carry comfortably, and he really didn't want to trust anything to the mails, sure though that might be. He settled on a matching pair of cognac glasses. That would be a lasting present, and a regal way to sip the cognac they both enjoyed.

He had been told to be sure to have something at Bewley's Café, the landmark stop for coffee or something stronger. And so, halfway up Grafton Street on the left, he did so. The restaurant was bustling and it was time for luncheon. He ordered a pint of Guinness draft and a platter of shepherd's pie and tucked into an enjoyable luncheon. Bewley's Café had been around for 80 years or so, and the announcement a few years ago that it would close had sparked a campaign led by the Mayor of Dublin herself to save this institution.

Robbie had a leisurely finish to his luncheon with strong coffee and an apple tart with cream. Then slowly, almost reluctantly, he relinquished his chair and walked along Grafton Street, taking in the shop displays, until he came to College Green and Trinity College. This, as his wife had said, was the absolute must visit of his stay in Dublin.

Robbie entered the great gate to the college, pausing to look at statues of eminent Irish university and literary figures that were planted here and there near the entrance and at intervals along the green inside the fencing. Here, college buildings attested seriousness of purpose and permanence. One of them housed a museum, and the most famous book in Ireland, and perhaps anywhere in the world, the Book of Kells.

It was a short line today, and so Robbie didn't have long to wait before entering the secluded space within the museum where the Book of Kells was kept. Along the walls were explanatory posters, telling of the times when the book was made, and the artist monks who had made it. It was a time full of extreme danger from northern marauders who respected neither church nor culture, the same Viking marauders, Robbie wryly reflected, who had really founded Dublin itself! It had been started, page by individual vellum page, on a remote island, possibly the famous Iona, before being spirited away for safety.

Finally it was his turn to stand before the exhibit of the Book of Kells itself, behind protective glass, one page clearly exposed at a time. Robbie supposed they were rotated occasionally, to protect the book. It was elegant, with superb attention to detail and craftsmanship, the letters alone an individual delight. But the pictures that adorned certain words and phrases, particularly at the beginning of the page, or a biblical chapter, were most striking. This treasure set the standard for medieval craftsmanship. Probably it was the donation of the book to Trinity College that had preserved its presence in Dublin over the years.

Lost in thought, Robbie left the Book of Kells exhibit, walked up a flight of steps, and entered the Old Library area, itself more an exhibit than a working library. Ah, there it was, the famous harp that had been found in the ruins of a former royal Irish site. It was said to be the oldest harp in Ireland. So what if grim historians disputed its authenticity? What did they know of the power of myth and music, anyway? This small standing harp was iconic, its picture even figuring on Irish currency in the past as a symbol for a people and their nation. In its way, it was certainly as celebrated as the Book of Kells. He walked back the length of the library after admiring the harp. Here were hundreds of old books, treasures to someone, surely, safe in their obscurity, he hoped.

Robbie reentered the gift shop from which he had entered the Book of Kells exhibit, this time from the other side, having crossed over the library area that formed the upper floor of the building, then come down the steps. Now he was attracted to the items for sale, and in no possible way did they strike him as touristy. He absolutely had to have that pin of the harp, and would sort out later who would get it for Christmas. His sister Evalyn, perhaps. An illustrated book on the Book of Kells was another absolute must. So was a silver thistle brooch with colored stones for the burrs, and he just had to buy a scarf with a perfect colored illustration from the Book of Kells. Maybe two of them? Which background color would go with Sylvie's complexion best?

No, get a grip, this was the FIRST stop on this trip, remember? He remembered tales of luggage almost bursting open from past diplomatic trips, and now he understood why. It was like being in a candy store. You wouldn't be paying for the trip itself, or for your accommodations or even for most of the meals, so you couldn't help but feel rather flush, with money to spend on nice things, like these presents. What he didn't want was for his credit cards to be maxed out before they even got to the second capital on their itinerary! Safe and sane, he put back the second scarf, and selected half a dozen postcards instead. He'd write them on the plane.

Leaving Trinity College, he still had a hour or so, and started walking back towards Grafton Street. Then he paused. What did he want to see most, in the short time still available? He remembered talking with a guard at Trinity College, when leaving the library. "For our real history, go to Kildare Street, the National Museum there. It's not far, and it's worth seeing."

Robbie decided to follow that advice. With luck, he could then duck in at a corner pub for another pint of Guinness. He followed Kildare Street back towards St. Stephen's Green, and then found the National Museum of Ireland, actually one part of it. Here was located the collection of archaeology and history, and as part of its collection, a treasure trove of gold ornaments from the early Bronze Age, set in cases around a dimly lit central hall The work was breathtaking, probably jewelry of some sort or breast plates, the gold hammered wafer thin. Robbie was reminded of gold work that he had seen at museums in Athens, and once, at an exhibit of early art in Bordeaux. It was superior work from an ancient culture, perhaps a culture common to what was now Ireland and France. Had it really been fashioned on these islands before they were islands, and even before they were Celtic?

Another room held a treasure trove of early Christian work. Here Ireland's actual rich history came fully alive once again. Robbie saw the Tara Brooch, the Ardagh Chalice, and other treasures from Ireland's remotest Christian antiquity. The brooch was the one that he now saw everywhere, with variation, for sale at museum shops and less scrupulous stores. He was doubly glad to have bought one at the gift shop at Trinity College, and would now have quite a story to tell. This branch of the National Museum had many more treasures to explore, including galleries devoted to both Medieval Ireland and Viking Ireland, but Robbie had had his share of high culture for the day. It was definitely time to find a friendly pub and make a start writing his postcards from Dublin.

That one on the side street leading from Kildare Street back to Grafton Street would do very nicely. Robbie found an empty chair at a table outside, in the pleasant warming sunshine. As a bonus, when he glanced at the menu, he saw that it contained a reference to James Joyce. Beyond that, there was a quotation from *Ulysses* that referred, by name, to this very pub! Robbie ordered his pint of Guinness, and when the waiter returned, said how he pleased he was to have found a Dublin pub so closely associated with Ireland's great writer.

"Well sir, that's as may be," said the waiter, "but the truth of the matter is, that it's devilish hard to find a pub in Dublin that ISN'T associated somehow with James Joyce. He was that thirsty!"

— — — — — — — —

After a late morning's sleep, Rudolphe Carlisle had spent an enjoyable morning. First breakfast, then by arrangement with a nearby stable, a brisk canter around Phoenix Park. The horse was frisky and wanting a good workout. Carlisle was glad to have brought some riding togs and his boots with him. They had been purchased new for London, but that hadn't worked out. He had been a generous contributor to the last campaign for the White House, but Carlisle was not in the same financial league as the hedge fund manager who become Ambassador to the Court of St. James's. So what if Phoenix Park wasn't Rotten Row? It was probably, from the standpoint of riding and exercise, even better than that fashionable central London riding area.

He enjoyed his canter, returned the horse to the stable, and went back to the residence to change clothes. Luncheon had not been served at the residence, since both Ambassador McGowan and her ranking guests were lunching in town with the American business community. He had an Embassy car take him to a restaurant near Phoenix Park for luncheon. Why was corned beef and cabbage supposed to be the great Irish specialty, when the lamb was so delicious and freely available? He glanced at the newspaper someone had left at the next table. It featured the Secretary's arrival, and the national soccer news. Then he had walked back to the Ambassador's residence, a pleasant few miles in the sunshine. He found in his luggage a book to read, the one he had started on the plane.

The residence was quiet. There would be several hours before the staff started to prepare for the reception that evening. Carlisle was enjoying his rest in Dublin before proceeding on to Riga. He was a thoughtful guest, and would help out where needed with conversational openers at the reception. All this fuss for the Secretary's visit didn't bother him, and the chance to meet some new people who counted, and had money to spend, was always a plus. They would remember meeting him when he was an ambassador, long after he had relinquished that title and had rejoined the commercial art world, locating antiques and selling them. Too bad the London visit had been postponed. That had been his real objective, where there was so much money once again available for art purchases, but the Secretary's schedule had been reshuffled. Well, it was good seeing Mary McGowan again.

He would be leaving Dublin a day or two after the Secretary's official party had left. Mary McGowan had asked him to stay, so that as a personal friend, she would have more time to be a proper hostess, and show him something of Ireland. The travel liaison office at the Embassy had made arrangements for his onward flight from Dublin, and he had sent a first person message to the Deputy Chief of Mission, acting head of the Embassy at Riga until Carlisle arrived and presented his credentials. He would still arrive several days before the Secretary's party came in from Moscow. Would that be sufficient time for him to present his diplomatic credentials from the President?

The DCM's reply was coated with diplomatic maple syrup. It said that the Latvian Government had been most accommodating. The necessary protocol and formalities would be taken care of after his arrival and before the Secretary's plane landed. Have a good holiday.

He suspected that is what any good DCM would have arranged. No disagreements, no acknowledgement of inconvenience, just find a way to accomplish what the new Ambassador wanted to do, and was going to do in any event. Well, he would bear that in mind when he made a recommendation for the man's next assignment. Carlisle was cautious enough to realize that assuming they got along well, the DCM should stay for long enough so that Riga and its history and politics were clear to him. Well, that young Consul,

Stan Bartlett, would help as well. He seemed like a good worker, and the sort of person who makes friends easily. Having him as a friendly subordinate would send a helpful message to others on the junior staff.

His book was turning out to be less interesting than its back jacket blurb had promised. With a yawn, he tossed it aside, got up from his overstuffed wing chair, and decided to go outside for another stroll around the grounds. He walked down the stairs, then paused as he came to the landing. There on the ground floor was that secretary, looming up like an unexplored miniature Gibraltar. Perhaps a closer look was in order.

He approached and studied it carefully. The top portion was unexceptionable, a middle nineteenth century addition, convenient for stacking books and stationery. It had some exterior carvings. Surely they were machine made? The legs and bottom portion seemed similar. They were probably designed to accommodate the middle portion, the desk portion, which extended out from the base of the secretary. This portion was carved oak, nearly blackened with time. That clearly was the interesting part, if any of the piece was worth a second look. It had interested the Victorians enough to give it a second life as an integral part of a quite different piece of furniture. But then, as he had implied earlier, the Victorians really enjoyed the Gothic look, which this piece seemed to have. The question now arose, though, whether this really was just a Victorian fake, as had been his first impression, or whether the carved oak middle portion was genuinely something older.

Carlisle squinted at the carving on the front outside lid. It seemed to be rather naive and somewhat pretentious, but charming for all that, and perhaps because of it, like most folk art. He could just make out a lion, and what seemed to be another beast. Was that a unicorn? No, the central horn on the forehead was lacking. Anyway, if this piece was as old as Carlisle was now beginning to suspect, it was centuries before the lion and unicorn had become the royal coat of arms. From the size and length, he suspected that it was a carving of a beast that the carver had never seen, because it didn't exist. A dragon, perhaps?

That would be a very odd motif. It was certainly not a religious one, not by itself, without St. George. The desk certainly had not been designed for use by a clergyman, and that in itself would be of interest, because most literate people then, Carlisle knew, were clergy of one sort or another. Something carved for use by a literate person who was not attached to the church was itself unusual. It made him wonder.

He opened the lid, which opened backwards. There was a stick and catch, he suspected a recent addition, so that the lid would remain open. When the desk itself had originally been made, there was no top portion, and the lid had just swung back and stayed open, resting down on the table behind the desk. Now that there was a top portion on the secretary, that was impossible, so a way had to be found for the desk to remain open while it was being used. That was clear enough.

What wasn't clear was the dimension of the desk. It was hard to tell how deep it originally had been. For that matter, the desk itself was so full of clutter that it was impossible to examine carefully. Magazine clippings, old newspapers, a family picture here and there, whatever had struck the fancy of generations of owners. You couldn't even see to the bottom of the drawer. It was a heavy mass of outdated material, of no earthly use to anyone. And if Carlisle were not already rather bored by too much vacation time on his hands, he would have given up the examination then and there.

But it was interesting and unexplained, and he did have some time on his hands. After the Secretary's party had left Dublin, perhaps he would have the leisure to explore the matter further. Surely Mary McGowan couldn't spend several entire days touring with him around Ireland. He had seen enough of Embassy life to realize that the work was constant. So this would be something interesting to do during Mary McGowan's inevitable sessions at the Embassy. A sort of diplomatic *Antiques Road Show*. He almost looked forward to the research, but probably, like that popular PBS television show, the likelihood of finding anything of real value was very small.

CHAPTER FOUR -
Irish Eyes Are Smiling

THE EVENING RECEPTION AT AMBASSADOR McGowan's residence found everyone in a good mood, anxious to please, or have an interesting time, or both. The Embassy officers and their wives were all present, and the occasion was clearly a festive one for all concerned. For several hours before the event, caterers had supplemented the household staff, hiding their mobile kitchen with its warming ovens on the lawn behind the residence.

They all had gone through security checks; at least, that was the theory. The catering firm had been doing catered affairs for the American Embassy for twenty years. The standing instruction hadn't changed over the years. "Serve good stuff, and don't try to stint." Over there by the side windows, a small ensemble played some light classical selections, for a pleasant background rather than for musical enjoyment. Even the ornamental trees and plants around the room had been trimmed and freshened up. They were probably impervious to spilled alcoholic beverages by now in any event.

Ambassador McGowan, Secretary Adams and Assistant Secretary Palmer formed the receiving line. As diplomatic ritual demanded, Ambassador McGowan was first in line, so that she could perform the introductions. She was amused to think that she was the highest ranking American official there, as the personal representative of the President. That was a distinction that every ambassador quickly overlooked when the Secretary of State was in town! DCM Smiley and Political Counselor Sullivan were in close attendance, whispering to Ambassador McGowan notes on the guests as they approached, or as she turned towards them, having momentarily forgotten someone's name or office. In reserve, Ambassador O'Malley, with a coterie of officers from the American Desk at the Foreign Ministry, tended to similar duties for his principals.

The conversation kept moving throughout the reception room, and was pleasant, fueled by fine *hors d'oeuvres* and wines, and choices of soft drinks, Irish whiskey and Maker's Mark bourbon. For those who did not know American bourbon, Ambassador McGowan, a native Kentuckian, was ever ready to explain the healing properties of the beverage, particularly when it was graced with branch water, a touch of sugar, nicely macerated with fresh mint and served on Kentucky Derby Day.

And, Robbie reflected, it was all in English! No straining to recall which verb tenses and persons and idiomatic expressions Mr. Petropoulos would have had to teach for this sort of occasion, in the recesses of FSI. That was a real plus. In Bordeaux, the language hadn't been a serious problem, except for his accent, which was still more Boston than Bordeaux. But he also remembered his early days in Budapest, struggling to hold even a rudimentary conversation in Hungarian.

That was life in the Foreign Service, a sort of perennial starting over. When you knew the territory and were beginning to get somewhat comfortable with the language everyone insisted on speaking locally, off you went to a new assignment somewhere else. Usually, your new assignment took you to a place where your last language was not only not understood, but an impediment to learning the new one. So you acquired a different bizarre accent from the second language while trying to speak the third one!

Ambassador Carlisle struck up a conversation with a woman wearing a tailored blue suit and white frilly shirt with cufflinks, Kelly Martin, a lecturer in Celtic studies at Trinity College. She was no dour academic. In her thirties, attractive and fun to talk with, Kelly Martin was a popular addition to the diplomatic set.

"I'll be staying on in Dublin for a day or two, after the Secretary's party leaves," Carlisle said. "Ambassador McGowan has offered to give me a car for an outing. What should I see?"

She stalled while thinking it over. "Well, that's quite a question. If you had one day in New York City, what would you see? It almost becomes a matter of what you should exclude, and in this beautiful country, that's too sad a prospect."

Then she made up her mind. Talking while mulling things over was a classroom technique that she had mastered. "However, you asked. So I guess I would tell you to see the Lakes of Killarney. That's in County Kerry. It's a bit of a drive, but you'll find the scenery is worth it. And if you have more than a day, then stay over and drive around the Dingle Peninsula, or perhaps the Ring of Kerry. A lot of our history is there still."

"Still?"

"Well, the scenery of course. On the Dingle Peninsula you can still catch a glimpse of what the early dwellings were like for the monks, just made of stones they were, poor souls. They must have half frozen in winter. The Ring of Kerry is magic for the scenery."

"I thought you were implying that some things are no longer there."

"I was, but I am not sure it was the best of manners. If you go to Killarney, go to Ross Castle. It's worth seeing. Both the castle itself, and the furnishings. You said that you had a special interest in early furniture. They have some there, oak from the sixteenth and seventeenth centuries. Then, take a boat out into the lake, it's called Lough Lein. That means 'Lake of Learning.'"

"Bizarre name for a lake."

"Yes. There's a reason for it. If you are lucky, the boat will take you across the lake, and you will find Innisfallen Island. It's quite deserted now, but it used to be thriving as a sort of religious settlement. A bit like Mount Athos in Greece, I should think. For centuries there was an abbey there, throughout the medieval times, and what some call the Dark Ages, when our Irish priests kept civilization going."

"So I understand. I read the bestseller!"

"Yes. Thomas Cahill, *How The Irish Saved Civilization*. He puts the case, I think, with typical Irish understatement." They shared a laugh.

"You have heard of our Book of Kells?"

"Of course."

"Well, that's not the only one, although it is certainly the best known. There were many fine books carefully made on vellum throughout the Middle

Ages, that managed to survive the Viking raids. But to see them now, you would have to go to Oxford University. The treasure from Lough Lein is called the Annals of Innisfallen, from the island. You'd have to go to the Bodleian Library now to see it. But it's not the only one. There are others there too, quite a collection of our national treasures."

"I'm sure they are all well looked after and properly kept.'

"Yes, that has been the customary explanation."

"Well, now I'm most curious to see County Killarney."

She smiled. "There is no such place. Killarney is in County Kerry."

"See how you are furthering my education about Ireland? Now I'll have something to tell my new friends in Latvia - the ones still in Riga, who haven't emigrated to Dublin yet!"

They both laughed.

Robbie and Press Spokesman Charley Sherburne shared some *hors d'oeuvres*. "This stop must be an easy one for you," Robbie ventured. "That welcome was tremendous yesterday, and they like us anyway."

"Well, yes and no. In my business, you do cultivate friends, and try to make more of them. Lots more. But you must never forget, newsmen are out to write a story. They want to get published, and they want to be on the leading edge of a break. Scratch a newsman, even a good one, and you find a *paparazzi*. They aren't at all bothered by controversy - they go looking for it! The good ones, and that's the overwhelming majority, don't ever make things up, and they give you a break. By that, I mean that they will check with me for a comment before printing something damaging that they've heard. And even then, they won't go with, usually, without some credible confirmation. But a bad story can happen anywhere, at any time, and you can't let yourself be lulled by the nice surroundings, or the common language."

"Sounds like a tough business. Full of minefields."

"Well, it does make one raise a thirst. Waiter!" He hailed a passing waiter and took comfort in a large glass of Jamesons and ice with a splash of water, "just to keep the whiskey company."

The arrival of the ranking guest, Prime Minister Thomas O'Bryan and his wife, was apparent to everyone by the blaring horns of their motorcycle escort. O'Bryan affected an apologetic stance for the noise, which fooled nobody. He liked the fuss.

"In your country forty or fifty years ago," he confided to Secretary Adams in a stage whisper while shaking hands at the reception line, "I might have been Mayor of Boston! Think of that!"

Not to be outdone, Secretary Adams said that reminded him of a story he had once heard from Senator Henry Cabot Lodge. The story had taken place when Lodge had run against Governor James Michael Curley of Massachusetts for the United States Senate in 1936.

Lodge, 34 years old, had only served four years in the state legislature, following a stint as a journalist. He wasn't given much of a chance during the campaign, and Curley had been dismissive, not taking him seriously. "Don't send a boy to do a man's job," his campaign literature had said.

But Lodge had paid attention to detail. He issued strict orders that no sirens be used by his motorcycle escort when he was campaigning against Curley. Since Curley as Governor and, before that, as Mayor of Boston, had annoyed nearly everyone from time to time with his motorcades, that had meant a number of votes gained for Lodge! He ended up winning the election by a narrow margin, even though President Roosevelt carried the state for his first reelection victory, and Lodge was the only Republican in the nation that year to win a Senate seat that had been held by the other party.

"After all," Lodge had continued, "by that time, everyone had known what a bastard Curley was. But they didn't know me ... Yet!"

O'Bryan roared at the story. "Ah, but even against Lodge, the Irish won in the end - twice. With John F. Kennedy for the Senate in 1952, and then the White House just eight years later. Both of them against Lodge. It was a great source of inspiration for the old country, I can tell you." Adams realized that much more was being implied about Irish history and gradual acceptance in Massachusetts than was actually said.

Ambassador O'Malley and the Foreign Minister came up to escort the Prime Minister around the room. It really then became a political gathering in the guise of diplomatic reception. The careful diplomatic circumlocutions stopped, and the backslappings began. Robbie Cutler was in the direct line of fire as he reached for a glass of Guinness from a passing waiter, and the Prime Minister greeted him. "Yes, you were with the Secretary this afternoon. Cutler, wasn't it? Robbie Cutler?"

"Yes, Prime Minister. I was honored to be present."

"Well, you are a young man, and the fact that Secretary Adams brought you means that you'll have a fine future, surely."

"Kind of you, sir, but his Executive Assistant had a heart attack just before we left Washington, so I'm sort of a last minute replacement."

The Prime Minister was on a roll, and simply would not be rebuffed in his gregarious *bonhomie*. "Now, now, don't sell yourself short, Mr. Cutler. There will be plenty that you'll find who will be quite willing to do that for you. Mark my words!"

He was about to move on to the next group of people, when a thought occurred to him. He turned back. "Would you by any chance know or be related to Seth Cutler?"

"He is my Great Uncle Seth, Prime Minister. Do you know him?"

"We have had contact over the years from time to time. I hope he is well." On Robbie's nodded yes, the Prime Minister's smile broadened. "That's good news indeed. Tell him hello from 'Sauerkraut' O'Bryan. He'll remember the reference, I'm sure." Prime Minister O'Bryan, with a conspiratorial wink, moved on in his sweep of the room. He went towards the far end of the reception hall in an arc, and now was turning back towards the receiving line to complete his circumnavigation of the room. Robbie realized that he would be leaving as soon as the sweep ended, and that he would have spent barely half an hour there, yet managed to greet everyone. He even managed a nod to the waiters, who were all smiles. Well, why not? They were surely voters for the most part, whereas many of the reception guests were nonvoting foreigners.

Also, Robbie realized, the few moments that he had spent with O'Bryan had been concentrated on the two of them. O'Bryan had not once looked elsewhere. While he was with him, O'Bryan had paid him absolute full attention, looking him straight in the eyes. None of this looking over the shoulder stuff to see who else was in the room that might be more important. Well, why should he? It was the Prime Minister himself and Secretary Adams who were the most important people in the room, and they had already talked. By making his sweep of the room, like a grand ocean liner, O'Bryan had created a sea lane that brought everyone into its vacuum. He didn't have to go to them. They came to him. And if by any remote chance he might have missed someone at the edges of a group of people, his wife made sure that each was included. Every single person was greeted.

But beyond that, people came to O'Bryan for a reason. They probably had been doing so for thirty years, when he was just starting out, penniless and eager. He hadn't had anything to offer then, surely, except his hopes and their futures. Then he had won election after election. Was it now his office that attracted people? For some, surely, but the magnetism went beyond that. It seemed to be his gift of conferring his importance on others. That, and his genuine interest, or so it seemed, in whoever he was talking with at the moment.

This was the Prime Minister of Ireland, and he was really interested in what you had to say. He listened with close attention, and then he would add a laugh, or, as with Robbie, a word of encouragement or remembrance, which meant that there had really been communication between the two of you. It wasn't at all one-sided. There had been a back and forth, a spark, a contact. He wasn't just waiting to talk with someone else. You had your own moment. When the tale was told by people who had met O'Bryan, it would include that vital fact. "For a moment just, the Prime Minister and I had a *conversation*."

If this was the political art, it looked like great fun, but Robbie doubted that he would ever have the knack. He also realized that he would never forget the few words of advice that he had just heard. He could have drawn a picture of that earnest, friendly face easily, but aside from that, the image blurred. Robbie couldn't remotely remember what he wore, or even how tall the Prime Minister was. Beside that smile, and those eyes and that friendly voice, nothing else seemed important.

As the Prime Minister took his leave, other reception guests two by two began to take their leave as well. Then it was time for those who were attending the President's dinner to leave. Bob Starett had arranged for Embassy cars to ferry the guests the short distance across Phoenix Park. While they were gone, everything would be cleaned and the furniture again polished before the Ambassador and other dinner guests returned from the President's house. To any cursory inspection, except for a few crushed flowers near the driveway, there would have been no evening reception at all.

It was a nice evening, and if they had had the time, some guests might have walked the short distance along a Phoenix Park trail to the dinner. But at some point schedule worriers must have their way, and nobody wanted to be late to the dinner. Certainly not the one reporter with the trip who had been chosen by an informal lottery on the plane to attend the dinner. He would be the pool reporter for the event, covering it for everyone else. Well, some would have their own turns at later events during the Secretary's trip. They were all seasoned pros, not out of their leagues. Some would remember White House roasts like the annual Gridiron Dinners, now revived in full vigor with the President and First Lady once again in annual attendance, making healthy fun of themselves.

And so the dinner party drove the short distance to *Aras an Uachtarain*, Irish for House of the President. There was enough curiosity about the residence that George Smiley held a short seminar on the way over for the ranking guests, in their limousine. He started with some diffidence. "I don't mean to lecture, but I just thought that you might be interested..."

"No, no, Mr. Smiley," said Secretary Adams. "I appreciate your efforts. It will all be of interest, and give us something to talk about with our hostess. We don't want to be gawking tourists once we get there, after all!"

Thus encouraged, Smiley noted that it was a fine residence, literally a regal one, and nearly always had been. "It has a very proud history. Built in the eighteenth century in the days of British rule, when the Viceroy had lived in town in Dublin Castle, this had originally been a lodge, or summer retreat. You'll see how it has grown since then once you're inside. The Council of State Room was the original dining room. The present State Dining Room was built for a visit by Queen Victoria. But I'm getting ahead of myself.

"Later in the eighteenth century it became more of a viceregal residence, and then, it just got grander over the years, as it evolved from country retreat to residence. As you'd expect, there are portraits in the walls of past Irish Presidents (theirs, not ours), and furnishings added over the years. Extensions were built to the building as the times required, notably as I said for the 1849 visit of Queen Victoria. It continued as the official residence of the Viceroys until Home Rule began in 1922, when the Queen's representative, the Governor General, lived there. Since independence, it has been the official residence of the President of Ireland. Seminar over."

"Fine *précis*, George," Assistant Secretary Palmer said. "I can see why the cables you edit are so packed with useful information."

The limousine and other Embassy cars swung around to the rear of the imposing building, and pulled up to the formal entrance. As he was getting out of his car, Robbie's cell phone rang. He answered its insistent noise, irritated that it was still on in the first place. Wasn't this like being in a concert?

"Mr. Cutler? Ron Jackson, Executive Secretariat. I'm at the Embassy. Sorry to disturb you. But there is a cable you should take a look at."

"Shall I come right away? I'm just going in to the dinner." Jackson would understand where he was.

"Sorry. I know it is a royal pain. Excuse the pun. Tell you what. It is not operationally immediate, and from the context, more is on the way, but it's unclear when. Why don't we leave it this way. I'll wait for the next message, and then call again. If you are stuck, I'll courier them out to you personally. But if you are through dinner and you haven't heard from me, give me a call at the Embassy, and we'll take it from there."

"Thanks, Ron. Sounds like a plan. And the name is Robbie."

Robbie caught up with the end of the line of arriving guests. He hoped, really hoped, that the cell phone would not go off at some embarrassing moment. Then he remembered. It had a switchover, from the musical tone to vibration. Relieved, he took out the cell phone again and made the switchover. He was in the formal Entrance Hall in full view of Irish President Edith Quinlan when he had another mortifying thought. Now, if he had to leave a state dinner in the Irish President's official residence, nobody would hear anything, and everyone would just assume that he had diarrhea. How embarrassing would that be!

He tried to think of something gracious to say to President Quinlan, and blurted out how glad he was to be there, adding "It's such a grand evening, and I think the other capitals we'll visit will be very hard pressed to offer anything like it, Madame President."

She smiled warmly. "How pleasant, Mr. Cutler. And they tell me you're not even Irish! My sources of information are clearly wrong."

Robbie saw George Smiley looking about the entrance corridor at various allegorical stucco panels lining the walls. He caught up with him and they strolled over to the attractive inlaid marble fireplace, and large decorative traditional Irish harp standing near it. "Yes, it really reminds me of the one in the old Trinity College library," Smiley said, "but it is not so old. Last century or two, I think."

They were shown by a uniformed guard into the State Reception Room, just off the entrance corridor. "Quite a room," Smiley said. "It's my favorite one. I particularly like the carpet, even if it's not the original one. This used to be the ballroom. It's where President Quinlan receives ambassadors. Ambassador McGowan presented her credentials here, in a formal ceremony. I accompanied her. And President Quinlan has continued a very nice touch that one of her recent predecessors started. She invites schoolchildren to be present for these ceremonies. Rather nice, actually."

Drinks were served. Since they were just coming from their own reception, that would be rather *pro forma*, and dinner would shortly follow. But it was a nice opportunity to stroll around the State Reception Room and the Council of State Room just beyond it. Robbie and DCM Smiley went through the open doorway, carrying their drinks into the Council of State Room.

It was particularly charming. Smiley said that this room was part of the original house, built in 1751. It had been the dining room then. Now, there were elegant ceiling paintings from Aesop's *Fables*, while on the walls hung a painting of the Council of State, an advisory group to the Irish President. Robbie tried to marry the two in his mind, looking from the animals on the ceiling to the dignitaries in the painting. His college French literature class came back, and the writer, La Fontaine. In his *Fables* each animal had its own character, and all together, the animals comprised a sort of royal court, code language for what he dared not say too directly. The lion of course was the Sun King, Louis XIV. Who were the others, and what were they like?

Dinner in the State Dining Room was announced, and the guests checked for their dinner places on seating charts held by uniformed footmen on either side of the door leading from the Council of State Room to the State Dining Room. Robbie found his, fortunately not far from the door if a quick exit was needed. He was seated next to that pleasant Celtic studies instructor, Kelly Martin. Rudolphe Carlisle had introduced them at the earlier reception.

"I saw you looking at those pictures in the Council of State Room, Robbie, and I know just what you were up to. I've had exactly the same thought," she said as he sat next to her. "It would be fun to figure out the human counterparts of those animals on the ceiling. Which was which, really? Who is cunning and who is wise and who sucks up to power and who is kindly? But you know, the animals all look their parts, while the humans put on a show. So you can't really tell much about them except for the obvious fact that they were all distinguished, or hoped to be considered distinguished, which in the long run may amount to the same thing."

"Guilty as charged," Robbie admitted. "Is literature your field at Trinity College?"

"Celtic studies. If you will, the folk history of Ireland. And that does include a real kinship to Aesop."

"But it's not all fables, surely."

"Not at all. We're very proud of what our people accomplished. I like to think that our current writers are just continuing the traditions. You have seen the Book of Kells?"

"Absolutely. It was number one on my list to see in Dublin. After the Molly Malone statue, of course!"

"Cockles and mussels. She must freeze in the winter. Anyway, there are many Irish literary treasures. Many of them aren't even here, like the Annals of Innisfallen. I was talking with Ambassador Carlisle about that. They are in the Bodleian Library at Oxford now, and there are a number of them there."

"A pity they are not here."

"Absolutely." She smiled. "Well, Dean Jonathan Swift did try to get the major portion of those manuscripts deeded to Trinity College here."

"*That* Jonathan Swift?"

"Yes, that Jonathan Swift, who wrote *Gulliver's Travels*. A pity he didn't succeed, and they were auctioned off. At least Oxford got them. But it would be grand now for them to be better known and appreciated here. At least now they have been catalogued properly by our School of Celtic Studies. That wasn't done until 2001. But it's a good start. Now people can know about this collection of our history."

"I see the problem. Or rather, several problems. It all starts with the Elgin Marbles, which the Government of Greece wants to be returned. Then we could go on to these treasures. But it isn't even the British Government that owns them, if I understand rightly."

"That's what adds to the difficulty, yes. Maybe it won't ever be resolved. But what a wonderful thing it would be if these treasures could at least be exhibited here - all around this island. In addition to the Annals of Innisfallen there are others in early Irish, written beautifully and painstakingly on vellum. The Annals of Ulster, for example."

"I had no idea. What are they? Church records, for the most part?"

"Well of course there is that, and the work was done by monks, so painstakingly, one letter and word at a time. But also you have records of the early kings of the regions of Ireland, the nation's whole grand history. It's a treasure trove in every sense."

"Well, you've certainly convinced me. You know, we had our own scrap with the British over two centuries ago. When the British pulled out of Boston in 1776, some of the earliest and most precious Massachusetts colonial records were missing. That included the primary record of the Plymouth Colony, William Bradford's *Of Plimoth Plantations*. The book was finally located in England during the late nineteenth century, and its possession became rather a tug of war between our countries."

"Now it's my turn to say 'I had no idea.' I hope your story has a happy ending?"

"Well, of course, since it is America. That's what we specialize in." She saw that he was entirely serious.

"We did get it back. Now it is in the State House Library on Beacon Hill in Boston. I just wish it were still on public display, like our founding documents at the Archives in Washington."

"So it worked out very well indeed. Principle, I suppose, and bargaining power."

"That's what it needs for things that ought to be done to actually get done."

"I'll bear that in mind."

He gave her a puzzled smile.

"Well, if you can keep a secret, President Quinlan has asked me to give these issues some thought, you see."

Now he did. So that explained her presence here. She was clearly a friend or colleague of President Quinlan.

Then a squad of waiters entered the room. Some poured chilled white wine in the Waterford crystal glasses, while others served the first course, mussels with wine sauce, *moules marinières*.

She said, "You see how Irish folklore is important even here? This is Molly Malone at the *Aras an Uachtarain*, the President's House."

She smiled and turned to talk with the guest on her right.

— — — — — — — —

It must have been the luck of the Irish, even though I'm not Irish, Robbie thought. He had not been interrupted by a phone message during the dinner. It was afterwards, when the last courses had been served and cleared, the toasts given, and the guests risen from their tables that the vibrating cell phone had reminded him of the waiting message.

He was in the Council of State Reception Room sipping a Hennessy when Ron Jackson reached him.

"The second message is in, Robbie."

"Great. Don't bother to come here. I'll take an Embassy car now. Thanks for letting me get through dinner."

"Not my choice. If this one had come in earlier, you'd have known it."

"I'm on my way."

The Embassy car sped through Phoenix Park, across the bridge over the Liffey River, and into the Ballbridge section, Dublin's Embassy Row. Robbie entered the Embassy, went through security, checked with the Marine Guard, and met a waiting Ron Jackson, who led him to their adjoining upstairs offices.

There, in the secure room, lay the folder. It contained two cables, each marked NODIS SALADIN. The first was from Embassy Tripoli. It was short and to the point. It informed the Department of State that their deep cover Libyan contact would be checking in with his Embassy controller in a few hours, with important news. He was eliptical, clearly talking around the subject, but he seemed to be saying that he had been called to a meeting to find out more details.

Robbie saw immediately that Embassy Tripoli only vouched for the source's reliability, without giving details that might identify him. Was he a main player in whatever scheme was being hatched, or a go-between? Well, after the Embassy Tehran hostage takeover in 1979, that was only prudent. Robbie remembered that the Iranians who had overrun the mission then had spent months painstakingly putting back together cables and other secret documents that had been shredded. No more of that. It was better not to spell things out unnecessarily.

The second NODIS SALADIN came from the State Department. Embassy Dublin was the only addressee. Clearly the Department was summarizing some reporting, probably back channel, from Embassy Tripoli. It said that their informant had said that Al Qaeda was planning an important action against the United States, at the direct order of Osama bin Laden. What was involved, in the guarded language of the terrorist extremists, seemed to be assassinations. The source reported one chilling phrase. "It will be the most successful operation since Booth."

The source said that he was cutting off any further contact with the Embassy. It was not apparent whether he was doing so because of fears for his own security. Maybe he was just going to be out of the information loop. Or maybe, chilling thought, the informant was himself part of the plot, if there really was one, and this was all designed to mislead, while something else entirely was underway.

In any event, the Department assumed that enhanced security measures were in order. Let's see, Robbie thought, the 1865 Booth plot did kill President Lincoln. But it was much broader than that. They tried also to kill Vice President Johnson, and several key cabinet members. Surely the equivalents of today's Secretaries of State and Defense had been targets. And it had all been planned for the same night.

No wonder the Department was alarmed. Where do we go from here? He could imagine the frenzy that Washington was now in. Meetings of intelligence agencies as the Director of National Intelligence asserted his authority to try to get an overall assessment and any further information, without tipping off the enemy. Trying to control intelligence agencies would be like herding cats. Then there would be operational meetings, planning enhanced security. You could count on agonizing judgments by the Department of Homeland Security on whether to reinstate colors indicating the national threat level. Robbie could almost hear the arguments. In the end they would decide not to do so, in order not to have to answer questions that were unanswerable at present. And, of course, they must not tip off Al Qaeda that the United States was aware that anything was up. If anything really was planned.

The Department cable had said that it would start a new series of operational security messages, restricted access but not NODIS and certainly not SALADIN. Regarding the Secretary's trip, each Embassy being visited was asked to contact their host governments immediately, and redouble security. If possible, public events were to be curtailed. Don't cancel them unless absolutely necessarily. The point was to push security to the point of being annoying, without tipping our hands that a specific threat was being addressed.

For Dublin, since the Secretary was leaving the following day, there was a special note of caution. It's too late to change much, but be sure that the Secretary's public appearances are strictly limited. Well, that wouldn't be hard. Robbie remembered that the main thing was the late morning office meeting with Prime Minister O'Bryan. After that, it was basically wheels up in any event. The early morning was for packing. There seemed no need to move up the Air Force Two departure, even if that would be possible. They would just be running into the same set of security issues at the next stop.

Robbie thought about the tactical situation. It was his job to make sure that everyone was briefed, fast. But Clark Framsen would go farther. He would take immediate action. Robbie checked his watch. It wasn't very late, just 10:30 in the evening. It would still be late afternoon in Washington. They might always send a third message, and he had to keep everyone in the loop, with a minimum of backing and filling. After all, they all had their own jobs to do. Without the information that he was getting, they were blind to the possible danger. And just distributing cables was clearly insufficient. There had to be coordination, and at least the beginnings of a plan. You had to be on top of a possibly fastbreaking situation, not driven by events.

Robbie made a short list. Since the Department was taking action without reference to SALADIN, it was not his business to do otherwise. He added a name or two, then crossed them off. He was grateful once again for Ron Jackson's superb sense of organization. There in his personal folder relating to the trip was a contact sheet for everyone in the party, with phone and cell phone numbers and details on where they were staying. He also had contact information for Embassy Dublin. Then he reached for his desk telephone and called into the Embassy the head of security for Air Force Two, the Administrative Counselor for Embassy Dublin, Sam Jardine of Diplomatic

Security, who was in charge of the Secretary's personal security for the trip, and Charley Sherburne, the Press Spokesman.

When they had arrived, he told them that a generalized, but credible threat against the Secretary of State had just been received. Washington would be sending out instructions and, he assumed, a threat assessment. Other posts along their route were being instructed to approach host governments. Clearly, this visit was nearly over. But it was a matter of keeping heads up, and not taking any unnecessary risks. For Embassy Dublin, just redouble your efforts. No last minute PR public appearances. He said there would be a further meeting on Air Force Two after they left Dublin.

Charley Sherburne stayed behind. "What do you know that you're not telling us, Robbie?"

"We'll talk it over on the plane tomorrow. I'm sure glad you're not covering this trip as a news story, Charley. There wouldn't be any secrets left by the time we left Dublin!"

Robbie wondered whether to brief Secretary Adams now. It was a close call, but he decided not to play the cautious bureaucrat covering his rear end, and let Secretary Adams get a good night's sleep. No sense worrying about what he could not help. He would brief the Secretary directly after breakfast as he handed him the overnight cables, including NODIS SALADIN. He could also have a word with Ambassador McGowan then. She would probably know that something was up, from her Administrative Counselor.

That would probably annoy her deputy, DCM George Smiley. In good theory, things were supposed to go through the DCM, not directly to his subordinates. Tough. Robbie told himself that he couldn't notify everyone without sounding alarm bells, and he didn't want to do that. Besides, he worked for the Secretary of State, not Embassy Dublin, and that gave him a certain freedom of action. But he could see how it was tough sometimes to "come down from the seventh floor" and work into a regular Embassy diplomatic assignment, particularly one that you had visited working for the Secretary. It might still be payback time for the people whose noses were still out of joint from your visit.

Robbie yawned. It had been a full day, and he was tired. He wished he could share it with Sylvie, right now, over a glass of wine in their living room. Well, that would have to wait for a week or two. Then he remembered his conversation with Prime Minister O'Bryan. On a whim, Robbie placed a call to Uncle Seth. He caught him at dinner, at his home in Cape Ann, Massachusetts. Robbie could hear the voice of Annie, Uncle Seth's longtime housekeeper, as she greeted him, and then handed the phone to Uncle Seth.

"It's Master Robbie, Mr. Cutler."

"Master Robbie," indeed. He might still be twelve years old.

Then Uncle Seth took the phone. His voice as always sparkled with enthusiasm, retaining the youthfulness of his spirit. He greeted Robbie with delight, as though he had finished dinner instead of being interrupted in the enjoyment of one of his favorite dishes. Uncle Seth was the last flowering of the Teddy Roosevelt era, Robbie always thought. Everything was a grand adventure for Uncle Seth, from beating the Nazis to consulting for the White House. What would it take for that wonderful, goodhearted optimism to come again and lift a generation?

"Yes indeed, I remember 'Sauerkraut' O'Bryan. He was a scholarship student at St. Marks, at least thirty-five or forty years ago. He came to us from Dublin, or perhaps, from his village in one of the rural counties. Not a penny to his name, but always a winning personality. Even then he showed character, brains and real talent. I've followed his career with great interest over the years."

"How did he get that nickname?"

"Well, one day we were having corned beef and cabbage for dinner, and the boys were ragging him about it, being from Ireland. He said that back home, he would always have his corned beef with sauerkraut, since he didn't like cabbage at all. So the boys started to call him 'Sauerkraut' O'Bryan. I guess it didn't stick or wasn't known back home. A good thing. That wouldn't have helped him with Irish voters one bit!"

"Wonderful story. I'll tell him we talked at the meeting tomorrow. He specifically asked to be remembered to you."

"Fine. Please give him my best. And tell him to look after Secretary Adams carefully. Mustn't tarnish the Irish reputation for hospitality."

"Oh?"

"And give me a call sometime early from Embassy Paris. I take it you're going there next? Good. I'll look forward to a chat. You know my friends have given me a new phone. Helps to avoid long distance charges, and we retired folks appreciate that. Even with the federal telephone tax finally finished. Good night, Robbie."

"Good night, Uncle Seth."

Well, that was interesting. He had just been told that Uncle Seth, long a consultant for American intelligence agencies, and recently an advisor to the Director of National Intelligence, now had a secure means of communication. He also had been told that Uncle Seth knew that something was in the wind that he wanted to discuss.

Robbie had saved the best for last. He called Sylvie, to tell her all about the dinner.

Her voice was all smiles. She was delighted to hear from him. It sounded like she had been waiting for the call. He'd better remember that. After all, she could hardly call him, given his uncertain schedule and rapidly changing locations.

"It sounds like a wonderful event. Trust President Quinlan to lay on the sheer Irish charm. And who did you sit next to?"

Right to the point, as usual. "A very nice Celtic studies lecturer at Trinity College, Kelly Martin. She told lots of interesting stories about Ireland."

"I'll just bet she did. Who else did you sit next to?"

"I don't remember the name."

A brief pause. "Well, I hope your shopping was successful on Grafton Street."

It looked like he was going to need it!

— — — — — — — —

Osama bin Laden and Ayman al-Zawahiri considered the prospects for Operation Salah al-Din. The decision to include the word "Booth" referred to the April, 1865, attempt to kill leaders of the Federal Government, planned for a single night in Washington. By now, the Americans would have heard from their operative in Tripoli, and started their counter planning

Ayman al-Zawahiri had feared that the feint might not work as planned. A phased operation was perhaps too complicated. He had also argued against any leak that would inform the Americans that a plot of any kind was underway. Why tell them anything in advance?

But Osama bin Laden recalled that there had been criticism of the 9/11 attack. Many civilians had been killed, which had bothered the squeamish. More important, some had objected that the Americans had not been warned and given a chance to avoid the attack by changing their conduct. In response, there had now been at least six direct warnings to the Americans that bin Laden had issued. America's Crusaders must leave the holy lands of the Middle East. Furthermore, he had even repeatedly told the American President that he and his nation should convert to the true religion, their Islam. The West had dismissed this as propaganda. They had not understood that it was essential preparation for the next attack. Now, they had even been warned specifically. There could be no criticism this time from fellow believers.

Bin Laden liked the idea of a feint. That always seemed a good strategy against a stronger opponent. Since that was the case, why not create their own leak to the Americans? That way, they might anticipate and to a degree even control the enemy's reaction. For the truth was that American security had improved. They could never again assume that there would be another successful 9/11, and that a major new plot would not be discovered. Their working assumption had to be that there would be a slipup somewhere. Why not take advantage of that changed reality, and misdirect them, as an integral part of the overall plan?

"They will think that a plot against their President and Vice President has been planned. That will dictate their response, to protect their leadership. They will react accordingly. And it will cost us very little. The men involved do not expect to return to their homes. They are true martyrs, not just in the way they imagined."

Now, they must be careful to bolster the impression they had begun to create. Soon other carefully controlled leaks would be given, one by one. Create anticipation, then fear, finally havoc, and make the threat credible. Barring a detail here or there, the Americans would try not to be heavyhanded. Not at first. They would surely not reinstate their threat level, for example, those color codes that lulled their people into believing that they were accomplishing something.

The teams were in place inside the United States, and had been for months. The schedules of the President and Vice President were known. For the next week or two they were both keeping a number of public engagements, the President in Washington, while the Vice President had a three day early election visit to California. Make it seem as if they were the primary targets. That is what the Americans feared and would expect, in any event. An unguarded phone call or two, carefully orchestrated, should reinforce the trick.

The phone call messages, to be made by team members already in the United States, had been carefully choreographed, practiced again and again. The messages included words that would surely be monitored. Each man had been given an exact time and place for his message, as had the person called. The answers were also minutely scripted. The men were told that it was all for security's sake. They were establishing themselves for later contact as the mission proceeded, and then would receive their final instructions later. The first series of calls had already taken place that morning, American East Coast time.

These men were surely already being watched by the Americans. They had been carefully briefed before departure with enough small errors to ensure that the hounds would find and then track them, hoping for bigger game. It was a delicate game of balance on both sides. If the errors were too obvious, or showed them to be too important, the men might be picked up too soon.

In that way, new American security countermeasures would work against the Americans themselves. The better the NSA got at monitoring communications, the more secure they became. Instead of picking up their targets immediately, they would instead track an operative in the field, leaving him alone and hoping to be led to larger game. That also meant, of course, more time to feed them controlled misinformation.

Nobody in the field knew more than his exact assignment and the mission's stated overall purpose, so when they were all inevitably picked up, there was nothing further to be revealed. All they could say if they cracked under torture was that they were preparing for a decisive strike against the President or Vice President. They were the first phase. They had been told that once established, they would receive final instructions to do the killings.

The Americans would believe that. That was designed to feed their paranoia. They would surely never guess that it was all part of a larger plan. For with these captures, the real operation would begin. With luck, that would explode onto the world just when the Americans were trumpeting their success against Al Qaeda at one of those press conferences they were so fond of holding. But even if not, the "Booth" shadow play would create a false scent that would keep the Americans off the track. They would think the failed operation in America was the real one.

American security was increasingly tight. But the real operation, once launched, would be conducted under cover of the behind the scenes consternation that the bluff would cause, and if they were very fortunate, also under the relaxed security that would surely follow that plot's presumed failure. They were creating for the Americans an initial feint as a diversion, and then Al Qaeda would launch its actual attack. They would eliminate the American Secretary of State while he was on his first trip abroad, trumpeting American power.

The operations plan for killing Secretary Adams was twofold. The inspiration had come from recent experiences in insurgency operations around the world. They had seen that an initial explosion would create damage and confusion, and set the stage for the second, larger one. That had been the case everywhere - in Cyprus, in Algiers, in Saigon, in Africa, and in Baghdad. People stumbling out of a building or a restaurant after an explosion, or out of an Embassy, for that matter, would clog a narrow street or entranceway, desperately seeking safety. They would then fall easy victims to the second, larger blast.

Adapted to their American enemy, the result would be lethal and devastating. With good fortune not only Secretary Adams, but most of the high ranking American diplomats who traveled with him would be eliminated, all in one stroke. Instead of "innocent civilians," this time most of the American diplomatic establishment would be wiped out.

And Secretary Adams, doubly dangerous because he was reasonable, who had already infuriated them by insisting that Guantanamo be closed, and had maintained that position strongly despite all obstacles, was now raising the American image around the world once again. Well, he would no longer stand in their way. Alive, he stood in their way. Dead, he would serve their cause, for recruiting for Al Qaeda and the final victory would accelerate as the Americans blindly retaliated.

With Allah's help, Operation Salah al-Din would succeed as planned.

Just over one week remained.

PROLOGUE (PART TWO)

WAS HIS WORK REALLY DONE? It was far too soon, and yet, there had been so many adventures. Christopher Marlowe knew that he had lived with the times. His plays were a source of gratification and income. If only he had had more talent for organization and the necessary patience, perhaps his own company, like Will Shakespeare's, would now have been a possibility.

It was not a matter for real regret that he had spied for Sir Francis Walsingham. The times had seemed to demand it, and it had been an adventure. Those of the old religion could indeed be treasonous in their intent: some certainly were in their deeds. But still, the doubts came, now more frequently, late at night.

He had participated in enough spy missions to know the signs: a remote place, well out of the way, meeting with people of uncertain loyalties. He was not even sure who would be there. And so the summons to Deptford bothered him. No, it was more than that. He was possessed by a sense of foreboding.

Did they know that he was uneasy in the new faith? He had put it about that he was a rakehell, unsure of any faith. But that smokescreen did not fool everyone. Some indeed took it as a mask behind which he might still harbor loyalties to the old religion. And in the year of Our Lord 1593, the old religion might well mean disloyalty to the English Crown.

In a way, he thought, it was his learning and quest for knowledge that had caused the problem. While he was in Rheims on one of his missions for Walsingham, scouting out who were the English Catholics, he had run across a former acquaintance from Corpus Christi College. The fellow had left Cambridge surreptitiously. It had been one of Marlowe's tasks to run him down, and find out his loyalties, or rather, to secure if necessary proof of his disloyalty.

The fellow had recognized him immediately. He was joyful on seeing Marlowe once again.

"So, Kit, well met! I knew that behind that facade, you were loyal to the true Church."

So it had begun, and it had lasted half the night. Finally they had gone for a walk outside the tavern to relieve themselves in the garden. Then they walked down the country road a bit. That is when the fellow had told Marlowe about his mission. He was being sent back into England to prepare the way for others to follow, well trained native Englishmen who would spread the true faith. He was gleaming in faith and sincerity, and he was pale and sickly, scared almost to death.

That is when he had asked Marlowe to keep something for him, something he had been given to peruse to strengthen his faith and courage. Now there was no time to return it safely. Would Marlowe keep it safe until his return?

It was a document written four centuries earlier, at the time of the crusades. It was a stirring testimony of faith. It was written, or probably dictated to or composed by a scribe. It was, he said, the *Confiteor* of Baron Robert Crecy. The document began with a confession of doubt and error, in Latin. Strikingly, it then continued in French and in Latin.

Baron Crecy was a French nobleman, a Knight Templar who had participated in the crusade that had gone terribly wrong. Led on and on by the wily Venetian Doge, Enrico Dandolo, the western armies had been lured into fighting, not the common enemy, but fellow Christians at the great city of Constantinople.

That had been in 1204, Marlowe remembered. He thought for a moment through the legends and epic stories that he had heard. Yes, that venture would have been the fourth failed attempt to reestablish a commanding Christian presence in the Holy Land. It had come to nothing amidst the ashes of a ruined and looted city, once the finest in Christendom. Venice, of course, had profited accordingly, and many of the looted art treasures were now part of St. Mark's Cathedral.

But not all of them. For what Baron Robert Crecy had described in his *Confiteor* was a cloth made of linen, a long folded cloth, which had been known for centuries. His *Confiteor* then gave the cloth's chronology in Latin, with dates and places. Its voyages to Constantinople from Jerusalem, by way of Edessa, were stated. To Marlowe's astonishment, mention of the Shroud at the Battle of Hattin in 1187 was also noted. Marlowe thought that this chronology might originally have been a separate document that had accompanied the cloth on its journeys. It seemed a reasonable assumption. The hand was not the same that had penned the *Confiteor*.

And then in French, Baron Crecy described the cloth and his understanding of its meaning. This was clearly a personal document. And this linen cloth that men had given their lives to protect over the centuries - was the burial shroud of Jesus. The very image of the Saviour was said to be imprinted on the cloth, shining through in full body length. The *Confiteor* also mentioned a separate cloth that had wrapped loosely around the Saviour's forehead, and that had been separated from this linen cloth centuries earlier.

Baron Crecy had searched his conscience, and then taken the linen cloth, as carefully as he could, home to his estate in France when the crusade ended. It was safer in his hands. If he had left it, it might have been destroyed by casual looters looking for gold or jewels, or even abandoned as baggage on the return voyage by some adventurer. God only knew, there were enough of such scoundrels.

He had terrible doubts about the failed crusade and his part in it. He hoped that if he had done wrong, his Saviour would take his intention into account. He had saved what he could, this precious fragment. Could that have been the purpose of his own crusade, after all? And there the *Confiteor*, dated May, 1207, ended, with the attestation of a scribe and the Baron's seal and mark.

Marlowe had been stuck by the tone of the *Confiteor*. This was not written down as a great secret. It was overall a compilation of details and places and occasionally, dates when the writer or writers knew them. But that was just it. It was a record of what people still knew and understood, put down in an authoritative form, so that they would be clearly remembered. It was written with evident reverence but not as a mystery. It was the truth as Baron Crecy was given to understand it. And through the document came the striking faith and personality of Baron Crecy.

"And," Marlowe said to himself, "if I am any judge, it is also a literary masterpiece."

He had agreed to keep the *Confiteor*. He had also violated his agreement with Sir Francis Walsingham, and failed to report this man and his mission. That had not been so very long ago. The man, inevitably, had been caught and publicly executed. Had he named Marlowe? Was that why he had now been summoned to Deptford, on the grimy dockyard outskirts of London?

He could not rule it out. He also must make sure that the *Confiteor* was safe, for a better age, when the fanatics were gone and its truth would be understood. Now it was in the deep hidden drawer of his desk. But even that would not make the document safe if he had been betrayed. The Privy Council agents would surely search his few belongings carefully and repeatedly. They were used to finding what they set out to find, for they knew that many people had tried to hide things, priests, papish literature, anything that suggested an adherence to the old religion and perhaps, to being an enemy of the Queen.

Marlowe thought carefully for a moment. He must lay a careful trail that would lead to the *Confiteor*. In case he did not survive the Deptford appointment, the precious documents could still be saved, for a better age. He thought carefully for a moment. Yes, Isaiah would do perfectly.

He opened the desk front. He took from the open drawer the slip of paper on which he had written the date that the desk had been made, and his whimsical notation that Peter Quintus had made it. It was now necessary to signal the existence of a secret drawer. A Latin motto would do nicely. He wrote *Per Lux Lunae ad Veritatem* on the paper. That should be a sufficient signal. It might lead an informed man to the first hidden drawer.

Then he pressed the crescent moon. The hidden drawer rose. Marlowe thought carefully, took a fresh piece of paper, and then wrote from memory two verses from Isaiah in church Latin, which any cultured man would understand. It was a sufficient indication to the priceless treasures hidden deep within the desk.

But still, something was missing. Marlowe thought again, and wrote the story of his encounter at Rheims. That might count for forgiveness, surely needed for his soul's sake. He wrote in detail what his doomed college friend had told him, the story as he understood it of Baron Crecy. Now, as the lawyers would have it, there was a perfect link of custody of the *Confiteor* and its attestations.

Leaving the first hidden drawer open, Marlowe lightly pressed the carved dragon figure on the front lid. With a slight click, the second drawer slid partly open. There it was, the Baron's *Confiteor*, and its attestation of faith, and the mysteries of the Shroud of Turin and its voyages from the Holy Land. Marlowe signed and dated his his own document, and placed it with the *Confiteor*.

Then he carefully closed both hidden drawers. They were as safe now as he could make them in an impious age. The Latin motto properly understood would lead directly to the first hidden drawer. Once there, the quotation from Isaiah would lead an educated person to the realization that a second and deeper secret existed, perhaps even a second drawer. That was as far as he could safely go.

Then Marlowe went out from his room in search of a drink. It was an overcast day, already quite dark. He thought for a moment, then returned to his room and picked up his desk. It was certainly time now to presume on an old friendship.

CHAPTER FIVE -
A Tale of Three Cities

ROBBIE ENJOYED HIS EARLY BREAKFAST. Pancakes with real maple surup, and slabs of bacon. Trust a Kentuckian to know about genuine American hospitality. Last night's dinner and reception had been a shining privilege, one of those rare diplomatic perks that he would always remember. To make up for it, he would probably have to endure many endless receptions south of the equator nursing watery gin drinks before his career was over.

The meeting at the Embassy had been a tonic. It made him sure that he wasn't just tagging along to deliver papers; he was earning his keep. Scratch Robbie Cutler, he sometmes thought, and you'll find Holden Caulfield. Well, the meeting had given him a real sense of accomplishment. He couldn't wait to compare notes with Clark Framsen, to see how he would have handled the situation.

And on top of that, he had really had a good introduction to Dublin, a fine and memorable free afternoon, and now he looked forward to coming back with Sylvie. He suspected that she was the family sophisticate. Well, Dublin would give him the chance to show her something wonderful. And if this was what Dublin was like, just imagine seeing the Irish countryside. He had tended to dismiss the well known folk songs as teary Irish romanticism, fueled by memory and Guinness. Now he was a believer. If anything, they didn't do this wonderful country justice. And, as President Edith Quinlan had said, he wasn't even Irish!

Charley Sherburne caught up with him as he strolled back and forth on the lawn behind the Ambassador's residence, walking off his double helping of pancakes.

"Have you briefed the old man?"

"No, the Secretary's not up yet. I'll let him have some coffee first. I can see the dining room from here. Then I suppose we'll go in to the Embassy, and he can read the cable traffic himself. There isn't anything for him to do, in any event. At least, there wasn't last night."

"Sounds like a plan. Well, I'll miss Dublin. But I didn't miss the key pubs after our meeting last night. What a time! Say, did you see that looker at the dinner?"

"You mean Kelly Martin? Yes, I sat next to her."

"Good thing you're an old married man. I had a word or two with her, and she's charming. She spent lots of time with Carlisle after the dinner. You'd just left, I think."

"Yes. I had just been called to the Embassy for those messages we talked about." Come to think of it, he had had an undisturbed night's sleep. That certainly meant that the Executive Secretariat team hadn't received any more rockets during the night that required immediate attention. Surely otherwise, Ron Jackson would have called him.

"Carlisle will be staying on for a day or so after we leave today. Dollars to donuts he and Kelly Martin have something planned by now. He's a bachelor. Something of an *artiste* I guess at that auction house. He makes me puke. Ambassador and a bachelor and rich, too. Some guys have all the luck."

Robbie grinned. "C'mon, Charley. What's it to you? Besides, you're in over your head with Sheila. She's much too good for the likes of you. Talk about dumb luck! The real story is how you managed to get her to marry you in the first place. So, live and let live."

"It's not in my DNA." He paused as they walked along the pathway. "But who would have taken Carlisle for a birdwatcher? I thought they were outdoor types."

"Why do you say that?"

"Well, it was last night. I heard him exclaim something about sparrows.

'Five sparrows!' Something like that. He sounded quite excited. The odd thing was that it was very late at night and even with the security lights playing on the lawn, there weren't any birds out there. Strange."

"As you say. Well, there's the Secretary, just coming in for breakfast. It's time for me to ruin his digestion. See you later."

Robbie entered the residence through the reception room back door, then walked into the dining room. He said good morning to the Secretary, then nodded as Rudolphe Carlisle came in and took his place at the table with Ambassador McGowan. Four for breakfast. Well, that was fine. Save him the trouble of separate briefings, particularly since Carlisle had better be briefed before he got to Riga, and McGowan should be told immediately. Robbie waited until their breakfast orders had been taken, and the waiter had disappeared into the kitchen. Then they started exchanging some chitchat until their breakfasts arrived.

It was impossible to wait any longer. Robbie leaned forward in his chair. "I have some news, Mr. Secretary," he said almost conspiratorially.

"Sounds like a prelude," Carlisle said. He was smiling, but smiling through a load of Irish whiskey from the night before.

"Yes. We have a security alert. A serious one, from the Department. Another two cables have come in, in that series, Mr. Secretary. It looks like Al Qaeda is planning something big against the United States, and so to be on the safe side, the Department is also concerned about your own safety." He looked at McGowan and Carlisle, who nodded, and stared at him intensely. They wouldn't repeat what they shouldn't have heard.

"We don't have many details, but it sounds urgent. The Department is sending out more messages separately regarding security for this trip. I'm sure the Embassy will have them. So should Embassy Riga, Ambassador Carlisle, and our other stops on the trip. I got the warning cables after the dinner last night and met at the Embassy with some key people dealing with security. I didn't want to bother you last night, Mr. Secretary. There didn't seem to be any need to do so." That should also do for Ambassador McGowan. "But security measures for today are being reinforced. Fortunately there was nothing public on the schedule anyway. Now there cannot be."

That fired up Ambassador McGowan. "I'll check that out at the Embassy right away." Her reaction shook loose the freeze frame that the little group had become as it absorbed Robbie's news.

"Thanks, Robbie. I guess we'd better finish breakfast and see what's come in overnight at the Embassy." The Secretary finished his coffee, made a pass with his fork which missed his scrambled eggs by two inches, then touched his face with his napkin, stood and walked towards the entrance door.

Ambassador Carlisle stood with them. He mumbled something about speeding up his plans and arriving as soon as he could at Riga. Tomorrow or the next day should do. He decided to go with them to the Embassy, and then give Kelly Martin a call.

— — — — — — — —

The Embassy Marine Guard on duty came to stiff attention as the Secretary of State and his party arrived. They went directly to his office. Robbie got last night's cables from the safe, gave them to Missy Bronson for the Secretary, and then went to see Ron Jackson for the morning's cable traffic. Sam Cartwright, the junior member of the Executive Secretariat team, was on duty, and he handed Robbie the cable take.

"No more of that series, Mr. Cutler."

"Robbie."

"Robbie. But there is an all points cable about security. The Embassy has already picked up their copies, and DCM George Smiley is holding a meeting."

"I just bet he is," Robbie thought. He returned to his office and began to leaf through the cables, marking them in the usual three groups. The security cable, downgraded to EXDIS, would be seen by everyone who should read it, at every Embassy they were visiting. In theory at least, EXDIS (Exempted Distribution) implied a limited distribution, one that was exempted from the usual distribution pattern, not automatic. More people would see it than a message marked NODIS (No Distribution). In practice, it depended upon who wanted to read the messages. The new cable cited enhanced threats without being very specific, and then called for a redoubling of security measures related to the trip and the cancellation of any public appearances "if that could be done with discretion."

In other words, just do it, and swallow the diplomatic fallout.

Dublin wasn't affected now, but that would surely upset plans in other cities. No review of the *Garde Républicaine* in Paris? Not very likely. Robbie was sure that other posts would chime in asking for exceptions, unaware of the nature of the warning and the threat that had been posed. Come to think of it, wouldn't the cancellation of previously published plans be an absolute giveaway that they were reacting to a specific threat against the Secretary of State? And if so, wouldn't Al Qaeda just bide its time, and strike when we were less prepared?

He assembled his cables and went to give them to Missy Bronson. He knocked on the door and heard a muffled permission to enter. There was the Secretary, Assistant Secretary Donna Palmer and Charley Sherburne. They were on a conference call with the Executive Secretary in the Department's Operations Center. It seemed to Robbie that they wanted more details than the Department seemed willing to give or could give for the time being.

Robbie tried to make sense of the one-sided conversation.

Worst case, should the trip be cancelled and rescheduled? No, there was no credible excuse. How about cutting it short? Well, they couldn't skip London, which was the last stop. How about Moscow? This was hardly the time to offend the Russians - just imagine not going to Moscow for security concerns! How times had changed. There was an unsatisfactory general feeling that they should continue to wing it. And, of course, each Embassy along the way was now under the gun to tighten its procedures. Each was ordered to approach its host government to do what could be done to reduce the threat that had surfaced.

"Yes, thanks." The Secretary hung up the phone and turned to Robbie. "They said I've got full authority on SALADIN messages. What on earth does that mean?"

"That means that you can initiate them. More important, you can send them to another Embassy. By the rules only the Department can do that, usually the Executive Secretary personally. It's a good idea. It gives us the flexibility we may need."

"How about the press play, Mr. Secretary? These guys are always on the scent. Any changes, and the stories will start being written from Air Force Two."

"All the more reason not to overreact, Charley. Let's meet this afternoon on the plane with security and go over the trip in detail. There is a very short suspense reporting time on this cable from the Department. Every Embassy is supposed to reply by midafternoon on what steps have or should be taken, and they are each then supposed to coordinate with us."

— — — — — — — —

Prime Minister O'Bryan welcomed them warmly at the entrance to his first floor office on Upper Merrion Street. The building's entrance hall featured a fine staircase and stained glass window, which, the *Taoiseach* proudly explained, had been part of the Irish national exhibit at the New York World's Fair in 1939. It showed a traditional Irish harp, and the emblems of the four ancient provinces of Ireland.

The visitors were the minimum necessary - Secretary Adams, Assistant Secretary Palmer, Ambassador McGowan, Political Counselor Sullivan, and Robbie Cutler. The Prime Minister was joined by the Irish Foreign Minister, and two men whose names Robbie didn't quite hear. The grimfaced man was probably there for security. The other, designated as notetaker, looked like a pleasant, open faced fellow, surely a coming man in the Irish diplomatic service.

Robbie was last in line to enter the office and shake hands with the Prime Minister. "I talked with Uncle Seth last night, Prime Minister. He remembers 'Sauerkraut' O'Bryan very well indeed, and sends you his best regards." O'Bryan broke into a broad and ingratiating smile.

Inside his office, waiters unobtrusively served coffee, then left the room, silently closing the door behind them. O'Bryan was all business. "Last night was a pleasure, Mr. Secretary, Madam Ambassador, Madame Secretary," he began. "But today, it's back to business."

He sipped his coffee, and then continued. "For now, I gather that your own security is being tightened during this trip. There were some consultations, I'm told, throughout last night between my people and your Embassy. All as it should be. There wasn't much to change for your visit here, though. The public appearances had already taken place yesterday."

Secretary Adams opened his hands in a gesture of resignation. "Couldn't be helped, I'm afraid. Apparently people start getting nervous when I'm out of Washington. They think there may be an attempt on my life. Well, that exaggerates my importance, perhaps, but people have to assume the worst. Anyway, so much for New Business. Now let's hear what you think about the G-20, and the other matters that brought us to Ireland this fine day."

The meeting proceeded through the agreed agenda. Then, as it concluded and the guests were rising, a button under the Prime Minister's desk was pressed, and photographers entered the room to record the scene. The solemn aide to the Prime Minister pulled Robbie aside. "A private word is needed with Secretary Adams now," he said. "You and I will stay on. Here is my private number." He gave Robbie a nondescript business card containing an address, a phone number, and the name, Robert Dillman.

Pictures were taken, and then the party and photographers were artfully led from the Prime Minister's office. Last in line were Robbie Cutler and Secretary Adams. Robbie took the Secretary aside. "He wants a private word with you, sir. His aide Robert Dillman and I will stay." Secretary Adams nodded, then signalled the others to wait for a moment. "Just a detail or two to iron out before the joint press conference. We'll be along presently." The door closed.

The Prime Minister leaned forward, as if to hide his conversation from the very walls. Perhaps he was, Robbie thought. "We hear that Al Qaeda is stirring once again against your country."

Secretary Adams nodded, and O'Bryan filled in the blanks. "We still have a few connections from the old days," he said. "Deep cover, you would put it. I am told that the memories go back very far, to training camps in Libya. Or so I am told." He glanced at the stonefaced Dillman. "Well, we sometimes hear things, or more precisely, we are told things. I suspect, though, that the things we are told are what the other side wants us to hear, and expects that we will transmit."

Secretary Adams decided it was a time to share confidences. "We have heard that Bin Laden is launching another attack against us. This time, it seems to be more personal. Hence the security worries."

Prime Minister O'Bryan nodded in agreement. "Yes. But we have heard something more extensive, that there will be an attempt to assassinate the President. Possibly yourself as well. No further details, except that it will happen fairly soon."

"Do your sources indicate any reason for this? I mean, for this attempt. Obviously it suits them, but why now?"

"No. Our own agent put in a personal word, saying that Al Qaeda, meaning Bin Laden and that other fellow, really hated your Administration more than any previous one. They've talked about it a lot. The agent's guess was that America seemed more reasonable to the world now, and therefore was far more dangerous to their ends."

Robbie noticed the contortions that O'Bryan was going through to avoid saying "he." It would be interesting if the Irish agent in place with these fundamentalist fanatics was a woman!

Secretary Adams sighed. "So, we try to lower the temperature, and the world becomes for us an even more dangerous place."

"That's the way it is with fanatics. They precipitate events, make things happen, drive the conflict and make it impossible for things to be settled reasonably. We know something about them here in Ireland. So do you, in your own history. People like Sam Adams in Boston during your Revolution. Or Rhett or Yancey, egging on the southern states to secede, setting off your Civil War. Fanatics require a sense of desperation, a roll of the dice. Otherwise the far more numerous reasonable people who want peace and quiet will prevail. And reasonable people in power, like you and the President, are their greatest enemies."

"Thank you, Prime Minister." Secretary Adams turned towards the door, then stopped, as a new thought occurred to him.

"Can your agent explore matters with the other side?"

"I am told that is not possible. It's just for listening to what they might have to say. Anything more active would at best cause suspicions and at worst, put the agent in a position of unacceptable danger."

The Prime Minister stepped closer to the Secretary. "Having said that, Mr. Secretary, of course, let me know if anything like that is ever required. I believe Mr. Cutler can be in touch with Mr. Dillman."

The Prime Minister and Secretary of State shook hands with an odd and stately formality. It could have been something more than a farewell. A good thing the photographers were not there to record the scene, Robbie thought. It was starkly different from the light humor and conviviality of yesterday's mood. He wondered if the stage was being set for the rest of their journey. The door opened, and with beaming smiles the Prime Minister and Secretary of State took their respective places to hold their joint press conference.

— — — — — — — —

Rudolphe Carlisle put down the phone. He was trying to remain calm, while he jumped out of his skin. Now that Secretary Adams and the rest of the party on Air Force two were leaving, he was nervous and afraid that he showed it. He couldn't wait for them to go. Then he would have enough uninterrupted calm to take another look at that secretary. His second look had happened when he had returned to the Ambassador's residence in Phoenix Park the previous night. Everyone seemed to be either still out on the town, or perhaps already in bed. But he had wondered about that odd piece of furniture, and now seemed like the best opportunity to examine it more closely.

By all means do so, Ambassador McGowan had said, an amused smile on her face. She was looking forward to a full report at their dinner, and would receive one. Carlisle was rather amused to discover that he was already missing his former profession acutely. There was a real thrill about the antiques world. You were looking at something that might or might not be promising, and then, something happened to clarify matters. It could be a style or flourish or a trademark of some sort, something that enabled you to see past the present and into the past.

American dealers of course preferred their antique furniture absolutely pristine, no repainting and precious little repair work. The Europeans had, he thought, a more sensible point of view, and wouldn't mark down a piece's value unduly if it had been cleverly repaired or cleaned. It might even raise the value a bit. That was the way it should be, Carlisle thought. Wine is meant to be drunk, not collected, and antiques are meant to be enjoyed. They can't be if they spend their useful lives decaying and being ultimately forgotten in some attic.

And so he had gone back to the secretary at the foot of the stairs, brought out a chair from the dining room, turned the hall lights up, and started to examine the piece, inch by inch. Yes, it was obviously put together during the early Victorian period. With their flair for Gothic, that was nearly inevitable. He smiled as he recalled that tracts from the time are still in existence that counseled doing exactly this, so that old furniture would be reused, not wasted.

Well, this piece was right from that school of parsimony. Someone had taken an old portable desk and reused it, made it the base for a secretary. In the process, some of it had changed, he supposed, but not essentially, not in its characteristic detail. The question always was whether something undeniably old was also worth anything. The old furniture makers were just as capable of turning out junk as present day assembly line furniture makers. The only difference was that yesterday's junk was sturdier and tended to last longer, so many people assumed that it had more than sentimental value because it was old.

He had sat in front of the secretary and opened the desk, propping it open with the stick that now served that purpose. He saw the stacks of magazines and newspaper articles that cluttered the desk's interior. Morbid, those Victorians! Half the clippings seemed to be regional death notices, from Oxfordshire and Gloucester, it seemed. They were of no conceivable interest. But he might as well give a thorough examination of the piece, and so he took out everything that cluttered the desk. Dust remained, and crumbling bits of long forgotten newspapers. What a mess.

He sacrificed his linen handkerchief to cleaning out the dust, very carefully, from the desk's interior, and then the back shelf. Then he saw it, just on the back shelf. First a crescent moon, and there in a line above it, what looked like birds. He brushed the area quite carefully with his handkerchief. Did that have a meaning? He tried to remember. Then he wiped the back shelf with his handkerchief, and counted the birds. There were five of them. They seemed like robins, or perhaps sparrows.

Of course! The Sparrow brothers! That must be carefully checked out with his friends in the Carpenters Guild in London. One of the first guilds, their records from the period were excellent. He couldn't believe it. Carlisle counted all five. That must refer to the best of the lot, Peter Sparrow, the fifth brother. Active in the early seventeenth century, and a decade or so before, his work was well regarded, if not particularly prized. Solid, built to last, rather than decorative or fancy. Still, it would be worth something, probably more than anyone realized, perhaps mid five figures at least. He would have a good story to tell Ambassador McGowan after all. He put the ancient clippings back into the drawer.

The next day after breakfast, Carlisle had rethought and rearranged his travel plans. Despite the morning's alarming news, he wanted to see something of Ireland. And he needed more time in Dublin. The Secretary's party was leaving early that afternoon, and he would certainly not be expected to see them off at the airport. After all, he would be welcoming Adams in a little over a week when Air Force Two touched down at Riga.

But then, this security alert had changed his priorities. Or had it? Would a day or so really matter? Probably so. He would advance his return to Riga by one day. That meant that today, he could spend the day in Dublin, and have a quiet dinner with Ambassador McGowan. That should be pleasant, and in view of their past friendship, would give him some leeway for a further look around the residence. His interest in the residence furnishings had already been put down to a former auctioneer's excentricity. This was his best and perhaps only chance to explore matters further.

He then planned to have an early start to spend the following afternoon in County Kerry. The Lakes of Killarney did sound entrancing, and he was intrigued by the stories that Kelly Martin had told him about Lough Lein and Ross Castle. For that night the Embassy travel office had pulled a few strings, and he had a reservation at Glin Castle on the west coast for the night. It helped that the Knight of Glin had vaguely recalled meeting Carlisle during a celebrity auction held a few years previously in London. He would stay at Glin Castle for one night, and then take a midmorning flight the following day out of Shannon. There was a connecting flight at Heathrow that could put him in Riga by late afternoon. If he missed it, there was a later flight. Carlisle was a worrier about details, and so he conjured up a vivid image of himself trying to match wits with an airline ticket agent at Heathrow after he had missed the connection to Riga. He shuddered, and made arrangements for the later connecting flight. He then wrote a brief cable informing Embassy Riga, called to confirm his Glin Castle reservation, and then dialed Kelly Martin.

"Oh yes, Ambassador Carlisle. Yes, it was a pleasant evening."

"And my friends are leaving today. As I mentioned, I will have another day to see something of Ireland. You had strongly recommended the

Killarney region. Is there any chance of your spending the day with me there tomorrow?"

"Let's see. Yes, I think so. I can rearrange a few things. What's the agenda?"

"I'll be driven out in an Embassy car early in the morning. Say, I could pick you up at eight o'clock? Then the afternoon in County Kerry - see, I did remember there is no County Killarney - and then I'll be going on to Glin Castle and leaving from Shannon the next morning. You're welcome to join me, if you could. I'm sure the Embassy could get a reservation there for you. I know the Knight, just enough to impose. Then the Embassy car would take you back straightaway to Dublin from Shannon."

There was a moment of silence.

"Of course if you prefer, I could rent a car to take you back directly from Killarney, or make some other arrangement. But Queen Victoria has stopped frowning over Ireland these many years, and I'd enjoy your company a bit longer. They say that the candlelight dinners at Glin Castle are simply wonderful. So is their wine cellar."

She smiled. "Thank heavens for that. I'll make my own reservation. Here's the address to pick me up tomorrow morning at my flat in Dublin. Eight o'clock, I believe you said?"

Carlisle smiled. It would be a most pleasant trip, just Kelly Martin and himself driving around County Kerry.

He put down the phone. Then with a start he had remembered, something ticking away from his past studies of furniture. There was something more about that desk. Peter Sparrow was the fifth brother, and he was well known for putting a secret compartment into the furniture that he made. Nobody knew why, but sometimes a crescent moon marked such pieces. The reason for that was not known. Why use any mark, and if you did, why a moon?

Carlisle remembered the speculation. Perhaps Sparrow could deny any complicity in his purchaser's use of the secret drawer, if he had openly indicated, for his records at least, that the secret drawer existed. As an excuse, it could be used once. Possibly the moon was meant to be emblematic of secrecy. Certainly those times gave a reason for secrecy. If you were catholic or protestant your political loyalties were also defined by your religion. Carlisle wondered just what was hidden in that desk. He couldn't wait for everyone to leave Dublin, so that he could explore the desk more minutely.

— — — — — — — —

Inspector Juris Jurovits knew this trip was going to be nothing but trouble. He could feel it in his bones. He sighed and reflected that he was just below the line for diplomatic invitations, but right at the cutting edge when it came to doing the actual work in preparation for the visit. He didn't believe that in the case of any failure, those above the line would be blamed. Well, the Americans had rediscovered the Baltic states, and that was probably to the good.

He was optimistic enough to glory in his nation's refound independence, and cynical enough to wonder if it would all last, and if so, for how long. Well, visits like this one by the American Secretary of State were reminders that Latvia was no longer a dead history lesson. It was a nation once again, coming alive, with a broad network of powerful friends. Let the Russians stew about it. It was Baltic persistence and will that had kept nations like the United States from recognizing the forced incorporation of their homelands into the Soviet Union. Sheer single issue politics had paid off. Now they must keep what they had.

Meanwhile, there was much to be done. He rose as the Political Officer from the American Embassy came into his office. It was the third time this week. "You like my coffee, I see, Mr. Saunders," said Jurovits. "Well, I better, since I'm getting so used to it, Inspector," Saunders replied with a grin. They admired once more the fine view of the old square from the office window, one of the finest views in Riga. "You'll miss this view when you are promoted, Inspector," Saunders said. It was the old joke, which elicited the old reply.

"Try me and see," Jurovits replied.

First Secretary Roger Saunders got out his notebook. "We've heard again from the Department, and we've been asked once again to go over security preparations for the Secretary's visit next week." Since they had done this in previous visits, Saunders added, almost apologetically, "Not just Riga. They are asking all Embassies on the trip to double check security arrangements."

As soon as the words were out of his mouth, Saunders regretted being so specific. What did he care if Jurovits was bothered? That was his job, and no justification was needed. But he couldn't recall the words.

"So, something specific is up? What, precisely, have you heard? Is there anything you should be sharing with us?"

"Nothing specific. Just new instructions. Washington is nervous, and in particular, wants us to take a second look at public events. For obvious reasons. But I will pass on your question."

"It's worth it. If we are guarding against something new, something more than the usual oddball assortment of malcontents that we will pick up ahead of time in any event, we will want to know about it. Fast. Like surgeons, we don't operate best in the dark." Then he added, "Of course, you remember, Mr. Saunders, that the day in our countryside would be the most difficult to be changed. Politically, I mean. Obviously we would not want to do that."

Once again Saunders and Inspector Jurovits went over security preparations for the visit, day by day and event by event. They paid particular attention to public events, of which there were three scheduled in addition to the arrival and departure ceremonies; a wreath laying, a visit to the university, and the afternoon in the country that Inspector Jurovits had just mentioned.

This outing had been included in the schedule at the personal suggestion of the Latvian President. He thought that it was high time for a distinguished American visitor to get outside of Riga and see something of the beauties of the countryside. And after a scenic drive, they would spend several hours at Rundale Palace for the official Latvian state reception.

It was a fine choice. Rundale palace, built during the reign of Catherine the Great for a court favorite, was one of the glories of Latvia, well worth the visit, and a reception setting that was second to nothing in Vienna or Paris. Secretary Adams had personally agreed. So that might be at the same time the hardest event to cancel, but the most difficult to justify from the security standpoint. There was just too much open territory to patrol with any degree of assurance. Saunders could already read the cable that he would have to write. If only Ambassador Carlisle were there to weigh in personally! Perhaps they might send him a message in Dublin. Then he could perhaps put in a word before the Secretary left Ireland.

— — — — — — — —

Paris was familiar territory for Robbie. He knew the city well, and had enjoyed his visits to the Embassy on the Place de la Concorde when he was Consul in Bordeaux. Once in his office at the Embassy, just down the hall from the Ambassador's office, he thought about the short flight over from Dublin.

As expected, no post wanted to change a single event. It was said that local security in capital after capital had been beefed up. "They are playing the local equivalent of diplomatic roulette," Robbie had said at the meeting they had held on Air Force Two. Still, several events had seemed rather marginal, their value outweighed by the potential security problems they might pose. A few had been cancelled. It was all like hunting in the dark. Secretary Adams mentioned that just before they left, Ambassador Carlisle had had a personal word with him, on behalf of Embassy Riga. An afternoon in the countryside had been saved. Adams just didn't have the heart to say no to the first request from a new ambassador, and one who had a fair amount of personal charm.

There were no new NODIS SALADIN cables, and aside from those pertaining to trip security that they had already gone over on the plane, nothing serious that related to the trip, just some inevitable details that pertained to scheduled meetings with foreign officials. That, and new material for briefing papers. Well, let Ron Jackson worry about that. He would give me the corrected and amplified briefing papers at the right time for the Secretary.

Robbie remembered that he owed a call to Uncle Seth. After a word with the Political Section, he located a secure phone in a nearby small office and dialed the White House switchboard, which put him through to Uncle Seth's private number. Things certainly had changed since the early days of Robbie's diplomatic service, when he and Uncle Seth had had the leisure to communicate with a book code.

"Hi, Uncle Seth. Greetings from Paris. We met this morning with Prime Minister O'Bryan, and he was most pleased to hear from you. He was glad to hear that you are well and remembered 'Sauerkraut' O'Bryan."

"Good. A sound man, all that bluff and bluster is beside the point sometimes. You'll find him one of the sharpest people you'll meet on this trip. Helpful, too."

"So we learned."

"Robbie, there is something that you and the Secretary ought to know. It concerns security. Possibly yours."

"Well, we do have a security alert and are trying to tighten things. But I gather there is a lot more to it than we have heard."

"NSA is tracking some people that are here. I've seen the messages. The target is on Pennsyvania Avenue." So even with a secure phone, Uncle Seth was trying not very successfully to be elliptical.

"Well, good thing that we now have the people and the right priorities to catch them early. I guess that lesson got well and truly learned after 9/11."

"Yes. I've seen the transcripts already. For some reason they wanted my view. Since I don't speak the languages involved, that puzzled me. But the problem is real. What the translator gave us, word for word, was a call that tracked POTUS. That seemed straightforward. There were not enough details to pick the speaker up yet, and nothing to indicate that action was imminent. What NSA is hoping to get is the contact, since the person making the call seemed to be waiting for someone else."

"Sounds reasonable. I'm glad we have such a sure lead. They must be very secure to keep him loose."

"For the time being, anyway. Maybe just a day or two longer. But that wasn't the problem. At least, it was not why they contacted me, and maybe one or two others, for all I know."

"What do you mean, Uncle Seth?"

"It was the translator's note. He said that on paper, it all sounded important and urgent. That, he said, is what really bothered him. Because, he added, the tone of voice of the person on the phone didn't sound urgent or excited at all. Not even, as you might expect from a fanatic, calm and detached. He sounded bored. Bored! As though he were reading a script. The exact words were, 'He sounds like a bored tryout actor who already knows he won't get the part, and is just going through the motions.'"

"Tell me what you know about the translator."

"The best we've got. Storybook credentials. American citizen. A Moslem patriot with a PhD from Columbia. "

"What do you think it means, Uncle Seth?"

"I think it means you had better be very, very careful on this trip."

Just down the hall, since a new Ambassador had not been selected to replace Ronald Adams, the Secretary had settled in comfortably into his old ambassadorial office. Nothing seemed to have changed. The personal pictures were gone, but Adams liked to carry a set with him. His first gesture was to open his briefcase and put pictures of his wife Pamela and their children on the desk. Now the store is open for business, he thought.

He wished that hs wife had come with him. Drat. Why not, anyway? She was tied up later in the week, but not for the next day or two. What's more, she would have enjoyed coming to Paris. He glanced at the schedule of formal events and called for Missy Bronson. She entered the office briskly, notebook in hand.

"Missy, I'm having second thoughts about being a bachelor on this trip. I see the Foreign Minister's dinner will be the day after tomorrow, sort of the high point socially of the trip. Pamela should be here. Would you ask Political to fix it up with the Foreign Ministry? Then please get Pamela on the phone for me."

"Certainly, Mr. Secretary. Will you want to inform the other Embassies that we will be visiting?" Might as well clue them in as soon a possible, she thought.

"Not necessary, I think. She's pretty well scheduled to the hilt at home later this week. But she'd hate to miss Paris. Maybe if we hop to it she can get on an overnight flight tonight."

Missy was out of the door almost before he finished the sentence.

Robbie knocked on the door as Missy was leaving the room, and was waved into the room. She stared at the files of cables, which he held. He nodded, a signal that he would not give them to the Secretary directly. Better deal through her, and she would be back shortly. She smiled.

Robbie entered the room. Should he relay what he had just heard, or not?

"Just a word in private, Mr. Secretary," he said. Robbie felt like a courtier in Medici Florence, about to convey news of the latest assassination. Secretary Adams nodded and followed him a short distance to the Embassy secure room, a bubbled enclosure that, in theory at least, was safe from prying ears.

"I've had some news that seems to bear on SALADIN, Mr. Secretary." Adams nodded and leaned forward. "From Uncle Seth. He's been called in. As we heard from that early cable in Dublin that I briefed you on this morning, his news tends to confirm a plot against the President." Robbie gave him the details of the message. "But the catch is the translator's view that this is too rehearsed. He made it sound as though it might be a sham, or some sort of feint."

"Why would Al Qaeda want to do that?"

"If it is a feint, maybe to misdirect our attention. I just don't know. Anway, it's a new detail to add to the little that we already know. I expect we'll be getting some more cable traffic on this, but there was none in that series waiting for us when we arrived here this afternoon."

"What was Seth Cutler's advice?"

"He said that you should watch your step very carefully, Mr. Secretary."

"So I shall, Robbie. So I shall."

— — — — — — — —

Ambassador McGowan greeted her guest for dinner. Rudolphe Carlisle was in high spirits. He clearly had enjoyed himself in Dublin, and was sorry he could not stay longer. But his plans were made. He would take the Embassy car tomorrow, have a leisurely drive over to the Lakes of Killarney, and then leave from Shannon the following day. His hostess said she was sorry that she really couldn't go with him. The Killarney region was gorgeous, particularly this time of year. But there was just too much to attend to, some loose ends from the Secretary's visit. She was sure that Ambassador Carlisle would have the same impression in a week or so, after the visit to Riga was over.

"Sorry you couldn't come along. I did ask that lecturer Kelly Martin to accompany me for the day after you pleaded the press of business. She is the one who talked me into going to Killarney in the first place. Great tales she told of the lake and Ross Castle and the Annals of Innisfallen. I'm quite looking forward to soaking up that atmosphere."

She took several slices of the *Châteaubriand* passed by the residence waiter. The wine was from her own cellar, a nicely aged Bordeaux from St. Julien. "You promised me a history lesson from the residence furniture."

"Ah yes, that was a real treat. Let me tell you what I found."

She leaned forward in anticipation. Carlisle certainly knew how to set the stage. No wonder his auction catalogs had always been so readable, and now, so keenly sought after by collectors.

"The first impression I had was that the secretary - you know, the one at the foot of the staircase on the first floor, just off the reception room - was early Victorian, and not terribly interesting." She nodded.

"Then I examined it more carefully, when your other guests left, and I had more time to take a careful look. It's quite clear now that its present format, as a tall secretary, does date from Queen Victoria's early years. I wouldn't be at all surprised, if you could check the *provenance*, to discover that it was put together about the time of her visit to Dublin. That would have been 1849 or so, if I remember the history lesson that your DCM George Smiley was giving us last night. It may have been purchased in connection with her visit. Perhaps it was even presented then."

"I'm sure that everyone has forgotten exactly, but there should be some papers around. Perhaps we could even discover which firm did the assembly."

"That would be interesting. I think your administrative man Starett said that it was now American property. At some point the furnishings were purchased?"

"Yes. Some items that came originally with the residence were purchased. Others were collected by my predecessors and left here as gifts, so to speak. It's not a piece that I bought. It was here when I arrived." They savored their history with the perfectly done dinner. The wine, a Château Beychevelle, was at its peak.

Carlisle went on. "When I looked more closely at the secretary, it became clear that the lower desk portion had been added to the secretary, which served as a sort of frame. The desk top still opens, and the drawer is full of accumulated junk, magazines and newspaper articles for the most part. Anyway, the desk is a portable desk, from the late sixteenth or early seventeenth century, doubtless made in London."

"How exciting! How do you know all that?"

"It is made of nearly solid oak, and has aged for centuries. Viewed on its own, the style fits the period. People didn't have nearly so much furniture then. Tables, a bed, benches, were about it. Desks were portable, in part I suppose because the court moved around a great deal. The French even called items like this desk *mobiliers*, and we still in law speak of movable and immovable property. That's why.

"Open it up, and you see the open drawer where papers were kept, and a shelf, I suppose for quill pens and sharpening tools. But it was the decoration that got my interest."

"I seem to remember something on the outside, the front lid."

"Yes. Rather presumptuous. A lion, and what seems to be a dragon. The carving isn't very good. They probably had never seen a real dragon, you know! But that was another possible clue to the desk's actual age. The dragon was the symbol for Henry Tudor, who became Henry VII after the Battle of Bosworth Field in 1485, when he defeated Richard III, the last monarch of the House of York, ending the Wars of the Roses. The dragon was the Tudor symbol. The lion and the unicorn didn't become official symbols of English royalty until much later, under the Georges, I think."

He took an appreciative swallow of his wine. "Ah yes, but that reminds me of something even more exciting. Did you know that there were also carvings on the inside of the desk, on the back lid?" She remained silent, fascinated by his emerging story.

"There are five birds carved there. Five birds, and a crescent moon. I remember some specialized research I once did in connection with the period, with the help of the Carpenters Guild in London. It's one of the very oldest, you know, medieval. Twelfth or thirteenth century if I recall rightly. Anyway, they had long been in business when this desk was carved. The birds refer to the Sparrow family. There were five brothers. The last, and most skillful, was Peter Sparrow. Unless there is an elaborate hoax being played out here, which seems unlikely in the extreme, he carved the figures, or had them carved in his shop."

"How extraordinary!"

"Yes. Then I remembered something else. It was a period, of course, of extreme danger in English history. Your religion, whether the old religion or the emerging protestantism, was thought to dictate your patriotism. The wrong side might be grounds for execution. And so Peter Sparrow became known, for certain clients, for hidden drawers in his furniture. With some, he put in a carved signal. It was a crescent moon. Why he did that is beyond me. It would seem to be a dead giveaway if the authorities ever came knocking. But perhaps that was the very reason for the carved symbol. He could then say that he clearly was not responsible for what was hidden in the desks that he had made. The authorities could look and see that he was showing them that there was in fact a hidden drawer. That should let him off the hook. He was not colluding with his customer in the least. That's only a guess on my part, of course. Nobody knows."

"What fun. And did you find the hidden drawer?"

"Let's go and take a look after dinner. But I'm afraid that you are going to be disappointed."

"Let's not wait. I want to take a look now." She rose from her chair, went through the dining room door in the direction of the reception room, and entered the entrance hall where the secretary stood. "Let's see."

Carlisle pointed to the desk and showed her the lion and dragon symbols which were carved in the front. Now she could see them clearly, despite the centuries old discoloration of the wood. He opened the desk and removed the contents of its drawer, old newspapers for the most part, setting them carefully on the floor. His fingers pointed to the back panel. There was a distinct crescent moon, its concave shape facing upwards at an angle, and above it, what seemed to be a collection of carved birds. They were not easy to make out, but with his small flashlight, Carlisle traced the contours. Yes, there were five of them. The crescent moon was just below the second bird from the left.

"Yes, I see them now," she said. "The five birds. Sparrows, you say? We'd better take that on faith. They look rather primitive to me. Now, what about that hidden drawer? Did you find it?"

Ever the art historian, Carlisle's tone became professorial again. "At that time, hidden drawers were rather new, but they did become fairly common over the years. They depended upon a primitive spring mechanism, which usually involved wooden springs or slots of some sort, held together by pressure or perhaps a hook. The trick was to disengage the hook or the wooden spring. You have to find the pressure point and press it at the right spot. Then the hidden drawer would in turn be released. Like this!"

He pressed the crescent moon. There was a very slight sound as something within gave way. The front portion of the drawer itself slid up towards them. It revealed another thin drawer underneath. Here they found a few more faded newspaper clippings. At the very bottom of the drawer were two handwritten notes.

Carlisle showed the two papers to Ambassador McGowan. They seemed to be property records, tracing ownership of an estate, Thorpe Hall in Gloucestershire. He joked about the old miser, bent and beaten, gloomily wasting his life. Then he carefully replaced the papers in the hidden drawer, and closed it.

"That's where the story ends," he said, emphatically and rather offhand. "I really should have opened it with you in the first place, but I just couldn't stand holding off the excitement of this discovery of a hidden drawer, and you were out at the airport with the Secretary. Anyway, this should add to the value of the piece, mid five figures I would say, and to its interest. What a shame, that the secret drawer just contains the hopes of a poor deluded soul, someone right out of Charles Dickens. But who knows who could have owned this desk in the past?"

She nodded, eyes narrowing. "It's a trite thing to say, but it seems to fit. If only this desk could speak to us now!"

CHAPTER SIX -
From the Vulgate

HAD HE DONE THE RIGHT thing? Shouldn't he have leveled with Mary McGowan? Was it too late to do so even now? Carlisle was very short of answers. Gradually but steadily his qualms about the situation yielded to his fascination with what he had discovered. Surely nobody had seen this material for centuries. Certainly nobody had seen it who had the least idea of what it might mean.

As a trained furniture antiquarian and appraiser, Rudolphe Carlisle tried not to get too far into speculation. At the same time, he was having a losing battle fighting the dawning supposition that he really had discovered something. Was this the find of a lifetime, or merely a banal old piece of very little value? He reviewed what he knew.

He hadn't slept at all the previous night, but it made no difference. He felt the way he had many years ago in college after pulling an all nighter cramming for exams, fueled by strong black coffee. He tried to factor that into his judgment, and slow down. Impossible. He read for the fiftieth time the copies he had made of the two papers that he had found in the desk's hidden drawer, and for the fiftieth time, he wished he had paid more attention to his high school Latin class. Latin he had always supposed was something that you could pay a researcher to do for you. Now he didn't want a researcher. He wanted precise translations and some answers. He had replaced everything in the desk as it was after making exact copies of his discoveries.

Carlisle hoped that his handling had not damaged the papers. He remembered how he had come across them. He had very nearly missed them entirely. That, surely, had given him the idea of replacing them in the drawer. If he, a trained and experienced antiquarian, had nearly missed their significance, surely they would be safe from other prying eyes.

There had been a small collection of junk in the hidden drawer. It was a continuation of the dismal country newspaper funeral notices that had cluttered up the main drawer as well. Presumably a pious and half mad owner somewhere along the line had run out of room for them, stumbled upon the hidden drawer, and stuffed them in. Come to think of it, the papers, some of them, had been folded, to judge from the old crease lines. So they had been too numerous for the original drawer and the owner, taking them out, had hit upon the crescent moon carving by accident, and been doubtless pleased to find another drawer in which to squirrel away his idiotic funeral notices.

He had looked more closely, and found that they did seem to have a pattern. The same estate, Thorpe Hall in Gloucestershire, was mentioned in several of the notices. Then there were occasional notations by the side. "Now to Sophia's child," for example. And here was "This line now extinct." It was rather like the film *Kind Hearts and Coronets*, without, as far as he could tell, a murder plot to get rid of prior claimants to the property desired.

He had stumbled on an obsession, and not a healthy one. Carlsle could picture the aging miser gradually losing hope, having deferred and then abandoned long ago his own chances for personal happiness or a career, as he tracked, year after year after year, the fortunes of the owners of Thorpe Hall. Then it all just ended. The last clippings were dated in the 1860s along with, Carlisle was fascinated to notice, some mentions of the battles of the American Civil War. The earliest clippings traced back at least thirty years prior to that time. The obsession had gone on for decades.

What that seemed to mean was that the owner had been possessed of the desk before and after its transformation into the secretary in early Victorian times. Perhaps the cabinetmakers who had restyled the desk into a base for the secretary had discovered the hidden drawer and told the owner about it. Very likely. And he had then wanted to use the hidden drawer as a safe repository for his collection of clippings, proving, so he thought, his gradually maturing claim to Thorpe Hall. There must, therefore be something that tied the clippings together.

Then Carlisle's eye had caught the very last papers in the drawer. They were on the bottom, and he nearly missed them. For on one side, spreading over the two papers, was the most secret aspect of the drawer, a genealogical line that traced Thorpe Hall over the centuries and then, the decades of the mid-nineteenth century. Now it was possible to tell the identity of the obsessive claimant. He was Richard Thorpe, a cousin of the possessors of Thorpe Hall. Tracing the line and the clipping with Richard Thorpe's hand drawn genealogical chart, Carlisle could see the competing claimants who were scratched out, and the dates of their deaths. There were even, and he could imagine the pain that caused Richard Thorpe, notations of late marriages and the unexpected birth of a final male heir, in 1864.

It was the very last notation in that curious, cramped handwriting. With that, Richard Thorpe seemed to have given up. Carlisle would hardly have been surprised to find Richard Thorpe's own name also crossed out, and a date given, on that chart. Presumably the secretary had been sold by his heirs, who would have been more than glad to get rid of it, with the morbid, unhealthy obsession that surely was no secret from his own family. They probably pictured him at the secretary, perpetually frowning at being interrupted by some pleasant family event.

Then, almost absentmindedly, Carlisle had turned the papers over.

Face down from the Thorpe entries was another world. Towards the top of the first page were a few lines printed in Latin, which he failed to understand. The message read, *Nunc ingressus scribe eis super buxum et in libro diligenter exara illud et erit in die novissimo in testimonium usque ad aeternum.* Then on a new line, the Latin message continued. *Populus enim ad iracundiam provocans est et filii mendaces filii nolentes audire legem Domini.*

There were two sets of messages on the second piece of paper, this time in handwritten script. In a careful hand, *Petrus Quintus Fecit Anno Domini MDXCII* was written. Then below it, in what looked like the same handwriting, he read, *Per Lux Lunae Ad Veritatem.* "By moonlight you shall find the truth," was the best he could do, and it made no sense.

That was it. There was no name, or initials, except for the reference to Petrus Quintus, or Peter Quince, whoever that might be. Carlisle first wondered if this wasn't some elaborate prank. Surely over the centuries the hidden drawer must have been found, and more than once? No, why not take it at face value? The piece even as a secretary wasn't very attractive. Its main purpose would be to hold things. Cleaning it out and inserting comparable family junk probably had become one of those family errands saved for a boring rainy Sunday afternoon that was eternally postponed. And so it seemed that the saga of Thorpe Hall had slipped from memory, and the paper, if genuine at all, had escaped notice over the years.

He was glad that he had brought some notepaper, the habit of a professional lifetime when he was making careful appraisals. His first impressions, carefully noted, often held insights that more careful study might have missed. So it might be here as well. After making careful and exact copies, Carlisle had replaced the papers in the hidden drawer. Had he retained any sense of humor throughout the long night he might have mused on the fact that the other side of these very same papers had long fueled an obsession. Now this side was to weave its own spell.

He looked at the copies again, taking apart the elements, isolating them. First, there were two printed Latin sentences, which he must have translated. That shouldn't be too hard. It looked to him as though a quoted text of some kind was meant. This wasn't a Latin grammar exercise as far as he could tell, not something laboriously written by a reluctant schoolboy. It was a received text, all written off in printed letters, presumably for added clarity, for an audience that would understand its meaning. At the same time, it was by its nature hidden. How curious. That surely said something about the times. Then there was the second paper, with several parts. First there was the claim that a man named Petrus or Peter Quintus had made the original desk in 1592. Then the Latin motto followed. That was all.

Just before dawn Carlisle got up, went downstairs and made himself some instant coffee. He took another long look at the secretary as he descended the stairs, and then, once again, before going back up to his room with his mug of coffee. Mustn't forget what he already knew, before discovering the paper. How did things fit together, if they did?

There were several clues. Then it came to him. Quintus was Latin for Fifth, while Petrus of course was Peter. Peter Sparrow was the fifth brother.

So this was probably confirmation of his guess that Peter Sparrow was the carpenter who had made the original portable desk. Furthermore, it was now dated 1592. Why put his name in Latin, and add the number rather than whatever the Latin was for Sparrow? Perhaps the writer was just protecting the furniture maker's identity. It was thin but plausible, and Quintus for the Fifth did make sense, particularly for someone who knew Latin.

Carlisle seemed to recall that those who had some education, would have had a thorough grounding in Latin. That is what education meant in those days. That was always one of the rejoinders to those who maintained that Shakespeare was too unsophisticated to have written the plays. His grammar school education at Stratford had been first rate.

Shakespeare himself? He almost dropped the mug of hot coffee. There was nothing to indicate that. On the other hand, he was quite sure that the date, if accurate, was of Shakespeare's time, which included the reigns of Elizabeth I and then James I, he seemed to remember.

Now as to the Latin motto. The *lux lunae* meant moonlight of course, or the light of the moon. What about the crescent moon, which was the way he had opened the hidden drawer? *Per Lux Lunae Ad Veritatem.* "By moonlight you shall find the truth." Of course it must refer to that. But if the hidden drawer held the truth, why would this piece of paper centuries old that indicated the hidden drawer be *inside* the hidden drawer? That made no sense at all.

Almost absentmindedly he made a second copy of the two Latin sentences. He would need some help understanding them. Perhaps Kelly Martin? She was trained in ancient documents, and therefore must know Latin. He would ask her, at an appropriate moment.

There were several possibilities. Had he discovered clues to a treasure of some sort? It seemed quite possible that the papers that he had found had not been inside the hidden drawer at all to begin with, but had been placed there later, either or both, possibly by Richard Thorpe. He would have done that in order to conceal any suggestion that a hidden drawer existed. Once he had found it, the hidden drawer had become his own hiding place. He clearly had failed to understand the meaning of the two ancient papers. Either that, or originally the hidden drawer must have held something else, some valued treasure long since lost. Perhaps Thorpe had sold or destroyed it, not realizing its value.

The other possibility, of course, was a second hidden drawer.

Carlisle decided to give the secretary one last, thorough search. He picked up his pocket flashlight and went back downstairs. He took a chair from the dining room and sat in front of the secretary. Then, once again, he laboriously took all of the clippings and articles out of the drawer. He looked at the carved figures on the back of the desk shelf. He pressed every single spot on the desk, both inside and out. Except for the crescent moon. Nothing moved. Then he pressed the crescent moon. Slowly, as if tired, just for a bit, just once more, the hidden drawer opened. Carlisle looked inside it. No further hidden drawer there.

He thought long and hard, and then with care and deliberation replaced the original papers beneath the nineteenth century clippings, exactly as he had found them, genealogical side up. Now his conscience was clear. Or was it a matter of conscience? Not entirely, not even mainly. As a trained professional appraiser of many years standing, he regarded separating the original paper from the desk as a sort of desecration. That was something that new money did. It wasn't right, it diluted value, and it removed evidence that should remain with the desk. It could be said for conscience that, new to diplomacy, Carlisle considered that some things were beneath the dignity of an Ambassador. Grand theft was one of them.

Besides, more prosaically, he couldn't remove the desk, and he was out of time. If the Latin inscriptions meant anything, he would think of some way to contact Ambassador McGowan. It would be an easy matter to have another look, turn the last two papers over, and discover the writings which he had overlooked the first time. He closed the drawer, and could just hear a very soft click as the ancient wooden mechanism, whatever it was, slid into place. Carlisle wondered how much longer it would work.

That, of course, was another thing. This was no modern piece of machinery, carefully calibrated, with fallback redundant systems, so that if one failed, another would take its place. No, if the hidden spring, surely made of wood, should fail, there might be no other way at all to open the hidden drawer again. That meant that he must caution Ambassador McGowan. Open it from time to time if it amuses you, but be sparing. Some day it will surely stop working altogether. It is a miracle that it has lasted this long. Probably it was opened with some frequency in Richard Thorpe's day. Perhaps that was the only time it had been used. Who could tell? But that also would mean that nearly a century and a half had elapsed since the hidden drawer had last been opened. Special care must be taken now not to overuse the mechanism, surely in fragile condition.

These reflections made, once again, slowly and with maddening deliberation Carlisle went over every inch of the desk, inside and out, pressing for another hidden catch, for a second hidden drawer. There was none. He nodded and gave up, having done his best. Now for a few hours stolen sleep, and he could go in peace on his trip to Killarney. He looked forward to it. Ireland certainly wove spells. It was best not to get too wrapped up in any one of them.

— — — — — — — —

Robbie woke up with a jolt. "Sorry, Robbie. It's Ron Jackson at the Embassy. There are some messages that you should see. I'll send an Embassy car." Robbie rolled out of bed and dressed quickly. He couldn't remember when the Embassy snack bar opened. Some coffee would be good now. Anything. He had spent the afternoon getting caught up on the cable traffic, all of which would certainly get ahead of him once again in the course of the day. Most of that was really not necessary. He was just paying the price for being too conscientious. "Stick to what's important," Clark Framsen would have said. Well, this was important.

He nodded off and then woke up again in the Embassy car, went through security, giving a half wave to the Marine guards on duty, and sprinted up the stairs to his office. There sat Ron Jackson with the cable traffic. There were three messages in a special folder, marked NODIS SALADIN.

The first was from Embassy Tripoli. It was short and to the point and had been sent by the highest possible precedence, FLASH. Robbie noted that the Department had authorized Embassy Tripoli to send it laterally, here to Embassy Paris. The short text merely said that the original informant had surfaced, and added that the assets were now in place, within the United States, for the operation.

The next two cables were from the Department of State. Sent

IMMEDIATE, they were addressed only to Secretary Adams in Paris. The first looked like another message had been grafted onto a Department of State cable. That was surely it, since it was clearly a report of an intercepted telephone call. The caller was referring to POTUS, the President, and had pinpointed his movements for several days later in the week. Instructions were requested for the "action," and the response of the other male on the phone was that they would be given quite soon. The gloss on the report said that these were two Middle Eastern males, who were legally in the United States. They were known (now, Robbie assumed) to be Al Qaeda operatives.

The second cable purported to offer some context and guidance. It was a personal message from the Deputy Secretary of State, Quentin Armbruster. It said that the President had convened a meeting with the Director of National Intelligence, several other intelligence gurus, the Director of Homeland Security, the Secretary of Defense, and, in Secretary Adams's absence, Deputy Secretary of State Armbruster.

All had agreed that these operatives, who were being closely monitored, should be kept on a short leash but not arrested for a while, to see if their communications, all of which would be closely monitored, led to a larger Al Qaeda ring within the country. They could still be picked up whenever that step was needed. Armbruster added the personal note that several other experts had also been consulted by the White House. He didn't have all of the names, but understood that Seth Cutler was one of them.

Nothing at all was said about the issues that Uncle Seth had raised with him over the secure phone, Robbie noticed. He wondered whether they had even been surfaced within that lofty group, or whether everyone, for the sake of Bob Woodward's next book a year or so down the road, was just protecting his turf by acting as tough as needed. No action was requested of the traveling Secretary of State. Neither was there any specific warning as far as the trip was concerned, except for a boilerplate injunction to keep security high and make sure that each post visited understood that all was to go smoothly.

"That doesn't mean they hope that something positive will be achieved on this trip," Robbie realized. "Their short term definition of success is that the Secretary of State must get back in one piece." Well, that too.

The telephone rang. It was seven o'clock, and it was Secretary Adams on a secure line from the residence. He seemed pleased that Robbie was there.

"Yes, there are a few new messages, Mr. Secretary. Nothing to come in for directly. No action on your part is needed.".

"Good. In that case, I'll go out to Charles de Gaulle and surprise Pamela. It's the least I can do. She did manage to get on a flight at the last minute. I'll come directly back to the Embassy. See you about nine."

Fine. Robbie eased up his tension with a few isometric exercises, then sat down and skim read all of the remaining messages, making his standard three pile cable collection. For some reason, the first, must read pile seemed thickest today. Everyone was weighing in, it seemed. Well, fine. He handed the package back to Ron Jackson and left the Embassy to walk along the park that bordered the Place de la Concorde, and find a good shady cafe for *café au lait* and *croissants*.

An hour or so later, Secretary Adams entered the reserved area at Charles de Gaulle Airport. A diplomatic security officer accompanied him. Adams was not yet used to the subterfuge of pretending that the security man was not there, although sometimes more private moments would have been appreciated. Ah, there was Pamela.

It never ceased to amaze him that after a long, overnight flight, she looked absolutely fresh and rested. She was wearing a light blue traveling suit and had packed light, just one bag and her bulging handbag. For only two days, who needed more? This was going to be a pleasant interlude in this busy series of capital stops.

"Now I know how President Kennedy felt when he introduced himself as 'the man who accompanied Jacqueline Kennedy to Paris,'" he said. His wife smiled broadly and rewarded him with an unwifely kiss smack on the mouth. The security people had already arranged a lightning move through French immigration and customs. It was done so effortlessly that she hardly knew it had happened, and half wondered when she would be going through customs. "Ah well, now I'm the wife of the Secretary of State. That proves it!".

The Secretary's security man called his car. When it arrived, they quickly proceeded through the only open area, a few yards from the VIP reception area to the vehicle pickup point.

Not many people observed them at this early hour. One who did, a conservatively dressed businessman arriving business class from Amman, Jordan, stared in surprise. He muttered to himself that this had not been on the schedule. He stood there for a moment holding his carryon leather suitcase.

Something was wrong. She was not supposed to be here. Had things gone wrong, or the schedule been changed? He had better doublecheck. One thing was certain. He could not stay here staring at them. Then he moved on. He hoped he had not overdone it. Up to a certain point, curiosity was expected when a person unexpectedly ran across a public celebrity. Not paying any attention might have been perhaps more suspicious. But staring too long would indicate some other intention, and would alert those security people.

And so he made a snap decision. Rather than proceed to his final destination in a few hours, he would first check to see if the Secretary's schedule still held. No sense being in the wrong place, and no sense going on just because the necessary equipment was in place. After all, they had assets everywhere. He moved quickly away from the arriving cars, and hailed a taxi.

— — — — — — — —

The Foreign Minister opened the meeting with a friendly little speech of welcome. Everyone knew Secretary of State Adams, and friends of the United States were pleased that the former American Ambassador to Paris had become the man in charge of implementing American foreign policy. What he didn't quite say but clearly meant to convey was that he hoped that the long period of official estrangement, papered over for the sake of form as the last Washington administration ground to its unlamented end, was now truly and finally over.

Secretary Adams replied in kind. France was the first ally of the United States of America. Indeed without French help in "the vast strategic chessboard" of the Virginia campaign and the naval battle of Chesapeake Bay which President Mitterand had evoked during his bicentennial visit to Yorktown in 1981, American independence would not have been achieved. The best way to resolve differences was to work through them. He wanted to restore the old cooperation. That was why he had hoped to include Paris on his first trip overseas as Secretary of State. And that is why his wife had insisted upon joining him as he did so.

Smiles broke out, and the tension eased. Maybe they could get back to business after all. It was a good start.

"And so, let us compare notes on the Middle East," Adams began. He knew they would disagree on several points, but the fact of disagreement was expected. The new consultation might produce some helpful results. After all, as the French never tired of reminding the world, they had had some history there themselves. It was foolish not to take advantage of their own experiences, all the more when, as in Indo China, their colonial period had ended badly. Perhaps there was some reservoir of knowledge or goodwill or even local assets that might be helpful. One never knew. And when American lives might be at stake, every diplomatic path should be explored, thoroughly and seriously. At the very least, that was owed to brave American fighting men and women. If it didn't work out, little was lost.

"The essential problem, it seems to us," said the French Foreign Minister, "is that the problem of terrorism has metastisized. That is where we have in the past disagreed so sharply, as to the causation for these growing problems."

"We may still continue to disagree," Secretary Adams answered. "But now, I want you to know of a change in our approach. It will be announced shortly at the White House, but I wanted you to know about it confidentially before the announcement." He took a sip of water, fully aware that everyone in the entire room was silent, fixing him with total attention.

"This Administration's priority in the Middle East will be to achieve a secure Israel and a just settlement for the Palestinians. We will be evenhanded as we pursue this goal. For one thing, we will return to the policy adhered to by administrations of both parties over decades, to opposing any settlements by Israel in occupied territories. If some other arrangement is to be worked out by the parties themselves, that is another matter. But the conventions on occupied lands are very clear. Israel has no right whatsoever to take over occupied sovereign territory pending a settlement."

The silence in the room grew even more profound. "This will cause us enormous problems in the short term. But as time goes on, it is the only hope for a secure Israel, which includes the strengthening of moderate Arab states."

"Yes," the French Foreign Minister replied. "I was sorry when that long established American policy changed. We all were. And I quite agree that the strengthening of moderate Arabs is essential. They are now fed, day after day, with distorted views of what is going on in that area, both Israel and what might be Palestine. Heaven knows little distortion is necessary. The reality is bad enough. But at the same time, you must be absolutely sure that the change of American policy is not taken as weakness. How will you manage that?"

"It must and will be done by the President. We will reinforce our security commitment to Israel. Let there be no confusion about that. We of course fear that the situation that we have inherited is a deteriorating one for Tel Aviv. We want to reverse that, and strengthen Israel while there is still time, before they are both outnumbered from within and opposed by fanatics from without. Time is not on Israel's side if we continue to let the situation drift. And Israel, a democratic Israel that can still be a beacon of hope, shouldn't have to choose between its democracy and its existence. Our ties with Israel are historic and right and will therefore be strengthened, lest anyone get any false ideas that our commitments will not be faithfully kept. Also, as they have long wished, we will move our Embassy to Jerusalem, and recognize that city as the capital of the State of Israel."

There were some gasps around the room. Adams continued. "But we will say at the same time that Jerusalem, whether all of it or a part of it, will also be considered the capital of the Palestinian state. When it emerges, the same Embassy will be dually accredited to that government. It goes without saying that what has been the Palestinian section will have a fair allocation of revenues for their daily needs, transportation, water, sewage, everything that makes possible the civilized living that we all take for granted. Or presence should guarantee that."

There was a gasp. "It is a great gamble, Mr. Secretary, one worthy of your great country. We deeply appreciate your consultation, and will keep these matters in strict confidence. But I am sure that you are also thinking that you will have two forces of hurricane strength to deal with."

He paused for effect. "One of course, will be those supporters of the State of Israel who will read this new policy not as a means to peace, but as a betrayal. The other, of course, will come from the fanatics like Al Qaeda, who fatten themselves on what they say are your encroachments on Moslem territory. They prosper on perceived injustice towards the Palestinians. They will immediately think of their recruiting. I shouldn't be surprised if they already were concerned, after the President's courageous and correct decision to close the prison at Guantanamo. The last thing they want is an America that does not fit their acid caricature.

"In short I fear, Mr. Secretary, that in the short run your policy, which is farsighted and courageous, will only fuel fanaticism. So beware the temptation to make 'midcourse corrections,' which would make everything far worse. I also wonder," he brushed his unfashionable goatee with the back of his hand, "if the terrorists will try to stop you in some way. After all, if your policy succeeds, their recruiting may well dry up. They cannot be in that position and still survive over the long term as a danger to all of us."

Secretary Adams nodded in agreement. He thought for a minute. He wanted to get it exactly right. He wanted to convey meaning and nuance, but more important, conviction and sincerity. If they could see how much he cared about this, they couldn't fail to help. Cynics to the contrary, the French were like that.

"Well, the way our people see it, is that if matters continue to drift, time is no longer on the side of our friends in the Middle East. Israel itself may well go under. That is why we are changing course. We are most concerned about the deteriorating situation if nothing is done. That is why I say that time is not on our side, if nothing is done to effect events. The stakes are just too high for the *status quo* and political posturing. It also simply just isn't good enough for anyone, let alone for this Secretary of State, to hope for the best. Sponsoring showcase meetings that raise expectations and accomplish nothing of substance are a diplomatic fraud. It's time for action. Walls of course solve nothing."

He took another long drink of water. "And no more headline hunting shuttle diplomacy without addressing the core problems of the area. That may sound good for potential political campaigners, but I can't see that any stability has been achieved. Quite the reverse. It's time for serious, painstaking diplomacy, secret where necessary, open where it helps the process, and always with an eye towards the needs of the people, on both sides. We'd welcome your help, *Monsieur le Ministre*, in New York and elsewhere, as we gear up for this."

He coughed softly, and added a personal note. "You know, my friend, my grandfather was here in 1918 at Château Thierry, and my father landed at Normandy. These memories may be overshadowed from time to time, but they run deep. Very deep, indeed."

"As someone once said in one of your films, Mr. Secretary, 'Welcome back to the fight. This time, I know our side will win.'"

— — — — — — — —

The meeting over, Robbie excused himself to go back to the American Embassy and check out the cable traffic. It wasn't a long walk, and he now had a spare hour or two. It would be nice to see something new, or rather, something old that he hadn't had the opportunity to see before. Paris was full of such things. He had seen the Conciergerie, the sad prison of the Revolution. He had several times enjoyed the Carnavalet Museum of the City of Paris over by the Place des Vosges, the finest square in Paris and probably the earliest. There wasn't enough time to go up to Montmartre. And he was in a museum mood anyway, but definitely not the Louvre. He would get lost there in its treasures, wanting to see just one more favorite painting or sculpture, and lose track of the time. No, something smaller scale was needed.

Then he remembered the Cluny Museum. It was close by, and its size, he had heard, was manageable. Also, he hadn't seen it. But Sylvie had, and the Cluny was definitely on her short list of things he absolutely had to see if he had any free time at all during his stop in Paris.

He even remembered why she had recommended it. In the Middle Ages, France had had magnificent religious and architectural art, everywhere. The mindless destruction that had wantonly occurred during the Wars of Religion and later during the Revolution was a source of real national regret, or should be, he thought. What had been saved during the initial assault had later largely been smashed. Some of the best that remained was at this small museum on the Left Bank, which had originally been an extensive series of Roman baths. In the twelfth century, the Burgundian Abbey of Cluny had acquired the property and built an imposing residence.

It was open, and Robbie picked up a brochure. It was here, he read, that Mary Tudor, eldest daughter of King Henry VII and the wife of Louis XII of France, was kept a virtual prisoner by a jealous François I, who feared royal offspring that would take precedence over his claim to the throne. He needn't have worried, Robbie remembered. Her husband, many years her senior, soon died. But there had been a highly unusual happy ending for her, as she had been allowed to marry the Duke of Suffolk, a love match and her choice all along.

Small though it was, the museum contained treasures, not all from the medieval period. There was even some hammered gold jewelry from the Gauls, which reminded him of the fine display he had seen in Dublin. To his untutored eye, the workmanship seemed similar, although these were somewhat later.

Then came treasures.

Here were some of the original stained glass from the Sainte Chapelle, the chapel built by Saint Louis on the *Ile de la Cité* to house the Crown of Thorns. They had been saved from the revolutionaries while other stained glass panels had either been smashed or removed and sold. Here they could be seen at close range, genuine in their primitive lead encased craftsmanship, and still brilliant in their colors. Robbie wondered if we in this new millenium even knew how those colors had been produced, or if this was a secret process that the craftsmen of the Middle Ages had taken to their graves. He rather hoped that they had. There were too many smartass scientists around today to suit him. There were still some mysteries, despite attempts to demystify them.

He remembered the ossuary found near Jerusalem a year or so ago with an inscription that might have referred to Jesus. It might not have. Robbie gathered that the name was not uncommon then. But why, just why, were there so many people who wanted to debunk the very notion? He was suspicious of the tests that had followed. They had not seemed professionally carried out. It was unsatisfactory, particularly for a century that seemed to pride itself on validation by science. Maybe that was the problem.

Then, chief amongst the mysteries of time, Robbie thought, must be the Shroud of Turin. Even though he was the descendant of generations of Yankee Protestants, and of English dissenters before that, he didn't share all of the plain religious preferences of his ancestors. He loved stained glass, for one thing, and not just for its beauty. He remembered the poem of François Villon dedicated to his illiterate mother, who couldn't read or understand the Scriptures, but who could look at the colored glass pictures on the walls of her church, and find her beliefs, puzzling out the lessons through the stories that she saw. Like the old Classic Comics for the Middle Ages, Robbie thought.

He remembered in Bordeaux, what a revelation it had been when he was being made a member of the wine society, the *Confrèrie du Médoc et des Graves.* The day's feasting had begun with a walk across an old bridge over a narrow point on the Gironde River. He and some diplomatic friends were being inducted, and they were happy and self important in their new borrowed crimson robes and white woolen (for ermine) collars. The service in the little church across the river was pleasant enough. But what had caught Robbie's eye was the stained glass. There were representations of grape growing, the harvest of the grapes, and inevitably, the crushing of the grapes. It was a very long way from New England.

Robbie had no idea whether the fabled Shroud of Turin was genuine or not. He rather hoped that it was. It was traceable for centuries, but the chain of proven custody broke sometime in the fifteenth century or so, he thought. He couldn't remember precisely. Then came the debunkers, and the tests for aging, themselves far from conclusive, and not well conducted.

It puzzled Robbie that he actually wanted the Shroud of Turin to be proved genuine. He was not Roman Catholic. Did that make any difference now? He liked to think that there had been an era when mankind, or much of it, was united. That wasn't ever true. And if it were true, it would hardly be benign. Somebody would inevitably seize power, and it would then be hard if not impossible to loosen that grip on power. And there would probably be pogroms, crusades, whatever. But he still wanted to believe that it could be true, that people could be united.

He focused on the exhibits once again, and the period of rampant destruction from which these remnants had been saved. Not everybody's motives were revolutionary, Robbie recalled, not by a long shot. He remembered the jewelry exhibit at the Museum of Natural History on the Mall in Washington. There was the famous McLean diamond, the "French blue," which had once belonged to Marie Antoinette. It had disappeared when the revolutionary harridans had invaded Versailles to force the King and Queen of France to return to Paris. And it had resurfaced to be sold in London years later, within a few weeks of the expiration of the statute of limitations for its theft!

Astonishingly, there was also an exhibit of the statues of the kings of Judah which had once adorned the exterior walls of Nôtre Dame Cathedral itself. They had been pulled down, the statues beheaded, during the French Revolution. At considerable risk an aristocrat, sickened by the loss, had gone to Nôtre Dame and secured 21 heads and safely buried them. They had been forgotten for centuries. Then, Robbie read, in 1977 they had been discovered by workmen doing some excavations for a renovated bank building. The fact that the discovery was made on April 1st, and France also has April Fool customs, meant that the original discovery was not taken seriously. Add to that the coincidence that the excavation foreman had the same name as the President of France, Giscard d'Estaing, which didn't help. Finally someone was sent to check out the discovery, which was found to be genuine, and the statue heads had at length been removed to the Cluny Museum for display.

But the Cluny Museum had other treasures. It was here that the famous Unicorn Tapestries, rich in beauty and symbolism, were displayed. He remembered that these fifteenth century tapestries, woven in Flanders and in France, doubtless the most famous in the world, had been rescued by the writer George Sand.

He entered the great room that held them on its walls.

This was worth a trip to Europe.

There were six large tapestries, still magnificent in their composition and coloring. They hung from ceiling to floor, filling the room. They were filled with depictions that must have been rich in associations at the time, rabbits, lions, heraldic flags, crescent moons, banners, people and animals, an entire world in vibrant blues and browns and crimsons. The series was called The Lady and the Unicorn, and five of the tapestries were thought to represent the five senses: Taste, Sight, Touch, Smell, and Hearing. The sixth tapestry, "To My Only Desire," was an elaborate and beautiful mystery. He looked at them in awe.

Definitely the Cluny Museum's offerings made the cut for Christmas presents. His Visa card was in prime working order, and in the gift shop, he made the shopgirl's day by purchasing a machine embroidered reproduction of the sixth Lady and the Unicorn tapestry, about half actual size. The colors were fine, and there were straps at the top so that it could easily be hung on a wall. It would make a nice Christmas present for Sylvie. She didn't insist upon it or make a fuss, but she was very observant, and liked traditions. That was a common element, across the cultural divide, France and New England.

This would make a nice Christmas present, he decided again. Robbie arranged to mail it to himself, so that he wouldn't be stuck with carrying the tapestry reproduction across five countries.

Then he left the Cluny Museum, hardly noticing the surroundings, so lost was he in thought of the beautiful works of art, and the evidence of vandalism, that he had just seen. Thoughts of the present century were inescapable. He wondered what else would be lost in our own time to fanatics, and what would be saved for future generations to marvel at.

— — — — — — — —

The morning was a fine one, and Carlisle had had just enough sleep to take off the rough edge. He was still drowsy, but not unpleasantly so. Ambassador McGowan joined him at the breakfast table.

"Good morning, Madame Ambassador."

"Good morning, Mr. Ambassador."

They both chuckled, almost conspiratorially, as if to say, "Where but in the United States could a horsebreeder's daughter from Kentucky and a selftrained antiques trader from Peoria rise to ambassadorial rank, to have breakfast in this fine setting in Dublin's Phoenix Park?"

"Mary, I've been thinking about that secretary. It looks sturdy, and from the outside, probably still is. But I'm not at all sure about that inner mechanism, the wooden spring or chip that holds the hidden drawer in place. It must be centuries old by now. I'd say, don't open it too often. I think it risks no longer working at all. It might well just crack or turn into sawdust. But I'd like to do some research, and then spend some time looking it over. So if you can stand it - and me - perhaps I can come back and take a more careful look sometime in the future."

"You mean, after the Adams visit is over and things have calmed down a bit."

"Yes. In the meantime, once I get my bearings, you must come and join me for a vacation in Riga. I'm looking forward to seeing the Baltics again. A cruise once took me to the region, and with shore excursions I went to Helsinki, and also to Riga, Klaipeda (the old Memel) in Lithuania, Tallinn in Estonia, and finally St. Petersburg, which has certainly been cleaned up since the old Soviet Union days. It wasn't much, but at least it gave me a thin layer of familiarity with the region, and that certainly helped with White House Personnel and then with the Foreign Relations Committee. You, on the other hand, just charmed them off their feet ..."

"... As you are doing now. Certainly. That would be fun. I'll look forward to seeing you in Riga. Meanwhile, good luck with the Secretary's visit. I still think you are cutting it a bit close."

"Probably so. But my DCM said they are all geared up for my presentation of credentials, and I've had a look at the Secretary's schedule. I'll be there late tomorrow night, flying from Shannon and then the connecting flight from Heathrow. So it all should work out well. Meanwhile, this day in Kerry and Limerick should be fun. I just wish there was time to do one of the great scenic drives as well, say the Ring of Kerry or the Dingle Peninsula. But that really would have been stretching it.

"Meanwhile, many thanks for the car and driver. He'll be back tomorrow afternoon. Sorry you can't join me for the day, but there we are."

He finished his coffee and she walked with him out to the car. He gave her a smooch on the cheek that nearly missed as she was turning her face towards his ever so hesitantly. "Men are really so dumb," she thought, and not for the first time. And not for the first time she told herself that the waiting game was one of her strengths. She hoped that that was still true. Then, with a smile, she brightened and gave a small, wistful wave of her hand.

"We'll always have Riga," she thought.

He smiled goodbye through the car window, at the same time giving the driver Kelly Martin's address. They drove carefully into Dublin. She was ready on time, quite excited about their excursion. It was a three hour drive or so by American road standards, just 185 miles from Dublin to Killarney. But that was not taking Irish roads into account. Sometimes, what had seemed like a main thoroughfare sort of funneled into something smaller. The roads leading off the main road were mysterious. Some seemed to have no names at all. Signs pointed in oblique directions, as though they were fending off spirits from the fields and not winning. Carlisle was very glad that he had not decided to do the driving himself. She could surely have done it, but he just as surely would have gotten hopelessly lost.

She chattered merrily away about the classes that she was teaching, and added a few words about her research projects. Now that Ireland was independent and prospering in the information age, there paradoxically was fresh interest in the nation's history and folkways. That had created a useful academic niche for her interests.

The scenery was pleasantly bathed in greenery. The Irish folksongs hadn't exaggerated, Carlisle thought. It really is a beautiful countryside.

She seemed to read his thoughts. "If you think this is nice, then you have quite a treat coming in County Kerry," she said. "The Killarney lakes were saved from development. Actually it was our first national park. Really. The story goes that a wealthy American had bought property on one of the lakes for his residence, to bring his wife. But she died suddenly. Unable to bear the idea of building a house as they had planned and living there without her, he decided to give the land instead to the Irish people. At the time, we didn't have any national parks, so the politicians had to decide how to create one."

"Like our Congress with Yellowstone and the Grand Canyon," he said.

"Yes, exactly. Anyway, the final result was that the region was saved. Let's turn left here," she said to the driver. He made a left turn off the main road into the Killarney Golf Club. "I don't play golf at all," she said. "This is for the view. It's the best one of the lake. If I lived here I'd learn how to play golf, just to see this view."

They drove along the sloping driveway which bordered the lake. It was beautiful. Carlisle found the word inadequate. It was the finest vista he had ever seen, certainly in Europe. They drove up to the main club building just for the view, parking the car and walking around for a few minutes. Nobody bothered them, although a few functionaries looked closely. Clearly it must be the Embassy car and license plates, Carlisle thought. That gave him an idea. They entered the building and Carlisle went to the front desk.

He asked the man leaning towards him across the club's reception counter, "I wonder if, by the least chance, my American golf club in Washington is a corresponding club with your own club?" Well, a search of the corresponding club registry revealed, the functionary lugubriously announced, that sadly it was not. Then Carlsle remembered that he also belonged to another club, this one in upstate New York. Since he never played golf, he had quite forgotten that it even was a golf club. He seemed to recall that the club bartender was unexcelled at making mint juleps. Surely Mary McGowan would approve. After a moment, he was rewarded with a patient and approving smile by the club employee. He had caught the word "Ambassador" and decided to waive the requirement for a note of introduction. Ah yes, the New York club was indeed a corresponding club, and they would be most pleased to have them stay for luncheon. They were right on time.

Their salmon was freshly caught and deliciously prepared. They enjoyed a white wine of recent vintage from the *Graves* region of Bordeaux. It was substantial enough to go well with the salmon, and light enough so that they would be able to enjoy the afternoon's planned sightseeing without getting sleepy. Raspberry crumbles and coffee completed their meal.

It was at that point, almost diffidently, that Carlisle took from his coat pocket the slip of paper that he had been meaning to ask her about the entire morning. The problem had been, when to raise the matter. He had wanted to do so earlier, but reading in a car was impossible for him. It gave him a headache, and he feared that it would bother her as well. Now that they had had a pleasant luncheon, and were enjoying a few moments before setting out to see the Lakes of Killarney seemed like a good time.

"I wonder if you would do me a favor and take a look at this," he said. "I was sent it recently. All I can make out is that it is Latin, of course. I must confess, though, my Latin is years behind me. Not that I did well at it when I was at school. It always seemed like too much of a chore. I wonder if you would have a look. I'm told it is from a paper that is centuries old."

"Well, I'll give it a try." She was intrigued. She took the paper and studied it for a few moments. "Mind if I jot down some notes?" He didn't.

"It looks to me very much like vulgate Latin. Some call it Church Latin. You're not Catholic?"

He shook his head, no.

"I would go even farther. It seems to me that quite possibly it is a biblical passage."

"In Latin?" He was surprised.

"Yes. One of the early Popes ordered St. Jerome to translate the earlier Greek and Hebrew texts of the Old and New Testaments into Latin. That was in the fourth century. Now, we tend to think that Latin is a dead language, and having something in Latin means it must be obscure. In the time of St. Jerome, I think the exact opposite effect was intended. Latin was the prevailing language of educated people and scholars, and of the Church. So putting the books of the Bible into Latin meant making it available to the broader Church community."

"Fascinating. What do you make of this writing?"

"Well, first, as to the general tenor of it. Somebody is highly annoyed. That comes through right enough. Indignation at this level is pretty magisterial. It would come perhaps from one of the early prophets. Or from God himself. Or from the first, speaking for the second. It wouldn't be too hard, if I am generally right, to find the exact reference, unless of course it was one of those apocryphal writings that are now popping up. My offhand guess, and without research facilities it is nothing more than that, is that this is from somewhere in the Old Testament. If in fact it is St. Jerome's translation, it should be even easier to locate precisely."

"Why is that?"

"Well, his translation is well known. It's even on line!"

"So, unless this is really ancient, dating back towards that time or close to it, it's not really very interesting?"

"Well, that might be true, except for an overriding factor. You said that it was from an original that was centuries old. That shifts the context. It could even bring up the history of Protestantism and the Counter Reformation. You are surely aware of the religious controversy that England got into before they began to instruct Ireland regarding our own religious failings?"

He made no reply. It was best not to start down a conversational alley that wouldn't advance matters.

"Well, during the Tudor times, and the gradual formation of the Church of England, the Catholic-Protestant split was the national issue. Where you stood indicated whether you were a patriot or not, since, of course, Henry VIII's divorce, not recognized by Rome, made his subsequent children illegitimate in the eyes of the Church. Mary, 'Bloody Mary,' was all right, but Elizabeth certainly was not."

"But he had a son."

"Yes, Edward VI, by Jane Seymour, even later. There was an Act of Succession passed by Parliament at some point. Edward got the throne first, then the eldest daughter Mary I, 'Bloody Mary,' the daughter of Catherine of Aragon, Henry's Spanish wife, the legitimate sole heir, in Catholic eyes. Then came Elizabeth I, his daughter with Anne Boleyn. A son, a Catholic daughter, then the younger Protestant daughter, numbers one and three illegitimate in the eyes of the Catholic Church. The reasons for this succession must have been fascinating. The male heir first, then legitimacy even though a Catholic came to the throne - possibly steering the Tudors in another direction entirely, a sop for English Catholics I suppose. Then Elizabeth, the younger Protestant daughter - I'd love to know how the voting went!

"Mary, Queen of Scots, was a pretender to the English throne if you were a Catholic. She was Elizabeth I's cousin, and not rendered illegitimate in Catholic eyes by any divorce. There were plots galore at the time, including what now seems a preemptive one by Sir Francis Walsingham, Elizabeth I's spymaster, to discredit Mary, a devout Catholic. Finally she was tried and then executed. And that bought on war with Spain, and the Spanish Armada."

"Quite interesting, but how does that fit in with that Latin writing."

"In all probability it doesn't. But it might. The point is that Catholics and Protestants alike fought a battle, the Reformation and Counter Reformation, with duelling versions of the Bible in their arsenals. You of course know the King James Version. That's the Protestant Bible, and it was translated as far as possible from known original sources, at the time of Elizabeth I's successor, James I of England. What I think you have here, if it is Church Latin from St. Jerome, is the version that was translated on the Continent by English Catholics in exile, at Douay and Rheims. The English version became known as the Catholic, or Douai Bible."

"When did it come out?"

"In stages. The Catholic Douai New Testament came out in the sixteenth century. Sometime around 1580 or so, I think. Then there was a real battle of translations. Now it's coming back to me. The Douai Bible Old Testament came out later, in 1609 and 1610. The King James Version, both Old and New Testaments, came out the following year, 1611."

"So this wouldn't have been from a Protestant source, this Latin sentence or two."

"In all probability, no. The St. Jerome Latin translation probably went from being the received text to being the basis for the Catholic Bible in English, a matter of high controversy. The Protestants then made the case, you see, that they were going beyond the Latin translation of St. Jerome to original texts."

"Imagine, a translation being such a controversy."

"Well, it was. A matter of first importance, and lives, not to mention souls, depended upon it."

"Which of course takes us back to this writing. You were making some notes there. What do you conclude?"

"'Conclude' is far too strong a word. As I've said, it seems to be one of the Old Testament prophets, tossing fire and brimstone. Not literally, but that is the idea. The people that he is talking about were clearly unworthy. So the truth will be rejected by them. They are lower than low, because they do not realize the truth. So, if I've got it right, this prophet says that the truth shall be hidden away from them. It will be written down and kept in a book in a secret place forever. Then, I suppose, it will be revealed in a better time, although I don't think he says that, exactly."

"I think you're quite right. The history and context are fascinating, but the text isn't. Just wanted to know. I'm an antiques man by profession, you know. Despite my new job, I still get offered things to buy or appraise. It's thought to be a free service, like annoying a doctor at a cocktail party. This scrap of paper, the original I mean, is fairly old, but I can see that of itself it really doesn't have much value. You were very good to share your knowledge with me. It's impressive. Now the homework is done. Let's enjoy ourselves, and see what we came to see."

Carlisle was pleased that they took his credit card. They left the building, walking towards the lake for a few minutes, then rejoined their driver and went back through town, driving to Ross Castle on Lough Lein. Along the way, she pointed out Killarney Cathedral, a Gothic Revival nineteenth century church. It saddened Carlisle by its lack of antiquity, and by its own history, for she explained to him that work on this cathedral had stopped for years because of the Potato Famine. They entered it for a moment. She lit a candle for a private moment of meditation, and then they continued driving towards Lough Lein.

It was as she had said, a glorious lake on a perfect afternoon. Ross Castle, they read, was a chief stronghold of the O'Donoghue family, and it had remained such for centuries, until Cromwell's army came, in the seventeenth century. Fulfilling an ancient prophecy that said that the castle could only be taken by sea, they read that a coordinated artillery attack launched from rafts floated across the lake had caused the castle to surrender. They entered the castle and found a great hall, some outer ramparts, and a few period furnishings. There was one portable desk. Carlisle smiled and almost physically had to restrain himself from taking a closer look at it. It looked seventeenth century, perhaps even earlier. Could this be another piece by the Sparrow brothers?

A small excursion boat took them pleasantly across the lake. This one landed on Innisfallen. He remembered what she had told him at the President's dinner about the Annals of Innisfallen. He wondered how far he might share what he had found out about the desk and its hidden drawer. He decided fairly reluctantly that he could not do so. Mary McGowan didn't know, and there was no reason for Kelly Martin to know either.

They docked and walked across the little inlet to the remains of the early medieval religious sanctuary and center of learning that had once been here. Lough Lein was the "Lake of Learning," and now the evidence of that learning was locked away at the Bodleian Library at Oxford. That didn't seem quite right. It was worth thinking about. He was bewitched by this setting, and convinced that some day he would return, spend more time, and see the Ring of Kerry. He wondered who might accompany him then.

CHAPTER SEVEN -
Change of Plans

RUDOLPHE CARLISLE HAD A DOZEN hours to kill at Heathrow Airport after his flight from Shannon, and he knew exactly what he wanted to do first. In transit in the international terminal, he flashed a pass and was ushered into a VIP lounge. There was a short wait for a free computer terminal. He ordered a drink and thought about his day in Killarney and Castle Glin. He was sorry that there had not been enough time to see the Ring of Kerry, or drive around the Dingle Peninsula. Kelly Martin had told him that either route was well worth it, in fine weather. They were almost conspirators, planning to meet again in unspoken agreement. That seemed a given.

The drive to the River Shannon had left the green countryside of County Kerry and criscrossed areas that were more built up. It was not an unpleasant route, but it was no longer magical. The conversation had become prosaic.

Glin Castle, on the other hand, was something else. It was a family residence with a larger history, including a touching exhibit of a promising young scion of the family who had not returned from France in the Great War, another poignant, irreplaceable casualty of the Somme Offensive of July, 1916. Carlisle was touched by this exhibit of the family's private grief. This was the way not taken for the family, as it had been for so many throughout these islands. Were these sacrifices still remembered, or were they now subsumed into memories of later conflicts? And what were the appropriate conclusions to be drawn from so much sacrifice? The castle grounds were private and well kept, just up from the River Shannon, and perfect for an after dinner stroll. Except for the intimidated group of Chinese businessmen at a large table over by the window, he and Kelly could have imagined themselves there by private invitation.

Kelly Martin had been wonderful company, pretty and bright and erudite in her field. She had looked particularly nice that evening, over dinner by candlelight at Glin Castle. He had enjoyed showing off his knowledge of wines, and she had let him do so. Their conversation now was light and amusing. It had not gone farther than that. Carlisle did not value short term relationships, and neither did she. They had not returned to the subject of the paper and its Latin inscriptions. There had been no point, really.

When they had parted at Shannon, it had been with a sense of shared adventure and a possible future. He left the Embassy car and entered the departure area, turning once to wave goodbye, but the car had already left the passenger dropoff area, to return to Dublin. The check in procedures were routine. He remembered to check his bags all the way to Riga. Let the Embassy people worry about getting them. He was well rid of them. He never liked the bother of worrying about baggage in the first place, even these new bags with rollers that were supposed to be so easy to use.

It had been a short and uncomfortable flight from Shannon to Heathrow. The engineers who had calibrated leg distances between rows of seats for this airline must have used Munchkins from *The Wizard of Oz* for their standard passenger sizes. He couldn't stretch his legs at all. Even isometrics were hard to do in the cramped space. Fortunately it was a short flight. By noon, almost before he knew it, before his leg cramps were too uncomfortable, he was in the Heathrow international transit terminal, with lots of time to kill.

Carlisle realized that he could still make that earlier connecting flight to Riga. But why bother? He had something else in mind. Now there would be ample time to do some Google research. He stood up and looked around the lounge for the twentieth time. If only a computer terminal were available! He sat down again and skimmed through the London *Times*. He drummed his fingers impatiently on the arm of his chair. At last, there was a terminal free.

Carlisle sat down and placed the Latin sentences where he could see them easily. Then he went onto his service provider, and saw that he had too much accumulated mail to read. Out of curiosity he opened the new mail and saw a long, dreary looking list of messages. Then out of habit he began deleting messages from the overflowing spam collection, but grew bored with doing so. There was nothing from Embassy Riga. Well, that was not surprising, since he had not given them his private email address. Nothing else seemed worth opening. He closed the new mail window and googled the first few words of the first Latin sentence.

To his surprise, an answer came up almost immediately. Really, the computer was a marvel. Here he was, researching fourth century Church Latin in the middle of an airport transport lounge! It was hardly the calm setting, the prelude to piety that St. Jerome had imagined, he was sure of that.

She had been right, "spot on" as the Brits would say. The reference was from the Book of Isaiah in the Old Testament. It was

Chapter 30, verses 8-9. He made a note of the reference, and looked up the translation in the Douai Bible. There was something about writing on "box" that he didn't understand. This wasn't getting him anywhere.

He then searched for a more idiomatic English translation of the Book of Isaiah in the King James Version. That was more familiar. That is what he remembered from his church going days, the familiar text and cadences, scripture translated into magnificent English. That is why the King James Version had been such a formidable weapon for the new Church of England. The Catholic authorities seemed to have come to the same conclusion. Kelly had told him that the Catholic Church now used an English translation, issued by an English Catholic Bishop in the eighteenth century, that had also used the King James Version for reference!

Isaiah was writing, it seemed to him, out of anger and disappointment. He seemed to be voicing the anger of God Almighty against those who trusted in Egypt and false gods. This was no candy coated sermon to do good. It was a judgment. "Now go, write it before them in a table, and note it in a book, that it may be for the time to come for ever and ever: That this is a rebellious people, lying children, children that will not hear the law of the LORD."

What did it mean? Well, "table" might mean "tablet," or perhaps papyrus in those days. Surely they didn't have paper. The context seemed to mean that these were unworthy people. Therefore, they should not receive the message of God. Instead, it would be written down and saved for a future time, when it would be understood "for ever and ever."

Something for which people were not ready, that had to be safeguarded. And the reason was that the people had lost their way. He remembered what Kelly Martin had said, about the Tudor period and the religious civil war in England, for that is what it surely had amounted to. For that matter, she would also be looking up the reference, and would find that it was the Book of Isaiah. She also had his private email address.

Then he had another thought. He remembered another part of the writing. He typed in *Peter Quintus*. There was nothing of any immediate interest. Maybe a scholar could make something of these few obscure early church references. He certainly could not do so.

As an afterthought, he idly typed in *Peter Quince*. The result astonished him. He almost shouted aloud. For Peter Quince turned out, in the sole reference that Google provided, to be a bit player in Shakespeare's *A Midsummer Night's Dream*. He was a carpenter! Feverishly Carlisle did some more searching, to entries for William Shakespeare and his plays. Peter Quince only appeared once. There were no other specific references to carpenters. He looked up the play, and saw that Peter Quince, like Snug the joiner, had just a few lines.

A Midsummer Night's Dream was in the First Folio, published in 1623. That was seven years after Shakespeare's death in 1616. What did we know about his plays, what was genuine and what was apocryphal? Here there was room for much speculation. Carlisle seemed to recall that Shakespeare's company had put together the First Folio from their scripts and acting notes. This was the gold standard. Plays in the First Folio were definitely the work of the Bard of Avon. How old was the play? An even earlier reference to the play had been found. It was generally thought to have been written in 1595 or 1596.

He started pacing up and down. The reference to something hidden haunted him. So did the possible reference to Shakespeare's carpenter. Was it all a dream? Was there really another hidden drawer, a deeper one, that he had somehow failed to find? Well, there was nothing he could do about all this now. Or was there? He was in a fever of excitement. He had to act now.

He glanced at his watch. His flight to Riga did not leave until late evening, many hours away. Would that be enough time?

— — — — — — — —

There was another NODIS SALADIN message from the Department of State when Robbie returned to the Embassy from the meeting at the Quai d'Orsay. This one was a personal message from the Deputy Secretary. It had a breathless feel to it, almost smug. It said that a second series of telephone intercepts inside the United States had taken place. There was sufficient information to identify all Al Qaeda members of this operation.

They had been so indiscreet as to mention the arrival plans of the killers themselves. It seemed that those on the telephone had had stalker missions, making sure where the President and the Vice President would be, and finding the best positions for their shooters. That had all been done. The shooters were arriving that very day on separate flights at LAX, Los Angeles Airport, from Jakarta. The time for the assassinations was set for the day after tomorrow.

With this much information, no further waiting was needed or desirable. The shooters would be picked up at LAX upon arrival, and those already in the United States would be taken at the same time. They were already under heavy surveillance. Timing was of course crucial, so that if they were in contact, neither those arriving nor those already in the United States would have the time to warn each other. It would be rolled up promptly and completely.

Robbie nodded at Missy Bronson as he entered the Secretary's office. His grim look dispelled Secretary Adams's pleasant mood. "I think we are starting to turn things around here," Adams was saying on the telephone. "And what we've done here, we will do elsewhere on this trip, with allies and the Russians alike. At least they now know they can talk with us and not get brushed side. Diplomacy is back!"

He put down the phone. "So much for the *Herald-Tribune.* Charley will be pleased." He saw the grim expression on Robbie's face. "Wait. Robbie, what's the matter with you?"

"It's this message, sir." He passed it to Secretary Adams, who scanned it quickly.

"I gather that you're going to tell me that the news is too good."

"Absolutely."

"Well, give my regards to your Uncle Seth."

It took a while to locate Uncle Seth, who was now in Washington, and to arrange for a secure call. Then, Robbie spoke quickly with Secretary Adams and the Embassy *Chargé d'Affaires,* the man in charge pending the arrival of a new ambassador.

As Robbie finished his calls and meeting, the man from Amman was just a few blocks away, checking into the Ritz Hotel on the Place Vendôme. He signed the register, Hassan al-Massoud, and gave the registration clerk a credit card from his private bank. Al-Massoud was amused by the clerk's comical double take, on seeing the picture of his client imprinted on the credit card, and the name of the issuer, the Al-Massoud Bank of Amman. Service, always excellent, became instantaneous.

The Ritz was his preferred stopping place in Paris, and the more costly it became over the years, the more he became wryly amused by the contrast between his missions and his means. He would indeed give all for Al Qaeda and its goals, but he saw no reason to do so in discomfort. He had had quite enough of that in his youth, in Cairo. But his own private fortune was substantial, and his financial advisors in London had multiplied the money several times. Diversification, including his surprisingly profitable private bank, had assured the rest.

There was no reason not to spend his money. To the contrary, as he had explained to his suspicious handlers, there was every reason to do so. The Americans and their allies with their profiling of suspects simply would not be looking for a clean shaven, conservatively dressed businessman who travelled first class and spent money quite freely. Not that he ever wasted any. He knew how to spend money and buy what he wanted. He would never do so in a manner that called attention to himself, as a matter of both taste and discretion.

He went to his room, tipped the bellboy generously, ordered a bottle of Dom Perignon, and took a leisurely shower. The champagne arrived, and he savored it as he dressed in a clean suit. He would tell the housekeeper to pick up his travelling suit for pressing when he left the hotel. That way, it would be ready should he have to leave shortly. Al-Massoud was always ready to leave at a moment's notice.

He looked at his hands and frowned. They would never be healed. When he was young and serious about reform and anxious to learn more about the prophets and his religious inheritance, he had been a student at Cairo University. The Moslem Brotherhood had seemed earnest about its goals, and ascetic about keeping to the true religion. From his moneyed background and his sybaritic experiences on vacation in Beirut, he had found the contrasting rigors of the Brotherhood attractive.

It might all have ended there, had he not been picked up in a police sweep at a Moslem Brotherhood meeting near the university. It was not the first meeting that he had attended, but he was still motivated more by curiosity more by conviction. His family had not been able to intervene in time, for the police had started their beatings and their tortures immediately. And this, he thought bitterly, is the gang that the Americans sent their own prisoners to, for "extraordinary rendition." Horrifying torture was more like it.

His lifelong souvenirs from those six months were a pair of barely usable hands, and fingernails that had been ripped out. When, much later, he had been contacted by Ayman al-Zawahiri, Osama bin Laden's deputy in Al Qaeda, he had been able to share his experiences with similar ones that al-Zawahiri had suffered in the same prison. It had not taken any persuasion for al-Massoud to join Al Qaeda.

But he had done so on his own terms. Perhaps the organization was not yet strong enough to impose its own will in all things. They had seen that in Iraq. Or perhaps, his preferred explanation, what he had to offer was something unique. And that was money and status and *entrée*. His money had gotten the records in Cairo changed, so that no formal record existed of his ever having been imprisoned. And it also managed, in Switzerland, a series of surgical operations that returned to him nearly the entire use of his hands, complete with interchangeable sets of cosmetic fingernails. It had been long and painful and expensive, but what is there that is really worthwhile that doesn't cost serious effort, time and money?

And, with the aid of professionals in Al Qaeda's technical branch, his cosmetic fingernails had been fitted as small tubes that still fit perfectly, and were sealed with a pointed tip that, like a tiny dart, would pour out the lethal poison it contained whenever he chose to shake hands and press the other person's inside wrist tightly with his index finger. With practice, he could sense where the victim's wrist veins were, by touch. Death, as he had discovered with several trials using captured Al Qaeda prisoners, including one American soldier taken in Mosul, was invariable, and almost instantaneous. Judging from the unholy rictus expressions clinging on the faces of the victims, the poison must also, for the short spell preceeding unconsciousness, have been extremely painful.

He had cotton gloves, a rather fussy accessory. That was to hide the fact that his hands did not have usual fingerprint patterns. Had that been known, the search for the killer that he had become would have narrowed, and memories in Cairo even now might have been awakened. The lethal index fingernail just poked through the cotton glove. However, al-Massoud was perfectly aware that his cotton gloves would be spotted in any situation where alert security forces were present. And so he was quite resigned, as a suicide gesture, not to use the gloves, and to shake hands with the right target, as his final mission.

That target was the new American Secretary of State, Ronald Adams.

His only worry, and that was a constant one, was that there might be some error, some factor they had not foreseen. All had gone smoothly to date. He was a known quantity and a highly respected banker and middleman who smoothed the path for Europeans and, let it be said, their governments, to those in Jordan who as middlemen themselves were helpful in deciding oil allocations with Saudi Arabia. Transshipments then were a matter of routine, and the grateful recipients were happy to shower al-Massoud with invitations at the highest level.

That was why he was on the list for a reception in Paris to meet the Secretary of State, as he also was in Moscow. He had asked himself whether this created new risks, and decided that if so, the risks were worth taking. He was, after all, exactly what he purported to be. He helped several governments, including amongst others the French and the Russians.

The French, of course, needed the oil. The Russians, with their huge reserves of oil and natural gas, did not. What they did want, and paid well for, was the right to determine which other client nation actually got the oil. That reinforced their own tactics with their neighbors. A neighbor who could no longer be controlled by military force could with less cost be kept on the leash through economic coercion. They could by this means not only control their own oil export, shutting it off for a neighbor when necessary, but they could at the same time be sure that that neighbor could not readily obtain Saudi oil either. It made a nice economic weapon, helpful at the United Nations, the European Union and elsewhere, multilateral forums where an indirect hand was diplomatically useful. Not everyone connected the dots, to realize that a small country's vote was determined by their oil supply from Russia.

There was no record of his earlier incarceration. And it gave him two possibilities to kill Adams. It seemed unlikely in the extreme that guest lists from two separate countries would be crosschecked. He looked with some satisfaction at the ornate invitation from the French Foreign Ministry, which his office had accepted at his direction, to meet the Secretary of State at a reception that evening. It was, as the Americans would have said, the hottest ticket in town.

He idly wondered whether he should attend in any event, whether or not he was to kill Adams there. No, that would be tempting fate. Surely the American security people would recognize him at a later reception in another capital, and wonder what he was doing there. It was better to save his presence for the actual task, when it counted.

Having checked in for the day, he signalled his usual Paris contact, then met her at an outdoor table of the Café de la Paix on the Avenue de l'Opéra. It was one of his favorite haunts. He enjoyed both the view of the Opéra Garnier just across the street at an angle, and the memories of the superb performances he had enjoyed there. His meeting lasted just twenty minutes. She would inform their friends of his change of plans, and ask whether he should proceed to Moscow. She would also attempt to find out whether there were any changes in the itinerary of Secretary Adams.

How she was to do this was not his concern. She usually managed to handle even more difficult assignments on short notice. There was time enough for him to take an afternoon nap, his preferred habit, and then go to the reception at the Foreign Ministry. He could instead leave for an evening flight from Charles de Gaulle Airport if necessary, although that would entail an inconvenient arrival time in Moscow. If the mission were not changed to take place here in Paris, he would prefer to spend the night and leave for Moscow tomorrow afternoon. He trusted that they knew that. He suspected that the way to get an unpalatable order was to suggest what he in fact preferred. Let them figure it out instead.

He had insisted on taking this mission himself, and knew precisely what was involved. He assumed that he would not return. The important thing, the only thing that mattered, was that he succeed in killing the Secretary of State. By now, the Americans would have tracked the men already in the United States. They should be arrested within a day or so.

What had to be determined was the Americans' next move. The assumption was that after the plot was exposed in the States, Adams would continue on his trip, now with a further patina of triumphalism, guard perhaps lowered. That was the plan, and that is why any detail that threatened to derail it had to be weighed carefully for its implications. But what he was suggesting, in fact reversing the order of assassinations, should suit Al Qaeda equally well. If the Americans hadn't yet moved against Al Qaeda's people in the United States, the element of surprise would still be with Al Qaeda.

He was not a free agent. He could not act by himself. But he wanted to succeed, to make his gesture count. Was it better to continue with the mission, and go directly to Moscow? He half expected to be told to move it up to Paris. That was what he would now be waiting to hear in any event. He wished the French could make a decent martini. Even the bartender at the Café de la Paix had to be guided through the process, step by step. He finished his drink and walked down the Avenue de l'Opéra to the Place Vendôme and after glancing at a few *couturier* shop windows, returned to his room at the Ritz Hotel and fell fast asleep.

He was awakened some hours later by the insistent ringing of his cell phone. It was his contact. Astonishing, that she had heard anything so very soon. In a calm voice, she told him that the champagne served at the Foreign Ministry was indeed a special *cuvée*, really excellent. She wished him a fine evening. He checked the time. It was late afternoon. He had enough time to do everything that was necessary. He could even, if he wanted to, walk to the reception. It was a beautiful day in Paris, one to savor. He would enjoy that.

For the first time in years, Hassan al-Massoud recited his prayers. He used a spare Ritz towel for a prayer rug, then did his ritual ablutions. He redressed with care. Then he turned on the hotel television set. Coincidentally a few blocks away, Secretary of State Adams and Robbie Cutler were watching the same television broadcast.

They saw that all hell was breaking loose on the television news, first in the United States, and then around the world. Every channel turned into CNN with immediate coverage as the Secretary of Homeland Security announced the arrest of an assassination ring in the United States. There were six Al Qaeda members involved, two from Saudi Arabia, two from Indonesia, and one each from Iran and Iraq.

The Secretary's live announcement had a tone of triumphalism. It seemed that the Department, in cooperation with the Director of National Intelligence, had traced the four members of the plot within the United States, and then, having analyzed their communications, snatched the two late arrivals, the Indonesians, as soon as their planes had arrived in Los Angeles from Jakarta. It was carried out with intelligence and precision, and with no injury to any passersby.

The Secretary announced that the group had been instructed to kill both the President and the Vice President. The entire plot had been foiled. Again and again, the arrests were shown on television, and commentators recited the obvious for hours, until their dwindling audiences could have recited the known facts in their sleep. At the end of the day the President gave a short address from the White House, covered live by all networks. Few stopped to consider that the remarks were so carefully crafted, lacking any sense of spontaneity or excitement, that the President must have had the speech ready for days.

Robbie flicked off the switch on the television remote. Uncle Seth had been far from sure that the problem was now finished. There was something just too contrived, too pat, for this schoolboy effort to be the most serious Al Qaeda plot in the United States since 9/11. It just didn't ring true. Uncle Seth had advised extreme caution because the old intelligence officer's instinct had led him to suspect that the plot was not finished. Far from it: it might be just unfolding, in its first stages. He hoped that he was wrong, but it wouldn't cost much to be on the safe side.

Robbie had agreed entirely. He then briefed the Secretary on the steps he had taken since the receipt of the last NODIS SALADIN messages. Robbie told the Secretary that the Foreign Ministry reception for early evening was still on. There had been no convincing reason to cancel it, regardless of security considerations, even if they were sure that was the right thing to do. All of the guests had been checked and rechecked anyway, the Embassy had been assured. However, Robbie had made a few points. For one thing, there should be no receiving line. With security in abundance, that limitation of personal contact was probably the best that they could do. And since the reception was not being cancelled, that also limited any damage that the press might otherwise sniff out. Frankly, with the reception still on, different nuances of handling such as the cancelled receiving line would be an expected reaction, not amounting to much of a story.

Charley Sherburne had agreed. "Nobody can make anything of that," he had said.

Then, Robbie recalled their private message with Prime Minister O'Bryan. Perhaps this was the right time to see if their contact could get any further information. An assassination plot against the President raised the stakes skyhigh. O'Bryan had said that in an extreme case, they might try, and he had given Robert Dillman as the contact. Robbie suggested to Secretary Adams that this was the time to find out if the Irish could get more information as to a possible assassination attempt. He should probably go personally. Reluctantly Adams agreed, and Robbie took some notes, to begin drafting the brief cable to Embassy Dublin announcing his midnight arrival there. He would be back the next day, he hoped before their departure for Vienna. Embassy Dublin was requested to send a car to the airport, and to arrange accommodations and secure his appointment with Dillman.

— — — — — — — —

There would, indeed, be just enough time.

Carlisle checked the departures and arrivals timetables. Dublin was slightly over an hour from Heathrow, and there were constant flights. The round trip flight from Heathrow would get him from London to Dublin and back with hours to spare, even including security delays. With luck he would have several precious hours on the ground. It was just possible, if everything worked like clockwork. Which in his experience, it never did. Whoever had invented that old saying had surely meant it sardonically.

He was too excited to think carefully, but this he knew: there was a second hidden drawer in the ancient desk. The only problem was to find it. If he went back to Dublin, this was not stolen time from Riga. He would be there as planned. He looked at his watch. It was too late now to make the afternoon flight to Riga in any event. His original thought had been to avoid a close plane connection. And on the positive side, he could then have a leisurely dinner at Heathrow, at one of the nice starred restaurants that seemed to be popping up in the international terminal. But his prior planning now furnished him with a new opportunity.

He exchanged a 500 euro note for pounds, and then bought a round trip ticket to Dublin, paying cash in pounds. He was glad that he had also brought his American tourist passport, which, he had recalled, was supposed to be used for personal trips in any event, by Department regulations. Well now, his foresight meant that he would not have two trips to Dublin on his diplomatic passport. That one would simply be stamped with his arrival on Air Force Two, and then with his departure from Shannon that morning. Later, if he was on time, the departure from Heathrow would be duly noted on the same diplomatic passport. As far as anyone could tell, the record of his travels for that day would be fully recorded on his diplomatic passport, without a single stop missing.

Why be so secret? It was, he told himself, a concession to his reputation. This was really, in all probability, a fool's errand. It was also, undeniably, a personal matter. There was no need to get his official status involved, and in fact, every reason not to do so. Given the fact of the Secretary's visit to Riga, he must not and should not change his arrival plans there. Given that, was this side trip necessary or wise? Probably not. Was it worth it? He certainly did not want it known. But if he found what he suspected might be in that desk, it would be the adventure of a lifetime. All would then be made public. And Riga, he suspected, would be his first diplomatic mission, but far from his last one.

It was a puzzled Ambassador Mary McGowan who met him at her residence in Phoenix Park. Even allowing for an antiquarian's quirks, this was odd behavior. He hadn't even requested an Embassy car! He had arrived by a Dublin taxi, having switched on O'Donnell Street from an express bus from Dublin Airport. He was still flush with euros, but remembering his days when the ladder only led upward, he was miserly in small expenses.

Humoring him, she had dismissed the residence staff for the afternoon, as he had requested when he had telephoned her from London. Well, she blushed to recall, it wasn't for the first time. But this was really odd, on Carlisle's part. No sooner left than returned! It's a good thing he wasn't going to head Embassy Tokyo. Relations with that Asian tiger would go downhill in a hurry, with Carlisle at the helm!

Together they went to inspect the secretary once more. It was just an antiquarian's hunch, he had said, but he couldn't get it out of his mind. There might be something there. The desk drawer was emptied, and Carlisle pressed the crescent moon. The hidden drawer opened, almost reluctantly. As it opened, Carlisle carefully put the clippings to one side in a tidy pile. Then he stopped cold. He found at the bottom of the small pile of clippings in the hidden drawer the paper which mentioned Petrus Quintus and the motto in Latin. The paper had sustained a small rip from handling. The rip had not been there when he had replaced it in the drawer.

Where was the second paper?

Mary McGowan looked at him with suspicion and concern. What would he do now? This was the worst acting job she had ever seen, and she had seen a number of them in her day. She listened as he improvised. Where was he going with this? With a practiced diplomatic smile, she had been forced to agree with him. There must indeed be something else hidden.

Indeed, there had been. After he had left the previous day, she had taken to heart his warning that the desk's secret drawer was rather fragile and should not be opened often. That was probably true, but what an odd thing to say. He was no sooner out the door when she had returned to the desk, removed its contents, and opened the secret drawer.

She found the last two papers in the drawer, first noticing the odd references to the Thorpe legacy and claimants to that estate. She remembered that Carlisle had joked about the old miser, before replacing the papers at the bottom of the secret drawer. Fascinated by the Thorpe puzzle, she almost absentmindedly turned the two papers over, noticing their great age. The other sides were quite different. She tried to analyze them. Her remembered Catholic upbringing had been helpful. These must be Latin biblical references. At least they seemed biblical to her. An expert would know. Her friend Kelly Martin certainly would know.

After dinner, alone in her residence, with just a consoling glass of bourbon whiskey for courage, she had painstakingly gone over the old desk. Carlisle was probably right. It would not stand many more openings of the secret drawer. Surely it had been opened more in the past few days than in the previous century and a half, judging from the dates she had noticed on the Thorpe genealogical papers. She slept badly, mulling things over.

After Carlisle's call from London, she had known something was up. She then had called Kelly Martin.

— — — — — — — —

Al-Massoud enjoyed his walk to the Quai d'Orsay. Across the elegant Place Vendôme and along the River Seine, he glanced at the city with affection. He hoped that it would be preserved. So this was the climax of his training. His senses were heightened. He looked forward to the hour ahead.

He stopped at one of the *bouquinistes* along the river, and perused some old volumes. The sun was beginning to set, and there was a clear view of the Pont Neuf. He decided to cross the river there, and walk along the left bank. There was the *Conciergerie*, where prisoners had been kept during the Terror of the French Revolution. And there were the towers which in the early Middle Ages had held the nation's wealth and arms. Now there was the Justice Ministry and, of course, the *Sainte Chapelle*. Al-Massoud could afford to be generous towards a religion that he was sure would be gone soon.

He walked he knew not quite where. It was time. There was the Quai d'Orsay just in front of him. He started to cross the street and, for the fiftieth time, felt the invitation in his pocket. Reaching the other side of the street, he paused and stared back at the River Seine and the city. He remembered that he really should turn off his cell phone. They would probably be confiscated at the entrance to the reception in any event. As if in protest, the cell phone started to ring the moment he removed it from his jacket pocket.

It was his contact. There had been a change. Perhaps he had seen the news? She hoped that he retained his taste for fine vodka.

— — — — — — — —

Carlisle had begun with his customary bravado, but it all sounded tinny and false. He had had an antiquarian's hunch, he stammered. All of a sudden, what had sounded so convincing when he had rehearsed what he was going to say over and over on the plane, now indicted him.

He had gone through the motions of emptying the hidden drawer, and had found just one paper, not two. He looked again and again. Only one paper, with its references to Petrus Quintus and Peter Quince, was there. But it had sustained a rip. And the second paper was missing.

He closed the secret drawer. It didn't take a Sherlock Holmes to figure out what had happened. Even Dr. Watson could have figured it out.

Then it had all unraveled, all of the pretense. He saw immediately from the gloating look on her face that she knew, KNEW, that there was a treasure hidden in the desk. She herself had removed the second paper, the reference to Isaiah. She had tried to hide her satisfaction at seeing him so frustrated in his search. Well, he had been too clumsy. His warning not to open the desk had signalled the exact opposite, of course. She then had looked and found them, and had known immediately that he had seen them earlier. That was why he had returned. Leaving them had been his great mistake.

Her reaction now had told him that not only was there, as he had suspected, a second hidden drawer, but that she had surely discovered it. And so he had asked her directly, shouted it finally, and was told that he must be mad. Yes, he knew that she must have found it, and it was the find of a lifetime, anybody's lifetime!

He could not recall afterwards how things had gotten so out of hand. He had struck her, and she had in falling hit her head on the secretary. Furious, now, he had put his fingers everywhere on the desk. His heart wildly beating, he had pressed every inch of the desk, inside and out. Nothing moved, except, maddeningly, the one secret drawer, creaking open.

With desperation he looked again in the open drawer. The minutes passed. There was nothing else there at all. Nothing.

Ambassador McGowan started to revive. This was impossible, a nightmare getting worse. She wakened and tried to get up, balancing herself unsteadily on her elbows. Her eyes were wild and out of focus. Her voice came back, and she started to scream. His hands were still powerful after many years of handling furniture. She was dead in a few minutes.

He remembered hearing about the residence basement, the spare freezer. Someone had made a reference to it at the reception for Secretary Adams, so very long ago. He hoisted McGowan in a fireman's carry and brought her downstairs to that basement. The spare freezer was open. He went in, switched on the light, and there in the corner, behind several sides of beef, deposited the body of the American Ambassador to Ireland. With luck, it would not be found for days.

Carlisle used his handkerchief to wipe all areas where he thought prints might have been left. He managed a grim sort of prayer for his dead colleague. He hadn't really meant to hurt her in any way. But what was done, was done. Back in the first floor corridor, he put the old newspaper clippings back into the hidden drawer, and was relieved that it still clicked back into place. The secretary was soon as it had been.

He had thought about the *Per Lux Lunae* paper, and decided to replace it. After all, she might have told someone else about it. If she had, and it was now also missing, that would be a signal to trace anyone who knew about the hidden drawer. As a furniture expert, his name would make the short list. And he did have exact copies of the writings. Not that he needed them. Every word, even the Latin, seemed carved in his memory. So it must now be left in the hidden drawer, exactly as she had left it. But what had she done with the quotation from Isaiah?

Now time was getting very short. He had to get back to the airport. What she had taken out of the desk was surely in her office at the Embassy in any event. What a pity. Well, the priority now was not finding that missing paper. It was getting to Dublin Airport in time to make his return flight to Heathrow.

He left the residence and walked the short distance to the main Phoenix Park road, that bisected the length of that enormous city park. He had the idea of checking to see if a bus was available, or hailing a taxi, but he was in luck. Sheer dumb luck. He saw a pleasant looking couple just passing in a new Ford, and stuck out his thumb.

They were Americans, on their honeymoon, and full of midwestern goodwill, they stopped and let him in. Madge and Bill would be pleased to give him a ride to the nearest taxi stand, just outside the entrance to Phoenix Park, so that he could continue going downtown. They would be turning off for their trip to County Wicklow. He had almost enjoyed their company, and he hoped that his invented *persona* would be totally forgotten in their honeymoon week's memories. Fortunately, they were the only Americans on view that day who were not camera mad.

His luck held. He waved goodbye to Madge and Bill, and when they were out of sight, he crossed the street. There in front of another taxi stand was a bus schedule. He found an express bus for the airport listed, stopping there within minutes. He got on, and arrived at Dublin Airport with time to spare for the return flight to Heathrow.

He was on pins and needles now, hoping that he would not be recognized. He made a grim study of how not to call attention to himself. He didn't need to exchange any money, and he already had his ticket. He didn't even want to buy a newspaper. Fortunately, there was one left on a bench. He picked it up and scanned its contents, which failed to register with him. He read a lead paragraph six times and couldn't remember what it said. The television monitors were droning on, and then exited television commentators were showing some action endlessly repeated. The sound was off, and he was not interested enough, and perhaps not capable, of focussing on the running printed commentary at the bottom of the television screens. Something about arrests in the United States.

Enough time had elapsed. He went through the security area in a deliberate fashion and then walked to the boarding area for his flight to Heathrow. He half expected at any moment to be stopped. He willed his pulse to slow down. But there was nothing to trouble him. The flight was smooth, and in slightly more than an hour the airplane was landing at Heathrow. He got off the plane and went into the transit lounge.

—   —   —   —   —   —   —   —

Robbie had decided to skip the reception. There wasn't enough time in any event, and he hated to rush things. He had quickly packed an overnight bag and shoveled the usual toiletries into his Dopps kit, then tried to enjoy the ride to the airport. One of these days he would have to take the Chunnel, the train linking Paris and London. His parents had done so, and said that it was very enjoyable, just whizzing along, and there was good food to be enjoyed, as well.

With the Embassy travel and security staff paving the way he was at Heathrow waiting for his connecting flight to Dublin almost before he had finished the magazine article from *The New Yorker* that he had been saving to read. It was a very late connection. He had just missed the earlier one, and so decided to kill some time in the transit lounge. Maybe the duty free shop had something tempting. After all, he wouldn't have that much shopping time despite all the stops they would be making, and his Mother's birthday was coming up shortly.

He saw someone familiar, and then, with a broad grin, Rudolphe Carlisle strode over to say hello. Yes, he had come over from Shannon earlier in the day. If he had thought it through, with more attention to the schedule, he might have stayed in Western Ireland a bit longer, and perhaps even spent another day at Glin Castle. But it had been a pleasant holiday, particularly in Kelly Martin's delightful company. Surely Robbie remembered her? Yes, indeed.

Carlisle asked about Robbie's travel plans. Odd, wasn't it, leaving the Secretary? No, just following through on some old business in Dublin for the Secretary. Robbie looked forward to seeing him in Riga. "Until then!"

Carlisle's flight to Riga would be boarding shortly, and so they shook hands and went their separate ways.

Quite a bonus, seeing Robbie Cutler, Carlisle thought. Just imagine, having this young diplomatic sleuth, with a service-wide reputation for his detective skills, now an eyewitness to his being hundreds of miles, indeed an entire country, away from the death of the American Ambassador in Dublin. That was really a lucky break.

CHAPTER EIGHT -
Reappearances in Dublin

RUDOLPHE CARLISLE GOT UP FROM his cramped seat, stretched and yawned in the aisle, and did some isometric exercises. His flight to Riga was nearly half empty. He had tried to savor his late snack, polishing off several small bottles of white Bordeaux wine, which had been well chilled and hence passable. In a few minutes he would be landing in Riga, a moment that he had practiced so often over the months since the White House call, that he had memorized his arrival and could have choreographed every step.

His moods ticked back and forth like a stubborn grandfather clock. The trouble was that now it was early morning, before daybreak, and he would not be met by anyone of consequence. But that was not really so bad after all, all things considered. It had all worked out rather well. There would not be anybody here to notice his nervousness, if he had been the least bit nervous.

He wasn't, and that rather surprised him. He had liked Mary McGowan, and her death was a tragic waste. The waste was compounded by what she must have known. What was hidden in the desk? Surely she had found it. Her expression, and the missing Latin text of Isaiah proved that. If only she hadn't reacted so violently! Well, he couldn't undo the past. What was done, was done. Now he had a hand that he didn't want to play, but that was the hand that he held, and he must go on from there. Nothing he could do now would bring her back. It would only harm him. He started to imagine various adolescent penance scenarios, wherein after suitable bouts of haunted guilt and self flagellation he donated his salary for worthy causes, or found the document, whatever it was, and gave it away to the nation.

Screw that. Carlisle thought that people who brooded over what might have been were pathetic. Look closely at what you still had and could surmise, and go on from there. That was the positive approach, the one that led to results. It was time for a cool, dispassionate look at where things stood. Both sides, and then he could take it from there.

Number one. It was unlikely that he could be connected with the murder. He wasn't even in Dublin at the time. His travel had been as anonymous as he could make it. He had used his regular passport, not the diplomatic one. He had put nothing on any credit card that could place him in Ireland after his departure yesterday morning from Shannon Airport. Quite to the contrary, he had paid cash for all expenses. His transportation had been public, except for an American couple who would probably never even hear about the murder. He could document from his diplomatic passport his departure from Shannon, arrival at Heathrow, and then his departure from Heathrow. As he had requested, the Phoenix Park residence staff had been dismissed, and he was sure that nobody had seen him there. And as a great piece of luck, Robbie Cutler himself had seen him at Heathrow Airport.

The only downside he could conjure up was the fact that his name would appear on the flight passenger manifest to Dublin and back. But who would think to check such a detail? Most likely, the police would go off on some unrelated wild goose chase. He was glad that he had asked Mary McGowan to dismiss her staff. That might even cast suspicion elsewhere. Most of the ambassadors he had met in the Foreign Service Club had mentioned dismissing their household staffs for an afternoon or so from time to time. That was how it was done. Surely women ambassadors could pull the same stunt, and in this case, cast suspicion on someone else entirely.

The thought was not only comforting; it was rather funny. Some Irish stud would probably be called in for a quiet chat within a few days. He could just picture the scene playing out in a dingy Dublin police headquarters!

Let's see, what else? Well, he had called her, of course, from Heathrow. Had he used a cell phone or a public phone, from the lounge? He couldn't remember. There would be a record of the call, surely. It was easily explained.

All perfectly normal. He was calling as a courtesy, as her former houseguest, to thank her for her hospitality. No problem there. "By the way, Inspector, why are you asking? Has anything happened?"

The great problem now remained, not the murder, but how to get at the desk. He was sure that it had contained something cherished and valuable. Had Mary McGowan found it? Probably not, or she would have thrown that fact in his face, triumphantly. In which case, it was still there, awaiting his return. But where on earth was the Latin fragment, that two verse quotation from the Book of Isaiah? She surely had found that, and removed it. The other paper, with its dated reference to *Petrus Quintus*, was still there. But try as he might, he couldn't entirely dismiss the possibility, however remote, that she had indeed understood the Isaiah quotation, and then located a second hidden drawer in the desk. Amateurs sometimes did make lucky finds.

He was upset that he had had no time at all to go through her bedroom and the private office that he was sure adjoined it. Yesterday in his hurry it had seemed more likely that she had taken both the Latin fragment and the hidden document, if that is what it was, and put them away in her office at the Embassy in Dublin. He might have done that.

On the other hand, if she had discovered something, it had only been on the previous day. Her curiosity on finding the two papers, the *Petrus Quintus* dated notation and the Isaiah Latin inscription would have been whetted by the realization that he had found them first, and skipped over them without telling her. Why would he have done such a thing? He was too meticulous an antiquarian not to have found them at all. He had left them for a reason. Perhaps they were not the important thing. They only led towards it.

His mind kept racing, piling supposition upon supposition. And then, why shouldn't she look further? Suppose she had found it, the manuscript. What would she have done then? Her first reaction might well have been just to keep it handy, and try to make out herself what it was. That would be more likely at her residence. Later, when she had satisfied herself as to its contents and meaning, she would have removed it to her office at the Embassy. Then she could have thought about what to do next, when she had double-checked and was absolutely sure of her discovery. It was sheer speculation, just going around in circles.

But that wasn't speculation. It was hardheaded deduction. Surely the police would soon have the list for the past few days of her calls, and start tracing them. If she had had a good look at the document, and not been sure of what it was or what it meant, she might have had time to consult an expert. That was an interesting thought. At the very least, she would make some calls and troll a hypothetical or two. "Suppose this sort of document came onto the market ..." Whom would she call? That would probably come out during the police investigation, another lead that went nowhere, but would be meaningful to him.

He tried to think about who the experts were in this field, whom she might have contacted. But which field of specialization, exactly, was involved? Was it the furniture part, and the hidden desks? Well, maybe so after all. Perhaps she had been smart enough to figure out that there was a second hidden drawer, but had, like himself, failed to find it. That was logical. He himself had, after all, gone all over the desk in a relentless and ultimately fruitless search for the second drawer. On the other hand, perhaps she had found the second drawer, had also taken out its contents, but hadn't understood either what she had found, or its value.

In that case, the Isaiah paper and whatever had been in the second drawer were now together somewhere, probably in her office. If they were not, that surely meant that she had not found the second drawer after all. Its secrets had remained buried in the desk.

In either event, as to the existence and location of the second hidden drawer itself, or as to its contents, she might have called an expert. That expert's name might be recoverable through the phone records. And that would be a certain clue to the Dublin mystery. After all, he knew experts by the dozens. As to those he did not know personally, there were standard directories listing experts in various fields of arcana, their names and contact information. That information, if it were made public, would give him a vital clue as to what the desk might have contained. Speculation within speculation, it was leading in circles.

Wait a second. How did a police investigation work when diplomats were involved? Didn't her diplomatic immunity mean that the Irish couldn't investigate? He really didn't know. And how about his own diplomatic immunity? That probably wouldn't kick in until he had formally presented his credentials here in Riga to the President of Latvia. All the more reason to move forward quickly. This question of diplomatic immunity was intriguing, an interesting detail, one that would delay things a bit, enough time for the traces to grow even colder in Dublin. Speaking of cold, he wondered how long it would be before her body was even discovered.

Where would he go from here?

But had she even realized the meaning of the Isaiah paper? He had been assuming that she did. Perhaps not - perhaps she had not progressed even that far. She might not have realized what it was that she had found. If he could somehow search her private office and find both the Isaiah fragment and the second document, whatever that was, all well and good. If he just found the Isaiah fragment, then she had not found anything else at all, and he should return to the desk for another search from the beginning.

He had to get back to Dublin somehow, once he was sure that it was safe to do so. He had to explore the desk and the house and have a good look for the Isaiah document. Then a new thought struck him. What if it were there all the time, and he had just missed it, and she had known nothing about it at all? Did that look on her face was only mean that she had no idea what he was talking about? She hadn't been hiding anything at all? No, no, that was not possible. It wasn't all for nothing, the killing. It couldn't have been. Could it?

He had to see if the Isaiah quotation was there, to prove that he had acted from necessity, even, in a way, justly. It wasn't all for nothing. It couldn't have been. At least, he knew that he was looking for something. Nobody else even knew that. And so, there was no real hurry. All the more reason not to seem hurried. He was, after all, an American Ambassador, reporting in to his post. There was time to do everything just right, both in Riga and in Dublin. Above all, there was no need to panic. None at all. He, after all, had left no traces. Surely he could now manage the less difficult task of returning to Dublin, outraged and saddened like Mary's other friends, and anxious to do her memory honor. Yes, that would give him excellent cover to search for the missing Isaiah document. And he could try once more to find the second hidden drawer, that must be hidden, buried somewhere in the old desk.

He looked out the airplane window and saw the landing lights of Riga Airport stretching out below. The fasten seatbelt light flickered on, and with it, the predictable droning pilot's announcement that they were arriving. The plane landed with a practiced series of bumps, one large one and several ever smaller ones until the plane was firmly planted on the ground, slowly taxiing towards the airport terminal.

Carlisle secured his briefcase from the overhead compartment, grinned at the sleepy stewardess, and got off the plane. He saw that there were no busses to take passengers into the terminal. It all seemed small scale. There were ramps, and then a short walk.

"Welcome to Riga, Mr. Ambassador." He recognized the voice, and then saw a familiar face. It was Stan Bartlett from the Embassy. "Give me your ticket stub and we'll arrange for your luggage to be brought to the Residence." An engaging and very sleepy blonde young woman stepped forward and wordlessly handed him a bouquet of flowers. Must be from their Office of Protocol, he thought. She escorted Carlisle away from the rest of the drowsy passengers and through a special VIP lounge. Then, seeing that the Embassy was taking charge, and with a brief bow and fetching smile, she vanished. Just like that, a Latvian Cheshire Cat.

"You're not missing much at this airport," Stan said, as they settled into the Embassy limousine. He explained that it had been gussied up somewhat for President Bush's visit in 2005. They had spruced it up, so that the collection of old Soviet era relics, planes and helicopters and whatnot, which had made this airport something of a museum, no longer gave the impression of a vintage film set. They turned down the airport access road a few miles while Stan Bartlett gave a running travelogue. The car turned right onto the highway coming from Jurmala. Bartlett told him that in daylight hours they would be seeing some nice, unspoiled vistas, with even a remnant of birch woods on the left, just before the left turn onto the road leading to Riga.

Stan said that some paint had been slapped onto the rather dilapidated wooden buildings that lined the road at the time of President Bush's visit, and for a later NATO summit meeting. "A very mixed bag," he said. "Some of these buildings are very fine and have been well restored, I'm told. Others should just be torn down." He said the area was called Pardaugava, "on the other side of the Daugava," the river dividing Riga. This was the residential side, although that distinction would be lost if the planned skyscraper expansion really took place. They came to a suspension bridge looking towards Old Town Riga, and he said that like Los Angeles, the traffic was usually so intense that stalled motorists would get lots of time to enjoy the view. Or curse out their neighbors.

"The outskirts and new sections are not entirely devoid of charm I suppose, but Old Town Riga is something else. A pleasure to wander in. Some nice restaurants, too. That's where your residence is located." His voice trailed off, as he saw that Carlisle was beginning to yield to the effects of the late flight. He was nearly asleep as they drove towards the city, skirting it, and then towards that part of Old Town close to both the Parliament building and Riga Castle where the American Ambassador's residence was located.

Carlisle woke up, sort of, as the car slowed, as they approached the Swedish Gate. And there was also the American official residence. Picturesque to a fault, Bartlett explained, in keeping with its surroundings, the residence was in the very center of the so-called Swedish Barracks, a 200 meter long, renovated eighteenth century building containing offices, boutiques and coffee houses. Very chic.

Carlisle was reminded of the Crescent at Bath, England, without, of course, the crescent shape. But it was very stylish. He could get used to this quite easily. Bartlett told him that he would have some diplomatic colleagues for company in the Swedish Barracks. It seems that for neighbors, the Dutch and European Union Embassies were also located there, as was the residence of the Italian Ambassador. He closed his eyes again, revelling for a moment in his good fortune, imagining fine Italian dinners and bottles of vintage Barolo with his new colleagues.

Carlisle opened his eyes, aware that Bartlett had stopped in mid-sentence. "Afraid I dropped off for a moment, Stan. I must apologize for getting you out so late. The flights weren't convenient. At least it was fairly comfortable. Am I all set to present my credentials?"

"Tomorrow afternoon, sir, end of the day. We were sure that today, you would want to sleep in. The car will be waiting to take you to the Embassy after luncheon, whenever you say. You could walk, but security doesn't like it. Actually it isn't far at all, just a few minutes, across the park. Then there will be a brief staff meeting after you settle into your office and meet the front office staff. Late afternoon, you will have a short meeting with the Foreign Minister. That is to present him with a copy of your credentials. He will then advise you officially regarding the credentials ceremony itself.

"But we already have the details. Everything is laid on for the credentials presentation tomorrow afternoon. You'll be able to get through it all in a few hours, then get some rest and have the chance to get acclimated to Riga for a few days before the Secretary arrives. You will have some remarks to make then. And oh yes, there will be a full press contingent at the credentials ceremony."

Bartlett wanted to go further, but it wasn't really his job. The DCM would take care of that. Besides, it was perfectly obvious that Carlisle was exhausted and should spend some time, once he had rested for a day, with his press advisor, and the political officer. Riga was friendly but like any foreign capital, it could be a public relations snare. There would always be someone in the press corps who wanted to stir up controversy, and have a rough question ready for the new boy. It was all part of the diplomatic game.

The Embassy had to test this new man, and do so very quickly. Was he fast on his feet? Stan Bartlett had told the DCM that he was. After all, he had handled the Senate Foreign Relations Committee hearings with ease. But then, Washington had been overshadowed with the death of the last Secretary of State, and the need to confirm Secretary Adams in a hurry. Carlisle really hadn't been challenged. Still, he hadn't folded under the pressure, either.

Any Embassy had its internal problems. With any degree of luck, Carlisle would find out about them fairly quickly, and sort out those he had to handle, and those he would just discreetly monitor. Some of the officers were there because they were oldtimers settling in for what they assumed would be an undemanding post, while others were still bound for the diplomatic fast track, eager to learn some Latvian, and to study the country and its history and people. Bartlett included himself in the latter category.

And Latvia had its political issues. Any and all nations had theirs as well. Some, the United States could help with, and some were no win situations that should be avoided. And with instantaneous worldwide communications from any pinpoint on the globe, a diplomatic blunder, if juicy enough, could be front page news tomorrow whether it originated in Riga, Baghdad, or Paris.

In short, he hoped that Carlisle was a discriminating leader in the good sense, and that he was a fast learner. It seemed so, but they would all know, soon enough.

"Sounds good. We'll take it one day at a time."

Carlisle put his head back on the cushioned seat. So far, all had gone well. There was nothing to indicate anything wrong, let alone any melodramatics like murder. He imagined that Embassy Dublin must be missing their Ambassador by now. He wondered when the search would begin. Not for a day, possibly. They must surely think that she had gone off with a gentleman friend. Not good form, but nothing that anyone wanted to call any attention to, either. But it wouldn't be so very long before someone, perhaps that DCM George Smiley, would start getting antsy and suspicious.

Then the search would start. First, there would be some low key looking about. A few telephone calls would be made to her known Dublin friends and associates. Carlisle tried to imagine what they would possibly say. "Pardon, but have you possibly seen Mary McGowan? We seem to have misplaced our Ambassador" didn't seem to quite do. Then, there would be something a bit more organized. Possibly a call to someone trustworthy in the European Bureau in State. He couldn't think who that would be and, of course, the Assistant Secretary for Europe was now travelling with Secretary Adams. They would still be in Paris, he remembered.

The car was nearing his residence, Bartlett said, and Carlisle suddenly felt a desire to see something of the city. He told Stan Bartlett, and the chauffeur eased into a parking area near the Old Town's cobblestone streets. It was predawn, and the town had come to life. There were restaurants, night clubs with live music blaring, colorful period streetlights, and a festive atmosphere. Carlisle smiled with appreciation. He was going to enjoy life here.

"How about a first look at Old Town Riga, Mr. Ambassador?" At Carlisle's nodded assent, Stan went on, "Here is where it all begins. Your residence is right over there."

Carlisle took an appreciative first glance at the Swedish Barracks. "Looks just wonderful," he said. "Let's see something of the town."

"Fine, sir. The driver can take care of your hand luggage while we go exploring, if you like." They got out of the car, walked through the Swedish Gate, and entered Old Town.

"Let's stop over there." Carlisle pointed towards a sidewalk restaurant, colorfully decorated, with tables looking out over the square. An enthusiastic small orchestra kept repeating the strains of a well known Latvian tune, while those already seated at the restaurant sang or chanted the familiar lyrics.

Bartlett listened attentively to the song, then gave up. The tune was familiar, but the lyrics were baffling. "Sorry, Mr. Ambassador, my Latvian isn't that good yet. I think it has something to do with stealing chickens."

At Stan's suggestion they ordered sorrel soup and fresh rye bread with beer, "just enough to give you a taste of good Latvian food," without, he could have added, keeping you up the rest of the night. They enjoyed their supper with steins of Pilsener. Then, Stan suggested more Latvian comfort food for dessert, *Debesmanna*, a whipped cranberry dessert pudding with milk. With cups of hot fresh ground coffee, it was delicious.

"The Old Town has largely been restored since the war, and particularly, since the Latvians regained their independence," Stan offered. "I think it's the best part of Riga still. Lots of it has medieval echoes. And just outside Old Town - now the heart of the modern city - are the more modern cultural sections, museums and concert hall, which were built up after Napoleon's invasion in 1812. He destroyed everything outside the Old Town, I suppose to create fields of artillery fire against an approaching enemy. Then afterwards, across the river from Old Town, the more modern sections were built, with the Opera House and other landmarks. Think Central Park and the Upper West Side. Very nice. You'll see them all soon."

Carlisle was enjoying discovering his city. It all belonged to him now, thanks to that phone call from the White House and his campaign donations over the years. It didn't hurt a bit, although he didn't know it, that his name had come up for the appointment at exactly the time when two other ambassadorial appointees had embarrassed the White House by failing to show the least understanding of their countries of assignment, in their hearings before a testy Senate Foreign Relations Committee. Their mumbled and inept responses had fueled the national late night talk shows with comic relief for a solid week. With Carlisle, anyway, they were appointing a cultured man, somebody who would never, ever, embarrass the White House.

They left the restaurant and walked along the cobblestone streets of Old Town Riga. Later he would come back, many times, and make the geography second nature. But for now, Carlisle was just excited to be there. He wondered what treasures still lay undiscovered and uncatalogued on shelves beyond the shop windows. He smiled at St. Jacob's Cathedral, and half listened to Stan Bartlett's travelogue. This church extended back to the early thirteenth century, it seemed. He looked appreciatively at three stylish buildings side by side, "The Three Brothers," Stan told him, medieval residences that had been rebuilt in later centuries, when money became more plentiful, surely during one of the rare periods when trading vessels rather than warships explored the Baltic coast.

Down Smilsu Street they saw the Gunpowder Tower. "Just like Colonial Williamsburg," he thought, "only this one is older and genuine." "This is just the beginning," Stan said. "I'm particularly fond of the Cats' House. No, it really is plural. And it wasn't a brothel. It was named for the two cat sculptures on top of the house. The rich builder had just been denied guild membership, which was then a very big deal. He didn't like being excluded. Somehow, that explains the cats - their tails were originally lifted in the direction of the Guild House that had refused membership to the builder."

Carlisle smiled in appreciation. It was just the sort of cute insider anecdote that visitors loved. But he was getting tired. It was time to go to the Residence and get some sleep. Then he remembered how the long day had started, from the overnight at Glin Castle to the drive along the River Shannon to Shannon Airport, then the flight to Heathrow and, of course, his back and forth to Dublin. He tried not to replay every detail of that afternoon, and by and large succeeded.

At some point, there would have to be a notification to the Dublin police, very discreetly done, of course, and to begin with, rather tentative. The search would then begin, low key at first. Then word would leak. It always does. Then they would find her body. It might take several days. Who would think to look in a disused freezer in her Residence? The discovery might even be when the Secretary was visiting Riga. That would suit Carlisle very well. Then he would be part of the official American reaction to this terrible crime. So would they all.

— — — — — — — —

Robbie was tired but keyed up. He had hoped to relax during the flights from Paris to Heathrow, and then on to Dublin, but it hadn't worked out that way. His sixth sense was acting up again. Something was going on, something that would demand concentration and an effort of will and imagination. He felt for all the world as though he were entering another crime scene, not embarking on a sensitive diplomatic errand. Well, he thought wryly, nowadays there was little to distinguish the two!

He remembered the other cases, that financial manipulation in Singapore that he had uncovered when he was a newly minted Vice Consul at the Embassy on that fascinating island. Then there were the Basque terrorist murders in Bordeaux, and ETA's attempts to blackmail the vineyard owners of Bordeaux. On to Embassy Budapest, and the traitor from the Hungarian Revolution group of Freedom Fighters on Barat Street who had pulled in the Russian Mafia in an attempt to kill him. No break even on his honeymoon, in the scenic Dordogne, when he and Sylvie had found themselves stalked by a vicious killer trying to keep a secret of wartime murder and grand art theft. If only that lost Van Gogh would turn up!

All in all, it really didn't seem like a diplomat's *resumé*! Robbie sometimes wondered if he were in the right profession. There had been that crime in Providence when he was a student at Brown, the armed robbery that he had helped solve. Maybe it had been the confident manner of the investigating detective, or his real appreciation for Robbie's help, or the intriguing *noir* world that he had allowed Robbie to share briefly, discussing old cases over a few bottles of Sam Adams beer. Whatever it was, Robbie had become fascinated by crime detection.

When he had entered the Foreign Service, the last idea in the world that he would have entertained was that he now had a broader canvas on which to trace murder cases. But that had turned out to be the case. More than that, he had discovered that a diplomat has access to many secrets, across cultures, and because of that sometimes can see quite clearly what is going on as far as criminal investigations are concerned. He could put together a puzzle, since he had all of the pieces, including key ones that others lacked. That was particularly true when American citizens overseas were the perps, or were involved as the victims.

Robbie would never interfere with any local investigation. It wasn't why he was posted at an Embassy, and he would have been the first to admit that he didn't have the detailed local background that only a lifetime would burnish. But sometimes, when others were stumped, he could lend a hand. And when an American Ambassador asked him to liaise with local police, his other diplomatic work took a back seat. For a while.

Well, that certainly wasn't going to be the case in this job. He was a Special Assistant to the Secretary of State. Somebody else was going to have to handle the murders for a while. His job was too important, and certainly too time consuming, to get hung up on murder cases, no matter how fascinating they might be. That was for sure.

Landing in Dublin, Robbie quickly went through customs, holding his single carry on bag. Yes, there was the Embassy driver. Robbie smiled hello at the man holding the sign, whom he thought he recognized. Soon they were out of the airport.

"Mr. Smiley thought you might want to have a quiet place to stay, a bit out of town in the diplomatic section, rather than one of those Grafton Street hotels," the chauffeur said. He handed Robbie a nice welcome note from Deputy Chief of Mission Smiley. If he was supposed to confirm the arrangement the note didn't say so, and in the absence of anything to the contrary, the driver drove to Smiley's house.

It was late but not quite too late when Robbie entered the residence, being greeted first by Smiley's security man at the door. "Very nice of you to have me," Robbie said to his host. He didn't know whether to call him Mr. Smiley or George. It was awkward being a high roller with a low rank. Smiley said something gruffly gracious, then showed Robbie his room and suggested he "have a wash," get comfortable, then come on down to the library for a highball. Hmmn, been overseas for a while, Robbie thought. The usual tipoff that somebody was overdue for home leave in the States was when an American diplomat started using local slang. And it was pretty clear that drinking was not what Smiley had in mind. Or, not primarily.

Ten minutes later Robbie was in pajamas, slippers and borrowed robe, and being handed a Jameson whiskey with a splash of water. He sank into the leather chair opposite his host, who poured his own drink and drank a hefty swallow before beginning the conversation. "We're both pros, Robbie," was the opener. What could be next? It sounded ominously like Smiley was putting his career on the line. Robbie guessed that it was not a policy matter. Whether one survived a policy disagreement or not in the Foreign Service depended upon a host of factors. Sometimes, with a change of administration, a known policy disagreement with the previous political team meant the reverse, a promotion. No, Smiley had something else in mind. Something delicate, something that if badly handled, would make him look very bad, even awkward - and in the Foreign Service, that was not recoverable.

"What is going on, George?" Clearly the first name use was indicated. Smiley was going to tell him something whether he wanted to hear it or not. By using the first name he was not being presumptuous. He was encouraging the confidence that he was going to hear anyway, whether or not he wanted to do so. There was no choice except to hear the entire thing, as accurately and fully as possible. There would be no second chance, in Robbie's experience. Get it wrong the first time, and the other fellow with the confidence to share would start, in just the tiniest way, to engage in mental evasions. Let's hear it now. All of it.

"Ambassador McGowan is missing. She has been gone for about twelve hours, and I have no idea where she is. She was at the Residence in Phoenix Park this morning. When she doesn't have office appointments she usually likes to come into the office in the early afternoon or late morning. Just what I'd like to do, frankly, given half the chance. But today, your cable came and I got it, and arranged your meeting with Dillman. But the Special Assistant to Secretary Ronald Adams just doesn't leave the Secretary's party in another country and fly off to Dublin. I thought Mary should be informed immediately.

"Anyway, I called the Residence, and she wasn't there. Nobody answered, I mean. I called again ninety minutes later. Still nothing. That bothered me. So I took a car out to Phoenix Park. The dinner staff was just coming on, and there was a caretaker who had just returned. He wanted to finish some work while it was still daylight. He is the one who told me that Ambassador McGowan earlier in the day had given the staff the day off. No, it was more than that. She had virtually ordered them away from the Residence for the day. That had never happened before.

"Well, fine. Boys will be boys, and I'm learning, girls will be girls, too. But here it is after midnight in another day. No Ambassador McGowan. So I put two and two together, wondered about your coming in, and thought it better that you stay here. For one thing, your cable was pretty cryptic. It didn't say why you were coming, just that you wanted an appointment with a Mr. Dillman in Prime Minister O'Bryan's office. He's not one of our usual contacts."

He took a long sip. "Sorry if I'm out of line, Robbie, but - as you'll surely learn one of these days - DCMs are professional worry warts. We like calm and predictability. What we don't like, because we don't understand it, are missing Ambassadors."

Robbie took a long drink of his own. It was a time for shared confidences. They were going to work together. He was sure that he didn't really have the authority to broaden the list of those authorized to know about NODIS SALADIN, but he was equally sure that Smiley was the man in charge, there was a serious local problem, and that it might affect security for the Secretary. So, his back was covered. He decided to level with Smiley.

"As to why I'm here, that's top secret. But I think, sir, that you need to know." The "sir" was just right. It removed the thought of talking down to a senior officer and it reinforced the confidence that Robbie was about to make and the need to keep it. It also told Smiley that he had been right to trust Robbie Cutler. Not bad for one three letter word and a lilting touch of respect in the inflection as it was pronounced. The scientific linguists at the Foreign Service Institute in Arlington would have applauded.

Robbie took another drink of his Jameson and, rare for him, accepted a refill. "As you know, we had a special security alert a few days ago, when Secretary Adams was in Dublin." Smiley nodded. "Also, of course, Homeland Security has arrested a group of Al Qaeda operatives in the United States who were planning to assassinate the President and Vice President."

He paused. "Well, when we were here, Prime Minister O'Bryan told us that a long standing Irish agent in place had heard about the assassination plan against the President. He also mentioned Secretary Adams. This is an agent who was left over from the old IRA training days, possibly now in Beirut. Just left in place, why, I have no idea. Anyway, the Secretary asked whether we could put any questions to the agent. The Prime Minister clearly didn't like the idea - I wish I knew more about O'Bryan's own background, by the way - but he did say rather reluctantly that it might be just possible, and he gave as a connection the member of his staff that I asked to see. Robert Dillman."

"Yes. You'll be seeing him at nine this morning."

"Good. And there's something else." He leaned forward. "It may be way out. Or maybe not. One theory we have heard is that the plot inside our country was essentially a diversion, to pump up Homeland Security and give us all a false sense of security. Then, just after the press conferences and the congratulations, the real target would be hit, very thoroughly. It may sound fanciful, but then, who would have believed 9/11? Anyway, that's what I'm doing here. I can't stay, obviously. So it would be good if you would go with me to the meeting and be the contact for their answer, if there is one, from their agent in place."

"Their answer to what question?"

"Where is it that they are planning to take out Secretary Adams?"

"Now *I* need a refill. This sure puts Ambassador McGowan's disappearing act into perspective. Just the time for a damn fool female romantic intrigue."

"Well, maybe. Suppose there was a crime?" Robbie didn't share his earlier premonition about entering a crime scene. "We don't lose anything by being careful. It strikes me that the possibility of finding out what really happened to her will get less and less as time goes on. Look at it this way. If she is all right, no problem except her own embarrassment. If not, we must try to find her, in house and with discretion at first, then if necessary professionals have to be called in. The main thing is not to blunder around and destroy any possible evidence, clues that might tell us where she is or what happened."

"Could this be related to your fears as far as Secretary Adams is concerned? I mean the attempted killing or snatch or whatever Al Qaeda has planned for our amusement?"

"Frankly, I wouldn't rule anything out at this point. Also, I think her Residence should be gone over, inch by inch. That Administrative Officer, Bob Starett, seemed to have a light touch. Maybe he would be the man to task. As Administrative Officer, there would be a certain logic to that, anyway. He is supposed to look after Embassy property."

Smiley agreed. "I'll put him on it. First thing. Now let's get some sleep. It's going to be a very interesting day, one way or another."

"Absolutely. Mind if I make a call first? I haven't talked with my wife since we left, and it's still the middle of the evening back home."

"Sure. Go right ahead." They were now in it together, and Smiley could barely suppress his sense of relief.

The phone rang a few times. That must mean that Minouette, the family Siamese cat, was in Sylvie's lap, and woe be to anyone who dislodged a family goddess without the utmost gentleness, phone call or no phone call.

"Hello?" Her voice was musical, and not the least bit sleepy.

"Hello Sylvie, it's me. I'm in Dublin." Impossible man, with years of New England reserve to be undone. He found it so hard to use the usual terms of endearment that every time he came back from a trip, he had to be retrained.

She was instantly on the alert. "What on earth are you doing in Dublin? Was there a change of plans? That schedule you left indicated that you would be in Paris now. Or is it Vienna?"

"I came back to Dublin."

"Why?"

Well, that was the trouble with being married to a trained television investigative reporter. One minute into the conversation and he was already looking for escape routes before he blundered into saying something top secret, and into an insecure phone at that.

"Can't go into that now. I'll only be here a day or so. Then back to Vienna."

"Somebody lost something?"

"Well, now that you mention it, we do seem to have mislaid our ambassador here, but I'm sure she'll turn up in the morning."

"Joker. Say, you're *not* joking, are you?" He already regretted the slip.

"Look, I just called to say 'I love you,' and ask how things are going."

"'Things,' as you so delicately call our not quite first born, are making their presence known. Or just maybe, their presences. It's hard to believe that just one baby could be making such a fuss. Anyway, the baby is a nice pillow for Minouette. Who says hello. So when did you lose an ambassador? That seems a bit careless."

"I'm sure she'll turn up."

"You said that." They were jousting for position in this conversation. Had he been home and intentionally shared the confidence, she would have had a suggestion or two by now. "You are repeating yourself, which means you just found out, and you hope that it will all go away. Does everybody know about this?"

He gave up. "No. You're right. I'm just finding out."

Interesting. Sylvie realized that meant that he had returned to Dublin on some other errand entirely, and been told upon his arrival about the missing ambassador. Also, he had blurted out the one fact in order not to mention the other one, his reason for being there. What on earth could be more vital than a missing ambassador? It was a fairly apocalyptic thought. Better not pursue that inquiry now, or he would clam up entirely. She would find out soon enough in any event

"Well, *mon chéri*, you are certainly the one to find her. But a woman that wants to be missing will stay that way for a while. I wish I were there to help you. I can just imagine a bunch of men stumbling about. Don't trample on any clues." She was smiling now, awake and interested.

"I'll try not to."

"Does she have a boyfriend?"

"I suspect we're about to find out."

Sylvie thought for a moment. Something else occurred to her.

"Well, at least that will give you an excuse to call that Kelly Martin woman, the one you told me about. You probably should anyway. If she really is a close friend of your missing lady ambassador, as you told me a few days ago, she probably has some idea where the woman is. Or what her habits are. Anyway, it's a start. Women like to confide in other women. It goes with the territory. What is her name, by the way? I mean your missing ambassador."

"McGowan. Mary McGowan."

"Oh yes, the lady from Kentucky. Well, I hope you find her soon. And stay safe. Did you have time for any sightseeing in Paris?"

He was pleased to answer that he had played hookey for an hour to see the Cluny Museum. It was worth the trip to Europe by itself. "Yes. I went to the Cluny. The Unicorn Tapestries were breathtaking, as you said."

She was pleased and said so. It was so sad, the old things that were destroyed, and a miracle that a few masterpieces, like those unicorn tapestries, had survived the mobs. But Robbie was very tired, and started to miss the thread of her conversation. He was afraid that in another moment he would yawn, and she would hear it and take it badly, or start to lecture him about getting proper sleep, or maybe both.

"Well, it'll be a big day tomorrow. And I'd better be sharp. I have the feeling that it is going to be one of those days. Good night, Sylvie. I love you."

"*Je t'aime, moi aussi.* Now, don't forget to remember what she says, so you can tell me everything she tells you!"

— — — — — — — —

The next day, all hell broke loose.

George Smiley met Robbie at breakfast, and told him that Bob Starett had already been briefed and was at the Phoenix Park residence. He had called to say that Ambassador McGowan had still not returned, and that he was beginning the discreet search that Smiley had ordered. As if there could be anything discreet about an exhaustive property inventory that began at seven thirty in the morning!

The Embassy car deposited Robbie and Smiley in front of the rather nondescript government office on Robert Dillman's business card, just down the street from the Prime Minister's office, at two minutes before nine. The door opened by itself, it almost seemed, and they were led through a hallway and into a small office. It had a window and basic furniture, but no pictures, either artistic on the walls, or of family, on the desk. There was just one framed photograph on a side table, in clear view of the visitor's chair by the couch, of Prime Minister O'Bryan and Robert Dillman. Clearly that was all that was needed.

There were no preliminaries, and Robbie came right to the point. He first introduced "George Smiley, our Deputy Chief of Mission, who will be our contact. I'm still travelling with Secretary Adams. When we were here, you'll recall, Prime Minister O'Bryan told us that an agent in place had warned about an assassination plot against our President, and also against Secretary Adams."

Dillman nodded in acknowledgement.

"Well, as to the President, as we've just seen, your agent was right on the mark. Thank you again for the warning. Now I've been asked to see if you could get any further details about the possible attempt against Secretary Adams. For example, is it to take place this week, on this trip? If so, where? The itinerary is public. He is now in Paris, leaving shortly for Vienna. Then he is going to Moscow, Riga and London. Anything that could be found out would be highly appreciated and helpful, to say the very least."

Well, that was the message. It was not necessary or advisable to mention that their earlier confidence had not been the first time that the American side had heard about the plot against the President. Better to give the Irish full credit for untangling things. It encouraged more confidences.

"Yes, well. As the Prime Minister implied, the agent is a sleeper, left over from previous days, if you will. It is one thing to pass on something that is said in the agent's presence. It is quite another, and highly dangerous, to have the agent make inquiries. For one thing, it calls attention, too much attention."

Robbie noticed that once again, the use of a personal pronoun had been avoided, this time rather awkwardly. The agent must be a woman. Either that, or Dillman's semantic skills were extraordinary.

"Certainly. We all appreciate that."

Dillman nodded and took George Smiley's card. That effectively ended the conversation. Dillman was not one for small talk, apparently. It was appreciated, the Americans thought, that neither had stressed the importance of a fast response. Some things were too obvious for comment, and comment would therefore annoy.

As they left Dillman's office, Smiley's cell phone went off insistently. "Never use the bloody thing," he said. "I nearly always forget that I have it. Can't always recall what button to press, and when I can, the damned things are so small, that I don't press the right one and the call is cancelled."

That sermon over, he found the right button, pressed it, and impatiently put the cell phone to his ear. "Yes, Bob. WHAT THE HELL? Say again? Are you sure?

"Of course, stay put. Don't notify anybody until we get there. We're coming now. And don't touch anything, for God's sake. We'll be right there. A few minutes. Just hang on. We're coming right now."

Ashen, he barked at the Embassy chauffeur to drive to the Ambassador's residence in Phoenix Park. Then he turned to Robbie. "It's Ambassador Mary McGowan. She's dead. Murdered. Bob Starett has just found her body in an old spare meat freezer in the residence in Phoenix Park."

PROLOGUE (PART THREE)

Kɪᴛ Mᴀʀʟᴏᴡᴇ ᴇɴᴛᴇʀᴇᴅ ᴛʜᴇ Mᴇʀᴍᴀɪᴅ Tavern on Bread Street, ordered a pint of ale, and went to their usual table. It was early, and his friends were either still working, writing, or had stopped off at another tavern to have a pint before coming to the Mermaid, so that few would keep count of their ales. As if he cared. The food was good here, largely fish, and the meals not as expensive as at the galleried George Inn near Southwark Cathedral.

Nor was the clientele here quite so fancy, just a group of writers. Himself, Ben Jonson, Will Shakespeare, that young fellow Donne from time to time, who was a puzzle, Thomas Coryat, a few others. Nothing to attract attention. Which was a good thing, since they all had been raised in the old religion, and all understood what was not said but intended. All except, possibly, Donne. He was not sure.

Where did Donne stand, regarding the Church? His conversation was always guarded. But the man could write! It was a different sort of writing, not for the stage certainly, highly personal, not declamatory, not written for an actor. There were just a few poems, circulated by hand amongst friends.

Well, it was best to be circumspect in this year of Our Lord 1593. Donne's brother Henry Donne was said to be an unrepentant Catholic who was now in Newgate Prison for his pains. Marlowe shuddered. Newgate was a death sentence, a wretched festering hell where life could not be sustained for very long. And yes, the Donne brothers were descendants of Thomas More, after all. No wonder young John was now reading law at Lincoln's Inn. He would probably end by stifling his writing gifts entirely and earn his keep by writing the suffocating and barely comprehensible legal prose of writs and actions at law.

There was Will Shakespeare, sitting idly by himself, at their writers' table. Marlowe hailed him and sat down.

"What's that you've got with you, Kit?"

"It's my desk. You've seen it before."

"Aye, but not here."

They must be circumspect, and lapsed into silence. So many Englishmen were eager to curry favor by reporting a loose conversation to Walsingham's men. Since he had been one of them, Marlowe could hardly condemn the practice. Morality and survival were now in mortal combat. The old soul of England seemed at war with the Crown. There was no shortage of wrongs, fueling the agony, year by year. For agony it truly was to twist one's conscience, one's very idea of God, to fit the requirements of a state. Many would not do it, on both sides. And yet, putting personal allegiance to the Pope and to Catholic Spain above loyalty to England was treasonous. If there were any doubters, there had even been that near thing, the Spanish Armada, just five years ago. Thank God for Drake and English seamanship!

England had become a sad litany of injustice and martyrdom. It had started under old King Henry. And then there had been the burned Protestant martyrs under Mary. There were now Catholic martyrs, under Elizabeth. And holy ground and customs had been defiled on a massive, organized scale, and still were, as new men enriched themselves and the Catholic church was driven underground. *And now!*

The silence had gone on a bit too long. There were times when trust must be attempted. Marlowe decided to try again.

"These are hard times, Will."

"Aye, as we know. Some say it began with the earthquake that came to these shores just thirteen years ago."

"You mean the priest Campion? He returned to England then."

"I mean the earthquake of 1580, literally, and would not be misunderstood."

Marlowe nodded. Perhaps Will would open up a bit now that he had trod upon dangerous ground first. But then, that was standard technique to ensnare a man, as all knew.

"You are often misunderstood, literally, Will. It is a great talent, and I would imagine helpful for survival. But do not press them too far."

"Yes. One could end by being pressed by Topcliffe."

So the fencing was over. It was unavoidable in these times, both normal and sensible. Obedience to the realm was demanded by oaths, that twisted the conscience. Yesterday's friend could easily be today's enemy. There was fresh villainy from Court favorite Richard Topcliffe, who seemed to delight in the torture of Catholics real or suspected, and whose agents were everywhere. Some were pressed to death, by stones. And just last year he had consolidated his position with the Queen by triumphantly announcing the arrest of the most wanted Catholic in the realm, Robert Southwell. The new tortures that Topcliffe had devised for the wretched Southwell were said to have been appreciated even by the new Queen's Secretary, Robert Cecil.

"Or by the Queen's crouchback, Robert Cecil."

Now they were in too deep for explanations, and further confidence might just be possible. Kit's reference to Robert Cecil had hit home. Young, brilliant, ruthless and given to conspiracy, Robert Cecil was as clever in his twisted mind as he was crippled in body. And the Cecils father and son were making a fortune in properties and titles from the misfortunes of recusant Catholics.

Shakespeare knew that William Cecil, Lord Treasurer, was bad enough. But his son Robert Cecil had been just the sort to evoke the image of *Richard III*, according to the history of Thomas More: twisted, brilliant, wrapping the kingdom around his plots and murders. The Court could hardly object to that stage formulation, even though the martyred More was his source. After all, More's history of the last Plantagenet monarch formed the popular argument for the legitimacy of the Tudor dynasty itself!

"I fear there may be even harder times to come."

"I am uneasy in my thoughts, Will."

"As many of us are."

"I wonder who can be trusted these days."

"Only one's own talent, Kit. And for the most part, not even that." Shakespeare wondered, just what was the man leading up to?

"I have an appointment in Deptford, Will. I am not sure where it will lead, or how it might end." Shakespeare was silent. The fencing was over. "I have not accumulated much if anything. The future always seemed so long, so far ahead." Shakespeare nodded in agreement.

"But who is to say when the fates will cut that particular cord?"

Shakespeare remembered the Greek spirits, who were said to measure life spans, and then cut them. The matter was too serious for a flippant reply.

"And so?"

"And so I have brought my writing desk to the Mermaid Tavern."

"A handsome one it is, Kit. But I am sure that your concern is not over this furniture, but instead, for what it may contain. Who made it, by the way?"

"Peter Sparrow. The fifth brother. Last year. I put in a note to that effect. *Petrus Quintus fecit, Anno domini* 1592. I can't say the Latin for the years."

Shakespeare nodded. "Neither could I. If one were even sure which day and year this is! Rome seems to find us off by several weeks, and I must say, they have a point. I trust nobody will consider me heretical on that score. And what year is it, exactly? When does the new one begin? In January or in March? It's enough to raise a thirst."

He shrugged his shoulders and stared over Marlowe's shoulder. "But that gives me an idea."

Marlowe was aware that virtually everything gave Will Shakespeare an idea. He had the most fertile imagination that Marlowe had ever run across.

"I'm writing a new play. Not historical, more fanciful. Why not have some characters that people will actually recognize? A carpenter and a joiner. That's it. The joiner will have to be Snug, that's certain. And I'll make the carpenter Peter Quince. Let people just wonder where *that* name came from!

"But you seem uncertain in your own mind, Kit. Did you want to tell me more about this problem of yours, and how the desk forms part of it?"

Marlowe was changing his mind. He had been emboldened by Shakespeare's company. He might keep the desk after all, or better still entrust it to his own man, to be safely kept for just a short while, until he returned from Deptford. With Will, you always had the feeling that things might turn out well. His mood lightened and became more hopeful.

"Perhaps now is not quite the time, Will. But I will tell you this. You of course remember our good Edward Alleyn?"

"Certainly. A fine actor, and your principal in more than one play. Would you lend him to me? I'll certainly make him Peter Quince in my new play, at the very least! Probably that and a few other parts as well. There are several that would fit together well, separated by scenes so there would be no confusion." Shakespeare was lost for a moment in his new play, arranging the sequences, rearranging scenes to suit himself and the talent available. "He certainly learns with ease and memorizes to perfection. And he doesn't have the nasty habit, indulged by so many, of improving the lines that you and I have written!"

"You are quite right, Will. And he is a man to be trusted. I believe that I will leave my desk with him. And could I just ask, if you are in the humor to do so, should it be needed, that you have an eye on what happens to my desk? I mean, at some future moment, should it be necessary? I'll go more easily to my appointment knowing that Alleyn has the desk, and that you are surety against its loss."

"It is that important, Kit?"

"It is as important as the great globe itself, Will."

"Then you have my word upon it."

The two friends had another pint together in silence, and then, shaking hands rather solemnly, Kit Marlowe put on his cloak, put the desk under his arm, and went out into the now threatening weather to find his principal actor's quarters.

CHAPTER NINE -
"Vienna, My City of Dreams"

THEY ARRIVED AT THE RESIDENCE in Phoenix Park in record time. Bob Starett was waiting for them at the entrance, his face a ghastly grey pallor reflecting death.

"I can't believe it," he said, over and over again, his hands hanging disjointedly like a malformed puppet. "She's just in there, half standing up, her body leaning against a side of beef. It's horrible."

Smiley took charge. "Does anyone else know?"

"I don't think so. I just called you and then came outside to get some air."

"All right. Let's go in."

They entered the residence and went downstairs, brushing past the baffled house staff, which was bunched together by the kitchen. "Better take a deep breath," Robbie warned, "to steady the nerves. We'll need it."

They entered the spare freezer and there in the corner, just visible below a hanging huge side of beef, the feet of a slumped figure could be seen. If you were not looking carefully, you might have missed it.

"Good God!" They stared at the shoes. Smiley went closer, peered around the beef, and saw Mary McGowan's face. Robbie stopped him from moving the side of beef so that the body would slide to the floor. Smiley nodded, understanding. Robbie looked closely. There was no blood on the body. There were deeply colored subcutaneous stains along her neck, as far as he could see, in fingerlike parallels, with violet contusions where thumbs might have been pressed. She had surely been strangled.

"What do we do now?" Smiley said.

"Don't move her. Not yet. There's probably some evidence here that we can't see," Robbie said quietly.

"Wait a second," Starett said. He dropped to his knees and gave a brief prayer for the soul of Mary McGowan. Then he got up, and the three men left the freezer.

"Well," Robbie said, "this is a crime scene. She can't be moved. Of course, we don't want to leave her there. It's not right. On the other hand, the killer put her in there. It looks to me like death by strangulation. But there is a lot of detail that has to be examined. The position of the body, perhaps fingerprints, certainly the finger spread and whether it was done from in front or behind. All that might furnish leads as to the killer. It's a job for professionals. They have to go over this place with great care. It's the best chance to get an idea who could have done this. So for now, we must leave the body exactly as it is until that is done."

"Fine. Who should do it?"

"That's a judgment call. Let's think it through for a minute. This is a diplomatic scene, obviously. And the fact that an American ambassador has been murdered makes this highest profile. We could call in the FBI and we probably should. I think there is a detachment at Embassy London. But time is also of the essence.

"Look, we're going to be second guessed no matter what happens. I think we should do several things, and do them at once. George, I suggest that you notify the Foreign Ministry. Get the head of the American Department if you can. Tell him what has happened and ask for their best national forensics team, on the double. My thinking is that we must secure the scene to get whatever evidence might be still available. The investigations part comes next. We'll have to get some instructions on that.

"I will call Secretary Adams, tell him what has happened, and the first steps that we are taking. No, wait a second. Let me do that first. THEN, George, you call the Foreign Ministry. I will also tell the Secretary that we want the FBI to send a team, probably from Embassy London. They should liaise with Irish forensics.

"Bob, you stay here and monitor the crime scene. Obviously, don't let anybody enter that freezer who is not on the forensics team. Come to think of it, the residence itself should be vacated. We don't know where any prints or clues may be, that would be destroyed by the ordinary daily cleaning staff. So get people out of here and post guards at the doors. You're going to have your hands full monitoring traffic, I think.

"George, I think you should go to the Embassy now. I'll call Secretary Adams immediately and then notify you. Then you can put together the cable to Washington and to the Secretary and Embassy London, most likely. Better put the FBI in Washington down as an addressee too. Or ask the Department Terrorism office to do appropriate liaison. We don't know anything at all yet about this killing. Was it personal? Was it terrorism? I just hope this tragedy doesn't turn into a circus. But I'm afraid it just might."

"OK," said Smiley. "There's something else. Somebody has to notify her family. They shouldn't find out about this from CNN. You have next of kin files, don't you, Bob?"

Starett nodded, yes. His color was beginning to come back as he thought of things to do, ways that he might help.

"My secretary can get them for you. It's not a classified file, just Official Use Only."

"All right, I'll attend to that." They agreed to touch base on the half hour and exchanged cell phone numbers. "Here's her number, Robbie. She kept her cell phone in her office upstairs here at the residence, to recharge overnight. It's probably still there."

"OK. I'll go upstairs and call the Secretary. By the way, there isn't a secure phone here, is there?"

"I don't think there is. So, should you come on back to the Embassy and make the call to Secretary Adams from there?"

Robbie thought hard, and shook his head. "No. Time really is the important thing now. I'll call him from here. We'll just have to risk it."

Bob Starett called his office and barked orders for the residence to be secured. George Smiley took their car to the Embassy, while Robbie went upstairs very carefully, trying hard not to touch anything. There near the top of the stairs, was her suite. He remembered the geography. His own room during their stay had been just down that corridor, then turn left.

He almost knocked on the door, but then remembered that nobody was there to be disturbed. Here was a sitting room, which clearly must have led off to her private quarters, bedroom and bathroom, closets on the other side. Here there was a desk, feminine in its French style, Robbie thought, one of the last Louis monarchs, he wouldn't know which one.

The organization of papers on top of the desk seemed by contrast ruthlessly masculine, neat stacks weighted down by souvenirs from all over the Republic of Ireland. Clearly Ambassador McGowan had gotten to know this country at first hand. There were letters here, personal and business, and a few notices, and a writing tablet. He squinted and looked sideways at the writing tablet in the morning sunlight glancing in through the window, and was astonished to discover, ever so faintly, his own name, "Robbie," then a series of undecipherable scratches.

His nickname was not uncommon, but the coincidence was unusual, to say the least. Obviously any note to him, or mentioning him, had been recent, probably just before her death. If it had not been recent, it would have been covered by other writing. And of course she was murdered suddenly. There was no time to break away and try to write anything. Also, the writing did not seem rushed. His name had been written in a clear hand.

What was it that she could have written? Had the killer made a search and stolen that communication, whatever it may have been? He debated with himself, and curiosity won. He looked on the desk and found another neat little pile of correspondence, her letters that had been written and were ready to send. He found nothing there. That meant, just possibly, some second thoughts. Second thoughts could mean something hidden, something the writer was not quite sure about. Not yet. It could be something hidden, or something to be transmitted later.

He decided. The letter, whatever it was, must really be hidden somewhere. A bit of sophistry helped here. It was, after all, addressed to him. He had a right, well, some claim of right, to find it. And so with great care, using just his finger tips and disturbing the desk drawer pulls and the drawer contents as little as possible, which was surely too much, he started to open the drawers one by one.

He stopped before he began, his hand in midair. No, it wouldn't be that obvious. He thought about it again. If she were hiding something, it wouldn't be in that top middle drawer. Of course not. It would be in one of the side drawers, possibly either bottom one. They would be for stored, half forgotten items that were too personal to throw away and not current enough to be consulted. Those other items would be placed in the upper or middle drawers.

He found it in the bottom drawer on the left. She was lefthanded, he remembered.

It was a long manila envelope, standard nine by twelve inches, and it was just below an admiring Dublin magazine article about the newly arrived American Ambassador, Mary McGowan, with a fine, smiling cover photograph. The hopeful, confident and attractive picture was the strongest possible contrast to what he had just seen in the meat freezer.

The envelope was not sealed, and it just had his name, Robbie Cutler, on the outside. The name was however not in script but printed. He opened the envelope, and there was a brief message to him. His name and the message were handwritten, and this writing of his name seemed to match exactly the indentation that he had found on her writing tablet.

It was short and to the point. "Robbie," it abruptly began, "I have found this document in the old desk by the foot of the stairs. It was in a hidden drawer, and seems to be valuable. I will try to find out what it actually may be. Should I not succeed, there may be another mystery to be solved, and I will trust in your reputation to do so. Mary McGowan."

The note was dated, yesterday's date.

There was another paper, the enclosure that she had referred to in her note. It was a few sentences in Latin, written on very old paper. That was all.

There was a bustling downstairs, and Robbie came back from his thoughts. It was Bob Starett directing the staff out of the house, and telling them to guard the doors until his security team could arrive. Where was Ambassador McGowan's cell phone? Yes, he saw it over there, on that bookshelf, recharging.

He found Ambassador McGowan's phone number list, a neat Roladex arranged alphabetically. Here he was, just following up on one of Sylvie's hunches. Well, Ambassador McGowan was no longer missing, but the mystery was still there, worse than anything. So he might as well call her, as Sylvie said. Women do chat amongst themselves. Yes, there was Kelly Martin's number. He called, and was in luck. She answered on the third ring.

"Hello, Kelly. This is Robbie Cutler."

"I thought you had left, with the Secretary of State."

"Yes, we all did, but I'm back in Dublin for a few hours. Just some unfinished business." He hoped that she would forgive him when that lie became transparent in a day or so.

"I've found something rather odd. Something in Latin. And we did talk at the President's dinner about old manuscripts. So I thought that you might know what it is."

She chuckled. Odd reaction, Robbie thought.

"Can you read a line to me?"

"It seems to begin, *Nunc ingressus scribe eis super buxum* ... Sorry about my pronunciation."

"What is it with you American diplomats? Nobody has been interested in the Book of Isaiah for centuries. Then, inside a few days, three American diplomats ask me about it!"

"Really?"

"Yes. First, Ambassador Carlisle, on our little jaunt, at luncheon in Killarney. Next, just yesterday morning, Ambassador Mary McGowan. She called me in some agitation, actually. Now your call. If this keeps up, I'm sure that the Latin version of the Book of Isaiah will soon be the most popular book on Amazon dot com!"

"Fascinating. Can you tell me something about the passage, who translated it, and what it means?"

She did, in practiced professional terms. For good measure, she gave him some context, the fact that this translation had been used for the Douay Bible. The translation itself had a particular historic context. And it referred to another, deeper truth, according to whoever had written these words down for the future to puzzle over. So, there was something hidden. Clearly it could not be this document. This writing, this Latin excerpt, was simply a coded reference to it, showing that a secret document existed. Robbie thanked her profusely. He had the germ of an idea. Two ideas, in fact.

"So, you are leaving me with quite a mystery, Robbie."

"I'm afraid that it can't be helped, for now." He pondered for a moment. "One more thing. I'd appreciate it if you didn't mention this call to anyone. Except, of course, to the police. You'll see why very shortly." That should cover things for the time being.

"The mystery deepens." Now she really was intrigued.

"Yes. But you have been a tremendous help. Sylvie said that you would be."

"*Who is Sylvie?* It sounds like the title of a Renaissance song!"

"She's my wife. Talk with you again when I'm back in Dublin?"

"I'd look forward to it, if Sylvie gives the green light!"

Robbie hung up in total confusion. He was delighted that his sister Evalyn had not heard this awkward exchange. It would have reaffirmed all her worst suspicions about her brother's social ineptitude with women.

He turned with relief to safer ground, diplomacy and the need to solve a murder.

Fortunately the cell phone worked, even for an international call. He squinted and tapped in Missy Bronson's private cell phone number, and she came on immediately. Missy was unflappable. It was as though she had been expecting his call.

"Yes, Mr. Cutler. The Secretary is just here. I'll put him on and close the door."

"Hello, Mr. Secretary." Robbie's doom ridden voice discouraged any reply. "I am afraid that I have very bad news."

"Go ahead, Robbie."

"Ambassador McGowan has been murdered. When I arrived late last night she had been missing for twelve hours. George Smiley, the DCM, organized a very discreet search. We found her body at the residence just now. There is no doubt that it was murder. She was probably strangled. Her body had been hidden in a spare freezer downstairs." He might as well spare the Secretary of State some of the gory details. Adams could imagine them quite vividly on his own.

"Good God! When did you say you discovered this? And what have you done so far?"

"Well, sir, we have just found her body, not long ago, just twenty minutes or so. I'm at her residence now, calling from upstairs. We're posting guards around the residence so that nobody can come in, and the staff has been dismissed for the time being. The Admin Officer whom you met, Bob Starett, is doing that. George Smiley is at the Embassy. He and I believe that we should waive jurisdiction, at least preliminarily, and get a crack Irish forensics team in right now to secure the crime scene. That would also allow her body to be moved."

"Yes." That wasn't an authorization. Not yet. Adams was just taking it all in.

"We also think our own people should be involved, at least as liaison. There is, I think, an FBI office at Embassy London. We should signal to them to send a team to come to Dublin. Then we should let the professionals do their job."

"That sounds right to me."

Robbie felt obliged to point out the obvious, and then to nail down what had to be done. "Anything we do will be subject to criticism, sir. But I think that forensics must be called in, right now, both as a matter of respect for Ambassador McGowan, and in order to secure the crime scene immediately, so that it can be gone over by professionals. That means an Irish team, the best they've got."

"I agree, Robbie. And you know, before the Senate, I was a prosecuting attorney for a number of years. If that crime scene isn't secured we could maybe kiss goodbye the evidence that could nail the killer. If, indeed, it still exists. So go to it."

"Yes, sir. I'll tell Smiley. And my message here has been delivered. Smiley went with me. He'll send me their reply."

"It sounds to me like you plan to leave Dublin soon. I'm rather surprised."

"Well, sir, we should talk directly about this. But I would like your authority to float one more idea with Smiley, to take up with the Irish Government."

"What's that?"

"I think in a few days, it would be appropriate to have a memorial service for Ambassador McGowan. It should be held, I suggest, in St. Patrick's Cathedral here in Dublin. You might wish to come and give the eulogy. Her family would be touched and most appreciative. She was a distinguished

American and a friend of Ireland. It's fitting. We can restore dignity to her memory."

Then he went into Special Assistant mode. "The arrangements would be just mechanics. I'd just have to rearrange whatever needs reshuffling on your schedule, sir. I actually think we could cut a corner or two on the London visit, and return home by way of Dublin. That would give time for the memorial service, if you agree that is a good idea. I think that Prime Minister O'Bryan would attend, and that his office would help expedite whatever is necessary."

"That is appropriate and well thought out. But you're sure you shouldn't stay there and help with the investigation?"

"Sir, I think I'd just be in the way. But I have done what I can, for now." Silence.

"I look forward to hearing from you directly, Robbie. Make sure that Smiley sends copies of everything to me, including next of kin information. I'll call them. Now I'll call in Charley Sherburne and let him know, for the press. And I do like your idea of the memorial service. I should be there. If you're sure we can work out the timing. To hell with the timing. I should be there and I will be. I'll tell Pamela. She was preparing to fly home from Paris. She should come to the service as well."

The Secretary of State thought for a moment. "I don't quite know why, but as so often happens, what pops into my mind is something familiar, from Shakespeare. *Hamlet.*

"'The play's the thing...'"

"'Wherein I'll catch the conscience of the King.' Yes, sir."

— — — — — — — —

He had reported the gist of his conversation with Secretary Adams immediately by cell phone to George Smiley, to Smiley's considerable relief. He had not, however, mentioned either the memorial service idea, or his call to Kelly Martin and their brief conversation. The first should be discussed with Smiley in person. As to Kelly Martin, it might not amount to anything anyway, Robbie told himself. But basically he didn't want to show all of his cards at once.

Smiley had his cable in polished draft before Robbie arrived at the

Embassy. They talked it over briefly while Robbie filled him in on his talk with the Secretary in more detail. Smiley took on board the Secretary's instruction, for such it now became, of approaching the Irish Government for a memorial service to Ambassador McGowan at St. Patrick's Cathedral. Robbie said that Secretary Adams wanted personally to take part, and perhaps even deliver the eulogy. They would have to be in constant touch regarding timing, as it evolved over the next few days.

Smiley's call to the American Department at the Foreign Ministry went through in a few minutes. "No, I must speak with the Director personally," Smiley quietly insisted, in a voice full of authority. "It is extremely urgent." Then, "Sorry to get you out of your meeting, Mr. Ambassador," Smiley began. Then he explained what had happened to the shocked Irish career ambassador, and with the authority of the Secretary of State, requested the immediate assistance of an Irish forensics team at the American residence. That would be forthcoming immediately, he was assured. Smiley initialled the diplomatic note making the formal request for the forensics team, and dispatched it with a junior officer to the Foreign Ministry.

He then mentioned the desire of the Secretary for an appropriate memorial service. He made a point of not suggesting where it should be held. "Leave it up to them to give us what we want, which is fairly obvious, without our having to ask for it," he said in a side whisper to Robbie, his hand over the phone. "We'll follow up later with O'Bryan. By that time, I'm sure that you'll have arranged to send a message from the Secretary to the PM making that request." It wasn't a question. The Embassy's next diplomatic note would accompany the request from the Secretary of State.

Robbie nodded. "I learn something from a real diplomatic pro every day," he said, with an appreciative grin, as Smiley cradled the phone.

"If I may make a suggestion," Robbie began. He looked at Smiley's quizzical expression. "Something occurred to me. Done very quickly, it might help us. And I mean within a very few days. Before the memorial service, even."

"What's that?"

"I was a little surprised not to find any real security system at the Phoenix Park Residence. You know what I mean. Not necessarily the full bells and whistles. But certainly a security camera or two, well disguised to the extent that is possible. They should be on 24/7, recording who comes and goes. If it's done for shopping centers, and as we've seen, all over London, then why not for an American Ambassador's residence?"

Smiley gave him a long look. Clearly Robbie Cutler had a few ideas of his own. "It sounds logical. I suppose a minimum of people should be involved."

"Well, yes, just yourself and Bob Starett from the Embassy. It's his job anyway."

Smiley realized that he and Starett had just been cleared as far as Cutler was concerned. "I'm sure that you have an idea where the security cameras should be placed?"

"Yes, I do. Outside Ambassador McGowan's personal suite, upstairs. Then, just inside the entrance to the Residence. Actually, front and back. And near the bottom of the staircase, looking towards the downstairs hallway."

"I see what you mean. Four of them. As well disguised as possible, of course. I'll talk with Bob, and we'll put a rush on it."

"I don't want to get into the investigating team's job. But it does seem as though they will want to get on her phone records pretty soon."

He paused. "George, Secretary Adams reminded me that before he was in the Senate, he was a prosecuting attorney. He emphasized the importance of securing the crime scene. So I'm sure that he would want the book followed as closely as possible."

"Actually, that's pretty reassuring. I hadn't realized that. It'll save some explanations later." He expelled a deep breath of relief. That really was helpful. The Secretary was a pro who would understand what needed to be done.

Robbie went on, spelling out his stream of thoughts. "Also, of course, any close friends, that could explain why she had given her staff the day off. I gather she hadn't done that ever before?"

Smiley shook his head, no. "Well, it's touchy, but I hope the FBI and the Irish police will be able to keep something of a lid on that aspect of things. It is, of course, rather embarrassing."

"Not as much as murder. Say, I'd better arrange my own departure. It's getting rather late to catch them in Paris. I think Vienna would be better, the next stop."

He stood and mumbled his thanks to Smiley. Once again some

awkwardness cut into his voice, as he shifted from confident crime analyst to lower ranking diplomat. He had the feeling that they might work together again, perhaps on this case when the Secretary returned, and certainly at some point in the future. The State Department was like that. You worked intensely over a short period of time with a colleague and then were gone. You wondered if you would work together again at some other Embassy, perhaps sharing the latest Washingon instruction or sorting out some diplomatic traffic jam. Then he remembered why he had come back to Dublin in the first place.

"We need to go over one last thing, Mr. Smiley."

"And that is?"

"What happens when Dillman calls you back. You'll be sending me the information. It shouldn't be in clear. I'm not even sure about NODIS, to tell the truth. So we should have an easy code. That was my reason for coming here, after all."

"You know, Robbie, I'd almost forgotten!"

They worked out a short series of coded references. Then he went to the office he had used in the Embassy a few days earlier, and called the Embassy in Paris, and asked to speak with Ron Jackson on the Secretary's Executive Secretariat team. Since he would have arrived in Paris just as they were preparing to leave, which wouldn't have done anyone much good, it made more sense for him to leapfrog, and fly to Vienna directly from Dublin. Ron rather excitedly agreed to exchange roles with him for a few hours. With Missy Bronson's supervision he would pack up Robbie's files in Paris, and Robbie said that in return, he would start getting the office ready at the Embassy in Vienna.

"That won't really be necessary, Robbie, but thanks," Ron said.

So there would be a smooth transition in Vienna. And it helped that they both had been staying with the DCM in Paris, on a leafy avenue not far from the Bois de Boulogne. It would be a simple matter for the Embassy Paris car to swing by and secure Robbie's luggage on the way to the airport. Robbie left Embassy Dublin, picked up his overnight bag at George Smiley's residence, where he said hello to a rather flustered Mrs. Smiley, and went to the Dublin Airport. There he caught a midafternoon flight to Vienna.

He had left things in Dublin in the best shape he could imagine, on such short notice. He had to be right the first time, and, he reflected, it was probably to his advantage that he hadn't had much time. His first impressions, his gut instincts, were usually on target where serious matters were concerned. But give him a few minutes to think things over, and who knows whether he might not have changed his mind, and not for the better. And if his first instinct was wrong, he couldn't think that he had done any harm.

— — — — — — — —

Carlisle's first days in Riga were something of a blur, passed in a memorable haze of fatigue and celebration. He had slept very late, enjoyed an early afternoon brunch of eggs benedict prepared by the residence chef, and then walked across the park to the American Embassy, accompanied by a dour and muscular security guard. Along the way, he saw several memorial stones, polished boulders which were placed to commemorate the death of Latvians killed by Soviet Interior Ministry troops during the attempted Russian counter-coup in 1991.

It was a grim reminder of the history of the three Baltic nations, hostage to their geography. They had been swallowed up by the Soviet Union once again as part of an annex to the notorious agreement between Stalin and Hitler that had also carved up Poland. But FDR had refused to recognize the forced incorporation of Estonia, Latvia and Lithuania into the Soviet Union, no matter how it was dressed up by phony delegations and petitions.

This Baltic Nonrecognition Policy was emulated by other key nations, and so for decades the matter stood. In the United States, frozen Baltic national funds were used to keep aging emissaries and their diplomatic missions going, while energetic Baltic-Americans, sensitive to any political shifts in the wind, became skilled at teasing out messages of support from their elected representatives. And so, annually, the messages on the three respective national days from the Secretary of State reaffirmed American policy. That all paid off when the Soviet Union itself collapsed, and Estonia, Latvia and Lithuania regained their national independence and freedom of action.

It was a background to insure a warm welcome for a new American Ambassador. Carlisle met first with his Embassy staff, small and energetic, just a dozen members on his country team. The usual Embassy functions were covered, and he was glad to see once again the only person that he actually knew in the group, Stan Bartlett. His secretary was the highly experienced

Claudia Reynolds, a commanding black lady from Alabama with a presence to match. His DCM, he decided, a laid back Minnesotan named Stanley Gunderson, would have trouble if he tried to boss her around. Better realize that she was the boss, if this Embassy was going to function properly. He wondered about Gunderson's assignment here. Did he really want Riga, or had he been hoping for Stockholm?

A serious, broad shouldered Navy Captain, Norman Vezelay, his Defense Attaché, welcomed him aboard. Let's see, there were also two agricultural specialists. No, just one was assigned here. The other one was making a boondoggle tour of the region for the Foreign Agricultural Service. Then of course were the political, economic, commercial and administrative officers, and another consular officer. Was that it? It seemed so. At least, that was all that he could absorb for the first day, as they sat around a conference room table and introduced themselves, half listening as some put in a word or two for their pet projects.

A worried press attaché wanted a quick private word with him before his presentation of credentials tomorrow. Fine, ask Claudia to pick a time to meet. Claudia smiled at the "ask Claudia." The new man wouldn't be so hard to toilet train after all.

Later that afternoon, Carlisle and Gunderson went to the Foreign Ministry, where they met with the Chief of Protocol and the Foreign Minister. The Chief of Protocol was an affable gentleman who had lived for decades in the United States and was very well disposed towards Americans. They made small talk about their respective backgrounds, and searched fruitlessly for points of common reference. The Foreign Minister was a younger man who, Carlisle supposed, was making his name as part of the newer generation, who had not been part of the Latvian diaspora during the years of Soviet occupation.

Carlisle gave the Foreign Minister a copy of his credentials, and was officially informed that his presentation of credentials to the President of Latvia would take place at Riga Castle at eleven o'clock the following morning. It would be business suit, and it was customary to have two officers from the Embassy accompany the new Ambassador.

The next morning, the Embassy armored car pulled through the gates into the courtyard of Riga Castle on time to the minute. A second car followed with DCM Gunderson and Captain Vezelay. There was a Latvian Army honor guard at the exterior castle gates, and also at the main entrance. Two opened the car doors, while others stood at attention, flanking the entrance to Riga Castle.

It all worked as Stan Bartlett had coached Carlisle it would. Carlisle, Gunderson and Vezelay entered the building, where the Chief of Protocol met them and escorted the trio from the vestibule up the oak staircase into a waiting room, the Castle Salon. They passed other rooms that Carlisle glanced at quickly and with real interest. The furniture authority thought he spotted some pieces of significance that would be of credit to any auction house lucky enough to receive their consignment.

It was a magnificent, memorably decorated building, Carlisle decided. The Latvians, recapturing their national history, were showcasing some of it right here for visitors of state. It was a successful effort, well worth doing. Riga Castle itself had suites of offices, and was in fact the office for the President of Latvia.

The Castle Salon, the Chief of Protocol said, was "formerly a Turkish room which was now dedicated to the history of Riga Castle." That much was evident. Throughout the room were handsome etchings and engravings of the castle's various periods of construction beginning in the sixteenth century. It was well appointed with mahogany furniture, and a fine Empire style ampel chandelier. There they were met by the Foreign Minister. The men made small talk until some sort of signal showed that the ceremony was about to begin. Then doors opened, and the party was ushered into the Hall of the Coats of Arms, where the press was also ushered in, and stood by themselves towards the side of the room.

Carlisle was very pleased with the Hall of the Coats of Arms. Quite evidently, the regions and towns of Latvia all had their various coats of arms, and they were reproduced here, in full colors and with evident pride.

The room, he had heard, had mirrored Latvian history, having been used as a reception room by the Russian Governor General prior to the gaining of Latvian independence on November 18, 1918. During the interwar period, Latvian national decorations had prevailed, some of them probably similar to those used today. The earlier decorations had all been destroyed during the period of Soviet occupation. Now, however, there were once again coats of arms of Latvia's regions and towns, as well as portraits of former Presidents of Latvia, and a representation of the national seal. The total effect was one of national pride and exuberance.

Suddenly the doors at the other end of the hall opened, and the President of Latvia entered the room, and walked over and shook hands with the three Americans, who were introduced to him by the Chief of Protocol. It's all working precisely, Carlisle thought, just like those ceremonies I used to see on PBS. Everybody has a place and a function, and it comes together really very well. For a moment, his daydreams transported him to Paris, Tokyo, or Rome, wherever a grateful nation might send him in the future. He told himself that he would surely judge that fortunate nation's protocolary efforts by the class act that he was witnessing today in Riga Castle.

The Latvian President then stepped back, joining the Foreign Minister, for the formal presentation of credentials. He gave a short speech of welcome in Latvian which was translated, sentence by sentence. It was Carlisle's turn. He expressed his pleasure at representing the United States, its President and People, and then, having been carefully coached by Stan Bartlett, let a few phrases in Latvian tumble out. There were no red faces, and so Bartlett, as he had promised, had steered him clear of any phrases which his sorry pronunciation might have twisted into memorable Baltic *double entendres*. All to the good, but, Carlisle was certain, it had been done before. He handed the original of his credentials to the Latvian President. Another brief reply, this time more substantive, came when the President mentioned with feeling that the United States had never recognized his nation's forced incorporation into the Soviet Union.

It was time for photographs and champagne, sweet Latvian champagne, rather tasty if your taste runs to sweetish *demi-sec*. There were toasts back and forth, to Latvia and its President, to the United States and its President. It might have gone on for some time when the Chief of Protocol tugged at the Foreign Minister's sleeve. It was time to face the press.

The gaggle of press waited with their questions. This was the only moment that had concerned him. He didn't want to make a slip, and had rehearsed several possible answers to the questions that he might have faced. After all, it would be easy enough to find out that he had been in Dublin with the Secretary of State. But they didn't know about the desk, so he had to stop thinking about that. Something might spill out. For God's sake don't mention the desk!

He worried that there might have been an early discovery of Mary McGowan's body in Dublin. If that happened, these Latvian newshounds would surely ask him about it. But that didn't happen. Actually, they were quite respectful, and the Embassy press *attaché* had prepared Carlisle well on the matters of topical concern that they did raise. There were no real landmines. All was bilateral harmony and friendship and, in the sheltering arms of NATO, Latvia's future seemed safe and assured. So did that of Ambassador Rudolphe Carlisle.

— — — — — — — —

Vienna had had a shining series of face lifts since Robbie's last visits, a few years ago, when he had first driven through on his way to Embassy Budapest, and then returned for a conference. All around the Ring, the semicircular series of boulevards that encased the inner city, buildings were gleaming, their stone facings freshly etched clean. Here and there a monument appeared, usually a memorial to some past musician or statesman. There in a park was the Strauss Monument, gleaming in the late afternoon sun, the gilded violinist's bow raised for always, to begin the alluring strains of one of his waltz creations, while *bas relief* statues of beautiful women and their escorts prepared for the dance that awaited them.

A few streets further along the Ring, Robbie had to grin at a contrasting work of art. There was the statue in grim uniform of a Russian soldier, one arm held up. "We had to keep that up, sir," explained the Embassy driver. "It was part of the conditions when the Russians left Austria. The reason he doesn't hold up the other arm as well, is that then all the stolen watches he's wearing would show clearly on his wrist, halfway up the arm!"

Robbie chuckled appreciatively. "Is it hard to find one's way around Vienna?"

"No, sir. Actually, it's fairly easy. The usual way to orient yourself is just to get a Number One Tram. It goes around the four kilometers of the Ring. Don't forget to get your ticket at one of those machines before you get on the tram. Then cancel your ticket when you get on. It doesn't take very long to do the circuit, and you'll see a lot, the Parliament, the *Rathaus* - sorry, sir, the Town Hall, the Votive Church, the Opera, the Stock Exchange. It's comfortable, cheap and a good way to get oriented.

"Well, here we are at the Embassy, Boltzmanngasse 16. First time here, sir?"

"No. I came over once for a conference when I was at the Embassy in Budapest. It's a beautiful building."

"Well, have a nice stay, sir."

Robbie got out of the car with his hand luggage and laptop, and entered the Embassy. "Beautiful building" was something of an understatement. It had been built in 1901 by Emperor Franz-Joseph as a Consular Academy, replacing the mid-eighteenth century building erected by Empress Maria Theresa as an Imperial and Royal Academy to improve cultural and trade relations with the Balkans and Middle East. The building was in baroque classical style, and fit Viennese taste like an elbow length formal glove. How it suited various representatives of America's sometimes fractious democracy could perhaps be imagined.

The United States, which had occupied the building during the Four Power Military Occupation, had purchased it at a bargain basement price in 1947, in an arrangement negotiated by Eleanor Dulles, sister of John Foster Dulles, President Eisenhower's Secretary of State. And now it was the nerve center and headquarters for American relations with Austria. But Vienna's importance was even greater on the international scene. For here were also located the IAEA, the International Atomic Energy Agency, the group that had failed to find the weapons of mass destruction in Iraq that didn't exist, as well as various other European and international organizations of importance whose founders had discovered after 1945 the advantages of living and working in one of the most civilized locations on earth.

Robbie checked though Embassy security, and found the office suite assigned to the Secretary of State, and his own office, as well as that of the Executive Secretariat team. He was pleased to discover that the Executive Secretariat office was already operational. "We always do that when we can," said Sam Cartwright, junior officer on the team. "We leapfrog from one stop to the next, so that the Secretary's office is always set up and ready. Ron Jackson will be leaving Vienna a day early to set up Moscow. That's the way it goes with us. Want your cables now?"

"Yes," Robbie said. He picked up cables from this afternoon, plus information copies of cables sent earlier in the day for action to Embassy Paris, which the Secretary would have seen, but he had not. He decided to go through the earlier batch first, to get the continuity back. He did so quickly. Yes, there was George Smiley's report from Dublin. It must have hit the Department like a thunderbolt. It was astonishing that the discovery of the murdered Ambassador McGowan hadn't hit the international news yet. By tomorrow, it surely would be headlines. Nothing on NODIS SALADIN either.

This afternoon's batch was more interesting. A crack FBI forensics team was on its way to Dublin from Washington, and an investigative team was already in Dublin liaising with Irish police. The remains of Ambassador McGowan had been transferred and, with American official permission, autopsied. The body now lay at rest in the finest facility of the Irish capital, awaiting instructions from the family as to disposition. "Well, at least they were spared what we had to see," Robbie thought. His next thought was that he wanted to see a copy of the autopsy report as soon as it was available. He sent a message to that effect to George Smiley in Dublin. There was nothing yet on their call on Robert Dillman. He hadn't expected that there would be any message this quickly.

What else? Oh yes, there was a cable from Embassy Riga. Rudolphe Carlisle was well and truly official now, having presented his credentials to the Latvian President. The ceremony seemed interesting. Carlisle had had enough sense to avoid drafting an endless report. He'd probably let Stan Bartlett draft it for him. Either way, it was interesting and well written enough to catch one's attention without overdoing it and annoying the reader.

The cable also gave Robbie a touch of prospective nostalgia. He really looked forward far more than he would admit to the day when he could write such a cable, on his own presentation of credentials as an American ambassador. Carlisle ended with a welcome to Secretary Adams on his forthcoming visit to Latvia. A final message would follow shortly on arrangements. That, surely, was Stan Bartlett's touch. His former Vice Consul in Bordeaux knew the nuts and bolts of diplomacy thoroughly. Carlisle was lucky to have him in Riga.

Robbie went through the messages a second time, then a third, and made his prioritized selections for the Secretary's attention. Let's see. There was nothing on tonight. The Secretary, continuing his habit of getting a good night's sleep, was leaving after the last official function in Paris, a gala dinner and concert at Versailles that Robbie was sorry to have missed. Just imagine, a state dinner in the Hall of Mirrors, where the infamous Versailles Treaty was signed, followed by a concert by skilled musicians dressed in period costume in the former royal theater. Well, he couldn't do everything. Secretary Adams and the party on Air Force Two would be getting in around one o'clock, and going directly to their quarters. There was a note from Ron Jackson that said that the Secretary would see Robbie in the morning at the Embassy.

And so, he had the evening in Vienna free. And as he realized that, Robbie's jaw dropped. There, in the office doorway, stood his wife Sylvie, an endearing smile on her face. Her surprise had worked, after all.

"I couldn't leave you here alone, *chéri*. All those *frauleins* and you without a murder to solve! Anyway, I hope you're pleased. I flew over yesterday and checked into a wonderful hotel, the *König von Ungarn*, in the First District of the Inner City, very close to Mozart's House and St. Stephen's Cathedral. Much better than that dreary place where the Embassy had you staying. And we have reservations at the Hotel Sacher for dinner tonight.

"What, are you really speechless?"

"With delight, yes! What a surprise, a nice one. You've really done it, this time!" He kissed Sylvie, locked up the office, and they left the Embassy, their arms intertwined, he thrilled that she had come, and delighted at their unexpected, wonderful evening in Vienna, and she most pleased that her surprise was so welcome. The murder talk, he decided, could be left for later.

They checked into the *König von Ungarn*, a traditional and roomy hotel with antiques to spare in each room. It was said to be one of the oldest hotels in Europe, or anywhere, for that matter. Then they slowly walked the length of the Kantnerstrasse through the inner city, along fashionable shopping areas ("It's Grafton Street with Mozart and chocolates," Robbie concluded). The Hotel Sacher, just across Philharmonikerstrasse from the Vienna Opera, was a dignified and reassembled reminder of the great days of empire.

They walked around the hotel exterior. Here on the corner of Karntnerstrasse and Philharmonikerstrasse was the "Rote Bar" Restaurant, which they could glimpse through the window. It had the elegant ease of a private London club. Then, after the main entrance, came the Café Sacher, a cathedral of chocolate cake where the world famous *Sachertorte* was dispensed each morning and afternoon. Private dining rooms followed, and then they arrived at the Café Mozart.

"How about a drink before dinner? No, let's sit inside," Robbie said.

They chose a table inside and ordered drinks. Robbie recalled his Vienna visit when he had been Political Officer at the Embassy in Budapest. "I made a special effort to get to know the sights of *The Third Man*," he said. "You know, that 1949 Carol Reed film with Orson Welles. It is just full of atmosphere. The Brits once voted it the finest British film ever made. They'll get no argument from me. Anyway, the Viennese have a walk of a few hours, worth doing, to get the background for the story, and the places around the city where it was actually filmed."

"Yes, the Graham Greene story. Wasn't that the one that was based on his friendship with Kim Philby, the spy? And wasn't Philby the original 'Third Man?'"

He wondered for a split second how she happened to know about this spying episode. It seemed unusual for a young French woman, for whom the British were exotic foreigners.

"You mean, the Cambridge University spy ring. Yes, he was. And Foreign Secretary Harold MacMillan once denied in a speech to the House of Commons that Philby was the Third Man in that ring, come to think of it."

"Wasn't this Café Mozart used as a location in the film?"

"Yes, absolutely. Baron Kurtz meets the American writer, Holly Martins, here. He can't go into the Sacher because at that time, the most famous hotel in Vienna was headquarters for British intelligence, and off limits to Austrian citizens! The country was still occupied, of course.

"Anyway, I went on the *Third Man Walk* when I visited here. There are all sorts of sites connected with the film, that still exist, such as the sewers, for example, although Orson Welles wouldn't go near them. That's why they finished up filming in England, which explains what a London doubledecker bus is doing in the background of one of the scenes supposedly set in the Vienna Central Cemetery!"

He went on, lost in the film. "The inspiration for all of this was Kim Philby, as it turns out. He really was a Soviet agent, and had been since he lived here in the 'thirties when he was recruited by the Soviet *Comintern*. For a while he was actually Graham Greene's boss. It's said that he recruited Greene into MI6. He probably told Greene something about Vienna. Turns out that the police rolled up Philby's communist agents, and he helped some escape through the sewers here. You can't tell me *that* is a coincidental detail. It's the heart of the film. That, and the diluted penicillin racket, which actually happened. Quite a story."

They finished their drinks and left the Café Mozart, walking around the block to the main entrance of the Hotel Sacher. They looked forward to a romantic dinner. And so, usually an inveterate tourist anxious to share his discoveries, Robbie didn't call attention to the heartbreaking memorial in the small park just across the street from the Café Mozart. It was the Jewish memorial, a statue of a man on hands and knees scrubbing the street. Underneath was a memorial of a different sort, the location of a collapsed apartment building. A stray Allied bomb had gone down the elevator shaft of an apartment building, trapping those caught in the underground shelter below. They were still there.

Robbie and Sylvie walked through the main entrance on Philharmonikerstrasse, through the main lobby of the Hotel Sacher, and down the corridor past a cloakroom to the Anna Sacher Restaurant. This was Viennese elegance, a room that would be long remembered, with its late nineteenth century *décor* and its electric chandeliers, the first ones installed in Vienna. They were shown to the far end of the restaurant, a separate room within the larger room, with just four tables and a feeling of catered privacy. And no blaring popular music, either, Robbie was relieved to note. It felt like a fine dining room of the period in London. Or Paris. Or New York, for that matter. The tables were set for before 1914, when civilization seemed to reign and set standards. For those who could afford them, of course.

"Speaking of *The Third Man*, all this restaurant needs is the zither music, but we'll get that too, if we manage to get to the Grinzing section outside the city," Robbie said. She smiled. The Anton Karas touch wouldn't fit here at all, but she went along with his mood. They enjoyed a superb dinner with fresh Austrian white wines. The pike-perch, or *sandre*, was a favorite, and the venison *daubes* that followed with glasses of Burgundy were excellent. For dessert, only slices of real *Sachertorte* would do. The chocolate cake, melting in their mouths with just a touch of apricot for contrast, lived up to its reputation.

"Glad I came?" She smiled at his nod. Then, pleased, she called his attention to the other three couples who had just been seated at the other tables in their private alcove. "Look, *chéri*, an English couple, then French over there, and those are surely Russians. It's the Four Powers."

"Yes. It's just like *The Third Man*!"

CHAPTER TEN -
Dublin Calling

ROBBIE FLIPPED ON THE TELEVISION set in their suite for the early morning news, carefully pressing the mute button on the remote, so that Sylvie would not be awakened. The stern and unremittingly serious expressions on the faces of the news reporters cried out that this time, seriously, they had something to say that was worth your hearing, even at this hour. The creeping news letters in English at the bottom of the screen told the story. "The American Ambassador to Dublin, Mary McGowan, has been found murdered. Police investigations, jointly held by the Dublin CID and the American FBI, are underway. She has been dead not more than two days."

Then, lacking further hard news and, for the moment, officials to question, the television reporters in the field switched off, and news summaries of Mary McGowan's career were shown: the Kentucky horse farm, a snapshot of McGowan as a young girl astride the horse that had two years earlier come in second in the Belmont, final leg of thoroughbred horse racing's Triple Crown, pictures of McGowan in cap and gown as valedictorian of both her college and law school classes, and then her philanthropic and political background. She had never been a candidate herself, but those she backed seemed to have acquired the winning touch, in races starting with the state assembly to the recent White House campaign.

The President's own statement came next, clearly a personal and heartfelt effort, which promised an unceasing investigation and the inevitable bringing to justice of the murderer. All commentators noted an air of mystery about the killing. No motive for the murder was suggested. And yet it had taken place, and was said to have been brutal. No doubt further details would be disclosed in the days to come.

Sylvie awoke, yawned, smiled at her husband, and started to say something memorable about their evening. Dinner at Sacher's had moved from the wish list to a treasured memory. She stopped short, as she realized that he wasn't hearing a word that she was saying. Then she followed his hypnotized gaze and saw the television screen.

"Don't tell me you can even get the Red Sox scores here in Vienna?"

"It's the news from Dublin. She's dead. Oh, sorry, g'morning darling." He gave her an absentminded kiss on the cheek. At least it was aimed for her cheek. With at least one eye on the television screen messing up Robbie's peripheral vision, it had landed on her ear instead.

"What? Who's dead? Ambassador McGOWAN? Did you know about this? I just bet you did! What's going on, anyway?"

"Well, darling, I didn't want to spoil our nice evening at the Sacher. Please order something. I've got to get dressed and get to the Embassy. What time is it, anyway? Seven AM? Just about right. I better be out of here in forty minutes, tops."

He disappeared into the bathroom and she called and ordered breakfast, scrambled eggs and ham with toast, coffee and apple juice for Robbie, just *café au lait* and *croissants* with jam and fresh whipped butter for her breakfast. She hoped they would serve the *café au lait* the proper way, as her Norman grandmother used to do, steaming in a large bowl rather than a coffee cup. But that was probably too much to ask, even in this daydream.

Her husband quickly emerged from the bathroom, rubbed his head again with the towel, and sat down to breakfast in the fluffy white hotel bathrobe.

She allowed him to finish his apple juice before the barrage of questions started.

"You mean to tell me that an American AMBASSADOR was murdered, and you wouldn't even tell me about it!" He smiled, waiting for the storm clouds to pass. They darkened instead, as a new thought occurred to her. "Wait a second, Robbie, you went BACK to Dublin and just returned from there. You didn't stay in Paris after all. You returned to Dublin. Did that have to do with the Ambassador McGowan murder?"

"So many questions at once," he said, enjoying his breakfast and her discomfiture. "I can't even remember the order. Let me think. No, my going back there had nothing at all to do with her murder. I'm pretty sure of that. What I mean is, I went back on urgent diplomatic business. I had no idea that she had been murdered."

"But you knew about it last night. Didn't you find out about it when you were there?"

"Yes," he confessed. "Horrible business. She was strangled. She had given the house staff the day off, a rather suspicious thing to do. Anyway, it gave the murderer his opportunity. She was found in the house. I was in touch with the Secretary and the *Chargé*, a good guy named George Smiley - no, that really *is* his name - to handle the preliminaries."

"You said 'his opportunity.' Could it have been a woman?"

"Not likely, unless it was a very strong woman. She was strangled."

"Do you know who did it?"

"That's a hard question. I try not to think so. It might give me preconceived ideas, that would get in the way later on. Fit the theories to the facts, and not the other way around."

"Very Sherlock Holmes."

"Well, yes. He was the master sleuth. Anyway, you weren't out of the action at all. As a matter of fact, you gave me a tremendous insight. Remember, when I spoke to you from Dublin, you said to call Kelly Martin? Well, I did."

"You told her about the murder, and not *me*?" The annoyance, if not hurt, was palpable.

"No. I most certainly did not. But I did ask her a question. You were right of course about women confiding in their women friends. It seems that Ambassador McGowan had called her, probably not long before her murder. Which meant that she had a clue that she didn't know was important, or even a clue, for that matter."

"Wait a second. I remember now. When you called me from Dublin, you said that there was an American Ambassador missing, Mary McGowan, our Ambassador to Dublin. So you knew that something was going on when I talked with you then?"

"Yes, but not that she had been murdered. It was just a puzzle then. She might have gone off on some personal errand, for all I knew. There may have been a lover, which was none of our business. It was more embarrassing than anything else. When we talked, Smiley and I had just been trying to decide what course to take. Honest. Two embarrassed men trying to figure out what course to take, with his wayward boss. I certainly didn't suspect a murder. There wasn't any reason to think that."

"What happens next?"

"Well, I'm calling for an Embassy car. I think it's going to be a very busy day. Now we have not only the bilateral diplomatic stuff with the Austrians to sort out, plus the usual multilaterals you get into here, but also this murder. I wouldn't be at all surprised, by the way, if the Secretary goes back to Dublin at some point. I thought it might be fitting for Ambassador McGowan to have a memorial service there. He liked the idea."

"It would be at St. Patrick's Cathedral, of course."

"Yes, absolutely."

"Any idea what the murder was all about?"

"Really, none whatsoever." He remembered the note to him that Ambassador McGowan had written, and the enclosure. He walked over to the bureau dresser and took the letter from beneath his stack of freshly pressed shirts.

"Well, almost no idea. She did, however, leave a note for me, and an enclosure. Take a look. But please be careful, *chérie,* that piece of paper, or parchment, whatever it is, seems to be very old and fragile."

She took the envelope and scanned its contents. "The Latin seems familiar. I'm sure it is old Church Latin, you know, from the Catholic Vulgate. I can make out some of it."

"Don't bother. I got a translation. That's why I called Kelly Martin. It refers to the prophet's wrath against the children of Israel. The Prophet Isaiah says the truth must be hidden from them until a later time, when the more worthy will understand God's revealed truth. That's a pretty free translation, but that is the sense of it."

He hesitated. "There's one more thing. She said that Ambassador McGowan had also called her about it." He decided not to play all of his cards at once. He might need her fresh analysis later on, and better not bias it from the start. Besides, he liked to control the details.

"Kelly Martin even made it something of a joke, about American diplomats developing a sudden interest in the Book of Isaiah. Said that

Chapter of the Old Testament was going to top the charts at Amazon dot com, if that kept up."

"But she didn't know more exactly what the reference meant? Clearly it must be something hidden."

"That's what I think. Yes. It's designed to point out something. Possibly whatever it was, or finding it, was the motivation for her killer. But that's all guesswork for now."

The phone rang. "Thank you. I'll be right down."

He turned to Sylvie. "That's my car. Better have an easy day, sweetheart. I don't remember what the schedule is, but there is probably something tonight."

"Can you get me on the guest list?"

"I'll certainly try. By the way, Pamela Adams is here. She flew out to join the Secretary in Paris. She was just going to come for that one visit, for old times, since they had been our Ambassador and lady there. But now, I wouldn't be at all surprised that with the possibility of going back to Dublin, she may be staying on."

"Good. Maybe she'll want company for shopping or sightseeing while you people are playing Embassy. Don't worry, I'll find out where she is. Probably at the Residence."

"Any trouble getting around? Do you have some euros with you?"

"Silly goose. I've got enough for a while. And by the way, I speak German."

"I didn't know that! Why didn't you order *apfel strudel* instead of *croissants*?"

"Just today's revelation for you, darling. Sheer cultural chauvinism. Anyway, the *croissant* began here, in Vienna. Now run off and don't be late."

This time, his kiss didn't miss its target.

Robbie noticed it was the same Embassy driver that had picked him up the previous afternoon. Must be dedicated to us while we're here, he thought.

"Right to the Embassy, or do you want some sightseeing along the way?"

"Thanks," Robbie answered. "Better get to the store. It's going to be a very busy day." They arrived, and he bounded out of the car and through the Embassy's imposing front door. He said good morning to the security guard, who checked him out carefully against the approved list of official visitors and waved him through the security checkpoint. "Must have just put that through this morning," Robbie thought. "They hadn't bothered last night."

He glanced at the elevator doors and saw too many people waiting, so bounded up the stairs to his office. Ron Jackson was already there with the diplomatic cable traffic for the Secretary. There was a note from Missy Bronson, who was already in her office, that the Secretary was having a press conference at 9:30. Fine, there was just enough time to accomplish everything. He remembered that the Secretary's Press Spokesman, Charley Sherburne, had already been briefed in Paris. Now an updating would be imperative.

There were some interesting cables about European Union restrictions on American imports, and some IAEA traffic regarding Iran, the perennial problem. Best to let the experts, the Assistant Secretaries involved, brief the Secretary on what he needed to know on both topics. He remembered that Donna Palmer, Assistant Secretary for European Affairs, was with the Secretary's party. Would she handle IAEA and multilateral trade issues as well? Well, she was sharp enough to do so, even if they were not technically part of her brief. He'd ask her this morning. And he was quite sure that she would be buttonholing him about Dublin, in any event. By now the word would have surely spread about his return to Dublin. He wouldn't lack company for lunch, that's for sure.

There was nothing extraordinary in the NODIS SALADIN series, although there were a few cables. It was fascinating, Robbie thought, how very quickly an exotic reporting cable series was sluiced into bureaucratic makeweight and tedium. His father had told him that that was the way it had been with NODIS CROCODILE, the series of telegrams that set up the Paris Peace Talks that ended the Viet-Nam War. First there had been excitement, then tedium.

Robbie was sure that this series too now had far too many readers. Well, that's the way it goes with a bureaucracy, even a diplomatic one. Everybody not only wants to get into the act - they all have to cable their suggestions and wave the flag, wherever they are, anything to get noticed and seem relevant! His father had also said that at the time of the Cuban Missile crisis, all the bureaucrats had gone into Washington early, whether they had anything to do with handling it or not. Better to lose a few hours sleep than to have the neighbors think that one was out of the loop!

And all we want to know is, when and where are they going to try to kill the Secretary of State, and maybe along with him, everyone on his plane?

Here were the cables from Dublin. The Embassy was handling a messy situation about as well as could be expected. The FBI and Dublin CID were getting along well, at least for the time being. He made a note to talk with the Secretary about the need for a request for the memorial service at St. Patrick's Cathedral. There were no immediate clues out of Dublin. However, the list of her phone calls for the past several days had been secured, and the police were running down any leads. In other words, did Ambassador McGowan have any possibly berserk boyfriends? It didn't sound very likely. But there was a note from Smiley that she had been seeing someone, and had spoken with him the evening before her disappearance. He would be picked up shortly. It didn't happen every day that a Minister of the Irish Government was questioned on a criminal matter by the Dublin police. Not since independence, anyway.

There was also a cable marked personal, to him from Smiley. There was no news yet regarding the other subject, their meeting with Dillman. And, he reported, the 'spy cameras,' as he insisted on calling them, were in the process of being installed at the Residence. It was a good, artful, inobtrusive job. "Sure," Robbie thought, "and it's also a tipoff to everyone who works there." Well, that was understood from the beginning. He still thought it was a good idea, all things considered, but now the second thoughts were beginning to weigh on him.

Then, he sat upright at the next part of Smiley's message. The police authorities wanted to try something. There had been no announcements regarding the cause of death, nor where the body had been found. There was a question of smoking out the possible killer, who would be looking for a news account. Some doubt about what had been discovered might make the killer uncertain.

The authorities were disinclined to make public where the body had been found. They had in mind the morbidly curious, who ought not to know, and Ambassador McGowan's family, who should be spared this horrible detail being put in the public domain. Robbie agreed. She should publicly remain the energetic and intelligent American Ambassador that she had been. A murderer must not rob her of that, substituting ghoulish images and headlines in the gutter press. Her next public appearance should be in full dignity of state, at St. Patrick's Cathedral. The protocol surely required telling the family what had taken place. Candor should not extend beyond that. It just wasn't anyone's legitimate business.

The next part was more devious. The police were rather suspicious about the killer. They had run down all of the telephone leads secured from her use in the day or so before her death, both from the Embassy and from her residence. There had been a few international calls back and forth, of course. They were being checked, more for the sake of thoroughness than anything else, it seemed. After all, they were a back burner matter of small possible significance, while her calls within Ireland were being followed up vigorously right now. A comprehensive list could probably follow, if Robbie would find that useful. All the callers who were in Dublin and could be checked out quickly seemed to have witnesses as to their whereabouts at the approximate time of the killing.

There was the further suggestion, that the cause of death be stated to be not strangulation, which it had been, but a blow from a blunt instrument. The purpose would be to see what effect, if any, this might have on a possible suspect. If it brought someone in who thought that he had a measure of safety, well and good. If not, later on they could always, if attention was called to the discrepancy, say that further analysis had now showed that Ambassador McGowan had been strangled while standing, from behind, and in falling, had twisted her head, which had struck a piece of furniture rather violently on the way down.

It was worth a try. But he wanted to talk with the Secretary first.

He entered the Secretary's office, three stacks of cables in hand. There was Missy Bronson, acting for all the world as though she had always inhabited this office, in this Embassy. She reflected an assured, lowkey competence that everyone appreciated.

"Welcome back, Robbie. I hear things got out of hand in Dublin."

"It seems that way. We'll try to put things right. To the extent that it can be done, that is. Is Secretary Adams in yet?" She nodded, yes. "Then I better see him for a few minutes before he goes through the cables, if that's OK." She smiled, the gatekeeper's powers recognized, and pressed a button that signalled the inner sanctum, and Robbie entered the Secretary's office.

"Good morning, sir." The Secretary was finishing a phone call, and waved Robbie towards his desk. Robbie sat down and waited a few moments. "I've got a press conference at 9:30," he said. "Is there any more news out of Dublin? What cables do we have this morning?"

"Missy has the cables, sir. The FBI and Dublin CID are working well together, but that's about it. They are running down leads. By that, they mean her telephone calls over the last few days of her life. Turns out she was dating a member of O'Bryan's government. There has been no official report yet, autopsy or otherwise."

"Do you have any first thoughts on this?"

"Yes sir, one or two. I think it was a private killing, for a private motive, rather than a terrorist act as such. It's more likely, since the body was hidden, and there has been no claim of responsibility. The terrorists, particularly after a successful outrage, are inclined to crow." Secretary Adams nodded in agreement.

"But anything else is far too speculative right now, if you don't mind, sir. They are proceeding with installing security cameras at the Phoenix Park residence, which I had suggested."

"So you think the killer may be coming back?"

"It's possible."

"Of course, if the killer is already there, your security cameras will be something of a tipoff, won't they?"

"Well yes, especially if the killer is the person who installs them." He thought for a moment. Was he really so darned sure that Bob Starett, the administrative officer, was not a suspect? If he was, wouldn't this compromise things? Well, it was his best judgment at the time. "But I don't think there is much possibility of that. Still, it's a fair point.

"However, I am not at all sure that the killer might not return to the Phoenix Park residence at some point. That's what this is about. We're not there to control things, so this is a sort of proxy. With a camera system in place, we can track movements of anybody that shows up in the residence. That will give a lot of routine shots, but it might just trap a killer, especially as time passes and the heat cools down.

"Sir," Robbie went on, "George Smiley has started making some arrangements with the Irish Government. I think it would strengthen his hand to have a request from you for the memorial service to be held at St. Patrick's Cathedral."

"Fine. Of course."

"You'll have a draft cable to the Irish Government within the hour. Now, Smiley and I did meet with Dillman, their security liaison. That's why I went over in the first place. I'd almost forgotten, with this McGowan murder. He is finding out if it's possible to get any more specifics from his contacts. A long shot in my view, but worth trying.

"And here is something else. I've just got a cable from George Smiley regarding the investigation." Robbie summarized what Smiley had reported.

"Well, that rather goes against my instincts as a former prosecutor. What do you think, Robbie?"

"I rather like the idea, Mr. Secretary. Of course, it is unorthodox. But to have justice, you have to have somebody to prosecute. This is a trick, to be sure. If it lures in the killer through a false sense of security, it will be worth it. I say, go ahead."

"I'm not convinced."

Robbie got up and started pacing. If later, you had told him that he had done that while talking with the Secretary of State, he would have said, in sheer astonishment, that you had made that up. But that is what he did.

"Sir, there is a very unusual aspect to this case. I don't think it was a crime directed personally against Ambassador McGowan at all. I think she may have surprised the killer, who was attempting another crime, grand larceny of a sort. I'd rather not go too far, as it's only a hypothesis. Possibly the killer just didn't get what he was after. That is why the Embassy put in those spy cameras in the residence. If it is the case that the killer didn't get what he was after, he wants to return. He may not even be in Dublin now. A false scent may help smoke him out. Give him security to return. I say, let them go ahead. It's their best judgment."

The Secretary looked hard at Robbie, and then nodded his head, yes. He coughed. "Well, I had thought that our stay in Vienna was going to be more idyllic than it's turning out to be."

Robbie smiled. "Yes, sir. Well, I got a surprise yesterday myself. Sylvie has flown in to join me."

"That's nice. Call over and get her put on the reception list for tonight. It's at our Embassy here, no problem whatsoever. Pamela will enjoy the company. Now, better stick around. Charley Sherburne is about to appear. I feel it in my bones. He'll want to know the latest on the McGowan case before our press conference."

After the initial part of the briefing with Charley Sherburne, Robbie left the Secretary's office and called Assistant Secretary Donna Palmer. He went to her office and gave her a quick rundown on what had happened in Dublin. He also informed her of the Secretary's wish to attend a memorial service there. Since the Irish Desk Officer had flown back to Washington, Robbie offered to draft the Secretary's message requesting of the Irish Government a memorial service in St. Patrick's Cathedral.

Assistant Secretary Palmer agreed, and Robbie asked whether he could put her down as having cleared the text in substance, to save time. That was fine with her. He returned to his office, wrote the short, personal cable, and passed it to Missy Bronson a few minutes before Charley Sherburne left the Secretary's office. When Robbie got a quick acknowledging nod from Secretary Adams as his press conference began, he knew that his cable had already been approved and had been sent to Dublin.

— — — — — — — —

The press conference was dominated by the breaking news of Ambassador Mary McGowan's murder. Trying to foresee that, Secretary Adams had begun the briefing, held in the press room of the Embassy on *Boltzmanngasse* 16, with a short statement praising the deceased, and her record of service to the nation.

"Was this a terrorist act?"

"We have no definite information at present. Let's leave that to Dublin CID and our FBI, who are cooperating on the scene. It's probably safe to say that they haven't ruled anything out yet. They are gathering evidence, and more will be available from Dublin, I hope shortly."

"How was she killed? We haven't even heard that."

"Again, I refer you to the investigation. That information will be released shortly, I'm sure."

"Has it affected your trip?"

"We will proceed as announced, if possible. I would however like to return to Dublin for a memorial service for Ambassador McGowan. That is just a wish at present. There are no plans to that effect."

There soon will be, Robbie thought.

"Mr. Secretary, it seems much of your business here is multilateral. I mean, you are concerned with Iran and with Russia. Is that a fair statement?"

"Well, anytime that I return to the beautiful country where I met my wife has a special aspect to it. It's another illustration of the Hapsburg motto, *Felix Austria, nube*, I suppose. If you mean do we have important bilateral matters to discuss with our Austrian colleagues, the answer is yes."

Appreciative chuckles and knowing glances from the local Austrian press representatives. Local references, artfully inserted, were always a diplomatic plus. This reference, Robbie remembered, was to the Hapsburg credo that other nations had to fight for territory, while happy Austria just got larger through dynastic marriages.

The Secretary went on. "And so, we are proceeding with diplomatic business and consultations with our Austrian hosts, and with the multilateral organizations in Vienna. We are hopeful of productive talks with the IAEA, specifically regarding Iran's performance of their international obligations. We shall also be consulting with the JCG, our Joint Consultative Group, regarding the Russian adherence to the CFE, or Conventional Forces in Europe Treaty. As you know, Russia formally suspended their adherence to this treaty in April, 2007.

"We regard that treaty, which limits Russian and NATO troop deployments in Europe, as of first importance. The Russians also announced at the time that as a second step, they might reconsider their adherence to the Intermediate Range Nuclear Forces Treaty. This was the landmark treaty that removed an entire class of nuclear weapons. Not adhering to it would be a step backwards towards the dark days of the Cold War. Here and in Moscow, we will consider these matters, which are of first importance to the peace and security of our nations. Extending the START agreement and its verification measures is a mandatory beginning to controlling nuclear arms."

That set off a buzz of technical questions, which concluded the press conference. Robbie caught Charley Sherburne near the door.

"Well, that was a neat change of subject. Surely we don't put JCG consultations, important as they must be, on the same level as negotiations in Moscow? Things must be fairly technical here, for one thing, not political."

"That's right. This was a marker, to get their attention in Moscow."

"I assume they will get the message."

"Several messages, actually. You saw how the Secretary schmoozed the Austrians."

"It's quite genuine. He likes them."

"He is all the more effective for that. Also, he linked the question of a change in schedule to a service for Ambassador McGowan. If things don't go well in Moscow, that might come into play. He would have a fine diplomatic cover for breaking off talks."

"I never thought of that angle."

— — — — — — — —

Robbie's mouth dropped open when he saw the next person to enter his office. It was George Smiley. This was unimaginable, with everything going on in Dublin. Why would the man in charge pick this time to fly to Vienna, leaving his post, which was already in crisis? Smiley, ashen faced, closed the door and sunk into a chair facing Robbie's desk.

"We just heard back from Dillmann," he said. "Yes, I know," he went on, anticipating Robbie's thoughts. "We had a code, to cover where the danger might be, if we found out. But we don't have a place, and anyway, that didn't cover murder linked with treason."

"What on earth is going on?" Robbie noticed that Smiley hadn't even removed his topcoat.

"The Irish contact had two things to say. The first was, that there would be no more messages on this subject. Dublin assumes that it is just too hot and dangerous. His or her life may be endangered by our question. It certainly would be with any followup."

"And...?"

"The second message was, 'Just watch your own people.'" Smiley waited a moment for that to sink in. "What we were being told is that the danger may not be from Al Qaeda, or perhaps, not exclusively. This long time agent in place hears things. It's a sort of blowback, what they hear, or perhaps infer. And what this agent seems to have heard is that Secretary Adams may be murdered by one of our own people."

"Any idea why that would happen?"

"No. I'd only be guessing. This isn't the time for that."

"We better brief the Secretary immediately."

"Yes, and unfortunately, I don't know if we can even have his security people present. One of them just may be the problem. Or perhaps not," Smiley said, "if this is a disinformation scheme of some sort, designed not to heighten security awareness, but to destroy it."

"A nice mess you bring from Dublin, George. By the way, he is on board, but only just, for that idea you were floating from Dublin CID and the FBI about her cause of death."

"We do our best to oblige, Robbie. I'll get the word back as soon as we've talked with the Secretary."

— — — — — — — —

They had changed locations on a daily basis. The danger was palpable, all the more so because American attention was once again directed towards Afghanistan, its border with Pakistan, and above all, to the mountain fastnesses of Waziristan on the Pakistan side of the border that separated the two. Here Osama bin Laden and Zayman al-Zawahiri compared notes.

"The Americans are changing their strategies once again, it seems," Osama bin Laden began. "They have indeed totally lost control of events. They first seek elections, which did not benefit them, for change in our region would not tend towards their precious concept of democracy. Far from it. But then, they don't seem to like popular governments despite their rhetoric. Look at how they bragged about military action against Mossadegh, and the installation of that fraudulent Shah! And then in Pakistan, they sent in Benazir Bhutto.

Why? To destabilize their own ally? They are children playing deadly games in a region they do not understand.

"Their covert plans don't stay covert, and they fail. Then the Americans go back to seeking stability, and to do so, they again alienate much of the region of the Prophet, peace be upon him."

"Yes, once again, from lecturing Saudi Arabia and Egypt, they go back to financing their military. I have some personal experience of those prisons, as you well know. That is where the American money will go." Zayman al-Zawahiri shuddered at the memory of his long and painful imprisonment. "It's supposed to provide some sort of balance while they build up the regime in Israel. For the suffering Palestinians, as they themselves would say in America, just peanuts. The Americans play at diplomacy during their election contests, with quotations that fit on the back of automobiles, and then they ignore diplomacy or freedom too, for that matter, in practice. In short, they create the best conditions for our cause, and they do it vigorously, as they do all things. Sometimes I think they are our best recruiters."

Bin Laden smiled. "Yes, it is diplomacy by presidential term, not by national interest. One may chart what they will do by how much time is left in the term of the incumbent White House failure. First the innovative, amateurish beginning, setting the world right, with rhetoric from the previous political campaign. Then the giddy trips around the region and the globe by the new celebrity who sets out to dazzle the world with his or her inspiring life story. Then after their failures become obvious even in Washington, comes once again the diplomacy of guns and violence. That fails. Then they go back to exactly what they lectured the last president about, and start chasing the Nobel Peace Prize." They laughed..

"Now as to our plan. The cells in America were picked up, of course. And the Americans have made their announcement, crowing about their latest victory in what they sometimes still choose to call the War on Terrorism. Now is certainly the time to strike against this Secretary of State.

"Unfortunately, he seems to be a civilized adversary. He seems determined to take steps that will make his country more appealing to the rest of the world. Whether it is sincere or not, one cannot say. That is what makes him dangerous. That is why we must deal with him now. The reaction to his death from the American Administration will help us even more."

"Our plans are in readiness. We only await his visit to..."

"Surprise me, Zayman."

Al-Zawahiri turned to his chief with what passed for a smile. "As you say. It will not be long now, just a few days. All is in readiness, as is the backup plan. And there will be a certain historic fitness to it, you'll see."

"I look forward to it. By the way, what happened in Dublin? I authorized no killing of the American Ambassador there."

"That was none of our doing. It remains something of a mystery now. Apparently it was a private act, not a political one. But it does coincide with a very odd matter."

"What is that?"

"The Americans suspect something. I'm sure of it. Like an old blind dog scenting a familiar smell, looking around a yard, curious and not quite sure of things." He took a sip of his tea, holding the bowl in both hands, and blowing on it to cool the hot drink. Osama bin Laden waited for him to resume his thought.

"They do indeed suspect something. Sorry, I repeat myself. But it is odd. They have inquired in Beirut about our plans. They have activated an old agent in place, an Irish agent, left behind from the old days in Libya. He was there so long that even with the Irish matter settled, he couldn't or wouldn't go home. Wasn't at home there anymore, I hear. So he had stayed on in Libya, then moved to Beirut. We talk with him from time to time, indirectly of course. It's nothing secret or official, mind you. It's just a way to get a Western point of view.

"Well, occasionally, he must hear something. We don't know what, or what he may have passed on to his masters in Dublin, that we assume then reached American ears, since as you know Secretary Adams has just been in Dublin. What we do know is that there was an inquiry from Dublin about a possible attempt against the life of Secretary Adams."

"Why am I just hearing of this now?"

"I myself have just heard. No instructions were given. It seems that our people thought quickly, and told their agent to watch their own friends." He paused for a moment, for effect.

"Why would that be credible?"

"It's the new Secretary and his policies. He says to close Guantanamo and the secret prisons. It has even been said that he wants to see what American security forces have been doing. He has not excluded the threat of prosecutions under American law."

"That makes him a formidable enemy indeed."

"Yes." Al-Zawahiri paused, sipping his tea. "It also makes the idea of a killing from within their own American security forces a credible threat. So Adams must watch out, in several directions, both against us, and against the very ones who would try to protect him *from* us. That will surely help us in the execution of our own plan. He won't know whom to trust!"

Bin Laden smiled in appreciation. "That's ingenious! So now, the Americans will be concerned about their own security forces. They may even take their attention away from us, in their diversion. Well, divide and rule, as the British imperialists used to practice it." He thought for a moment. "I suppose it goes without saying that the message has now been reinforced?"

"Of course. Their agent has been killed, in the customary way. The video is ready anytime we care to use it, or to send it."

"A good idea. That will add credence to what they now believe."

— — — — — — — —

Ambassador Rudolphe Carlisle looked forward to his first full day as American Ambassador in Riga. The ceremony had been pleasant at Riga Castle. He wished, come to think of it, that he had taped the historic proceedings. It would be a wonderful family momento, if he ever married. Perhaps the Latvians had thought to do so. He must remember to ask the press attaché to look into it.

He had slept late beyond his usual habits, and who was there to stop his doing precisely what he liked? It was now just past noon, and following his shower, he had rung a discreet bell (a nice touch, that!) and a residence waiter had silently come to take his breakfast order, and then deliver it, "in the morning room, just over there, sir."

He looked around with satisfaction at the morning room where he was enjoying breakfast. There was bright sunlight coursing through the window, and he even rather liked the curtains, in a shaded lavender. Beyond in the courtyard there was a patch of tended rosebushes, just coming into bloom.

They must be the everbearing type of bush, Carlisle thought. Eveything conspired to give pleasure this morning.

His coffee was fresh, his fruit juice also, and the rolls and jam and butter were a great treat. Carlisle was not one of those snobs who insisted on imported foods, Normandy butter and English marmalade. It was a matter of knowing what was what, and the truly refined taste could tease out such secrets. These breakfast treats were Latvian, and the rolls were freshly made by a skilled bread chef. He wondered if they had been purchased, or made in his own kitchen. And if so, surely that meant that the chef could also produce fine pastries, *mille feuilles*, éclairs, fresh fruit turnovers and the like.

He pictured an ascetic tall chef with a saturnine glance, tempting the diner as a Faustian devil, turning attention from more praiseworthy pursuits towards the delights of worldly pleasures, one irresistible small step after another. No, on reflection, probably the chef was a fat peasant lady who only knew how to make rolls, in the good old way that her own grandmother had taught her in their smoky primitive kitchen! He laughed to himself and said that he would solve that mystery, at least, this very morning.

It was time for reality to intrude. Carlisle picked up his coffee cup and walked over to the television set. No, the remote was over there, by that comfortable couch. Even chintz had a place here, he charitably observed. He placed his cup on the side table, sat down and pushed the power button. An edifying bucolic Latvian scene unfolded. It seemed to be some sort of continuing saga, with no subtitles. Carlisle began to press the up channel button. A series of vaguely familiar channels succeeded each other. Well, surely there was a master guide to the channels somewhere. He looked more closely at the side table. Yes, there it was. He found the local channel indicated for CNN, and pressed those numbers on the remote.

Now a familiar channel at last, and thank heavens, it was in English, with subtitles in, well, whatever, that didn't matter. The worried announcer had on her most serious expression. Carlisle turned the volume up, and watched as a series of pictures succeeded each other, showing Ambassador Mary McGowan, her career highpoints and her early life. Carlisle braced himself.

The announcer repeated the main news flash as the coverage ended. Ambassador Mary McGowan, the American Ambassador in Dublin, had been found dead. Adding to earlier reports, there would shortly be a press conference with the early police findings. Waiting for that press conference to get underway, the television announcer stalled for time by repeating what was known. The body of Mary McGowan, American Ambassador to Dublin, had been found at the official residence at Phoenix Park in Dublin. At the request of the American Government, and in cooperation with the American FBI, Dublin CID had taken charge of the American residence, which was now viewed as a crime scene.

Cut to Vienna. The American Secretary of State, Mr. Ronald Adams, was shown beginning his press conference with a reference to the tragedy of Ambassador Mary McGowan's death. He mentioned her distinguished career and accomplished life. The Secretary said that he hoped it would be possible for a fitting memorial service in Dublin, so that her memory could be joyously evoked. In questions following the prepared statements he returned to the theme, regretting exceedingly that her service to the nation, which was surely just beginning in her first ambassadorial post, had been cut short by this incomprehensible act.

Well, Adams was a gentleman. That was to be expected. Surely, as a fellow Ambassador, and one who had just enjoyed the hospitality of the deceased in Dublin, Carlisle should send flowers to that memorial service. He started to make a note to that effect, when the tone of the television announcer became a bit more urgent.

"Now we take you, live, to the press conference in Dublin, that is just getting underway." The scene showed a nondescript conference room, with several grim bulldog officials near the microphone. First came the Dublin CID, Commissioner Flaherty.

"This is a sad day for us all. Ambassador McGowan met her death at the American official residence in Phoenix Park. We are asking anyone who was in that vicinity for the past 72 hours to contact CID Headquarters in Dublin." He added a number and address. "The cause of death, a savage blow to the back of the head, leaves no doubt that it was murder."

FBI Special Agent Simpson spoke next, briefly, his piercing eyes surveying the scene, then looking straight into the camera as though he could sense guilt or complicity in the face of any member of the television audience if he so chose. "There are indications that more than one murderer was involved. We ask that anyone having any information about this crime contact us immediately, at the number that Commissioner Flaherty has just given." He repeated it. The press conference ended with a slew of unanswered questions, as the police officials left the room.

"My God. *NOW* what do I do?" Carlisle's hand shook, and he forced it to stop shaking, as he pressed the television remote power switch. "What the hell is going on here? When I left her, she was dead. *Or was she?*" He couldn't decide whether to take the police announcement at face value or not. They didn't even have the cause of death right. Or did they? Was there really another person involved, a killer who came into the residence after he had left? If so, why? What possible motivation could there have been for anybody else to kill McGowan? Could she possibly have revived, and staggered out of that meat locker? He had left it unlocked, after all.

No, it must be a clever police smokescreen. They were trying to get him to come in and confess. That must be it. They really had no leads whatsoever. They wanted him to do their work for them.

On the *other* hand, it was intriguing to think that perhaps he hadn't committed the killing after all. Perhaps it really was a bad dream, a sort of waking nightmare. Somebody else had done it. But why? What possible motivation could there have been?

Suppose, again, that he could take the police press conference at face value. That didn't really mean that he had to confess to anything. Attempted murder, after all, wasn't exactly jaywalking. But surely, they would link the attempted strangulation with the blow on the back of the head. There had only been one murderer, and two methods. The first, strangulation, hadn't worked, and so the *coup de grâce*, as it were, had also been administered.

And if there were a private motivation for the second murderer (how Shakespearean that sounded!), that could mean that he could have another look at the old secretary.

He decided that, really, flowers were not enough. If there were to be a memorial service for Ambassador Mary McGowan, he would attend in person. It would be only fitting. Surely it would be held in St. Patrick's Cathedral. Perhaps, as an historic note, some music from Handel's *Messiah* would be played.

She would have liked that.

— — — — — — — —

There were a few loose ends to attend to before George Smiley left Vienna. He was quite sure, as he had told Secretary Adams, that the Irish Government would hold the requested Memorial Service for Ambassador McGowan at St. Patrick's Cathedral. Within a day or so at most, they should have the date. In the meantime, he had heard that the Dean of the Cathedral must be cajoled to rearrange a few prescheduled services. But that should soon be sorted out.

Robbie hoped that this successor to Dean Jonathan Swift was amenable to change, to letting the American Gulliver hold a memorial service. Well, why not? If the Dean were himself involved in the arrangements and the service, for what would surely, taking the television audience into account, be the largest congregation ever to experience a service at that venerable church, there should be no problems.

He reflected for a moment. This business of sorting out motivations like a perennial chess match had limits. He hoped that it was unworthy to think that there even might be problems about granting the request, or calculations of gain in doing so. That was the trouble with thinking as a diplomat, Robbie realized. It wasn't what outsiders thought at all. It was a *déformation professionelle*, as the French would put it, a way of viewing things, a sort of professional prism. You extended political motivations to everyone, whether or not they were appropriate, and extrapolated conduct from those calculations. That must lead to error. There must be a corrective for such thinking. Certainly there was, in the odd science of detection. And her name was Sylvie!

George Smiley had gone by himself to the airport. He had refused a courtesy escort, and even an Embassy car. "Best not to call too much attention to myself," he had grinned. "It's just what my sainted namesake would have done. See you back in Dublin." Outside the Embassy, he hailed a waiting taxi, just a rumpled man on his own. Was anything more conspicuous than that? He promised to let Robbie know if, by any chance, there was further word from the mysterious Irish informant, somewhere in the Middle East. They both doubted it.

The diplomatic business meeting began, in a gold etched formal conference room of the Austrian Foreign Ministry that surely traced back to the days of Empress Maria Theresa. Secretary of State Adams was amongst friends because they wanted to be such, and because he instinctively knew it, and embraced them with his inclusive speech.

"I have very fond memories of our time in Austria, Madame Minister. And I brought home the very finest souvenir of that summer, the lady who became my wife." The Austrian Foreign Minister was enchanted. Her own patrimony was Upper Austria, and so she knew well the Salzkammergut, the lakes region outside Salzburg to which Secretary Adams referred. The University of Vienna held a summer session on the lake at Strobl am Wolfgangsee, and that is where Adams, as a university student at loose ends for the summer before law school beckoned, had met his future bride, Pamela Higginson.

"The *Sommerhochschule* still holds its annual session at Strobl," she replied. "Surely they would be thrilled to receive you and your wife." Secretary Adams asked Robbie to make a note of the request, and try to sort out the timing for another trip. "I'm overscheduled for this one," he noted apologetically. "But it's a wonderful idea."

This was the open part of the meeting, with press allowed, and many pictures were taken. Then they departed, and the two sides addressed their bilateral business, a trade agreement and some nasty agricultural problems. It was businesslike, with some good back and forth. Nothing earthshaking, just professionally handled, with a small concession here, and an acknowledged point there. It seemed to go by rather quickly. Then there was a brief break, before diplomatic business was again taken up. Robbie had thought that he recognized an old friend on the other side, Georg Haussner. Yes, it was Georg! He picked up a cup of coffee and some pastry and nodded hello.

His friend was glad to see him, and pleased about the meeting, which was "remarkable." Georg Haussner had been part of the monthly political officers' luncheon club, that had met around town to compare notes on political developments within their host country, when he and Robbie had been assigned at their respective embassies in Budapest. The American, British, Austrian, Greek, Brazilian and Italian Embassy Political Officers had usually shown up, with others joining them from time to time.

They had all been anxious to understand Hungary and how its turbulent past was reflected in the give and take ("mostly take," Robbie once noted) of national politics, but it was not an even playing field professionally. The American and British Political Officers had had Hungarian language training, and the rest had not. One or two, with a Hungarian family background, could follow events and even something of the language, but that was the luck of the draw. Mostly the luncheons were a matter of drawing out what the trained linguists knew or could reasonably surmise. Georg Haussner was one of the sharpest and most personable of the lot. That was surely why he had been chosen to be Executive Assistant to the new Austrian Foreign Minister, whose background was in provincial politics, not diplomacy.

And Georg was really pleased by the way this meeting was going. He didn't have to spell it out, and wouldn't have done so. Some things were better left unsaid, and diplomats were also supposed to be able to communicate in silence.

The difference was not just that Secretary Adams knew something about Austria from firsthand experience, although that was helpful. His demeanor said that he would treat his Austrian colleague as a respected equal. Vienna was not, for Adams, a photo opportunity and a chance to show off, with a flashy joint press conference. It was an occasion for serious work, on the unglamorous bilateral problems that are always present. But beyond that, it was a time for candor and consultation. Nothing is so ingratiating as being taken seriously by a great power, particularly when the American Secretary of State also understands your nation's history.

They resumed the meeting. The Austrian Foreign Minister raised a broader matter. "We have noted that you intend to close the prison at Guantanamo, and abide by Geneva rules for prisoners," she said, testing the waters. Adams nodded firmly. Encouraged, feeling her way, she added, "It must have been a difficult decision. The terrorists threaten all of us. But you are doing the right thing."

She thought for a moment, and was silent. If he wished to comment, he could do so.

Secretary Adams replied. "When nations start to lose their way, it is in the name of security, and those without power or friends are always the first to pay. In the guise of protecting national security, those who are different pay a terrible price. For me, the finest thing about my country is not its wealth. It is our Constitution and our laws. When we start to break them, or try to get around them, or when we take a single step in the wrong direction, then something is lost. You saw that here in the last century. I think of that statue near the Café Mozart, the victims…"

He stopped speaking for a moment, a catch in his voice. Time stopped in the room as each person caught his breath. He added softly, "All the more reason for all of us to rededicate ourselves to the rule of law." The Austrian Foreign Minister, remembering what she had heard of those days, and the many family members that she had never known who had been murdered for their beliefs and their faith, nodded her head in silent agreement and reverie.

Then his voice returned in full conviction. "My country wants it firmly understood that the law protects all of us. When we give our word, whether it is a bilateral matter, such as we have just been discussing, or in a multilateral context, such as the Vienna Convention on Diplomatic Relations, or the Geneva Conventions dealing with warfare and its consequences, we will keep it, in letter and spirit. The alternative is not possible. That way, the enemies of civilized mankind win through our miscalculations what they could not possibly win through persuasion or on any battlefield. There will be no more 'extraordinary renditions' of persons held by the United States to other nations for interrogation. Unjust military commissions designed only for convictions are disbanded. Parsing words to inflict pain has ended and will not be resumed. Ever. You have our word."

There followed a stunned silence and then something that Robbie knew that he would remember for the rest of his life. It was without parallel for a closed diplomatic meeting. Those present, first the Austrians and then the Americans, started to applaud. Then the Austrians, still applauding, rose, and came forward, one by one, to shake the hand of the American Secretary of State.

"My God," thought Robbie. "This cuts deep indeed. This must have been the way they thought of Secretary of State George Marshall, when he came up with the plan that saved Europe."

Then he, too, joined the standing applause. It was an honor again to be an American diplomat. Further diplomatic conversation was simply not possible. The meeting adjourned on that high note, and both sides wandered back to their office suites, savoring the occasion.

"It seemed to go well enough, don't you think, Robbie?"

"Yes, indeed. I hardly know what to say about that reaction, Mr. Secretary."

They were alone in the Secretary's Embassy office, cleaning up a few details before the evening reception.

"Well, I think I do. Everyone feels better, and safer, when the biggest kid in the neighborhood is someone you can trust. It makes a real difference. Always has." He thought for a moment, and rapped his pen on the desk.

"It doesn't really seem to matter, those petty jealousies that are always there, sometimes beneath the surface, sometimes more obvious. That goes with the territory, I mean, our size and sheer power. We ought to discount that reaction, and not take it very seriously. It's nothing that cannot be handled with a few Leader Grants and press tours of our country. Besides, everyone thinks, given the opportunity, that they would wield power more wisely, more *justly*, than we have done. Perhaps they would, I don't know. But the history of the past few centuries tends to show that they would make similar mistakes. Maybe even worse blunders.

"But when we don't set the example, I mean a good one, one that the world *expects*, even those who do not wish us well, that's when the trouble starts. And no amount of clever public relations can ever set that right. I'm not starting a Revolution, Robbie. Neither is the President. All we want to do is to set our nation back on the right track. Fortunately, we can do that and still prosecute the fight against our enemies. In fact, we can do an even better job of it, if we play by our own rules."

He looked searchingly at Robbie. "You're the coming generation, Robbie. What do you make of this?"

"Thank you for asking, sir. I make two things out of it. The first is that, now, as you say, our nation is on the right track again. It will take a while to set things right, but it can and will be done. The bad residue is that, for years to come I suspect, people will always wonder what sort of people we really are. That Pandora's Box has been opened, and it is tough to shut it again. However, as we saw today," Robbie shrugged off a dismissive wave from the Secretary, "our friends, and there are lots of them, everywhere, want to have their idea of the United States revalidated."

Secretary Adams shook his head in agreement. "Yes. That's why that applause was not for me, not by a long shot. What is your second point, Robbie?"

"It's the reverse, sir, the dark side of the coin. If our coming back to the rule of law strengthens our country, and cheers our friends, it makes us more formidable to our enemies."

"There may be something to that. Where does that lead you"

"Again, two observations. The first is that our enemies actually may prefer it when we do not abide by the rule of law, whether it is secret prisons, torturing people, extaordinary rendition, the entire sickening lot. I suspect as a practical matter, such measures simply do not work, lurid television shows to the contrary. They also build hatred towards us, reinforcing stereotypes, particularly when those being mistreated are the target audience of the fanatical enemy. In other words, since our victims are Muslims, why should we be recruiters for the enemy? Examples, like Abu Ghraib Prison, will be over the internet and the airwaves and the television screens all over the Middle East, whenever they occur. If we return to our own values, they lose a valuable recruiting tactic."

"True enough. And...?"

"And, it follows that your policy of decency, Mr. Secretary, and that of the President, will put you both on the top of the Al Qaeda assassination list, for that very reason. It is exactly that policy that makes you both far more dangerous adversaries.

"So, if you were planning things for Al Qaeda, what would your next move be?"

"Well, we have already heard that they are planning an attempt against your life. We have also heard that our own intelligence service, for whatever reason, may be involved. There is a superficial logic to that. If the Administration was to start prosecuting people for what they did under the other, permissive, team in Washington, the logic goes, some disgruntled 'patriots' would want to stop it."

"You say the logic is superficial?"

"It sounds like a bad plot, payback time for Hollywood heavies. It came from a good source, Dillman told us. But who knows? We have never met him, or her. We don't know if this was from a free agent. Could it have been disinformation? I mean, something planted so that you would distrust the very people who are supposed to protect you - and at the very time Al Qaeda may be planning something? That's what makes sense to me."

"I have the feeling you're not going to be a very successful career bureaucrat, Robbie. You lack the instinct for covering yourself, in case something awful happens. And thank heavens for that! What do you think is our next move?"

"I say, a thorough go-round with our security people. Let them sort it out. We can start here, and continue tomorrow before we leave. Let me talk first with Sam Jardine from Diplomatic Security. He's the professional. I think we've got to trust our own people and widen the loop. Have him make whatever contacts he needs. After all, we've still got several countries to visit. Then tomorrow morning, a full dress meeting here before we leave."

"Good. Put it together with Sam and inform the Department. Don't wait to send it. You can put me down for substance. Then we'll see you and Sylvie at the reception, surely."

That was a real compliment. Robbie realized that not seeing the cable again before it went was a threshhold of trust that he had successfully passed. Even so, it was a flattering judgment, on a matter as important as this one. It was the sort of thing that Secretary Adams occasionally did with Clark Framsen, Robbie knew. It had better be the best cable he ever wrote!

"We'll do that. It's time for you to leave for the reception at the residence, sir, I think. Missy is ready to lock up your office for the night. I'll stay here and talk with Sam. Then we'll get the cable out. SALADIN series, I think. What time tomorrow morning do we leave for Moscow?"

— — — — — — — —

The reception was a tribute to Austrian hospitality and American ingenuity, or was it the reverse? Nobody would ever have known that the automatic lawn sprinking system had broken down once again, making the residence lawn into a swamp. It couldn't be dried in time, so the reception was reconfigured to be an inside event. None of the events had to be cancelled. The toasts of welcome and response were given, the cold drinks were refreshing, and the chamber music, by one of Vienna's prized groups, was thoroughly enjoyed. Some bilateral business was conducted by Embassy officers but not, Robbie supposed, very much. This was a feel good reception for a visit that had gone extremely well.

Sam Jardine was a tough professional, who let out a profane comment or two when Robbie briefed him. Together with Robbie, he put together a discreet NODIS cable in the SALADIN series to send to the Department of State. Let them worry about distribution within the Washington community. The cable also asked that Washington pass on so much of this information, disguising the source, as needed, to Embassies Moscow, London and Riga. Once again, special attention must be paid to security during the Secretary's visit. Robbie added, and in particular, for any public events, or ceremonies commemorating traditional historical ties. Why he put that in for Moscow and Riga Robbie couldn't quite articulate. Maybe something would turn up. And this time, it was really better to be safe than sorry.

Sylvie had said that she had no wish to go on with the official plane, which Robbie greeted with something like relief. She wasn't really authorized to do so anyway, and it wasn't right to ask, especially since Mrs. Adams had joined the group. Besides, given her health considerations, all things considered Sylvie thought it a better plan to spend another day in Vienna, and then fly on to London. She would be there for the visit, and then join her husband in Dublin as well.

Robbie had told her to meet him at the residence since he was running late, and would have to come directly from the Embassy. She arrived on time and was greeted warmly by Pamela Adams. There would be just time for a bit of careful shopping the following morning before the Secretary's plane left Vienna. Robbie couldn't help wondering, as they enjoyed the reception, whether this was a sort of calm before an approaching storm. If so, he wanted Sylvie well away from danger. But where was it?

After the reception, they took a taxi up to Grinzing, the rural district not far from Vienna where zither music, in the best Anton Karas tradition, greeted the visitor from the doorways of dozens of wine taverns. Flowers seemed everywhere, and the evening weather was perfect. It was a memorable way to pass an hour or two, drinking the new wine and listening to rollicking Austrian country music. Then they took a bus back to the Vienna Ring near the University section, and continued on a Ring bus halfway back to the hotel. They walked through the narrow and picturesque streets of Vienna's Inner City to the König von Ungarn Hotel, near St. Stephen's Cathedral. It was really a lovely evening, and became a nice memory of the city of dreams.

CHAPTER ELEVEN -
To Russia With Love

YAWNING AS HE PEERED AT the travel alarm, Robbie mentally went through the morning schedule. It was a sort of countdown, a reentry into the world of diplomatic details following the previous night's enjoyments. Let's see. There was time enough to check into the Embassy for cable traffic, and then to have last minute briefings in the safe room. Everyone would be packed, and their bags would be picked up after breakfast by Embassy trucks and taken to the airport escorted by American and Austrian security.

The Secretary and his party would leave for the airport directly from the Embassy. The Austrians would furnish again their elite national counterterrorist escort, the *Cobra* force. Robbie had missed it on the way in, since he had not arrived with the Secretary's party, but Sam Jardine had told him that it was an impressive outfit. They should be in Moscow by early afternoon, and check into the Embassy compound an hour or so later. Were there going to be airport statements, farewell (here) and arrival (there)? He couldn't remember. Charley Sherburne would. That was his job. Mine, he remembered, was to try to keep this Secretary of State on time - and alive throughout the trip.

"You're muttering. You're *actually* muttering!"

Robbie hugged Sylvie. "Yes, that's what I do. I'm the Secretary's Official Mutterer, so that he doesn't have to worry about things like schedules and briefings and whatnot."

"I'll just bet he does too. Anyway, one of these days I'll ask Pamela."

"It was a lovely night last night."

"Hmmmnnn..."

She watched the bathroom door open once again, and her half-dressed husband emerged and gave her a proper kiss. "All right, run along to the Embassy and play. I'm sorry to miss Moscow and Riga, in a way. I've never been to either place. But I'll look forward to London."

"Save your strength, darling. We'll have some free time there, and we'll have fun. Plus, I rather think we will be going back to Dublin for a memorial service, and you wouldn't want to miss that, either."

She was somewhat mollified. "What will I miss in Moscow and Riga?"

"It should be basically a tough time in Moscow. We're so far apart now, in just about everything. Riga should be old home week. Our Baltic nonrecognition policy means that they love us despite our warts, or maybe because of them. Who knows?"

"'Bye, *chéri*."

"'Bye, *chérie*."

Robbie set the course record for arriving early at Embassy Vienna. Missy Bronson wasn't even there yet! But Ron Jackson from the Executive Secretariat team was, and he brought Robbie the Secretary's cable traffic.

There were several in the NODIS SALADIN series. First, of course, was yesterday's outgoing cable from Embassy Vienna that Robbie had cowritten with Sam Jardine. It summarized the warning from the Dublin source and gave the Department their view that it was disinformation, designed to make the process of protecting the Secretary against a genuine threat that much more difficult. Then they had asked for another look at security measures for the entire trip. Robbie had added the possibility of a reschedule at the end, to accommodate a return to Embassy Dublin in the event that there would be held a memorial service, as the Secretary had requested, for Ambassador Mary McGowan. And, Robbie noted, the State Department had spread their news in a way that protected the Dublin source.

Embassy Riga was full of assurances, and reported that, on second thought, a prolonged trip through the Latvian countryside to Rundal Palace had been scrubbed. They would think of some excuse, but the fact of the matter was that over so much open country, there would have been too many possibilities for a grenade launched ambush, the sort that had been used with such devastating effect in Iraq. The Embassy didn't want to take the risk and neither, on reflection, did the Latvian Government.

"Good old Stan Bartlett," Robbie thought. "He's still on the ball."

Embassy London would go over everything with the British Government, as would Embassy Dublin with the Irish Government. Since both embassies shared their information meticulously with their host governments, that was to be expected. "I just hope they see it all with fresh eyes," Robbie said under his breath.

Embassy Moscow's reply was a bit stuffy, as had been their Russian Foreign Ministry counterparts when contacted in the middle of the night to review security measures, as the Department had requested. What Embassy Moscow seemed to be implying was that it wasn't necessary to give the Russian Government lessons on security. "Well, I'm not so sure about that," Robbie thought. "Being a police state and having excellent operational security could be two very different matters."

There were no public events scheduled as such in Moscow. The one sticking point, it seemed, was the Kremlin reception that evening. With great reluctance, the Russians had gone over the guest list with the Embassy. Their information was however, rather shallow. Of course, a number of the invitees were already known to the Embassy. Several of these were not known favorably, but not for reasons of operational security. Finally, the Embassy had raised questions about six of the invitees, and enclosed that list of names for the Department to vet on a crash basis with the Joint Intelligence Center, the Department of Homeland Security, and whatever other players might be useful in Washington these days. Washington was now doing so more thoroughly, after a quick initial check had proved negative.

"Anyway, there was now a precedent for some more detailed cooperation on operational security," Robbie thought. "Just wait until they remember that and start asking us!"

He turned to other cables. Embassy Dublin, replying to the Secretary's request for a memorial service, replied that the Government of Ireland would be honored to do so. St. Patrick's Cathedral would be the location, and the times suggested, Robbie noticed with a quick check of the calendar, would be possible with some rejuggling. That public event in Latvia that was not being held would save half a day. Should they leave Riga early? But that would mean playing hopscotch with the London schedule. He thought it through again. Diplomats were too complicated, Sylvie sometimes said. They tended to overlook the obvious.

Perhaps the best thing would be to go straight from Riga to Dublin, stay over in Dublin after the memorial service and then return directly from Dublin to London. That way, nothing in London would have to be rearranged, and the schedule fit would be precise. An afternoon and overnight stay in Dublin would be substituted for the second day and overnight in Riga. As to that, the afternoon program had already been cancelled, and the evening was not essential. Ambassador Carlisle was probably just inviting the usual suspects for a return reception. He couldn't know that many people there now, having only been at post for a couple of days. And he himself would surely want to return to Dublin with the Secretary to pay his respects to Ambassador McGowan. As a bonus, the trip would not be extended, so nothing on the Secretary's overbooked Washington schedule would have to be changed either.

Yes, that was a possible solution. It would fit together neatly. He would raise it with the Secretary now for a decision. It was time anyway for his overdue conversation with Secretary Adams about the return trip to Dublin. It would cause some havoc amongst the schedulers and the air traffic controllers, but they were used to it by now. Yes, that might well work out. He would have to call Sylvie about the change of plan.

Really, on these trips there was always too much planned, in too little time, and no, absolutely no room for maneuver. Robbie remembered his father's stories about Secretary William P. Rogers in the early Nixon presidency, before Secretary Kissinger claimed that office. Rogers looked after the troops, his father had said. He recalled that the last stop of their eighteen day trip around the world had been a golfing stop in Scotland, at Gleneagles. And they had seen Robert Burns's cottage. There had even been time for a look at Culzean Castle, where a luxurious apartment had been given by the Scottish people to General Eisenhower.

It had all been grand fun after a most strenuous trip full of multilateral conferences and bilateral meetings. The media had relaxed, and everyone had enjoyed playing diplomatic hookey for a weekend. Surely Secretary Adams would consider some flexibility next time, as a suggestion. If, indeed, there *was* a next time. Robbie recalled that he was on this trip only to fill in during Craig Framsen's illness. Well, it had been a memorable trip, and surely would become more so before it was over.

Robbie sorted the cables in the usual three piles. Then he looked up from his reading and saw that Missy Bronson was arriving. There she went, bustling down the hall towards the Secretary's office. He gave her a moment's head start, then followed her to the office, cables in hand. There would be just time to give her the cables, then grab some coffee from the Embassy snack bar before the Secretary's briefing. He wondered whether it would be watery American coffee or the rich Viennese blend. It turned out to be buyer's choice and, as a bonus, there was a nice assortment of breakfast pastries. "Can't afford the calories here," Robbie decided.

A grim Sam Jardine joined him at a table near the counter. "Anything back yet from our cable?"

"Yes, a good reply, Sam. Several, as a matter of fact. We'll go into it in the meeting in the bubble in half an hour or so." He leaned across the table conspiratorially. "Moscow may be a problem. Otherwise OK."

"So what else is new?" Jardine replied.

Robbie's morning meeting with Secretary Adams started off prosaically enough. Robbie summarized the "nice to know" traffic before getting to the NODIS series that he wanted to spend some time on. There was no need to go into the substantive cables, the matters that the Secretary would be raising in Moscow. That was the business of the Assistant Secretary for European Affairs, who would also have received her cable assortment, and could be relied on to defend her turf in the staff meeting. The same was true for more specialized security questions, which senior specialists in arms control and nuclear proliferation would raise directly with the Secretary, with updates based on their multilateral talks in Vienna.

Robbie knew that for the Moscow stop, he was essentially a facilitator. The substantive diplomatic business for Moscow dwarfed all but four or five other Embassy stops in the world: Tokyo, Beijing, New Delhi, London, and the ones to come, in the new century. But the facilitating was always important. Like many behind the scenes tasks, it was invisible when done properly, and very noticeable when it went wrong.

"Mr. Secretary, you'll note the cable that we sent out last night. There have been replies from the Department, and from London, Dublin, Riga and Moscow."

"I guess it helps to breathe down their necks a bit."

"Yes, sir. Nothing quite focuses an Embassy's attention like the forthcoming visit of the Secretary of State." He summarized the replies. Sometimes that did it, other times not. He waited while the Secretary read the cables.

"Well, I'm glad that Dublin is sorted out. Smiley is on the ball, a good man. What does that do to our schedule?"

"Sir, you may want to bring that up at the staff meeting, to get a sense of what the bureau people think best. I do notice that it would be possible, now that the Riga afternoon excursion has been scrubbed, to go directly from there to Dublin."

"How would that work?"

"Well, we could fly from Riga to Dublin and have a late afternoon or early evening memorial service, then stay over in Dublin, and continue to London the next morning. That would mean that your London schedule is not affected at all. You would, however, miss the second evening in Riga. "

The Secretary thought for a moment. "Yes, I see all that. But why not save a day and fly that same evening to London, after the memorial service in Dublin? You know I prefer to get a good night's rest before meetings, rather than going directly from the airport to another conference."

"Yes, sir. I had thought of that. That would, however, be a very long day, combining three separate places, Riga, Dublin, and London. But there is another consideration."

"Which is?"

"I still have a murder to solve in Dublin. And the extra time would be useful there."

The Secretary was amused. "So what you're telling me, Robbie, is that my presence overnight in Dublin is going to be a sort of diplomatic cover for your Sherlock Holmes?" It could have been a stinging remark, but it was not. Secretary Adams was genuinely amused at the thought. He was also intrigued, the former skilled prosecutor looking over the shoulder of the crime solver.

"Well, it would be useful to have the time, sir. I'd rather leave it that way, if you don't mind, for the time being."

"This gets better and better. All right, Robbie, we'll discuss this in the staff meeting. I mean the scheduling, of course, not your reasons for proposing the change. We'll keep that part of it between ourselves." Robbie nodded in relief. "Better have a cable drafted, to be sent before we leave Vienna."

"Yes, Mr. Secretary." He hurried past Missy Bronson to prepare the cable to the Department of State, and to Embassies Riga, Dublin and London. There was also an information copy for Embassy Moscow, so that they would know that no changes were planned for the stay there. Was that everything? No, not quite. Robbie thought for a moment, and then drafted a personal cable from Secretary Adams to Ambassador Carlisle in Riga expressing regret for the shortened stay there, and the thought that if Carlisle wanted to pay his respects to Ambassador McGowan with the rest of the party, that he would be welcome to join them on Air Force Two for the flight to Dublin.

Those cables were approved and sent after the Secretary's meeting ended. At Sam Jardine's insistence, the six names mentioned by Embassy Moscow were also to be vetted with the allies. Maybe some other nation had something that might be helpful. It was a worried, last minute cable, the sort that usually broke but sometimes made a reputation. Robbie saw no harm to it, and didn't bother the Secretary. He had enough on his mind with the substance of the visit to Moscow. Another worrying detail about his personal security was the last thing he needed right now.

— — — — — — — —

The welcome at Sheremetyevo Aiport in Moscow was stiff and ceremonial. Secretary Adams and Foreign Minister Chernyenko gave their prepared opening round speeches, staking out their ground. There was so much good will expressed in principle that even the most casual observer would have sensed trouble ahead. If there was so much agreement, why did it have to be underlined, and particularly by rather serious looking officials near an airport runway? Even the little girl who had flowers ready for Pamela Adams seemed a bit too rehearsed. But Mrs. Adams saved the day with a warm, genuine smile, and a hug for the startled child and her delighted parents. In the West, Robbie thought, that was going to be the picture on the television news report of their arrival in Moscow. And as he later discovered, it was.

They drove the forty minutes to the Embassy compound in Moscow, at

Bolshoy Deviatinsky Pereulok, in a convoy of armored cars. Robbie went with the rest of the party, while Secretary and Mrs. Adams were driven directly with Ambassador and Mrs. Cruikshank to the Ambassador's residence, Spaso House. That was where the Secretary's reception would be held the following night.

The new American Embassy, finally finished and occupied in 2000, had been the source of great security concerns. The whole world had noticed the bugging devices that riddled the early construction. Meanwhile, the Russians had their new Embassy in Washington, not far from the National Cathedral, on a small hill rise, perfect, it had turned out, for intercepting signals from all over Washington! Well, at least the new American Embassy here, now that the engineers had been over every inch many times, would be bug free, as far as security could determine. It certainly was a vast improvement over the compound that it had replaced, a grim rabbit warren that had resembled a lower East Side slum more than a diplomatic enclave.

Robbie remembered that his father, after a visit to Moscow, had turned down a career making suggestion from the then Assistant Secretary of State for European Affairs that he study Russian, go to Embassy Moscow, and build a career as a Russian specialist. "I didn't join the Foreign Service to raise my children in a slum," he had once told Robbie and his sister Evalyn. "So we didn't go to Moscow."

There were surely the inevitable second thoughts. Was that the assignment pattern that could have led to that treasured goal, an ambassadorship? Frankly, it hadn't looked like it at the time. Even for Moscow, it helped to be political, well connected, and rich. But nobody really foresaw the breakup of the Soviet Empire, one result of which had been the proliferation of the "Stans," new countries on the mapmaking horizon that all required a shiny new American Embassy, and a career man or woman to put up with the heat or cold, the bugs, and whatever else went in the newer world that the Soviet breakup had occasioned. A real roll of the dice, where you ended up, it seemed.

He went over the schedule in his mind. Grim topics in historic places, about summed it up. Well, not entirely. There would be bilateral meetings, of course, with a working session not involving the Secretary at the Foreign Ministry, a dreary semi-skyscraper which resembled a cylindrical package of Quaker Oats, on Smolenskaya-Sennaya Square, and a more extensive and highpowered meeting later in the afternoon at the Kremlin. That was the first day.

The second day had them returning for another, smaller bilateral session between the Secretary and the Russian Foreign Minister. Robbie could hardly conceal his pleasure at being included in that meeting, along with Ambassador Cruikshank, Assistant Secretary of State for European Affairs Donna Palmer, and Russian Affairs Director George St. Cyr from the State Department European Bureau. St. Cyr, a career officer, had had three tours of duty in Moscow, and his Russian was bilingual ("except for the latest anti-Putin slang, although I try to keep abreast of it"). Someday he hoped to be the American Ambassador to Moscow.

Robbie had sought out George St. Cyr during the flight from Vienna. He liked when feasible to get some first hand thoughts about countries they would visit from the experts, and George St. Cyr was certainly that. There was a Russian speaker that Robbie had heard of in the Foreign Service Institute named George Sears - legendary for learning the language thoroughly. Did St. Cyr know him?

"That's me, I'm afraid. I changed my name to St. Cyr, or rather, changed it *back* to St. Cyr. I did some family research after a family vacation trip to Halifax, and found out that we were Acadians, French, not from Scotland at all. It was the brutal expulsion of the Acadians by the British that caused so much misery, the *Grand Dérangement*. You may know it from Longfellow's *Evangeline*. Anyway, I got interested and found that sometime after that ethnic cleansing on our own continent, one of my ancestors had changed the family name to Sears. All I did was change it back."

So many stories in America, Robbie thought. It would be more than fitting to tell this story one day when Ambassador St. Cyr took his oath of office on the State Department Eighth Floor. Robbie wouldn't want to miss it.

Then they had gone over the schedule. High points of the visit would surely be the diplomatic reception at the Kremlin tonight, and the return American reception tomorrow night.

Driving towards Moscow, Robbie was greatly looking forward to seeing Spaso House. All of the diplomatic greats, including George Kennan, who helped guide the Cold War through to a bloodless final conclusion, had lived here. It was odd to realize how many of them were motivated not only by American patriotism, but also by a genuine feeling for the longsuffering Russian people. That was something that Robbie's father had noted about his service in Budapest years ago. "You couldn't help admiring the people while you despised the government that had been foisted off on them," he had said.

Protocol didn't really permit substantive bilateral meetings with the Russians at the new American Embassy, but there would, of course, be press interviews there, as the Secretary sent signals to his hosts by meeting with publications such as *Novaya Gazeta*, whose reporters had been recently murdered. The total number of such murders was rising - over a dozen by now, Robbie remembered. For a highly centralized police state in the guise of a democracy, that either meant implication of the authorities at some level, or a high level of police inefficiency. Take your pick.

There would also be meetings with the Embassy staff and their families, and a session with the jittery resident American business community. They had a lot to be jittery about, Robbie knew, and sometimes, business economics and profitability were the least of it. This was a town in which cutthroat competition sometimes really meant exactly that.

The motorcade neared Moscow. Some Embassy cars peeled off, taking people to settle in to their quarters, while others, such as Robbie, went directly to the Embassy. He had to check on incoming cables. Embassy Moscow, he was glad to see, was all business. The Executive Secretariat team was already up and in harness, for they had followed their usual routine of leapfrogging. One team finished a particular stop of the Secretarty, putting away cables and memos, while the second team travelled on ahead of the Secretary's plane in order to get to the next destination early, and set up shop. That way, there was never any time lost. They were always open for business when the Secretary's plane touched down.

Robbie found his office quickly, and within minutes, had his cable take for the Secretary. If there had been something that urgently required the Secretary's attention, he could have been with him in half an hour at most. Fortunately, there was no such message.

There was, however, one cable of particular interest. As sometimes happened, it was written by a relatively junior officer, and it didn't come from

Washington. The Department of State, in response to Sam Jardine's message, had indeed circulated the list of half a dozen names that Embassy Moscow had provided, as unknown quantities that might require further checking. An alert political officer at Embassy Paris had noticed that one of the names was duplicated on the official guest list for the reception that the French Foreign Minister had held for Secretary Adams. Names can be similar, particularly Middle Eastern ones, but this coincidence was too striking to be ignored.

The Embassy Paris political officer had realized the importance of the situation, and had sent a FLASH message, the highest precedence, flagging what they knew. Embassy Paris officials were meeting immediately with Foreign Ministry political and security officers at the Quai d'Orsay to find out more. To add to the mix, according to Embassy security records the man, Hassan al-Massoud, had been a no show at the diplomatic reception that the French Foreign Minister had given for Secretary Adams. For the hottest diplomatic ticket in town, that was unusual in itself.

Robbie immediately called Sam Jardine to tell him about this latest development. Sam said that with the next message from Embassy Paris, they would probably have enough to know whether to bring this up with the Russians. His inclination was to do so, in any event.

— — — — — — — —

Hassan al-Massoud watched the television arrival of the Secretary of State at his suite at the Moscow Marriott. There was Mrs. Adams too, receiving the flowers from the little girl. The arrival was exactly on time, and there was no reason to think that there would be any schedule changes here. Nothing had been cancelled or postponed. Things proceeded at a predictable pace in Moscow, as they always had done. It was appropriate, after all, that his work be done in Moscow rather than Paris, although such decisions were not up to him. The shock would be all the greater, if Adams could be killed in one of the most densely protected and famous buildings on earth. That would underscore the message that the enemies of Al Qaeda were not safe anywhere. The fact that the Russians were an old enemy of the true faith, and a recent adversary, in Afghanistan and Chechnya, was an added bonus.

He double checked for the tenth time, and there was his engraved invitation for the diplomatic reception at the Kremlin Palace this evening. It was beautifully done, the former communist state evoking the opulence of the imperial Russian past. In the same vein, the reception would be held in one of those grand reception rooms comprising the Hall of the Order of St. George, Georgievsky Hall, a magnificent setting for diplomatic receptions, worthy of the great nation that Russia was, and still is, come to think of it. Al-Massoud smiled in secret recognition of the truth that he alone in this capital knew. He was sure that tonight's events would be as important as the uprisings against the Tsar had been in shaping modern history.

He was ready to meet that destiny. His special fingernail was now charged with the fluid that could not be detected by the clumsy screening apparatus that all nations used, and once it met the target, the veins of the victim, relief and recovery were simply not possible. What happened after that, aside from his own bliss as a martyr, did not concern al-Massoud. Once again he turned from the television set, noting the people that seemed to have a security function. Then he turned off the set, arranged his prayer rug, and said his devotions. For the past week or so, he had returned to the rhythms of the faith of his younger years, with unquestioning devotion, tempered by injustice and suffering, and a feeling of ultimate vindication.

He kneeled on his prayer rug and concentrated. Then he slowly rose and went to his nap, a soothing half hour that would further prepare him for the events to follow. He was asleep within a few minutes.

— — — — — — — —

A second FLASH cable came from Embassy Paris, and Ron Jackson ran to Robbie's office to deliver it. It described Hassan al-Massoud, as a trusted figure from Amman, Jordan, who had been an intermediary in a number of petroleum deals between France and the Middle East. The message gave his background and description, and a recent photograph soon followed. Sam took the biographical information from the message and a copy of the photograph, and ran for an Embassy car, to join the working bilateral group at the Foreign Ministry. He called ahead to Embassy security officers to let them know he would be joining them.

When Jardine arrived, the officers were slowly slogging through details that probably should have been settled days previously. He was given the floor as an American security officer who wanted, once again, to go over arrangements for the reception that was being given by Foreign Minster Chernyenko for Secretary Adams that evening at St. George's Hall in the Kremlin Palace.

Sam put his cards on the table. Who was this al-Massoud, and why was he on the official invitation list? The Russians were outraged. This was their business, after all. Jardine was having none of it. This person had not been properly vetted. What did they know of his background? He did not play his trump card, that al-Massoud was on the official guest list for two host nations during this trip, just yet. But he did go over the background given in the cable.

He showed them the photograph. None of these people actually knew al-Massoud, but they did have a file with them, and consulting it, nodded in confirmation, that this was a photograph of the man that was on the official Russian invitation list.

"Yes, this is the man. It seems that you already are familiar with Mr. al-Massoud," said one senior Russian. "So what is the nature of your objection? Or are Americans just getting paranoid about security these days?"

"I don't think that we have enough information about him," Sam replied in a level tone of voice. Those who knew him would have realized that he was now at his dangerous stage, reining in a savage temper. "There must be something more in your files. Why not share it?"

The Russian backed off. "He has rendered distinguished sevices to our nation in the petroleum market in the Middle East," he replied. "He has proved trustworthy, at the highest level. He has also been quite loyal in his friendship towards our nation."

Jardine played his trump card. "That being so, just why do you think that he was also on the guest list of the French Government for their reception for Secretary Adams? By the way, he didn't show up there. I assume you have, as the French did, his acceptance of your invitation for tonight?"

The senior Russian nodded, yes.

"Then, I think the only reasonable course is to rescind the invitation, and put him in some sort of protective custody."

The Russian snorted. "So that is how things work in your so-called American diplomacy?" He laughed out loud. "Isn't that the sort of behavior that you condemn from every other government on earth, and practice yourselves?"

Jardine's eyes narrowed. "This is an emergency. The life of the Secretary of State is at risk. I have presented to you, after your repeated reluctance to cooperate fully, evidence that merits your entire attention. The modalities I of course leave up to you. But do you really want an assassination of the American Secretary of State to take place in the Kremlin itself, and done by an individual whom you had notice might try to do just that?" He paused and took a long sip from his glass of water. "And then have it known that you did nothing to stop it?"

The Russian shrugged, trying to be offhand. But he was getting just a bit uncomfortable. He began to see the bureaucrat's worst nightmare, the problem that is known in advance and not handled that comes back to haunt and ruin careers.

"I see your point. Ours is not an exact science, not, as you Americans say, by a long shot. By the way, I hope that one of you will tell me what that expression actually means! I think some reasonable measures are required. I propose that we act prudently. There are no grounds for rescinding his invitation. I cannot recommend that we go that far. But we can certainly be careful."

He drummed his fingers on the desk, thinking. Then he pointed to a junior, muscle bound assistant seated at the end of the table.

"You, Dimitri, are assigned to watch Mr. al-Massoud throughout the reception. You are to pick him up at his hotel, the Moscow Marriott, for surveillance, and discreetly follow him to the reception at the Kremlin Palace. From there, you will watch him throughout the reception. Pay special attention when he approaches any of our principals, Russian or American. And keep in closest touch with this American security officer, Mr. Jardine."

"Understood."

Sam Jardine almost sighed in relief. This was at least something. He left the meeting to report to Robbie, who was meeting the Secretary shortly before the bilateral session with the Russian Foreign Minister. He was glad that he had not had to play his fallback card, formally recommending that the Secretary boycott the reception itself.

— — — — — — — —

The bilateral meeting was not going well. There were speeches and replies from Secretary Adams and Foreign Minister Chernyenko. The Russians were, frankly, furious about what they considered the raw deal they had been getting from the West in general, and the United States in particular, in recent years. They were venting, causing what the summary of the meeting would call "a frank exchange of views."

What was unfolding before their eyes was a great power that had lost much of its prestige and authority, and was attempting to reconfigure itself in a newer world. In the back of their minds, one could trace the progression. It had been a mistake even to consider German reunification. That had been one of the very first steps, it now appeared, for the new Western power projections. Independent Kosovo was a slap in Russia's face if there ever was one. Had the West no sense of history? Other provocations were Ukraine and Georgia, possible NATO members. As to that, why can't we protect South Ossetia against Georgian aggression?

They were extremely suspicious of the United States and its motivations. American withdrawal from baseline security treaties such as the ABM Treaty in 2002, and their beginning to construct a global missile defense system was a signal to the Russians that the Americans wanted great power hegemony over this region too. American attention to the Baltic countries, Latvia, Lithuania, and Estonia, that quite obviously Russians still considered part of their own territory, rankled the Russians like an open sore. Not only were they separated from the mother nation, but now they had even been permitted to join that anti-Russian alliance, NATO!

If all that were not bad enough, the Americans had broadened their own defense sphere into Russian strategic territory, with a missile defense shield in their own back yard, with deployments and construction planned in Russia's neighbors! And the excuse given had been Iran! Iran had no nuclear capability, would not have one under the most pessimistic scenario for many years, and could not hope to have a long range delivery system for many years beyond that!

It didn't make any difference that the vaunted American missile defense system might not work. It didn't have to work to be useful, and the Russians were quite capable of understanding the strategy of bluffing. That immense cannon just outside the Kremlin walls hadn't worked either. If anyone had attempted to fire it, the huge device would simply have exploded, certainly killing the entire gun crew, and causing no harm to the enemy. But it had been quite enough to scare away a Polish invading army.

No, this was all a dodge, and a fairly transparent one at that. That was why, with regret, Russia had been required by its national interest to resume flights of nuclear capable aircraft over the world's oceans, for the first time in over a decade, expanding its own power projections once again. And also, with regret, that is why Russia had formally suspended its participation in the Conventional Forces in Europe Treaty that limited Russian military deployments in Europe.

Their message remained clear. If the United States continued its provocations, Russia's next move would be to withdraw from the landmark Intermediate Nuclear Forces Treaty, which had eliminated an entire class of nuclear weapons. This had been the historic first step taken by President Ronald Reagan and Soviet General Secretary Mikhael Gorbachev during their 1988 Moscow Summit. If the Russians went along with their threat and withdrew from the INF Treaty, we were indeed in unchartered territory.

Secretary Adams tried to stop this slide towards a diplomatic chasm between the United States and Russia. He mentioned the common interest in combatting terrorism. "Then why don't you support us in Chechnya?" was Chernyenko's hissed reply. "They are terrorists, and yet, you don't want to condemn them! Muslim terrorists, at that!" The Russian realized from Adams's startled look that he had gone too far. "We also look forward to an American proposal on joint missile defense, as President Putin has proposed," he said. "You don't move things forward by ringing our neighbors with missile systems!"

The meeting adjourned for a break. Robbie saw no real reason for them to reconvene. Perhaps things would go better tomorrow, now that this venting session was over.

This wasn't the best time, but there was no better time. Sam Jardine crossed the room and quickly whispered to Robbie. Then, huddled with Secretary Adams, Robbie and Sam Jardine talked together. Sam reported what he had discovered, what the Department and Embassy Paris had found out, and the eventual Russian reaction. Jardine showed the Secretary a copy of al-Massoud's photograph.

"Good work, Sam. That's beyond the call, I think. Please shadow me like a hawk at that reception tonight. You never know."

"You have my word, sir."

— — — — — — — —

It was a pleasant early evening in Moscow, the sort that makes the visitor glad to be there, and to breathe the air, fresh for once after a late afternoon shower. Hassan al-Massoud had dressed slowly and carefully, savoring each detail. He left his room, and decided not to take the elevator. He walked down three flights of stairs to the hotel lobby.

He was hypersensitive to police surveillance. Yes, there they were, three of them. There were two slouching over by the newsstand. That young fellow reading the newspaper near them seems to be in charge of the detail. There will be somebody else with a car nearby, the motor idling now.

Al-Massoud thought it through. It was useless to try to reason how he had been spotted. It was imperative that he think through the situation, and proceed with the mission. Well, if they are shadowing me, so much the better. They have not already cancelled my invitation, and therefore will not do so. It is a watching brief only. The proof of that is that I am not being detained or arrested. They are just watching. The proof will be, he reminded himself, if they do not snatch me right outside the hotel. If that doesn't happen, my luck will hold good. After all, they have no idea what I am going to do, or if they do suspect something, they do not know how I will do it. And so, they will probably watch me all the way through the arrival, and then, the reception line, when it will be too late. And there is, he reminded himself, no antidote.

He wondered for a moment if the Russians might call off the reception line. That hadn't occurred to him. There was no defense for that. He would just have to wait and see. Of course, if they did do that, it would mean that his usefulness as a special agent was finished. They would pick him up sooner or later, and he would never again have such access to senior targets such as Secretary Adams. Better have a counter plan if that happened.

Yes, he knew what to do. There would be some mingling, even without a reception line. Should he butter up one of his Russian contacts? There would certainly be three or four at this reception. Could they introduce him to Secretary Adams? Perhaps not. But it was worth a try.

Fortunately, his English was perfect. He could also easily manufacture an interesting conversation with another invited American guest, and from there maneuver into a personal introduction to Secretary Adams. That would be even better. For Americans, the urge to shake a proffered hand during an introduction was an irresistible reflex. Yes, as a fallback plan, that would work very well. With some self control he mastered the bravado that almost made him look at his Russian minder. He left the hotel, and the doorman hailed a taxi for him. The men following him, he sensed, were on the move, but keeping their distance. All to the good. There would be no snatch outside the hotel. A few blocks away, he looked into his small pocket mirror and saw the car half a block behind, shadowing him. All in a day's work.

The Grand Kremlin Palace, newly scrubbed since Soviet days, had regained its previous splendor. Attendants by the score, unfurled flags, an orchestra barely concealed in a reception hall near the entrance playing music suitable to both Russia and the United States, it all made for an impressive arrival. So Secretary Adams had remarked to his wife Pamela as they had arrived, following his rest for an hour at Spaso House after the bilateral meeting. She replied that, with Tschaikovsky's music for the background, it really was something of an American holiday.

"But then, I never could see why we always play his *1812 Overture* for our American holidays," she said. "Are we celebrating the defeat of Napoleon, or the victory of the House of Romanov, when we hear that music on the Fourth of July broadcast from the National Mall in Washington?"

"Neither one, I suspect, my dear. It's an excuse for those 76 trombones, and whatever else is in the orchestra, to cut loose for a celebration! Well, here we are." They entered the Kremlin and the Russian Chief of Protocol whisked them upstairs, away from the line of invited guests for the reception line which had already formed. He stopped frequently to answer questions from the delighted Adamses about the history of the Kremlin.

"Have you been here before, Mr. Secretary?"

"No, but a member of my family lived here on diplomatic assignment many, many years ago. He also was on a mission to bring our nations closer together. I wonder what he would think of all this."

They entered the Georgievsky Hall, which was named for the highest Russian military decoration. The room recalled Russian history, and some American history as well, of both rivalry and, occasionally, the attempted management of their differences. It was here that Yuri Gagarin, the first man to walk in space, had received his Hero of the Soviet Union decoration. Here also, Secretary Adams remembered, was where President Reagan and General Secretary Gorbachev had signed the INF Treaty, that seemed now to be in question.

The enormous room was ablaze with lights, which highlighted the lavish interior designs along the walls. The reflections danced along the room's parquet floors, which included many types of Russian woods. The ceiling, twenty feet high at least, was adorned with a series of crystal chandeliers. The floor space of this hall alone was the size of an entire American house. And the walls were decorated with innumerable marble plaques of Russian military units, names incised with gold, whose officers and men had been honored with the Order of St. George.

Pamela Adams remembered what the columnist George Will had once said about the British royal family, that they were in "the magnificence business." To an extent, the Russians had been and perhaps, she thought, still were, or certainly wanted to be. She whispered that observation to her husband. He smiled and nodded, filing it away for later use as one of his stock of well turned diplomatic compliments which cost little and pleased many.

There was the Russian Foreign Minister waiting for them, with his wife, in an antechamber just off the great hall. Ambassador and Mrs. Cruikshank were already there, and translators for both languages. The Chief of Protocol deposited them, introduced Mrs. Adams to the Foreign Minister and his wife, and took his leave. They declined the offer of some champagne. It was a time for small talk, but for once, words failed Secretary Adams. Small talk seemed banal indeed in these surroundings. All things considered, it was a rather awkward twenty minutes. "That's the last time I decline a glass of champagne," Adams promised himself.

Then someone unseen gave a signal and the antechamber door was opened, and the lights from Georgievsky Hall seemed to blaze even more brightly. The Chief of Protocol guided the Foreign Minister and Mrs. Chernyenko, and the Adamses and the Cruikshanks to their places in the reception line. Secretary

Adams looked about and saw that the working American party had already arrived and, of course, would not go through the reception line. There was Robbie Cutler hovering near the beginning of the reception line with Sam Jardine. Some midlevel Russians, probably security men, were not far away, and their faces were resolutely directed towards the guests, who were on the verge of being allowed to enter the room.

Secretary Adams wondered what had transpired during the twenty minutes that they had waited in the antechamber. Then, of course, it came to him. That line of visitors had gone through security. There was of course a double checking of invitations against a master list, then physical security, surely a machine of some sort, and the usual emptying of pockets of keys and wallets. It was time consuming, and surely had not ended by now. But they were beginning the reception line and, by the time they were finished greeting the first guests, the remainder would be through security. Much better than having everyone wait until the entire line was ready, Adams thought. The orchestra was now behind them in the recesses of the vast hall playing sprightly music. Or was it a separate orchestra?

The reception line basically consisted of the Chenyenkos and the Adamses, with the Chief of Protocol and the Cruikshanks hovering in close proximity as a matter of courtesy, to introduce guests as their names were called. They hissed a few phrases to their principals from time to time.

"It's Thornton Goodpaster, Mr. Secretary, formerly from the Joint Chiefs. He's here for Halliburton to explore the commercial prospects of a Caspian Sea cleanup."

"Ah, yes, good to see you, Admiral. Hope it works out. We've got to keep that caviar coming!" Adams had no doubt that the Russian Foreign Minister was doing the same sort of greeting. He always wondered whether his remarks were made to the right person. He didn't remember half the people identified by his aides, who whispered remnders into his ear. After a while, the game become positively enjoyable. Only one turned head indicated that just possibly, the wrong clue had been given, or the wrong wife identified.

The line was just ending, and a waiter hovered near with their glasses of champagne. "Well, this time I'm having one. It's certainly been well earned," Secretary Adams said.

"Hassan al-Massoud," the announcer's voice proclaimed, and Secretary

Adams looked to see a prosperous looking, smiling man of Middle Eastern aspect, whose custom made suit clearly had cost thousands, and pounds at that, not dollars, from an expert Savile Row tailor. "One of our Middle East middlemen, helpful with petroleum allocations," Chernyenko said to Adams through his translator. "A good friend to Russia." He stepped forward to greet al-Massoud.

Al-Massoud nodded to the Foreign Minister's wife and smilingly shook hands with Chernyenko, then turned to the Adamses.

Robbie saw in slow motion what happened next. Al-Massoud extended his hand to shake hands with Secretary Adams. There was a cry of *"NO!"* as Sam Jardine sprinted forth to knock away al-Massoud's hand. But he was already too late.

The earsplitting cry *"Allah Akbar"* echoed through the great hall. Hassan al-Massoud's hand tightened over that of the short, muscular Russian who had charged into the line from nowhere, shoving Secretary Adams aside. Then al-Massoud's own capsule exploded in his throat. In a split second, or was it an eternity, both Hassan al-Massoud and the young Dimitri, faithful to his charge, lay dead on the Kremlin floor.

CHAPTER TWELVE -
The Kremlin Thaws

CONFUSION BORDERING ON PANIC REIGNED. Nobody knew what had happened. The screams of the guests closest to the beginning of the reception line echoed throughout the vast hall. Two Russian doctors on the scene confirmed that both men were dead. One of them shouted that the crowd was to be kept back at all costs. How had the men died? Some poison seemed to be at work. Was it communicable and if so, simply by touch? It was best to keep everyone away.

And then, was this the only attempted assassination that whoever the enemy was had in mind? Nobody could be sure. Two sets of security guards, American and Russian, tried to guard their charges in the confusion. They followed their first instinct and cordoned off the scene.

The press, which had been covering the reception, leapt into action. Wildly Charley Sherburne tried to find Secretary Adams, who had already been shunted off with Mrs. Adams into the antechamber off St. George's Hall where they had awaited the start of the reception just a short time previously. George St. Cyr, the Department's Russian Affairs Director, meanwhile took informal charge for the American side. He had after all bilingual Russian and, from his several tours at Embassy Moscow, knew about everyone worth knowing.

Gradually, with the help of St. Cyr and Sam Jardine, Charley Sherburne put the pieces together. There had been, he found, suspicion on the American side that there might be an assassination attempt against Secretary Adams. Concerns had been brought to the attention of the Russians several times, and the response had been rather grudging. There had been, of course, particular concern about events where there was public participation, which meant this Russian Kremlin reception, and the American reception tomorrow night at Spaso House.

The Americans had put together a list of half a dozen names of concern, that were not fully vouched for, they thought, and had tried to get more information from the Russian side. The response had been grudging and only partly satisfactory. St. Cyr was oddly delighted that it had actually been the French Government which had given further information about Hassan al-Massoud, including a picture. It was that picture that all security men had been issued that evening with, he suspected, a brief to watch the man closely. But they could so easily have prevented his coming to the reception at all!

The second man, St. Cyr found out by listening to the agonized whispers of Russian security agents, was Dimitri Sergeivitch Popolov, a Russian professional security agent in his late twenties. Apparently he had seen something in al-Massoud that he hadn't liked, a gesture perhaps or a glance, that had told him to act. His instinctive gesture had been the right one - to take al-Massoud's extended hand and shake it as though al-Massoud were greeting him.

There was split second timing here. It seemed to St. Cyr that quite possibly al-Massoud's cry *"Allah Akbar!"* had been the spark that had forced Popolov to act. That would never be known now. What was sure is that al-Massoud had, possibly in his hand, some sort of horrific poison, and that he had intended to use it on Secretary Adams. Dimitri Popolov had taken the handshake instead, and paid for it with his life. Simultanously, al-Massoud had bitten his cyanide pill as the handshake began, possibly never fully realizing in the turmoil that he had failed to kill the Secretary of State.

So much seemed accurate, as far as St. Cyr could tell. Meanwhile the press was becoming more clamorous, and someone made the inevitable decision for a very brief statement to the press. Sherburne and St. Cyr, to their relief, found the Secretary shaken but unhurt in the antechamber, and briefed Secretary Adams on what they had discovered thus far.

Secretary Adams, shocked to learn of the death of the young Russian, authorized the Press Spokesman to make a brief statement. Adams dictated and Sherburne took shorthand notes.

"Don't get into the facts of what happened. We don't know enough yet. And I would stay away from any speculation about al-Massoud, and how he happened to be here. Certainly say nothing about the Russians dragging their feet in any way. Say that I applaud our Russian hosts for their speedy handling of this situation, and that I am forever grateful to the brave young Russian security officer, Dimitri Sergeivitch Popolov, who has given his life so unhesitatingly and so valiantly. America opposes terrorism. So does Russia. This cooperation on personal security matters shows that. We look forward to our meetings tomorrow, and will not be stopped, or even delayed, by fanatics such as this poor deluded individual. God rest their souls."

Charley Sherburne and his Russian countepart went to work, giving their brief public statements. Further comment was declined. Emergency medical technicians appeared, as well as the cleaning women that seemed to keep all Russia tidy throughout its history, and within a short time, all evidence of the tragedy had been removed. On an instinct - or was it at the direction of the Russian Foreign Minister - the orchestra at the other end of the hall started to play, something classical, rather slow, unmistakeably Russian, dignified but not dirgelike.

"Let's take our signal from that," Secretary Adams said, hearing the music. He and Mrs. Adams, trailed by a rather befuddled Ambassador and Mrs. Cruikshank, left the antechamber that had again served as their holding room. Together with St. Cyr, they found the Russian Foreign Minister. He clearly didn't know what to expect. After all, he had greeted the assassin personally and had tried to introduce him directly to his target! St. Cyr translated expertly.

"Mr. Minister, we are all grateful to your security service, and especially to the memory of this brave young man, for saving my life. The danger seems over, at least for the time being. Why don't we say to the world that we will not yield to terrorism for even an instant, and proceed with the reception as planned! Surely two great nations cannot have their plans stopped by one miserable terrorist."

Foreign Minister Chernyenko's face wreathed into an unaccustomed smile. He had been kept fully aware of the security concerns of the American side, and had personally dictated the Russian response. The decision to admit al-Massoud had been his. And, of course, he had greeted the man personally! Decidedly there was more to this Ronald Adams then he had thought.

"Absolutely, Mr. Secretary. It is good to stand together, as we did during the days of the Great Patriotic War. They should not stop our plans for an instant. And you are quite right. No one can defeat us when we are together. It will be an honor to continue. And my name is Sergei."

The line of visitors who had not yet been admitted were informed that the reception would continue, for those who wished to attend. That was at the request of the American Secretary of State, in memory of the valiant Russian security guard, Dimitri Sergeivitch Popolov, who had just sacrificed his life to fight terrorism. In his spirit, the reception would continue. Those who wished to enter were welcome to do so.

There was a moment of profound silence, and then something unexpected, and unprecedented in the long memories of Kremlin watchers occurred. The visitors began clapping, the applause continued to the end of the line as the news spread, and the applause was returned by the dignitaries within St. George's Hall. Quickly the line reformed, the music continued to play, now with merrier tunes, the champagne flutes reappeared, and some laughter, first nervous and then genuine, was heard. The reception would continue after all, and everyone there had the feeling of being part of something new, something thrilling and worth doing, which was just perhaps, a new beginning after so many false starts.

— — — — — — — —

The attempted assassination of the Secretary of State, the Kremlin press statements, and the reception held in defiance of the assassination attempt, crowded every other story off the front pages of the newspapers, dominated the radio and internet talk show forums, and stayed prominent for three news cycles. It was a newer world indeed, with both the dangers of terrorism and a gallant reply to it, both on display.

By joint decision, further substantive bilateral meetings had been cancelled. Instead, attention was turned to honoring the memory of the fallen young Russian. The Spaso House reception, however, was still on. That would be as much a thumb in the eye of Al Qaeda as it would be an opportunity to see if this Russian thaw could translate into something substantive and worthwhile.

"Tell me what I need to take up with Sergei then," had been Secretary Adams's instruction to the officers of American Embassy Moscow when he had met with them the following morning. "He and I will have a private session at Spaso House during the reception tonight, or just after it. Just make sure there is good vodka - I'm a bourbon man myself, and wouldn't know the difference!" The Embassy staff were as delighted by that comment, as they were by the fact that the Secretary and the Foreign Minister were now on a first name basis, a real one. Perhaps, this time, it might actually lead to something.

The memorial service to the young Russian security officer, Dimitri Sergeivitch Popolov, held the following afternoon in the former imperial church of the Kremlin itself, then dominated the news, with the rich strains of Orthodox music mingling with the views of commentators explaining the service. A brief biography of what was known of the young hero was broadcast, with pictures of his family and his *fiancée*. The Secretary of State made a short personal statement, translated sentence by sentence by St. Cyr. The Russian nation itself, and much of the rest of the world, came to a halt as the service continued. It was, Robbie later heard from Sylvie, one of the biggest news events to take place inside a place of worship since the wedding of Princess Diana and Prince Charles.

— — — — — — — —

"Was this the best we could do?" A furious Osama bin Laden asked the question, and his mood was not rhetorical. Far from driving the Russians and the Americans farther apart, and demonstrating to both the extent of Al Qaeda's reach, this martyrdom had achieved precisely nothing. No, it was worse than that. They had hoped, by demonstrating the power of Islam in Moscow, to force some sort of accommodation. There were still millions of the true faith within Russian lands, and other nations carved from the old Soviet empire which were largely muslim. These people had to be awakened to their potential power, and Russia had to realize that Al Qaeda was a force to be reckoned with.

It had been a lot to hinge on one assassination attempt, but this really had been something different, in its way, a Russian 9/11. Now the opportunity had been wasted, and worse yet, it seemed to have been turned around somehow to become the occasion for some new cooperation between Russia and the Americans. That was the worst possible result.

And to think, the Russians had even had the audacity to use the occasion for a ceremony at their false church. The nerve of it! That made everything far worse. Bin Laden knew that at one stage in their history, the Russians had even been on the verge of accepting Islam as their state religion. With that, everything else would have followed. An opportunity lost and wasted. And not just the Russians, but also the Americans, seemed to have profited from this botched assassination. He was sick to death of doing videos that promised action and failed to deliver, or even worse, just tried to be menacing with no specific threat announced, not for security grounds, but because they could not reliably deliver. They were not on a mission to frighten children. He went on until his voice tired, and began to be hoarse.

Nobody answered him. The small group of men, cautious in their glances and semihidden in their flowing robes, were sullen and silent. Bin Laden knew that these immediate men were not to blame, or not all of them, but the fact that nobody would speak in answer to his anger did little except fuel that anger. Here he was trying to hold together, and even expand, a revolutionary movement which had gloriously begun, and now when a problem occurred, nobody wanted to take responsibility, defend the action, or even to speak. Timid bureaucrats were even there in Waziristan, it seemed, like so many clerks in a Western European midlevel trade ministry, arguing subparagraphs about a grain allocation.

It was a problem that suggested other problems. In the name of the Prophet, nobody was indispensable, but still, what on earth would happen if he were no longer there to direct and take charge of Al Qaeda? Would someone else be chosen, or would these timid bureaucrats squeeze the life out of their own movement? Physical bravery, he knew, was not the issue. They had all proved themselves, time and again, first against the Russians in Afghanistan, and now against the Americans and their NATO hirelings. But moral courage and some foresight were now equally important. At last, looking around the group, he saw eyes darting, then a knowing expression, and a slight jerk of the head, from his deputy, Zayman al-Zawahiri. His expression had a touch of personal concern. It seemed to say, "Save your strength. It still must be rationed. Enough of it has been wasted for now."

Wearily Bin Laden dismissed the group, called for some tea and something to eat, and sat down with al-Zawahiri to consider matters. He lapsed into silence and they ate. Then he broke into a rare smile. "There was no reason to share our plans," he said. "Those who know will not be fooled," he said finally. "Those who do not know will be in wonderment. In the meantime, it helps from time to time to remind our friends that failure is not tolerable."

Al-Zawahiri shook his head in agreement. "Yes," he said, sipping his tea. "That was a target of opportunity. It would have been spectacular if it had worked. However, the plan was twofold. Let us hope that they are so spellbound by this Kremlin event that they will be less vigilant elsewhere."

They talked tactics, rehearsing the old argument, whether it had been wise or not to permit al-Massoud to receive two diplomatic invitations in two separate countries. That had seemed to Bin Laden to be risky, but al-Zawahiri had liked the idea, which had eventually prevailed. If only the Americans had not trusted their security service, it might have worked perfectly.

As it was, they would not be prepared for a more telling and resourceful strike. This time, the second strike would come in another country. It would build on the sensation that an attempted assassination inside the Kremlin had begun. And it would succeed, decapitating the American diplomatic establishment at one stroke. The effect would be colossal.

They permitted themselves a moment of reflection on that event and its inevitable aftermath. The Americans would strike back blindly, as usual. There would not even be any voice of diplomacy to present alternatives. Even the diplomats would compete amongst themselves to show how tough they were. The effect would cascade. And then, with the inevitable American military overreaction, new recruits would again swell their Al Qaeda ranks, and the day when the crusading Americans were expelled finally and definitively from the land of the faithful would be in sight. "They themselves will do the work for us," bin Laden often said. "It is a matter of leverage and provoking their fury."

He didn't have to add that anything that showed a more measured America did not work to their interests. That is what made this man Adams so very dangerous. Already the news accounts of his first visit to Europe as Secretary of State showed that he was improving ties with the European nations, surely at their expense. Let the Americans open more prisons, not close them.

"They are their own worst enemies," al-Zawahiri would say.

And bin Laden would add, "And so, we must keep them at their worst."

— — — — — — — —

Roger Saunders once more stared at the revised schedule for Secretary Adams's visit to Riga. It was truncated now, since the party would be going directly to Dublin from Riga after luncheon on the day after their arrival. Just a day and a half. It would almost run itself. The decision to skip that afternoon excursion to the Rundale Palace made sense, all things considered. Nobody in their right mind could have guaranteed the safety of a car convoy over so much open country. And a helicopter ride wouldn't have been that much safer and perhaps even less so, with hand held missile launchers readily available on the international arms black market.

"So, Mr. First Secretary, you have news for me?" Inspector Juris Pavlovis, the security expert called in for liaison by the Foreign Ministry, had expected the call. He had actually been on a brief holiday when the request from the American Embassy for a meeting had come. Between the request and the appointment had come the news from Moscow. It had caused jitters all over Riga. If that could come so close in Moscow - *Moscow* of all places - then what could a determined terrorist do here in Latvia! And so the Latvian Government had been almost relieved when the decision had been jointly made to skip that excursion. The fact that the consultation had come at American request made the backing down much easier. The sighs of relief from Riga Castle were almost audible.

Leaving for Dublin rather than staying over a second night in Riga seemed to follow, particularly when the Secretary was going to participate in a memorial service for Ambassador McGowan. Nobody could possibly object to that. What was one more diplomatic reception, more or less? Just crowd those who would otherwise miss meeting the Secretary into tomorrow night's reception at the President's estate at Jurmala, had been his suggestion. It had been accepted, and the new invitations issued, as those for the Carlisle reception had been rescinded.

Stan Bartlett got Ambassador Carlisle's cables first. He had been designated Ambassador Carlisle's executive assistant, and that chore came with the job. It was not that Carlisle needed one. That designation was due to the ego of the boss, not to the volume of the work or the size of the staff. So in the mornings, before he went off to his day job in the Consular Section, he sorted the cables for Ambassador Carlisle.

There was corridor talk at Embassy Riga. There always is Embassy corridor talk, for corridors are a sort of diplomatic no man's land between offices, where FSOs and staffers share possible diplomatic indiscretions. Sharing an office suite with a secretary and reception room between their offices, Roger Saunders and Stan Bartlett often compared notes as their coffee pot warmed.

Bartlett told Saunders that Ambassador Carlisle had reacted rather oddly to the Secretary's cabled invitation to join the party returning to Dublin. He had seemed lukewarm, at best, when Stan had mentioned it to him in his oral summary of the cables. He had remained somewhat hesitant when Bartlett had handed him the Secretary's cable. But then, thinking things over, he had agreed, and sent a reply affirming his attention to leave Riga with the Secretary. His return plans were indefinite for the time being.

— — — — — — — —

George Smiley was pleased and puzzled. The Irish Government had responded graciously to Secretary Adams's request for a memorial service for Ambassador McGowan, and there was so little time left before the Secretary arrived in Dublin once again that much of the fluff could be dispensed with, as the Embassy and the Foreign Ministry, with representatives from St. Patrick's Cathedral, got down to the business of planning for the return visit, and configuring the ceremony itself. This sad and poignant land certainly knew how to plan a dignified and beautiful memorial ceremony, Smiley realized. That was perhaps because their history had provided so many melancholy occasions for doing precisely that.

He hoped that something positive could come of this. As an old Cold Warrior whose idealism had long worn thin, still he was not surprised that in Dublin, not so far below the surface, hope triumphed over bitterness. He remembered something of the history of the first presentation of Handel's

Messiah here, and the hope that Handel's glorious music could do something to heal old wounds. Perhaps it had, at its first presentation, uniting Dublin's leading Protestant and Catholic choirs, and then, over the years, giving comfort to many.

He was puzzled by the assassination attempt in Moscow. Was this the warning that the Irish Government had first conveyed, while the Secretary was visiting Dublin? If so, what if anything did that second message mean, the one that he had flown to Vienna to convey, that implied danger coming from America's own security services? It must have been mistaken or, more likely, it was disinformation, and an indication that the Irish Government's source had been blown. Murdered was probably more like it.

He had seen Dillman at a meeting set up to plan details of the Secretary's return visit. During a break, they had talked briefly and cryptically. Dillman could not be sure, of course, but on reflection his personal guess was that the second message was not from their agent. That meant that their agent was either compromised, or dead.

The return visit would just be for the late afternoon, evening, a stayover, and then the Secretary's party would leave for London. Due to the circumstances, a reception would not be appropriate. Arrangements were made to cater a dinner for the arriving party. They would stay where they had stayed during their first visit. Smiley was brought up short when Bob Starett had questioned that arrangement. "After all, that's where she was murdered, sir." Well, yes, but the gruesome circumstances were not public. And he had checked it out with Robbie Cutler.

Ambassador McGowan's family, her parents and brother, would be arriving the next day, and Frank Sullivan would meet them and serve as their contact throughout their stay. Sullivan, as Political Officer, knew everybody, and had a deft touch for personal conversations. He could include the McGowan family in any appropriate social situation with no awkward pauses, a nice knack to have, which Smiley realized he himself lacked.

Frank had even thought to go over the seating arrangements at St. Patrick's Cathedral, and had asked the family, in his many phone calls with them before they left the States, if they wished to participate in the ceremony itself, perhaps with a few words from the family. They had appreciated the offer, but declined. Sullivan told Smiley not to make book on that, so a final meeting with the Dean of St. Patrick's Cathedral had been made for late the following afternoon, after the McGowans had arrived and settled in.

The investigation itself was spinning wheels, Smiley thought. Robbie Cutler would have a better feel for such things. So, for that matter, would Secretary Ronald Adams, as a former prosecutor. The FBI team and the Dublin police had run down an evaporating sequence of leads. The murderer had not left fingerprints. For a messy crime, it was fairly meticulous. They had carefully taken all of Ambassador McGowan's telephone records for days before her murder, and run them down, to no great effect.

They had also, with surprising discretion, investigated her romantic side, and discovered only one lead, aside from the sometime escort from O'Bryan's Cabinet. This other man was James Desmond, who raised thoroughbred horses on his farm in Killarney. That fit in with her Kentucky background, Smiley supposed. Ambassador McGowan had once visited this Irish thoroughbred for a long weekend during an Embassy holiday. Shown pictures, the Phoenix Park staff had identified him as the gentleman caller that one day, months ago, when Ambassador McGowan had also given the staff the day off. Shooed them away, in fact. But Mr. Desmond had been home in Killarney at the time of the murder. He seemed quite genuinely upset by her murder, and offered any help that he could give. Of course, he would be present for the memorial service.

Smiley had no knowledge of police or investigative ethics, if any such field could be said to exist. He did wonder about the false news concerning the Ambassador's death. Why on earth invent a cause of death as though two potential murderers had been involved? If it worked and helped solve the crime, this deception would be, if it was remembered at all, not just forgiven, but applauded. Nothing succeeds like success, in every field. Meanwhile, all persons who had been known to be anywhere near Phoenix Park on the day of the murder had been questioned, in an ever widening circle, whose waters seemed to grow ever more shallow. The police inquiries had even spread to airlines, and to car rental agencies. So far, nothing even potentially interesting had turned up.

From the security side, the return visit would practically run itself. Irish security forces would be out in unprecedented force, given the failed assassination attempt in Moscow. A private murder case was one thing -

and there was certainly no indication that the killing of Ambassador Mary McGowan was anything over than a private case - but a terrorist assassination was something else. They were not going to get away with it in Dublin. Every detail of the visit was checked and rechecked. Half the national payroll seemed to be going to the plainclothes agents who would haunt the streets, bars and byways of Dublin throughout the brief visit. Not to mention those who would help crowd the aisles of St. Patrick's Cathedral itself for the memorial service.

— — — — — — — —

Embassy London was used to high level visits. They could almost recite the drill in their sleep, which was the problem, DCM Alexander Smithson told his staff. "I don't believe that Embassy Moscow did their job. If they had, no damned Al Qaeda killer could have gotten within a country mile of Secretary Adams. So listen up! You are no longer in London. You are in some dank sweaty third world capital where assassinations are routine. That's the way I want you to look at it, every step of this visit. Question everything. Look at everything with fresh eyes. Every half hour, no, every *quarter* hour ask, 'Where is Adams?'"

He sipped his coffee and went on. Nobody spoke. When Smithson was in this frame of mind, nobody would have dared to interrupt. He glared at two officers in the back of the conference room, who had dared to chatter during his monologue. They started taking notes, as they realized that the third world was exactly where their next assignments were likely to be if anything went wrong. The Department of State knew of Alexander Smithson, and his first person telegrams to the Bureau of Personnel were legendary.

"So, here we are in the third world. Look at the visit that way. We are not at Parliament for an address: we will be at some godforsaken lodge in the godforsaken bookdocks. This isn't the British Army and their security services protecting the visit. It's somebody else, an outfit which has been heavily infiltrated with bad guys. Think. *Think* of what can go wrong. Take positive countermeasures. Run through the planning again, as if you had never done so before. Then do it all *again!*"

He nodded, out of steam. The class was dismissed for the day.

Joshua Running Deer, Political Counselor, had direct responsibility for the visit. That meant that he was senior enough to be in every meeting, but not quite senior enough to be able to affect policy for the visit. But he should be able to spot any flaws. That was, he suspected, why Smithson kept glaring in his direction during the visit. That wasn't really a sign of dislike, Running Deer told himself. At least, he hoped not. People who stood up to Smithson, did their best and met his standards, after all, had had promising careers. Smithson was not just a holy terror. He was a benign terror, who looked after his officers and saw that they were suitably rewarded when things turned out well.

People who knew that Foreign Service legend said that Smithson was this generation's Phil Habib. It remained to be seen whether his crusty demeanor would ever catch the attention of the top political brass in the Department, let alone that of the White House, as Habib had done with Ronald Reagan. That had been a high water mark for the Foreign Service, Running Deer had always heard. And that was an era that must come again, if the United States was ever going to have a foreign policy that matched the abilities of its diplomats.

But for now, the midlevel political appointee Clausewitz munchkins in State and Defense and Lord knows where else who dominated the national security reporting in the Washington *Post* still tended to run things. They probably got in the political route because they couldn't pass the Foreign Service Exam in the first place. His mood turned sourer. Why should these idiots be running things, anyway? It just leaves a mess for us to clean up. Not to mention what it does to the countries concerned, including our own.

Running Deer was convinced that political appointees couldn't tell one foreign country from another, and cared even less. In his experience, they would defend to someone else's death their right to be egregiously wrong. All the Foreign Service's painfully acquired wisdom of foreign languages, regions, religions, history, and national interest, let alone any humanitarian concern, never seemed to matter. Just get your office, stake out your territory, speak sharply, subscribe to whatever carried the day as the approved domestic political line, do your quota of damage, then resign and write your memoirs before the harm you have caused becomes obvious.

Joshua Running Deer's Bell Curve for Political Appointees, he called it. He had special scorn for the last bunch. Their "preemptive" war? The last and only American President to have tried that was Jefferson Davis at Fort Sumter in 1861. That hadn't worked out so well. He scoffed. "Neoconservatives" indeed! What they espoused was not new and it was certainly not conservative. Edmund Burke had begun modern political conservative thought. He believed in the value of history and traditions. He would have scoffed at the idea of imposing a political system on another country. And he would have clearly predicted the horrendous cost of trying to do so. As with Davis, the initial mistake would be corrected by better men after great suffering.

But maybe, just maybe, with Secretary Adams it might be different. He might get things off to a fresh start. He had, after all, made an excellent reputation as Ambassador in Paris. And he seemed to be starting off well now. Well, better make sure that this visit was a successful one, Running Deer told himself. At present, he defined "successful" as Adams surviving London, while Running Deer survived Smithson!

Let's see. It would be for two days. There was the arrival, now from Dublin. It would be at roughly the same time that they would have come in from Riga, although that should have been an hour or so longer flight. Running Deer guessed that meant that the Secretary liked to sleep in whenever he could. Clearly a man with a well developed sense of priorities. No talks at the airport, good. Security he would go over separately.

Drive to the Ambassador's residence, and briefings there. Running Deer was in charge of the briefing book, which meant that he would probably be shuffling papers to whoever was in charge for the Executive Secretariat. There was the name, Ron Jackson. He didn't know Jackson, but everyone knew or wanted to know Robbie Cutler, the diplomat and crime solver. He hoped there would be time to get acquainted, but frankly, that was doubtful.

There would be luncheon at the residence, then an afternoon meeting with the Brits. Their hosts would offer a reception that evening of course, an early one, and then they were all off to the Globe, at the Secretary's express wish. He hadn't seen it and wanted to see a play there. Fancy that!

The second and concluding day featured two events of importance. The Secretary was going to appear at Runnymede for a ceremony at the Magna Carta Memorial. He would return from Surrey and then offer a late luncheon at the residence. Then, in an extraordinary gesture, he would appear as a guest at the House of Commons, with leave to offer remarks on relations between the United States and Great Britain. The Secretary and his party would fly home in the early evening, arriving at Andrews Air Force Base somewhere around midnight Washington time.

All right, Running Deer said, it's a nice schedule. Now, just suppose I were a terrorist. They would get maximum value out of an explosion at the House of Commons, of course, but I think we can trust the Brits to have handled that end of things. There hasn't been a credible mass assassination attempt there since Guy Fawkes just over four hundred years ago. That leaves the residence, the Globe, and Runnymede. Embassy security could be trusted to monitor the residence, and for all that, the two guest lists were all well known people. Nothing to bother us, as happened in Moscow and might, he had heard in the corridors, have happened in Paris. Well, the French were like that. Charming, but neither particular nor careful.

It was time to check out the Globe and Runnymede personally. A visit to that wonderful theater, and then a nice afternoon in Surrey, would be just what his jaded spirits required. He called the Foreign and Commonwealth Office, American desk, and spoke with the officer handling security arrangements for the trip, Audrey Turner. They arranged to meet at the Globe the next morning. Yes, she had been planning on going to Runnymede again (he winced at that "again") in the afternoon, and they might just as well have a look together.

Duty done, Running Deer read through his briefing book once again, telephoned around the Embassy for last checks before his foray to the Globe and Runnymede, and left for the day. Might as well have an early evening. It was going to be a crowded final day tomorrow. And who knows what last minute requirements Smithson might level at him if he stayed at the Embassy too late!

— — — — — — — —

Spaso House gleamed for the reception. This imposing house, named for the Russian Orthodox Church that anchored one side of the square where it is located, was designed by renowned architects and finished just in time for the Russian Revolution. It had been the official residence of the American Ambassador in Moscow since diplomatic relations between the two countries had been resumed in 1933. It was about one mile from the Kremlin, far enough away to have been countryside in centuries past, but close enough to have allowed for hunting and other excursions. It was said that centuries ago, the area had been inhabited by the Tsar's falconers. By now, it had long been absorbed by the urban agglomeration of Moscow.

"Well," thought Robbie, "if their spirit still hovers near us, we could use some of the falconers' hunting prowess tonight." He had been fascinated with falconry ever since seeing it practiced in the rural back country of southwest France. The raptors and their handlers seemed to come from an earlier age. Well, they did, and they all had a sixth sense about hunting, both as hunters and as prey. Not that Robbie really expected another assassination attempt. If there had been anything planned, it might more logically and with more devastating effect have been as a follow-on to last night's failed attempt in the Kremlin Palace, adding terror and rumor to attempted murder. No, they had shot their bolt with that one, in Moscow at least. Or so it seemed. Or so it was comforting to believe.

It was an ostentatious house, built on a lavish scale for a wealthy Russian merchant in 1914, during the days when nascent Russian capitalism was poised to take off, and never got the opportunity. What happened to the original owner, Nikolay Vtorov, depended upon which legend you chose to believe. He could have been shot by a red revolutionary in 1917, or perhaps he made a deal with the new Soviet rulers and stayed on for a while. Nobody was quite sure. But according to the brochure that the Embassy had prepared for visitors, the transformation was soon made from the Soviet Central Executive Committee's official entertainment center (Robbie read that with a shudder) to the American official residence.

A ballroom wing was added a year or so later, an odd detail, Robbie thought, for a building in the Soviet capital at the beginning of the worldwide Depression. Still, the extra room had come in handy for receptions over the years, and certainly would do so again this evening. There had been some celebrated entertainments given at Spaso House over the years, including the first performance of Sergei Prokofieff's opera *The Love for Three Oranges*, conducted by the composer himself.

So this is where Harriman, Bohlen, Thompson, Kennan, Kohler and Robert Strauss had lived and conducted our national business. It had all ranged from the Soviet Union days, throughout the Second World War (when the resident American community's evacuation to the Volga city of

Kuybyshev far to the east had been arranged here, the community being convoyed to the Moscow railroad station from the premises), the Cold War, and then the transition, for the better one hoped, to today's Russia. During that long period, Spaso House had so far hosted five American presidents, three vice presidents, and, with the visit of Secretary Ronald Adams, ten secretaries of state.

The Spaso House interior was suitably imposing. It was built on a grand scale, with a main hall 82 feet long, boasting a domed ceiling from which hung an enormous chandelier of Russian crystal. Going through the front entrance, flanked by ceremonial flags, one was drawn into the compelling Chandelier Room, its paired white columns adding space and dimension throughout the room, while ceiling decorations in patterned light blue and green added space and graciousness to the hall. A staircase led upstairs to the private quarters, which were on a more personal scale, with moulded ceilings, chandeliers and carved wooden doors.

Other public rooms dazzled the visitor, as they were intended to do. Robbie had arrived early to take a good look around the premises. The music room was an enchantment in rococo style, while the State Dining Room, which seated dozens of diners around a long table curved at either end, fairly shouted Summit Visit. The table was set, for decorative purposes, including stemmed glassware for wines. Robbie's Bordeaux instincts kicked in, and he wondered which wines would be served for dinners here. Surely not French at the official American residence, but California perhaps?

He played with the idea of the wines that he might serve, if he ever had the opportunity to host a state dinner here. For white wines, perhaps an assortment from Chalone Vineyards? It was fun imagining. He next mulled over some excellent American red wines. For the meat or game courses, a Robert Mondavi Cabernet Sauvignon Private Reserve or the *Opus One* that Mondavi had jointly created with Baron Philippe de Rothschild of Château Mouton Rothschild would show well. So would a Heitz *Martha's Vineyard*, or a Stag's Leap Cask 23 Cabernet Sauvignon.

He decided upon Christian Moueix's *Dominus* from Napa Valley. The winemaking of Château Petrus was evident in those bottles, at a fraction of the price of that elusive Pomerol. *Dominus* was also a favorite, he recalled, of the *Washington Post's* Ben Giliberti. He and Ben had agreed that those Frenchmen really knew how to transfer their magic to California!

And over there, steps led to the Ballroom Annex, the first floor addition where receptions, including this one, were held. Clearly it would hold several hundred guests comfortably. Robbie also located the comfortable and imposing library, where Secretary Adams had told him that he would have a more private chat with the Russian Foreign Minister. It was hard to be too private when neither man spoke the other man's language, but the attempt seemed worth making, and the timing certainly would be right.

Robbie checked his watch, and went to the Ballroom Annex. Security was already in place, both at the entrance to Spaso House, double checking spotters along the main hall, and then at the entrance to the Ballroom Annex itself. Shortly Secretary and Mrs. Adams appeared, descending the staircase from the private quarters with Ambassador and Mrs. Cruikshank. They enjoyed a private glass of champagne and some *hors d'ouevres* in the library, and then emerged to take their places receiving their guests, with Assistant Secretary Donna Palmer. Robbie, Sam Jardine, and George St. Cyr floated near the receiving line, ready to intervene with an introduction, or some strong arming if that proved again necessary. Robbie suspected that Foreign Minister Chernyenko's entourage would include some of the late Dimitri Popolov's security associates, no doubt eager to defend the memory of their dead colleague.

An orchestra at the rear of the Ballroom Annex started to play its first melody, and the guests began to arrive. When they had gotten this far, the mechanical security procedures were finished. All that was left would be whatever those assigned to security duties within the room thought necessary. The Russian Foreign Minister and Mrs. Chernyenko were amongst the first to arrive, and at Secretary Adams's invitation, they joined the reception line.

Guests entered and introductions went smoothly, and Robbie noticed, without handshakes. Nods were the fashion of the day. There had been no security instruction to that effect. It had just happened that way. The first guest to arrive had been announced, and then had nodded at the Secretary, who had nodded back. That had been copied by all succeeding guests. Whether it was for security or, as Robbie suspected, was meant to be a silent tribute for Dimitri Popolov, nobody could have said. It just seemed right under the circumstances.

The music played, and the pool press correspondent, who was covering the event for the entire press party that had come with the Secretary to Moscow, having pulled the long straw and therefore had the luck to join the reception, conducted his interviews discretely. It was as normal a diplomatic event as could have been expected in Moscow. Drinks and *hors d'oeuvres* were continuously served. There was amongst the principals an absence of conversation. Neither George St. Cyr nor his Russian counterpart was called to translate more than half a dozen times, and not once for anything really substantive. That would all wait for the private drink in the library, Robbie was quite sure.

And so, eventually, that moment came. The few hours of the reception were passed pleasantly enough, and ranking guests began to take their leave. With a beckoning nod to Ambassador Cruikshank, Secretary Adams left the room, and his wife and Mrs. Cruikshank retired to the private quarters. Robbie entered the library with George St. Cyr, who had his notebook ready, and Assistant Secretary Palmer. Foreign Minister Chenyenko entered the library with Ambassador Monolov, Head of the Americas Department of the Foreign Ministry, an English speaker who had served as Russian Ambassador to Washington not that many years previously. A waiter took the last drink order, filled it, and left.

Now was the time for careful understanding. George St. Cyr had his hands full with both interpreting and notetaking, so Assistant Secretary Donna Palmer graciously took over the notetaking detail. Foreign Minister Chernyenko began by conveying the formal regrets of the Russian Government for the lamentable events at the Kremlin Palace, an apology which Secretary Adams turned aside with an expression of thanks for Russian security, especially for the young man who had saved his life.

"It was a time when we worked togther, Sergei. Just as we worked together in the war against Hitler. When we find the will and resources to do so, much good is accomplished. When we do not, we expend our treasure in needless competition, and neither side benefits."

Chernyenko shrugged, in an expression, St. Cyr would later tell them, not of indifference, but of peasant stoicism in the face of greater, uncontrollable events. Then the Russian sighed, and went off into what was, for him, a rather long speech. He talked about his youth, about the promises of social justice under communism, about the many sacrifices that the people had made, and specifically, about his own family, which for three generations had lost its most talented members to the world of the *gulag*. He uttered a profound sigh, then started to speak again.

"We hear this from the West time and again, Mr. Secretary - Ronald. And what happens? Russia trusts, and then is invaded, or chopped into bits, as it has been now yet again. You didn't appreciate our Warsaw Pact, but it did serve a purpose, after all. Now look at where we are. Our former allies - or at best, countries that we could control militarily - are now in NATO, an armed camp whose purpose was to destroy us. Has this changed? Look around you, from where we are sitting, right this minute. We are surrounded by enemies, equipped by the United States.

"And there is the United States, your country, withdrawing from the arms control treaties that made a reduction in what you used to call the 'balance of terror' possible. One after another, beginning with the ABM Treaty, you withdraw. I must say that your president has begun to talk the language of arms control. Perhaps it will be a new beginning, with some logical limitation instead of a new arms race. Why not? What is the mighty United States so afraid of? But I must tell you, when you speak of terrorists and surround us with armed enemies, we suspect the worst.

"And so we must do the same thing. We react the same way that you do. We follow your lead in this madness. We must, MUST, protect our Russia. And recently you even threatened us with missile bases on our very borders. Why not share them, if you are really worried about Iran, as you say?"

Chernyenko sighed again and took a long pull at his drink. Then he spat out something in Russian, and Ambassador Monolov took his empty glass and went to the door, in search of a refill.

"Sergei, I came on this trip to change things. On our side, there has been too much given away to fight terrorism that restricts our liberties. I have been talking about that side of things with our allies. There will be no more Guantanamo, as you know. There will also be no more secret prisons, or extraordinary rendition. That all makes matters worse. I will be setting this forth in full before the British Parliament in a few days."

Chernyenko nodded, appreciating the confidence, of what he already knew. He hoped that Adams would not suggest that it was time for Russia to handle its internal problems in the same easy, benevolent way. He prepared a reply along those lines, but it wasn't needed.

Adams continued. "But that isn't enough. It also isn't enough that Russia and the United States remain in a state of suspicious hostility. We have to begin to work together. I want to propose just that. I think that we have to see where, once again, we can start a fruitful relationship. We did it in the days of the Soviet Union because we had to. We should do it in the days of the new Russia because we want to. I think our peoples want that. I certainly think that in the spirit of the gallant young man who died yesterday, we can both certainly try."

Chernyenko's drink arrived, a real one, not a small Waterford crystal glass one-third full, but a tumbler full to the brim. He drained half of it at a gulp.

"Yes, I like that. It is prudent, respectful, and new. It might even work."

He went on, in so low a tone that St. Cyr had to lean forward, dropping to his knees to catch the Foreign Minister's words.

"And I saw what you did last night. You did not tell the full truth of what happened, why the assassin got so far. I appreciated that. You gave us full, and undeserved, credit. By the way, several people in our ministries are now answering questions on the matter, who the man really was, and how he could have gotten so far. We will share details with you as they emerge."

He frowned, and left the details to Adams's imagination. He finished his glass, and Secretary Adams continued, his voice rising emphatically as his sentence marched on.

"My idea is to bring our conversation to the attention of the President. It will be with the idea of inviting your government at the highest level to Washington, say within a year. Let us then and there negotiate our differences, the grand ones that separate us, if we can. We surely are smart enough to do that. Do we have the will?"

Chernyenko rose, a trifle unsteadily, and answered with a toast.

"To Dimitri Sergeivitch Popolov!"

The Americans rose and answered, "To Dimitri Sergeivitch Popolov!"

And so the reception ended.

PROLOGUE (PART FOUR)

I, John Donne, Cantab. Dr., Dean of St. Paul's, London, this sixth day of June, in the year of Our Lord 1630 and the reign of our dread sovereign Charles I the sixth year, do inscribe this memorial.

Well, that is how I thought it might begin. How stuffy I have become, how removed from the Jack Donne who wrote early poetry. I should begin, if this is discovered in an age that remembers nothing of Dr. Donne, whether Jack or John, by introducing myself. I am the lawful son of John Donne, ironmonger of Bread Street, that same street where sits the Mermaid Tavern, often the late meeting place for our Friday evening suppers.

Well, as to that poetry, man does change, and man must a living make. I circulated my poems by hand, you know, and many years passed before I would authorize them to be printed as part of my collected works, with my essays and sermons. I did this as I was being awarded my present position as Dean of St. Paul's, and many did object. Forget or deny that unruly past, they would say. Cut off your right arm, would have been more like it.

Preferment is not an easy thing to come by. Some say it was my marriage, the joy of my life and my undoing as well, that cast my lot in life. You have all heard about it. *John Donne. Ann Donne. Undone.* Yes, my father-in-law Sir George More, secretary to Thomas Edgerton, Lord Keeper, did wish to make an advantageous marriage for his daughter and yes, I was cast into prison for that usurpation of his right. But Ann and I lived through it all, although the years spent and the time wasted climbing that slippery ladder of preferment were hard. Very hard. It is not an easy thing to live, when the Lord Keeper undercuts you at every turn.

But when you have become, at long last, a deserved royal favorite, life's sweetness is manifest. James I, that fine and subtle soul, was rightly convinced that religion should be my ultimate calling.

My *Pseudo-Martyr*, published in 1610, paved the way. I rightly condemned the useless pursuit of Catholic martyrdom. The days had passed, or soon would, when a good Englishman could not keep his faith. And so, the Oath of Allegiance could be taken in full faith, as prescribed by James I. It was time to move forward and mend the nation, preserving our beloved England from foreign dangers and inner cankers. I was gratified by my preferment. But it should be known that the book was written from conviction. I had, after all, previously twice turned down the offer to become a clergyman.

Now, some profess to see amusement in this matter of "Doctor" Donne. It was neatly done, after all. Cambridge buckled at the thought, initially, but then the Vice Chancellor yielded to the persuasive force of his Majesty's logic. So shall it ever be.

Mine has been a life of the times. We were raised in the old faith, Henry and I were. My brother died for it, at Newgate Prison, of filth and neglect, a victim of the times. We are of the family of Sir - or should it be Saint? - Thomas More, after all. My Mother Elizabeth went abroad rather than forswear her religion, only returning towards the end of her life. She and my stepfather saw that Henry and I were well if irregularly schooled. We went to Oxford when I was just twelve. Why so early, you ask. Was I that precocious? Well I was, if you must know. But the point was to secure an education before the age of sixteen, when the oath had to be taken, an oath that would have blackened my conscience. We studied at Hart Hall and then, as sixteen approached, we went to Cambridge for another year.

But I sometimes fancy that my real education began after those formal studies were at an end. Not that I neglected my studies, you understand, even for the ladies. Well, not all of the time. Fortunately I didn't need a great deal of sleep and my mind was as sharp and focussed as my needs. I learned the great languages of the past with relish. And when it came time to look about for employment, something on the practical side, I formed my lifetime association with Lincoln's Inn. First, their student: finally, their chaplain.

And there was the great assault on Cadiz in 1596 with Lord Essex, and the less glorious expedition to the Azores the following year. My associations did not always help me, and I suspect that was particularly true when the net was cast, following Essex's failed treasonous revolt against Her Late Majesty Elizabeth.

And that was not the only time when things could have gone badly astray. That terrible Gunpowder Plot in November, just twenty-five years ago. The authorities were energetic, and rightly so, in rounding up sympathetic Catholics, many of them, it now appears, not remotely connected with the plot to blow up Parliament and with it, the entire government and royal household. But then I was on the continent, with Sir Walter Chute, in 1605 and 1606.

I had other interests beyond our borders. I put in an application to join the Virginia Company in 1609, but it did not succeed. I even had some experience with the world of diplomacy under James I, as secretary to Lord Hay in 1619, our mission to Germany being an attempt to stop hostilities and reverse the fortunes of the King's Protestant son-in-law Frederick. All to no avail. But I did find the use of a diplomatic cipher quite useful. I toyed with putting this letter to the future in cipher, but decided not to do so. I shall merely hope that its time to be made public has arrived.

I have had a long association with London, and now for nearly a decade, with St. Paul's. I remember the older days vividly, and it is my earnest hope that peace will prevail in this country, and that religion will not divide us further.

In my *Holy Sonnets* I talked about religion and spiritual loneliness. I must confess here to this unanswering sheaf of paper that I always looked for the sense of community, of wholeness and oneness with God. That was part of the old religion, regardless of what zealots thought. I hope it will be possible, through tolerance, to look to a sort of universality of religion, as a universal yearning that attracts us all, no longer dividing us, and certainly, no longer the excuse for hatred, war and murders.

I was ruminating about these matters, as an old man will do, when an even older man, my own son-in-law Edward Alleyn, came to see me in strict confidence. After the sad death of his wife Joan in 1623, he married our eldest daughter Constance. It was perhaps not an ideal match. She was 20 and he 57 (to my 51, come to that) when they were married. But she is content.

Alleyn is now a prosperous man. He was an actor, as you may know if you are reading this close to our times. He performed many roles and rather well for Marlowe, and was said to inspire, as a journeyman actor, the "rude mechanicals" celebrated by Will Shakespeare in *A Midsummer Night's Dream.* You know, Snug the Joiner, Peter Quince the Carpenter, and the like. Probably just a sop to the groundlings, but they seemed to enjoy it. Alleyn, who founded the Fortune Theatre, even says that he will give money for a school at Dulwich.

I would not, however, take him for a classically learned man. And so when he came to consult with me about the matter of Marlowe's desk, I was amazed, first by his story, and then, by the contents of the desk itself. For Marlowe was rightly alarmed by his summons to Deptford some thirty-seven years ago, that dreary and stinking port section of East London. He feared a Walsingham plot, and he was quite right. He died there, and the circumstances put about are barely credible. No, I fear the man was murdered. Was he murdered for this desk?

Whatever the truth of that might have been, before he left, Marlowe left his desk with Alleyn, his chief actor, for safekeeping. He also told Alleyn that in times of extreme peril, if he feared for the safety of the desk, he was to bring it to Will Shakespeare. What an extraordinary instruction that was! It is almost as though Marlowe and Shakespeare, the greatest dramatists of the age (I exclude Jonson) had made a pact of some sort.

Well, that contingency never happened. And what Alleyn said to me was most affecting. He said that he was a trustworthy man, but not a learned man. And he was right on both counts, as Master of the Bears and Bulls, a good fellow, not a scholar. He said that he had always suspected that there were papers that were hidden in the desk. He hoped that I would now take charge of the desk and its contents.

There was no question of turning down such a request from my son-in-law. It showed a certain dignity of place, and respect, I thought. I promised to take care of them, and thanked him for his confidence. He seemed relieved. He had fulfilled his promise well. The papers that I found had not been seen for thirty years, I am sure of that. If they had been, they would have been confiscated and surely destroyed. I praise God that they have been delivered unto my hands. I will do what I can to secure them for a future that is more worthy of them.

But in an old man's excitement I am not telling things in the rightful order.

First there was in the open drawer a paper notation of the maker of the desk in 1592, *Petrus Quintus fecit,* probably put down by the carpenter himself, or by Christopher Marlowe. The same paper had another Latin inscription, *Per Lux Lunae ad Veritatem.* I thanked Alleyn and he took his leave, with rather a sense of relief. His knowledge of Latin was slight, and he had clearly feared that the sentences had been a coded reference to the old religion.

I noticed the crescent moon shape on the rear lid of the desk, presumably the *lex lunae.* I pressed the crescent in several spots, and then as I had suspected, a hidden drawer slid up. It was empty except for one paper, containing two sentences in Latin. It was clearly from the Vulgate, St. Jerome's authorized translation of the early books which became the Bible. My library at St. Paul's is extensive, and the reference to the Book of Isaiah was found quickly.

The meaning seemed obvious. Something further that was also hidden was referred to. The trick was to find it. Clearly Alleyn himself, if he had a shrewd intimation of the first hidden drawer, had no idea that there was a second, deeper one. How could he? He had suspicions, surely, and he was fearful, but he had no Latin to understand the mystery. That was, as Marlowe his master had clearly intended, his margin of safety. But until we met, he had not dared share knowledge of the desk with anyone. Not after what had happened to Marlowe at Deptford.

I did the obvious things, to no result, and then thought a moment. The second drawer referred to by inference from the Isaiah quotation might well be unhinged in a special way. Could that be only when the first drawer was itself open?

At length, this worked. The second hidden drawer opened. In increasing excitement I held a document written by Marlowe, which told of his mission for Walsingham, his regrets and sense of doubt, and of the document with which he had been entrusted. And so I then found the *Confiteor* of Baron

Crecy, thus introduced by Marlowe. It is the holiest and most poignant discovery of my life.

The *Confiteor* states Baron Crecy's sins and hope for eternal redemption. First there is a sort of confession in the Latin. Then, in the French of the time, and in surprisingly legible writing, the document also traces his salvaging of a precious document relating to the Shroud of Turin. That earlier document, in Latin, is also present, partly in the now ragged original, partly copied by a later hand, preserving for our eyes where age had done its work.

I was not unacquainted with Baron Crecy's subject matter. I saw the Shroud displayed in Turin during my travels throughout Italy with Sir Walter Chute in 1605. I had even preached a sermon at St. Paul's on the Shroud, noting how it did retain the dimensions of the Saviour's body and evidence of His wounds.

Now, here was Baron Crecy's testimony of how he had taken the Shroud from Constantinople followng the revolting and unChristian sacking of that city in 1205. He was a Knight Templar and could not, in conscience, leave the Shroud there, to be destroyed. And so he had taken it with him! His account, infused with his ardor and religious feeling and hopes for redemption, rival, no, *surpass* anything in our own language on that most precious subject.

But there was more. The document that he salvaged, partly copied and partly still in the original, was a detailed Latin chronology about the history and travels of the Shroud. It had been taken from Jerusalem by Saint Helena, mother of the Emperor Constantine, and after centuries at Edessa, found its home in Constantinople.

I was moved to learn that with the permission of the Emperor, in a rare example of Christian unity, the Shroud had once accompanied the Crusaders back to the Holy Land from Constantinople. The presence of the Shroud, it had been hoped, would inspire the Crusaders against King Richard's most skillful enemy, Saladin himself. Alas, Saladin's skillful leadership prevailed at the Battle of Hattin in 1187, and Jerusalem was again lost to the Crusaders.

Then, astonishingly enough, came a miracle, stated to be sanctioned by Salah al-Din himself. Provided that never again would the Shroud be misused as a battle pennant, Saladin authorized its removal back to Constantinople, as an object precious to Christians. Saladin noted that their own Muslim holy writings mentioned Our Saviour and Mary with respect. He said that it would therefore be a crime against Allah for the Shroud to suffer damage or to be destroyed.

There is much more, that scholars may marvel over. But beyond that, there is a holiness of inspiration here. It must be safely preserved for the future. And so I replaced the documents as they were entrusted to me, in their respective compartments. I hope that Marlowe's desk and its precious contents will now remain secure until they may be safely and reverently revealed. I add this memorial to those of Christopher Marlowe and the Baron. They should just fit within the second hidden drawer.

Signed and dated: Dr. John Donne, Dean of St. Paul's Cathedral, London, June 6, 1630.

CHAPTER THIRTEEN -
Climate Change in Riga

SECRETARY ADAMS DICTATED SOME NOTES to Missy Bronson in the private compartment on Air Force Two. Waving an air kiss, Pamela had left the compartment to give him some time alone for his briefings and memos. It was not a long flight from Moscow to Riga. There was just time enough to take stock of what the trip had accomplished, and what needed follow through.

Charley Sherburne stuck his head in the doorway. "Got time for a talk, Mr. Secretary?"

"Sure, Charley. Come on in."

"I'd like a heads-up on London. It seems that something important is planned, and I ought to have the background. It's a matter of credibility with the press."

"You're right about that, Charley. Frankly, we want to start a new era in our diplomacy. We started from a pretty low ebb. But this President has some experience in great power politics, and a healthy midWestern respect for the views of others. We think that what the country really needs is not so much new daring initiatives but a return to the principles that had been proven right again and again throughout our history. Afraid this is beginning to sound like a lecture, Charley, and I was never much good at that."

"You're doing just fine, sir."

"I know that the really bad stuff has stopped. There have been internal

Justice opinions, and court decisions as well. But others might think, that could change back again. We want to lay down a marker, the President and I. That's what this is all about. Frankly, it is all so basic that it sounds like a page from the Boy Scout Manual.

"The United States of America does not torture people. It does not kidnap people and, averting its eyes, send them off to be tortured elsewhere. It does not create prisons where the law is said not to reach, and it does not hold prisoners in secret. It obeys the Geneva Conventions, and does not hide behind shallow legal opinions that rationalize torture and exempt the President and his agencies from civilized behavior. It stands for the lady in New York Harbor.

"Now, torture was not only practiced, but tolerated. For a former Army JAG officer like me, that was sickening. And America's law schools for the most part didn't even weigh in. In sharp contrast, I remember Erwin Griswold, Dean of the Harvard Law School when I went there. His book, *The Fifth Amendment Today*, had reminded an earlier generation, about the Constitution and the Fifth Amendment during the shameful McCarthy era.

"What do I get now from the Law School? They just send smug, self-satisfied fundraising letters.

"Anyway, that's the background. This is never going to happen again. Saying so publicly will make that crystal clear, and raise the stakes for any President who might be tempted to do this. We're closing Guantanamo, fixing Bagram, and setting up proper courts martial for trials. We are in touch with the Red Cross, the ICRC, regarding all these matters. And here's something else. We are going to move forward with the International Criminal Court. President Clinton signed that treaty and then shelved it. We're going ahead with Senate hearings. Am I making myself clear?"

"Loud and clear, Mr. Secretary. And it's an honor to be on board." He almost saluted as he left the compartment.

Well, Secretary Adams thought, this President was a decent person, a Jerry Ford. Thank God! Now, the repair work overseas was begun. At least, we can stop adding recruits to that cause by our own policies! This trip was a start to that process. What they all wanted and needed to hear, was that America was back. It was a message he believed in. If the politicians and talk show pundits at home didn't understand what was going on, perhaps the enemy overseas already did. They were targetting him as being particularly dangerous. He hoped they were right.

Then the image came to him of the young Russian, Dimitri Sergeivitch Popolov, who had sacrificed his own life to save him. The determined look on the Russian's face was like that of a runner stretching to reach second base before the throw. But this was far from innocent. Then, he remembered what he had heard about the manner of death, that fingernail needle and the poison that it masked.

Was it too early to ask that smiling steward for a martini? Clearly, yes. He frowned.

Dublin, Paris, Vienna, Moscow. Now they would soon be in Riga for their shortened visit. Secretary Adams was sorry about that. He wondered if smaller countries felt that they were taken for granted. It would be good to spend more time with them to prove the contrary. Then back to Dublin for Ambassador Mary McGowan's memorial service. That was a fine idea that Robbie Cutler had had. He wondered for a moment what else was up young Cutler's sleeve. Yes, there still was a murder to be solved. Or had Cutler already solved it?

Secretary Adams called the Baltic Desk Officer up to his cabin and asked for a briefing. The young woman was suitably nervous. Bet she could use a martini too, Adams thought. No, better not start the rumor mill by offering her one. It is early, after all. He couldn't imagine that early martinis with the Secretary of State would do much for her career. And what if she didn't accept!

She turned out to be a very attractive young woman of Lithuanian origin, Beatrice Jurmalis. She was well dressed, bright and proud as punch to be on this trip. She had had one trip to the region as part of her orientation, and could, if he so chose, be full of helpful information about Estonia, Latvia and Lithuania. He let her lead the briefing through generalities about the region, including the familiar and still inspiring story about the refusal of the three Baltic peoples to accept their forced incorporation into the Soviet Union after the Molotov-von Ribbentrop Pact, that division of the Baltic nations and Poland between two ravenous tyrannies.

It was all very nice for background, and interesting. But what was the main item of business for their stay?

"Well Mr. Secretary, as you know, the Latvians are heading the European Union now, so they will be involved in the next G20 Summit. Ireland is involved too, as Prime Minister O'Bryan is President of the EU Council. You briefed him in Dublin, I understand."

Secretary Adams shook his head, remembering. So much had gone on that he had almost forgotten discussing G20 issues in Dublin. At every annual meeting of the G20, the gathering of the world's economic superpowers, which now included Russia and a broad selection of regional powers, the multinational European Union also played a role. How much of a role, he wasn't sure. But it was always a good idea to get American ideas across and understand their point of view. Small nations liked being consulted, and were flattered at being courted by the American superpower.

Well, diplomacy was back now, thank heavens. The Latvian Government didn't have German Chancellor Angela Merkel's political clout, but they were still going to get the Adams treatment. Their economic woes were part of the larger picture, a danger sign for everyone.

Then he recalled that their visit to Riga was being cut short, in order to fly to Dublin for Ambassador McGowan's funeral. That was fine and logical from the standpoint of Dublin, but how would that go over in Riga?

She was unambiguous. "They are so pleased to see you, Mr. Secretary, that it is already smoothed over. Frankly, with one assassination attempt already on this trip (she blushed - did he think she was predicting another one?) they probably are even more pleased that you are still coming to Riga. And of course, the reason for cutting the trip short, the Dublin funeral for Ambassador McGowan, is well understood. I hear it was national news here, too, her murder. No problem, sir."

"What was cut out, or rearranged?"

"Sam Jardine from Security consulted with the Embassy, which weighed in heavily. The result was that the trip to Rundale scheduled for tomorrow afternoon was cut. It's too bad in a way. Rundale is a fine castle manor house an hour or so south of Riga. It's a beautiful place, something of a national showpiece, finished by Catherine the Great for a court favorite. You were going to drive out there for the Latvian President's reception. But it is highly insecure. It is the country's breadbasket, flat country, sugar beets, wheat, and increasingly, rape seed for the oil and now for biodiesel fuel as well.

"It is also ideal country for an ambush, flat and open. So there were sighs of relief about cancelling that visit. Security wasn't thrilled with that trip being scheduled in the first place, sir. I suspect that the shortened visit, and the need to consolidate, gave them the opportunity to do what they had wanted to do all along."

"Yes. Well, one or more shaped grenades aimed at our cavalcade, as they had been doing in Iraq, would have ruined anyone's day."

"Yes, sir. Anyway, now the reception will be held at the President's estate in Jurmala, on the seaside. It's not far from Riga, maybe a half hour drive. Our cavalcade can surely make it in less. The final guest list will be at the Embassy. There must have been a flurry of last minute planning when Latvian Protocol had to switch locations, but they are used to it. Most protocol offices are, I hear. Actually, the reception is not only switched - it now incorporates what would have been the American return reception, which Ambassador Carlisle was to have hosted the second evening, when you will now be in Dublin. It's all put together for tonight."

He thought for a moment. There was an opening, but it wouldn't be fair to ask her about Rudolphe Carlisle, if indeed she had heard anything about him. He had after all just arrived at post and so it was too soon, and she was too junior. It was better not to put her in the false position of either gossiping about her superior, or finding a way out of the conversation, which would end their talk in a minor key.

"Well, that seems like the main points. I appreciate your reminder about the Latvian connection with the EU and the next G20 Summit. It sounds like a lot of rearranging of our schedule was involved. As you say, though, I suppose that protocol people are used to it. I'm glad that Ambassador Carlisle went along graciously."

He smiled. "It will be fun seeing Riga. I've always wanted to visit the Baltic nations - all of them. But I hope no pyrotechnics are planned. I had enough of that in Moscow." He nodded in dismissal.

"Yes, sir." She smiled and left the compartment.

He sighed for his lost youth, just for a moment, and then more deeply, because the need was more pressing, for the martini that he hadn't dared to order. You may think what you want about being Secretary of State, but if it stops you from ordering a nice Bombay Sapphire martini shaken in fresh ice when you really want one, the job is overrated!

— — — — — — — — —

Ambassador Carlisle greeted the Secretary and his party graciously. The reception that he had planned to give the following evening was off, now subsumed into the larger event that the Latvian President would host that evening. But Carlisle had substituted an informal luncheon, catered at the best restaurant in Riga, with Executive Chef Eriks Pavlovskis, often the chef for official national dinners, supervising every course.

They were just over three dozen, visitors and Embassy staff and spouses. Carlisle greeted Mrs. Adams with genuine warmth. "You weren't on the trip to Dublin, Mrs. Adams. I suppose that Paris was irresistible?" Mrs. Adams was charmed, and said so. "Yes, I just couldn't miss this chance to return to Paris with Ronald. And I must say, as a former ambassadorial wife, I know how hard these functions are to carry off well. This is enjoyable and light and fun - and you don't even have a wife to help you arrange things. How is that possible?"

He smiled in reply, and greeted Assistant Secretary Donna Palmer as she joined them. "The truth is that Assistant Secretary Palmer left me a great staff. Her DCM and now mine, Stanley Gunderson, runs things very well, and even lets me think I am calling the shots. Which is pretty darn shrewd for someone who wanted Stockholm and got Riga instead. The rest of the staff is also helpful. Roger Saunders, the Political Officer, is good, but he's new here. He arrived just after you left, Donna, I think.

"And that young Consul, Stan Bartlett, has a real future. He told me that he served with Robbie Cutler, your husband's aide, Mrs. Adams, at the Consulate General in Bordeaux a few years back. He is a first rate talent. He sees problems coming long before they actually get here. A good man. But it was Gunderson who knew about this restaurant and the fine young chef, Pavlovskis. I hope he isn't considering a career in diplomacy, like his brother. That would be a real loss for gastronomy, if you ask me!"

Assistant Secretary Donna Palmer made polite noises in acknowledgement. She was delighted to revisit Riga. If truth were told, she would happily have remained here for a decade if the White House had not called with news of her diplomatic promotion. As it was, she was sorry that the visit would be cut short. She had hoped to find a few hours for shopping in Old Town Riga, one of her favorte pastimes. Despite the shortened visit, she had made and rearranged in her mind a short, indispensable list of shops to see. Christmas wasn't that far away, after all.

Consul Stan Bartlett and Robbie Cutler, meanwhile, were conferring in low tones at a corner table. "Yes, Ambassador Carlisle arrived in the middle of the night. I met him at the airport. He said that was the only available convenient flight. I find that very hard to believe. He must have had some shopping to do, or maybe just fell asleep at Heathrow and lost track of the time."

"Well, he was wide awake when I saw him at Heathrow earlier that night. I was flying back to Dublin from Paris on an errand for the Secretary. And there, in the international departure area, in a sort of holding zone, was Rudolphe Carlisle, big as life, reading the newspapers."

"Did he see you?"

"Not only did he see me, he made a special effort to make sure that I saw *him*. That's what struck me as a bit odd at the time. We were acquainted, of course, but not particularly friendly. Although, I must say, since I've had this job, I've developed all sorts of interpersonal skills I never knew that I had. Just everyone wants to be friendly."

"Unlike those of us who knew you before, I suppose."

"Stan, I suppose you are right about that. We didn't picture any of this when we were serving at the Consulate General in Bordeaux."

"Not a calm place then, not with the Basque terrorist ETA group making life miserable, and taking its chances at murdering you."

"And my sister Eva. Thank God we stopped that in time. You, Stan, in particular. If you hadn't yanked me out of the conference in Paris to get back to Bordeaux, I'm not sure what might have happened. I don't even like to think about it. And yet, now, that level of violence, the car bombing, seems almost quaint. The enemy now is much better equipped and more fanatic."

"You mean Al Qaeda?"

"Yes. I think they were responsible for what happened in Moscow. And it darned near worked. Thank God for a trained and brave Russian security man. If it hadn't been for him, the Secretary would not have survived. I'm sure of that. It's a grim business."

"Why are they after Secretary Adams?"

"I suppose because they want to show that they are in charge of the terrorism game, having failed so frequently lately. And they probably see his very reasonableness as threatening to their sick agenda. If what Adams has started continues, their recruiting base will start to dry up. At least, I think so."

"Was the McGowan killing part of all this?"

"I don't think so. Maybe it was supposed to look like that. Maybe not. But I suspect that it had nothing to do with Al Qaeda."

"Is that the real reason why you are going back to Dublin for the memorial service? To try to flush out her killer?"

"You're pretty sharp, Bartlett. No wonder I recommended you for promotion."

"And what do you hear about the security here, Robbie? Do you really think an attempt could be made here? I mean, you see all the highly classified stuff. Sorry - didn't mean to pry."

"No, that's OK. We have to talk about this stuff sometime. The route that was cancelled for tomorrow was ideal, I think, for a terrorist attack. And I'm sure that they have the means to carry it out. A flat meadowland area for an hour's drive each way through the countryside is just perfect for that purpose. Shaped grenade charges, deadly and hard to defend against. An attack could happen just about anywhere, and we have to be prepared for it. And I don't underestimate the risks. Terrible. But, you know Stan, I don't really think Riga was on their list for an attack. I think they want something far more showy. Like 9/11. No offence to Embassy Riga, but that is why the attempted assassination in the Kremlin would have been so spectacular."

"As an assassination would be in London! What is the program for that visit? I hope that Embassy London is taking a very hard look."

Robbie looked hard at Bartlett. He had to switch gears, past Dublin. Perhaps the real threat was yet to come after all. He would call Ron Jackson of the Executive Secretariat, who had the duty in the Embassy code room while they were having luncheon, and have him cable Embassy London for a revised copy of that schedule immediately

Bartlett continued his thought. "And we in the meantime would be thinking that their real attempt had failed, and just possibly, lower our guard?"

"Right as usual, Stan. I guess I'll have to rethink the rest of the trip. Thanks."

— — — — — — — —

Joshua Running Deer and Audrey Turner crossed the Thames, and looked over the Globe Theater on Bankside in Southwark with fresh eyes. Joshua decided that he would, once again, put in a recommendation against the Secretary taking in a performance at the Globe. He also knew that since the fact of the Secretary's attendance at the performance was now public, that it would be virtually impossible to cancel the stop. In the first place, Secretary Adams was a genuine theater patron who enjoyed the stage and had often taken in performances of the *Comédie Française* when he was Ambassador in Paris. For another thing, any cancelled appearance would forever be measured against the background of the Royal Family's heroic public appearances during the Second World War. It might also cast aspersions on British security capabilities. No, cancellation was not possible. And so they went over the theater minutely, even checking where the special security guards, men and women, would cover any possible approach to the Secretary and his party.

"It is a grand theater, one has to admit."

"Yes. Thanks to Sam Wanamaker," Audrey added. "He was surprised, so the story goes, that Shakespeare's original Globe no longer existed. But he had the will and the money and the clout to put up a replica. A very nice job, I think. It was the first time a thatched building had been permitted in London since the Great Fire of London in 1666."

"Yes. I enjoy going. And standing for the performance, as the Elizabethans did, is the best way to enjoy the performance. It really gets you into the spirit of the production. Cheapest way, too, at five pounds a ticket."

"Well, aside from entering and leaving the theater, Secretary and Mrs. Adams will be exposed to the public throughout the performance. They will be in the best seats in the house, the middle rows of the Upper Gallery. Also, the Swan, the restaurant portion of the Globe, will be closed off for the use of the Secretary and his party. It's not very far from their seats. Our people can cover them pretty well, and do so unobtrusively."

"What do we do when the Secretary decides to try the standing room in the courtyard? I just know he's going to want to do that! He's such a theater buff, and he won't take no for an answer."

"Just go with the flow. He'll get tired after a while and go back to the gallery. No chairs are allowed in the courtyard, not even cane seats, those 'shooting sticks' as we call them. And they say there are no exceptions."

They had stopped at the galleried George Inn for luncheon and pints of ale. "You were an inspiration to many of us," Audrey said. That was unexpected. He was surprised that she would have heard of him at all. But then, he was still surprisingly insulated from celebrity.

She was in her early thirties, some ten years his junior. Until now, they had just been colleagues, occasionally meeting privately for followup meetings to compare security notes on the visit. They were both sure that this visit would go like clockwork. All the more so because of what had happened in Dublin and, especially, Moscow.

"Well, I was thrilled to come to Oxford," Joshua replied. His Rhodes Scholarship had been the occasion for coming here, and his Seneca lineage had created a welcome. He then embellished his rowing credentials, honed at Georgetown. Rowing for Oxford, he had contributed to a defeat of Cambridge by the largest margin in a quarter century.

What happened next, when for the first time he had first rate athletic coaching in track, had created a sensation. "I thought everyone could do this," was his modest and sincere reaction when he returned an errant discus by hurling it further than the English national champion who had been exhibiting his skills at Oxford. Joshua had been standing outside his college when the discus had landed nearly at his feet. Wearing street clothes, he had hurled it back in the direction it had come from, with natural grace and great force, and a nice spin, which, he said later, had seemed the natural way to get good distance. A disbelieving photographer and an unanswerable tape measure showed that his discus throw had probably equalled the British national record.

The Olympics inevitably followed, as a member of the United States team, "since I cannot compete for the Seneca Nation." The fact that he was the younger son of the paramount chieftain of the Seneca Nation compounded the sensation. He became, in the eyes of the press, "Chief Running Deer," and he was hailed as the greatest natural track and field athlete since Jim Thorpe. The press accolades were right, for a change.

"I'm curious," Audrey said. "And forgive me if I'm intruding. But what led you into the diplomatic service?" He replied with a toned down version of his real motivations.

His decision to join the United States Foreign Service had been noted with approval by his legion of followers. Here was an Indian who was not going to fade away, they thought. He is entering an honored profession, and we'll follow his career from time to time. So we won't have to feel sorry for him once the cheering stops.

But rapid promotions followed, and here he was, young for a Political Counselor, at one of the most desired posts in the entire Foreign Service. His bosses had learned along the way that he was intelligent, and had the refreshing, rather undiplomatic habit of saying exactly what he thought. When he didn't, he seemed to be holding extended silent coversations with himself. His colleagues didn't know whether that was an Indian custom or not, so they let it alone. He was respected, admired, and often alone in a crowd. But he loved the English nation and made no secret of that. He was thrilled to live in London amongst so many friends, and to be the Political Counselor at the American Embassy, and said so. And he had developed an agenda.

Joshua Running Deer was determined to show the world that his nation could still hold its own in any arena. No handouts, gambling reservations, or tokenism. He was pleased to be a diplomat, but not grateful for the opportunity. He knew as the State Department team that inteviewed him for his Foreign Service Oral Examinations did not, that diplomacy was a natural career choice for a Seneca. They looked at it instead from the standpoint that the Foreign Service, once a privileged WASP sanctuary, was now graciously broadenng its breadth to include talented people of all backgrounds. The State Department made rather a show of doing so, Joshua realized, as though they were doing assimilated minorities a huge favor.

From his observation, they had a lot to learn about diplomacy. He doubted that many had any idea how skilled his own people had been at the profession.

The Iroquois Confederation of Five Nations, including the Senecas, had first banded together to assure mutual survival before the Europeans arrived in North America. They were joined by a Sixth Nation, the Tuscaroras from North Carolina, who had migrated north when the British settled in their country. As the Iroquois Confederation, the Six Nations had outmaneuvered the British and French for years before yielding to sheer numbers and territorial aggressiveness. No less an authority than Benjamin Franklin, America's first diplomat and Joshua Running Deer suspected, still the best, had cited their skill, asking whether his fellow colonists could not band together and parley as skillfully as did the Iroquois.

And, of course, the Iroquois Confederation's custom of hearing speeches and then adjourning for a day before replies were made, was a way to respect the speakers. You really were supposed to listen to what the other side had to say, and think about what you had heard before replying. Today's diplomacy, with fallback positions arranged far in advance, and final conference statements readied before the meetings had even begun, was no improvement over the past. That really ensured that no real attention would be paid to what the other side had to say.

Joshua Running Deer tried to put his people's customs into practice, as far as possible. Not that he could run his own Political Section at Embassy London with a full degree of democracy. But he had stuck with an old Iroquois Confederation custom, making sure that the most junior member of his section spoke his opinion freely. That opened up debate and participation remarkably well.

"So you see, Audrey, diplomacy is a natural profession for me. At least I think so. What the Foreign Service thinks about all of this remains to be seen."

"I think they are lucky to get you. What's next on our agenda?"

Joshua saw her faint blush. "Well, I can't imagine that the Secretary's more private venues will pose any security problems beyond the usual," he said. "Not after Moscow. Your people and ours have been cooperating fully. So the airport arrivals and departures, the receptions, the Foreign Office meeting, even the address to Parliament, all of that seems covered. I'm not thrilled by this Globe outing, but he'll do it anyway. You can count on that. I may be missing something, but at this point, we've been over the schedule so thoroughly and so often, that unless someone in the service itself, yours or ours, has been turned, I think we have done our jobs."

"Which leaves Runnymede."

"Exactly. Which leaves Runnymede."

— — — — — — — —

The Latvian Foreign Minister welcomed his guests, and settled back for a routine meeting with Secretary Adams, doubtless designed more for domestic benefit back in the United States, where the Baltic-American vote was still significant in the rust belt, than it was for diplomatic business. He looked benignly across the table at Secretary Adams, Assistant Secretary Palmer, whom he recalled from her residence in Riga, and now, Ambassador Carlisle. There were a few others on the American side, some doubtless for the press, and also a staffer or two, to pick up the pieces in case a principal misspoke.

It was too early to have formed much of an impression of Carlisle. He had the requisite surface amiability. What had he been? A political fund raiser for the White House, surely, that was how such things worked, he had learned. He was not personally very familiar with the United States. Foreign Minister Veloutis had passed his exile years, as he called them, in France, and so his English, although good, was not fluent. His appointment had even been interpreted by the sniffing media, desperate for news, as a Latvian step away fom the American orbit. It was nothing of the sort. It was taking care of the boys, Latvian style.

After the usual polite formulas, Veloutis put on the simultaneous translation headgear that was always available and very rarely used. If he caught it correctly, Secretary Adams was actually addressing the issue of global warming and climate change. "Excuse me, Mr. Secretary, would you make that point again? This apparatus was a bit slow to warm up."

"Of course, Mr. Foregn Minister. I was saying that the United States wished to congratulate your country in the leading role you have taken, after such a brief membership I might add, in the European Union. You will be participating in the next summit meeting, I believe."

"Yes. We quite look forward to it. The issues are important." What the devil was Secretary Adams up to?

"Well, we think that it could be a landmark meeting. We are also looking forward to The G20 Environmental Ministers meeting that will precede the summit. Our EPA Administrator will of course be attending. He will have instructions to seek practical ways to cooperate, so that working together, we may combat the threat that global warming raises to our welfare, to the planet, and to the environment generally.

"The President, as you may have heard, is a rather devout person. The stewardship that we have here and now is a matter of great concern, both for mankind and - I almost said 'even' - for the creatures with which we share our environment. We want to do what is feasible to make sure that we understand the problem, its dimensions, and what steps should be taken to address these problems. They are serious, of large scope, and they will not go away."

Foreign Minister Veloutis was not sure that he had heard correctly. He almost hit his headgear as though it was emitting static. Then he took it off and looked Secretary Adams in the eye. "If this means what I think and hope it means, Mr. Secretary, this is significant news indeed. What steps do you have in mind?"

"Well, in the first place, a clean environment should not be the pawn of politics. We all want that, or should. Within a few weeks, the President will be addressing our National Science Foundation. The address will highlight the importance of honest and thorough research. And it will mean that research papers will not be subject to political vetting by this Administration. Ever. We will hear what the best scientists have to say to us. And as far as the G20 is concerned, we will work with you to find solutions, if they are possible, to the great problem of global warming and environmental pollution that we face."

"Does that mean you are rethinking the Kyoto Protocol?"

"No. It still does not fit our needs. We are not yet convinced that mandatory targeted reductions in carbon emissions are the way to go, although they seem to have been helpful to some extent. It may be possible to find other means. Let the scientists tell us. But beyond that, we fear that if the problem is not handled expeditiously, it can only grow worse."

"Could you be more precise, Mr. Secretary?" Veloutis could hardly believe his ears.

"Yes. Petroleum technology has to come of age. It must be made cleaner. And we must bear in mind that the alternatives, in that not too distant day when oil reserves will begin to run low, are even worse. I think of the tar sands of the Canadian province of Alberta, for example. These immense reserves could be a boon to everyone. Or they could be a curse, as the landscape is fouled beyond redemption for the extraction of oil from that source. It will be far worse for the environment than the petroleum extraction that we know about. Light years worse. If nothing is done, we will look back on twentieth century methods as the good old days.

"In short, that seems to be the way that we are now heading. We must have a plan, and we must work together. Starting now. Will it be difficult? Of course. But who would have thought that with international cooperation, the problems of acid rain and ozone layer depletion could have been addressed? As for acid rain, I'm no scientist, but it seems that scientists studying the problem have figured out ways to curb or dilute the emission of sulphur compounds, which created the problem. And with the ozone layer, for years after the problem arose, there was handwringing. Then concerned governments set to work, and the Montreal Protocol some twenty years ago set a standard for cooperation and good practical results - results which should guide us now.

"The problem is hard. Doing nothing is far worse. Anyway, we'll disagree as we go along from time to time, you can be sure of that. But we will do our best to contribute to solving the problem, or at the very least, to managing it. That's my sermon for today."

"Mr. Secretary, I must say, your words are welcome."

"Well, Mr. Foreign Minister, it's not all going to be smooth sailing. But I am very afraid of the consequences of continuing to ignore the problem, or seeking to define it out of existence. These matters pose a serious security threat too.

"Just what will happen if global warming, to raise one example, changes patterns of agriculture so much that people cannot feed themselves? Who will manage the large scale droughts that we may see in the future? What happens to all of us, and let nobody imagine that the rich nations will somehow be immunized. The world does not work that way. The language of terrorism may be political, but it is rooted in the economics of despair. That must not happen. The problem is that if it does, we will be facing something that nobody wants to see. That's putting it in the mildest possible way."

"Mr. Secretary, what do we say about this now? Can we make your views public?"

"You are right to be cautious, Mr. Foreign Minister. For the time being, I would prefer some generalities. Mr. Sherburne - he nodded towards Charley Sherburns, who was furiously taking notes a few seats down on the American side of the table - is skilled at dealing with the press. Let them know that the subject has been raised and is seen as important by both sides. But, you'll understand, I can't preempt the President, and certainly not before he delivers his speech to the National Science Foundation. So I think for now we should keep the tone positive and the specifics muted. By the way, I will make sure that our minutes of this meeting, which you will have before we leave Riga - reflect everything that has been said."

Foreign Minister Veloutis smiled in pleasure. He was going to enjoy the job, after all. It just might be an era to remember. Certainly he would always recall with pleasure the visit of Secretary of State Adams to Riga. Perhaps that new American Ambassador, Rudolphe Carlisle, had brought good luck. He had the look about him of someone who was born lucky.

— — — — — — — —

Which was almost exactly Carlisle's mood. He had gauged his welcome by Secretary Adams, and it was warm and sincere. He hadn't had an opportunity to talk with Robbie Cutler, but that was peripheral. There was no need to emphasize their chance meeting at Heathrow. It was in the background, ready to be used in case of need. He felt safe here in Riga. It was almost a sanctuary. He was beginning to have second thoughts about the Dublin trip. Suppose it was a trap? And yet, he had agreed to go. It would look very odd indeed if he backed out now. There was no reason to do so, and after all, the next few days in Riga would be anticlimactic anyway, after Air Force Two had lifted off. No, all things considered, it was best to proceed as planned, but cautiously.

Carlisle looked through his portable daily calendar and reviewed the past several weeks. He saw Kelly Martin's name, and remembered their outing to the Lakes of Killarney. It would be fun to see her again. And, quite possibly, she might have the lay of the land. She might have heard of something regarding the investigation. It would be a natural thing to ask about. Yes, there was her cellphone number.

On a whim, he called her. She answered, pleased and surprised to hear from him.

She wanted to know how he was settling in, and what was life like in Riga. They chatted on, and he gave her a rundown of the ceremony at Riga Castle where he had presented his credentials.

"That must have been so nice. Thrilling. Our news here has been dreadful, as of course you know." Then, she made the connection with the recently announced memorial service. "Will you be coming back for the service at St. Patrick's Cathedral, then?" she asked. He thought he detected a note of hopeful anticipation in her voice. At least, he hoped that that was what he heard. He made up his mind finally.

"Yes, of course. Secretary Adams and his party are with us now, in Riga. They are cutting their visit short by a day, as I'm sure you've heard. I will be joining them for the flight back to Dublin from Riga tomorrow. Will you be attending the service? It's tomorrow night, as you know."

"Of course I'll be there. Mary McGowan was my friend. As a matter of fact, there was an odd coincidence. She called to ask me about that same quotation from the Book of Isaiah that we talked about in County Kerry. Do you remember?"

Pulse racing, he was silent for a moment, then mumbled something about their meeting, and perhaps attending the memorial service together. She murmured what sounded like a yes, and he said that he would be in touch the next day, when he had more details about their flight. Then, he realized that there wasn't much time to plan in any event. Better firm up their meeting now, if they could.

"Tentatively, how about 5PM at Bewley's Café on Grafton Street? I gather that the service will be a couple of hours later than that, so that should give us enough time to chat and have a bite of supper and a pint first." She agreed.

"What about the murder? What are people saying? Do the police have any suspects?"

"Not yet, anyway, nothing very definite. I hear that they talked with someone from the west country, a horseman and sometime romantic interest, but he seems to have been cleared. And that's all I've heard. Plenty of Dublin rumors, certainly, but nothing at all very substantial."

Kelly remembered in a rush her talk with Robbie Cutler, and that odd business about the old Church writing, from the Latin Vulgate. Carlisle would be interested in that, since he had asked her opinion about it as well, as had Mary McGowan. The very same scripture. What a coincidence! The first syllables were forming when she remembered something else. Robbie Cutler had asked her to say nothing whatsoever about her conversation with him. Nothing at all. She should only talk with the police. Why she had agreed to that, she couldn't say, but Cutler had seemed like an honest young man, if wired somewhat too tight. Perhaps this is what Robbie had meant. Anyway, the opportunity passed. Surely she would see Cutler as well the following day. The confidence could be kept until then.

"Until tomorrow afternoon, then, at Bewley's Café.

"5PM. I'm looking forward to seeing you again."

— — — — — — — —

Robbie Cutler examined the latest batch of cables from Dublin. Several of them were from George Smiley, and were marked for his attention personally. The new security system with multiple recording video capability was installed at the Phoenix Park residence, and it was unobtrusive, unless you were really looking for it. As Robbie had suggested, the members of the Secretary's party who were returning to Dublin would be staying at the Phoenix Park residence, as they had before, "for convenience." The rooms had not been changed. The private ambassadorial suite had been reserved for members of Ambassador McGowan's family, who had just arrived from Kentucky.

There was nothing in the NODIS SALADIN series, which seemed to have petered out. There was, however, extensive coverage of what had happened in Moscow, with personal telegrams from fifty American diplomatic missions, at the very least, wishing Secretary Adams well, and expressing relief at his narrow escape. That would make a great presentation book for Secretary Adams when he returned to the Department, Robbie thought. He would mention that to Sam Cartwright when he saw him. It was the sort of thing that the Executive Secretariat did very well. The Secretary would be pleased, he was sure.

The returning diplomats were actually half the number that had been in Dublin earlier, since various members of the delegation had already dropped off following their stays in Paris, Vienna and Moscow. One or two, including

Ron Jackson from the Executive Secretariat, would proceed directly from Riga to London in order to advance the visit, and get everything ready for the Secretary's arrival. That still left Secretary and Mrs. Adams, Assistant Secretary Palmer, Ambassador Carlisle, Press Spokesman Charley Sherburne, Sam Jardine of Security, the indispensable Missy Bronson, and Sam Cartwright, plus Robbie himself, and another half dozen souls whom Robbie did not know by name. They were part of the Secretary's personal security detachment, he supposed.

There would be a light buffet at the residence before the memorial service, as well as breakfast the next morning, and transportation had been laid on to and from St. Patrick's Cathedral. The service was at 8PM. Robbie glanced at the Order of Service itself, which the Embassy had received from the Dean of St. Patrick's Cathedral. He was pleased to see that Prime Minister O'Bryan was speaking, as well as Secretary Adams. The St. Patrick's choir would sing, and there would be some remarks from the late ambassador's brother, representing the McGowan family. It would be an appropriate service, a dignified coda to the life of an accomplished woman.

Robbie read what Smiley had written him regarding the investigation as well. The police were hoping that their planted story about the cause of death would give the killer a false sense of security. Perhaps he might even show his hand. They clearly believed the classic folklore that a murderer shows up at the victim's funeral, Robbie thought. But whether he would be amongst the official mourners or the general public was the question.

On a whim, he called Kelly Martin. He caught her sharp intake of breath. "This is my day for surprises, I guess," she said. "An hour or two ago I put down the phone from talking with Rudolphe Carlisle. He just called me out of the blue."

"Did you tell him about our talk in Dublin?"

She was candid. "I almost did, to tell you the truth. It very nearly slipped out. I had just mentioned that I'd had a call from Mary McGowan, about the same Isaiah fragment. But I remembered just in time, that you had asked me not to mention your call to anyone except the police. So I didn't. All very hush hush, I'm sure."

"What did he want to talk about?"

"*Really*, Mr. Cutler, is this necessary?" Her tone was playful, but it was arch.

"I think it may be. I hope not. I'll tell you more tomorrow, or the next day, in Dublin."

"Well, if you must know, I'll be meeting Carlisle at Bewley's Café on Grafton Street at 5PM for a bite and a pint before the service."

"Thanks. He is in great spirits, and I'm sure that you'll have a nice catching up."

"Spoken like a married man!"

He smiled. "Now that you mention it, I'm overdue to make a call, myself. Thanks for the information - *what information*, she wondered - and I'll see you soon. By the way, please continue to keep the lid on our conversation in Dublin, except to the police. This one as well."

"You are very mysterious."

"It goes with diplomacy. See you soon."

Robbie hung up the phone, and called George Smiley at his residence private number. Smiley agreed to arrange surveillance of Martin and Carlisle at Bewley's Café the following afternoon. Robbie wondered whether he should have warned her more directly, but realized that he had no actual hard evidence that would support such an intrusion into the private life of an American ambassador.

Here was a wrapup cable from Embassy London, containing the visit schedule. Nothing much had changed. Once more, the Embassy was recommending, or rather, forwarding the recommendation of the Political Counselor, that the outing to the Globe Theater be scrapped for security reasons. The tone was somewhat wistful, as if the writer knew that the Secretary would never heed that recommendation. Well, Robbie would bring it once more to Secretary Adams's attention. He was sure that he would receive the same reply. Aside from that, the Runnymede excursion needed one more security check, and that would take place the next day.

Secretary Adams would never want to cancel that trip, irrespective of what security thought, Robbie knew. In a way, that visit was to be the centerpiece of the entire trip.

— — — — — — — —

Ambassador Carlisle was enjoying the reception. The music was excellent, and the refreshments on a par with anything more affluent European capitals had to offer. His guests had melded perfectly with those that the Latvian Foreign Minister had invited. The official seaside residence, while it didn't have the history and architectural pedigree of Rundale Palace, was elegant and invited guests to enjoy themselves. It gave the visitor the notion of participating in a world of private elegance, without the suspicion lurking that at any moment, a cruise ship tour bus might hove into view.

He was very pleased with himself. The call with Kelly Martin had been a good idea. And her talk with Mary McGowan confirmed that she had found the Isaiah manuscript and removed it from the desk. That was nearly as good as finding it himself. Clearly she hadn't even realized what it meant. He was fairly certain that she had not taken it to the next step. It was now worth the gamble to find out. The odds were that whatever had been hidden in the second hidden drawer was still there, awaiting discovery.

Beyond that, Kelly clearly remembered him with pleasure and perhaps affection, and would be glad to see him. Bewley's Café was public and nonthreatening. He could get the lay of the land from her in their meeting, and then decide what to do. For one thing, she might know something further about this odd announcement about Mary McGowan's cause of death. There is often scuttlebutt with murder cases. Surely there would be talk around Dublin by now, and she would have heard it. She would certainly know what was publicly known about the murder itself. It was a good way to be read into the Dublin reality.

Increasingly, it struck him that the police announcement must be some sort of bluff. They must want to reassure the murderer. Why? So that he would return? Well, come to think of it, that curious announcement had figured into his decision. He mustn't let it go beyond that. He mustn't *assume* that the story of a second murderer was true, just because the police had said so, and let down his guard in any way. He would have a good talk with Kelly Martin, and take his cue from what she had to say. He wondered whether they would be shadowed, or indeed whether he was a suspect at all. Well, everyone had to be, to a greater or lesser extent.

There was the Latvian Foreign Minister, distinguished and old world, smiling his way. It would be rude, not to say impolitic, to ignore the man.

Rudolphe Carlisle bowed politely, then sauntered over to join the Foreign Minister. It was a triumphal moment for them both. The truncated visit had clearly gone well, and real substance had been discussed. Just a few words sealed their mutual satisfaction. They were now colleagues. The Foreign Minister remembered that he should have a word with Charley Sherburne to finetune some press aspects of the visit. He might as well touch base with the American expert. With a smile and a hearty handshake he left Carlisle and wandered over to join Sherburne, signalling as he did so to a junior aide who would introduce him.

Robbie Cutler entered the ballroom, and walked over to have a word with Secretary Adams. Once again free, Ambassador Carlisle sauntered over to join them. He just caught the gist of their conversation as it was ending. As he had hoped, it was about Dublin. And they had no problem with his joining the conversation. It was another good sign.

"So, Mr. Secretary, the Irish Government and the Dean of St. Patrick's Cathedral have arranged everything. I've just talked with George Smiley, and he has sent over the Order of Service for the memorial service tomorrow night. You will be speaking. Are you sure that you don't want some draft remarks?"

The Secretary shook his head, no. He was going to speak spontaneously about Mary McGowan. Perhaps that would be better than a more formal speech. Well, Secretary Adams was the master at creating a memorable occasion. Trust him to know and to do what was right and appropriate.

Robbie continued. "Prime Minister O'Bryan will be speaking, and so will a member of the family. They flew over from Kentucky and will also be staying at the Phoenix Park residence. Oh hello, Ambassador Carlisle."

"Hello, Robbie, Mr. Secretary. I'm glad that arrangements for the service worked out. That will surely be a comfort for her family. Secretary Adams, is there anyone you'd like to meet, or anything else I can do for you here in Riga? I think it's been a successful visit. And I must say, your talking with the Latvians as trusted grownups has raised quite a few eyebrows. Very, very favorable reactions, from what I just heard from their Foreign Minister. And that is even beyond the substance of what you had to say, which pleased - and I must add, *surprised* - the Latvian side."

"Thank you, Rudolphe. I'm glad the visit has gone well. There is just one thing. Pamela would like someone to go with her for some shopping and local sightseeing tomorrow morning. Say, nine o'clock?"

Carlisle looked at Robbie, who answered for him. "It's already arranged, Mr. Secretary. An aide and translator will be at your quarters waiting then. Once she sees how charming the Old City and its shops are, they say she'll only wish she had more time here! I know that Sylvie is sorry to have missed it."

He saw his chance to slip in a confirmation of the next day's schedule. "Now, tomorrow we'll have a wrapup meeting at the Embassy, then departure directly for the airport. The bags will already have been picked up. I gather that a light luncheon will be available on the plane."

"Yes. Thank you, Robbie. I'm glad you'll be joining us, Rudolphe."

"After her hospitality in Dublin, Mr. Secretary, it's the least that I could do."

CHAPTER FOURTEEN -
Return to Dublin

ROBBIE FASTENED HIS SEAT BELT and reviewed where matters stood in Dublin. He had a feeling that they were close to a conclusion. He had had this feeling before, and it was usually right. Tired though he was, the excitement of the case added an adrenalin rush. He had to conceal that, do his job, and mask his feelings. It was also time to brief the Secretary more fully.

He had put down the phone the night before, after his talks with Kelly Martin and George Smiley, with a note of triumphal purpose. As a bonus, he had called Sylvie in London. That had gone less well. She read him too perfectly, what he said and what he was concealing.

So they were actually going to catch the murderer, and do so in the next few days! Maybe even tonight. It was an exciting prospect. Getting Carlisle back to Dublin was crucial. But he had to stop thinking of any suspect in particular. Keep the mind and possibilities open.

For one thing, the surveillance tapes should soon offer some hard proof. But of what exactly? Surely the murderer, if he or she were part of the Secretary's party, would hardly go stalking about the Phoenix Park residence in the dead of night. It would be a total giveaway, and a pointless one at that. But would he be able to resist the bait of another search of the desk?

Robbie remembered Ambassador McGowan's note. It referred to finding the Isaiah quotation in "a hidden drawer" of the desk. Had she been aware that the quotation itself suggested a hidden drawer, logically a second one? Did her talk with Kelly Martin put her onto that possibility? And had she had time before the killer came to find it herself? What if the killer had opened the first hidden drawer and found that the Isaiah fragment was now missing?

He reviewed once again what Smiley had said about his last talk with Inspector Halloran and Agent Kulker. His daily briefings with the Dublin police and the FBI team had yielded very few leads, but they had a shared taste for speculation and evidently thirsts to slake while they were doing it. The talk poured with the Irish whiskey. Smiley reviewed with him their last chat, that had taken place just a few hours previously in his office.

The police speculation on a motivation for the crime was circular, ending just where it had begun, now with more than one question mark. Clearly, the fact that Ambassador McGowan had asked the staff to leave for the afternoon was important. Probably crucial. It couldn't just be a coincidence that a potential murderer had blundered in, at exactly that time. No, obviously not. Not to mention the fact that if that had been the case, the actual private visitor whom she had been awaiting would have raised bloody hell when he had found that she was not there. But he wouldn't have discovered the body, of course.

Unless he had been there first and already left! That was a new thought. No, most probably she was dismissing the staff in order to be free to meet privately with the person who had turned the visit into murder.

But that wasn't the only possibility.

The police had a record of telephone calls for the day, in and out. They were not many. She had had what had turned out to be a few social calls, that probably her staff would have filtered for her, had she been at the Embassy. Others she would have taken, for example, the call from Rudolphe Carlisle. He probably didn't even realize that the police knew about his cellphone call from Heathrow. But surely that was just what he would say it had been, a thank you call from a departing guest with a few hours to kill at the airport.

Ambassador McGowan had not made many calls. There were several to her Embassy staff, for follow-up action, routine subject matter: a play she wanted to see at the Gate Theater, and a guest list suggestion or two for the future. There was also that call to Kelly Martin. Smiley had learned that the two were chums, and talked virtually every day. No, the telephone links were something of a dead end. Anyway, that base was covered. Kelly Martin had been followed and her movements recorded step by step since the murder. And there would be special surveillance when she and Rudolphe Carlisle had their meeting. Could they be accomplices?

The police investigation had turned up Ambassador McGowan's sometime boyfriend. He was perfectly respectable and good-natured, and had not been anywhere near Dublin that day. Witnesses galore accounted for all of his movements for hours before and after the time of the murder. Besides, the household staff said that she had dismissed them for the day in a rather matter of fact manner, hardly the mood of someone clearing the way for a romantic interlude.

There were also some notes that she had made in her residence office upstairs, at the desk, clearly well before she saw her visitor. Nothing seemed to relate to her murder at all.

The hiding of the body in the spare freezer was bizarre. Clearly the murderer was trying to buy time. To do what? To look around the residence? Why, and for what? Or simply, had he intended to create more time in which to make his escape, before the staff returned? In which case, he knew that the staff had been given the afternoon off, and he wanted or needed even more time to get away. How would he know that? If he wasn't a lover, he would have had to *ask her* to give the staff the afternoon off. She wouldn't have had that idea herself.

That was a new thought. Why would the killer do that? He would have to ask Smiley to run that past Kulker and Halloran. And then, had she mentioned the reason for asking her staff to leave the residence to anyone else? It struck him that someone else might know her motivation for doing that, even someone who had not been there, and perhaps not thought the information to be important. Rudolphe Carlisle, for one. He had called her that day. Perhaps she had mentioned her plans to him? In any event, the police would want to know about their conversation, in considerable detail. It was a good thing that he was returning to Dublin.

What about the physical evidence? There were a series of tests being run, but so far the blood smears had turned out to be hers alone. Too bad she had not scratched her assailant. No DNA samples were found under her fingernails. That meant surely that her strangulation was a surprise, and there had been no buildup struggle. It just happened, and from behind. They had been talking, and something had happened to set the murderer off. But what could it have been?

How did the murderer come to the residence, and then leave? Here, the police work had been exhaustive. Taxis, rental cars, bus conductors, residents of the neighborhood had all been questioned closely. Nothing had yet turned up. The murderer had "vanished into air."

The announcement of her murder, he knew, had been international news, and that was still true, fanned of course by announcement of the Memorial Service, which had reawakened interest in the case. The television crews were still all on hand, augmenting what was already an ample set of reporters and photographers in the Irish capital. Smiley had said that he was glad that Charley Sherburne was returning with Secretary Adams. It would help having a steady and experienced hand in dealing with the press. The Embassy's resources were stretched beyond the breaking point. Let the pros take over.

Then, there was that business about the cause of death. Obviously, it had been strangulation. As to the police putting out a different story, that the fatal blow had been struck from behind, they were playing mind games with the actual murderer. Was the killer supposed to think that the local police couldn't tell the difference between two very different causes of death? No, clearly not. It could not be a case of police mistake. If he bought the announcement, he had to assume that his murder attempt had somehow failed. An insidious question would be raised in the murderer's mind whether he or she had been the actual killer after all. With luck, that might furnish sufficient cover to lure the murderer back. If he had ever left Dublin, of course.

The killer would wonder what was the other person's motivation, and there it fell apart. Two killers with two separate motivations all in the course of a single afternoon was just too farfetched. Or was it?

And he really had to talk again with Kelly Martin. That business about the quotation from Isaiah seemed to be a link to the killing. At least, it was something that Mary McGowan wanted to know about from Kelly - and Rudolphe Carlisle too. Any hint that Robbie knew about those phone calls, and Carlisle might have found some compelling reason to stay in Riga.

If the killer believed the story that a second assault was involved, and this time a deadly one, he would also think that Mary had partially revived after he had left. What had happened then? If a killer went to his victim's funeral service out of curiosity, how much more curious would he be if there were a second killer out there? That might even let the first murderer off the hook.

He would certainly want to know what the second person had found out, if anything. Wouldn't he assume that the second murderer had the same motivation, whatever it was? Surely Mary McGowan's first instinct would have been to warn him or her about the first murderer! She would have blurted out what had happened. It was only natural. That would mean that the actual killer would know the identity of the first assailant. He would have to find out about that, urgently. And having done so, he would then be free to have a look around the residence for whatever his motivation might have been in the first place. But this time, the surveillance cameras would be in place.

But what would happen if the murderer realized that there had been no second assault after all? And how would he come to that conclusion? Robbie shook his head. There were far too many imponderables. He almost looked forward to getting back to the tangled business of diplomacy. Even taking Al Qaeda into account, compared to murder, diplomacy was a straightforward business!

— — — — — — — —

Sylvie woke up too early, from a bad night's sleep. She had enjoyed her stay in London, and was looking forward to Robbie's arrival. But that was the problem, the waiting, and missing the action. Robbie had given her a roughed in official schedule, and she was going to be included in several events. She particularly looked forward to the performance at the Globe Theater. Shakespeare, of course, *A Midsummer Night's Dream*. She hadn't recognized the names of any of the actors. She was sure that she would have known several of the players across the Channel, whoever was playing Molière or Racine at the *Comédie Française*. But that would all come in time.

London was new to her, and she saw it with French eyes. There was the charm, a real British charm, if you knew your Dickens. And from what she had gathered, the countryside and residences there were rather fine. The people were odd, though, strangely welcoming and familiar at the same time. She was used to a bit more, what would the English say, standoffish behavior? Yes, that was it. It was what the Americans complained so much about when they were in France, but she saw a bit of personal reserve as normal behavior. That is probably what Robbie had meant when they were in Bordeaux, she at the newspaper and he at the American Consulate General. He had said that to find a real, proper Englishman, you had to see what part of Bordeaux he hailed from. That was about right, she thought.

He had called late last night, from the Embassy in Riga, full of unsaid news about the trip. She gathered that it was going very well indeed, and she looked forward to hearing more details, once the unreliable telephones no longer impeded their conversations. He had painted a detailed picture of the attempted assassination at the Kremlin, realizing no doubt just how much she, as a television journalist, had missed not attending the news event of the decade. It was a very near thing, and Robbie himself had been not far from the assassin when the attempt had been made.

The Moscow scene was vividly etched in her imagination. She had thought to ask whether the danger for this trip was finally over, an unanswerable question of course, and had been surprised by his reluctance to say the usual platitudes, reassurances which she had wanted and half expected to hear. The security situation must be even worse than she had thought. Shopping and theater plans, always fun in the rare instances when they could enjoy them together, were even more pointless in these circumstances.

He would be arriving with Secretary Adams from Dublin the following day. Let's see, they would be flying over to Dublin from Riga in a few hours, and staying over in Dublin after the memorial service for Ambassador McGowan. That made her own presence in London for today totally pointless. Well, she was not a Foreign Service wife, or rather, not exclusively so. She was a media professional. And she missed her husband, who was, as usual, where the action tended to be.

He would also, of course, be where the action was today, in Dublin. There, terrorists were not the only game. There was also a murder to solve, and she had the feeling that Robbie had an idea or two. Well, the last murders were during their honeymoon in the Dordogne, and he had missed some of the clues that she had caught. Then, the conspiracy, if that was the right word, was directed against Robbie himself, and without her help, he mightn't have made it home alive. Why should he be doing any better now? And if he really did have everything in hand regarding this fascinating murder, shouldn't she be on hand when he solved the case?

Of course. The heck with it. She called the front desk and rearranged her hotel booking. Tomorrow morning she would be on a flight to Dublin. With any luck, she would be there when he arrived. No need to bother him in Riga. She should have raised the matter during their telephone call last night, and she had not thought to do so. Too bad. Calling again, now, assuming she could even reach him, would be too much like asking permission. No way. She wasn't going to miss this one. They could then fly back to London together, surely, and complete the trip. It would be a story that she would tell and retell to their first child, after all..

She was feeling better already about the theater performance at the Globe, which they would see together when they returned to London from Dublin. They would both have earned the treat by then. Even if it wasn't Molière!

— — — — — — — —

Rudolphe Carlisle was reassured. When the Embassy car had deposited him and Charley Sherburne at the Phoenix Park residence, he had found his former accommodations quickly, laid out a suit and unpacked, and put his toilet kit into the suite's bathroom. He had decided to give everyone a chance to get settled, and then he would either leave the house for a breath of air, or settle in for an afternoon nap.

Then all was quiet, and he sauntered downstairs. He went carefully, looking back and forth, this way and that, pausing at every squeak the floorboards made. Then, nearing the end of the stairway, he stepped briskly to the secretary. It was still where he had left it. There were no signs that it had been disturbed. He leaned over and examined it carefully. Later, he thought, would come an opportunity to open it once again. If he had to do so, he would even wait for a later occasion. No, that wouldn't work. He would have, after all, no reason to return, as he would have had with Mary McGowan. No, if possible, he must open that secretary once again during their overnight stay at the residence.

That shouldn't be too hard. There was not a very large household staff, he recalled, and they did not seem to prowl around late at night. If he had the secretary's interior rightly figured now, it would not take long to find what he was looking for - always provided that Mary had not removed it. But if that were the case, surely the police would have found the document by now. Such a bombshell couldn't be kept secret - unless they didn't know what they had found!

He leaned towards the secretary, looking more closely. No, nothing had been moved, or even slightly rearranged. It was tempting to try to find the entrance right now, to open the secretary top and go on from there, to bring to light once again the magnificent Elizabethan desk that lay wedged carefully within.

Well, why not? Nobody was here now. He looked again in all directions, and saw nobody and heard nothing. Now was the right moment. It wouldn't take long at all. Then on an impulse he looked up, and froze. There, nearly flush with the ceiling, was a video camera. It must certainly be new. If it had been there during his last visit, it would have captured on film what had happened, and he would not be a free man now. No, they had had it installed precisely because it had not been there earlier.

Carlisle walked the length of the downstairs corridor. With careful looking, he spotted seveal more video camera recorders, all flush with the ceiling, and all except the one by the front entrance nearly masked by lighting devices. They had been carefully arranged. Their placement was reassuring. The video camera above the secretary was not obviously designed to catch someone at the secretary. It looked like it was designed to record the presence of people as they came down and went up the staircase to the private apartments of the residence. All to the good. That meant that they had not localized the need to see who was at the secretary. And in turn, that indicated that they did not know the secretary's importance. The secret might still be safe. And if that secret was still safe, then so, probably, was he.

The video cameras meant that they expected the killer to return. Either that, or more probably, the Embassy's Administrative office was having a case of shutting the barn door too late. In any event, it looked like there was no weighty suspicion pointing his way. Ambassador Carlisle with a positively light step hailed his cab and went downtown for his meeting with Kelly Martin.

She was glowing. This American Ambassador was really happy to see her. He absolutely oozed charm, and who would have imagined that they would be sipping champagne at Bewley's rather than cups of piping hot tea? It was flattering and fun, even if his conversation had veered inevitably towards the sad event that had really brought him back to Dublin, regardless of what his invitation to her had implied.

He alluded to the Isaiah quotation, but it only registered faintly as old business with her. Clearly she did not associate it with the desk, so Mary McGowan had not confided where it had been found. Kelly prattled on, unaware that she had eliminated herself as Carlisle's rival for what still might lie hidden within the desk. She couldn't be the second murderer either. He was now convinced that no such person existed.

Answering his questions, she hadn't paid much attention to what the police thought. She had certainly not paid attention to the cause of death. Those were conversation killers, as her short and forced replies gave him to understand immediately. Besides being unpleasant, it was sad and cruel. Mary McGowan had been her friend, almost a chum, nearly a confidante. She missed talking with her already. Finally Carlisle took the hint and the conversation became more friendly and relaxed. They left arm in arm to walk together down Grafton Street towards the park, there to hail a taxi for St. Patrick's Cathedral.

— — — — — — — —

"Well, at least you're glad to see me!" With this wifely warning, Sylvie gave her surprised husband a hug and kiss as he entered their room at the Phoenix Park residence, and found her there waiting for him, already unpacked.

"Darling! What a wonderful surprise! And a surprise it is, too. I thought we had decided to meet in London."

"No. That's what *you* had decided, Robbie. I suspect there is a murder case being solved here in Dublin. I couldn't miss it. And of course, I wanted to join you for her memorial service."

"Yes, of course. I should have thought of that. By the way, how did you get here so quickly? When we spoke late last night, I was still in Riga, and you were in London."

"Dublin is a short flight from London, Robbie. Via Heathrow Airport. Just a couple of hours ago I was still in London. They come and go constantly."

He seemed stunned. But he was also honest, part of the Yankee makeup, surely. "Of *course*! Well, darling, you solved the last mystery, in the Dordogne. I think you'll get at least part of the credit for solving this one as well."

He smiled and turned his back and made a quick cell phone call to George Smiley. Then there was just time for an hour or two together before the evening service.

— — — — — — — —

The memorial ceremony for Ambassador Mary McGowan would long remain in the memories of those who attended. St. Patrick's Cathedral had been designated the National Cathedral of Ireland, although it was not as old as Christ Church Cathedral. National observances took place there, much like those at the National Cathedral in Washington, including funerals for two Irish Presidents.

It was the largest church in Ireland, and it resonated from the unhappy past, as Protestant and Catholic had warred for control of the island over the centuries. The medieval background here was reassuring and welcome, as this chance congregation found solace in tradition, formulaic responses and, above all, in glorious music. It had to be Handel, of course, and as in 1742, when they were together for the premier performance of *Messiah* at the Old Music Hall on Fishamble Street, the choirs of Christ Church Cathedral and St. Patrick's sang together for this memorial service.

There were invitations for the leading pews with the best view from the transept of the ancient church, but so many people wanted to participate that television monitors were set up outside the church for the thousands waiting outside. Even the threat of changing weather did not stop them from congregating, umbrellas ready.

The service began with a processional of church dignitaries in full regalia, then the speakers, led by the Irish Prime Minister. The music, played by an experienced organist with a light touch, Sylvie remembered were a toccata and fugue by Bach. Then the procession reached the nave and settled themselves into their assigned chairs, facing the congregation.

The Dean, Jonathan Swift's present successor, welcomed the congregation, and read from scripture. Next came Prime Minister O'Bryan, who evoked the memory of Ambassador McGowan feelingly, and spoke of the warm relations between Ireland and the United States. He noted that her favorite hymn was from *Messiah*, and as his remarks concluded, the soprano soloist presented "I know that my Redeemer Liveth." Its notes seemed almost to arc gracefully up the ancient archways of the cathedral and cascade into heavenly sound as they then descended, in slight and harmonious echo.

Then Secretary of State Ronald Adams spoke. He told about the Ambassador's early promise and her career, and lamented the contributions that she could no longer make. He said that this was a new opportunity for the peacemakers, an era for peace and heightened struggle against the ancient enemies, fear and disease and want, and Ambassador McGowan would have done her part nobly. His words reminded Robbie of what had been said so many years ago at the dedication of the National Cemetery in Gettysburg. It was not a bad comparison, he thought. Then Robbie was not the only one to choke up when the moving bass solo followed, "Why do the nations so furiously rage together?" The music echoed the storm that had suddenly sprung up, drenching Dublin as occasional lightning dramatized the night sky.

The family was represented by Ambassador McGowan's younger brother. He added a third dimension of family to the picture of the murdered envoy. He said that it wasn't the time for details, which would be forthcoming as they were worked out, but he did want to announce on the part of the McGowan family the creation of a memorial fund. The final musical offering was the concluding chorus from *Messiah*, "Worthy is the Lamb," followed by a subtle segue into the concluding Amen Chorus.

The service had lasted just forty minutes. It seemed longer, because the experience had been so eloquent, and it seemed too short, because people had wanted to stay and hear more. It was just the mood to capture the loss of the young and vibrant Ambassador McGowan herself, the Dublin newspapers reported.

As he left the cathedral, Robbie caught sight of a frantic George Smiley signalling to him. Clearly there was some news. He excused himself to Sylvie, huddled with Smiley briefly, and thought for a moment. Then an idea occurred to him. Smiley smiled in agreement and quickly dialed his cellphone.

"What was all that, darling? More about this wretched murder case?"

"Sort of, Sylvie. It seems that there has been a power failure at the Phoenix Park residence. It may take some time to fix. Something about lightning and a power line down. There was a storm while we were in the Cathedral, as you possibly heard. So, those who want will be transported to other accommodations. They'll be spreading the word directly. As for the rest of us, there will be a candlelight buffet supper. Isn't that romantic?"

"It would be, if I believed a word of it. Now, Robbie, I want to hear from you what is really going on. Right now." She was indignant and insistent.

So he told her.

— — — — — — — —

Nobody moved out of the Phoenix Park residence after all, but that, Robbie knew, was hardly the point. The Secretary and the other dignitaries had had their buffet, and then, the luxury of a rather early night. After all, there would be an early call in the morning for the Air Force Two flight to London. One by one the guests retired to their apartments and the candles were snuffed out.

Rudolphe Carlisle was tense with excitement in the silent house. Hours passed, then one or two more. It was pitch black, with just a sliver of moon visible, lending atmosphere if not light. There really was no electricity, as he had found out when he had tried to flip a wall switch. It wasn't possible to go in search of the main fuse box, to see if this had all been contrived. In the first place, he didn't know where it was. And if he did go and was found out, what would he say?

Well, whether they had intended it or not, one thing was sure. The electricity did not work. Since it did not work, the video camera recording devices couldn't either.

What should he do? Carlisle for the hundredth time weighed the inviting prospect of checking that desk one more time. The problem, of course, was that he couldn't imagine another opportunity. Just when would he be able to return and look over the secretary once more? And would it even be there when he managed a return trip? Embassies were always selling off old furniture. It was impossible to say when someone's enthusiasm for unloading the old furnishings would go just too far, and deprive the residence of this treasure. It was too much to bear.

Carlisle didn't have to get out of bed, since he had never gotten into it. He rose from his armchair, took a candle and some matches, and ever so carefully, breath caught like an escaping prisoner from a maximum security prison, tentatively opened his door. Good. It hadn't squeaked. That meant it would not do so when he closed it again. It was a good sign.

He tiptoed over to the staircase, and waited in the silence. Still nothing. He hazarded a few steps down the staircase. Still nothing. He thought for a moment. This was surely the last opportunity to change his mind, and glide back into his room. The thought was tempting. Then he remembered the expression on Mary McGowan's face, afterwards. Was all of that really to be for nothing? And would what might actually be one of the great discoveries of all time be lost, because he was now frightened? No, it wasn't rational. In for a penny. He muttered childhood nonsense to himself silently, to give more courage.

He was at the bottom of the staircase now. Had he taken a single breath since he had opened his room door? No, it wasn't possible. Come to think of it, his walk thus far could still be explained away. He was still safe. For one thing, he might be sleepwalking, which would explain why he had not lit the candle that he held in his hand. For another thing, he realized that he was now heading in the direction of the kitchen. Surely he wouldn't be the first guest to raid the icebox for some savory leftovers in the middle of the night!

But there was the secretary, standing against the wall. That was it, of course. He had been idiotic not to have realized it sooner. In particular, that two line Latin message. It had been there to help, to illuminate, not to conceal. That was surely proof positive that his intuition had been right in the first place. There was a *second* hidden drawer. And that would be where the treasure, whatever it was, had been hidden. Unless, of course, Mary McGowan had already found it before he had returned from Heathrow, and secreted it in her office. That was just possible. But if so, wouldn't she have said something? At least, to try and stop him? That made sense. It would have been the only card that she could play. The fact that she hadn't played it meant that she hadn't found the document after all. So she had had no final card to play.

Carlisle approached the desk, and looked carefully around. It was too dark to see anything. Well, there was no help for it now. He found the matches and lit the candle. Then he held the candle up towards the ceiling. There was no movement, no flickering into life of the video camera. It was indeed dead. This was his chance, if he was going to take it. It was his last and only chance.

He found a side chair near the wall on the other side of the corridor, and carried it over to the secretary. He lifted the secretary's front lid, and placed the flickering candle on the space some Victorian furniture maker had providentially supplied for precisely that purpose. The appropriateness of it rather amused Carlisle. It was a good sign. Luck was running his way.

He opened the desk and removed its contents. Then he found the crescent moon and the five faint birds. "Hello, my five sparrows," he said softly. His fingers glided over them, and then he pressed the crescent moon. Once again, he was relieved to see, the hidden drawer came up, now ever so slightly. It was wearing out, the old mechanism, but the Elizabethan cabinet maker had done his work scrupulously well. It still worked, for possibly the very last time.

Carlisle took out the papers one by one, and sorted them into neat, careful piles on the floor by the desk. Coming to the end, he was relieved to discover the ancient piece of paper containing the now familiar, sloping script. On one side, it was covered by the nineteenth century notations of the miser who had followed the fortunes of Thorpe Hall with such industry. Turning the paper over, he read the two Latin inscriptions: *Petrus Quintus Fecit Anno Domini MDXCII*, and *Per Lux Lunae ad Veritatem*. That was all. But it promised a great deal more. Of course, that was the reference to the hidden drawer, that could be found by pressing the crescent moon.

What would then happen? The owner would press that crescent moon, as Carlisle had just done, and open the secret drawer. There, he would find the two Latin sentences from the Book of Isaiah. Surely, they were meant to lead to something else, something hidden even more profoundly. Fortunately, although Mary McGowan had taken that second paper, he still had the copy that he had made from the original. He took it from his pocket and examined it closely, reading it again and again. He could not be mistaken. It was a signal that the times were not yet right for what was hidden to be revealed, but that such a time would surely come, some time in the future. And what that meant, of course, was that there was a second drawer hidden somewhere in the desk. Carlisle could hardly speculate on what that treasure might be.

Now he had to figure out just how the second hidden drawer worked. He closed the hidden drawer and put his fingers slowly in turn everywhere on the desk. Nothing whatsoever happened. Then it dawned on him. *Of course!* He opened the hidden drawer once again, and then pressed every inch of the desk in turn, inside and out.

And then he heard it, a very faint sound, just barely audible in the still darkness of the night. It couldn't be the first hidden drawer. That was already open. It had to be something else, and he looked for it. There was no sign of any second drawer, anywhere. He looked thoroughly at the desk, from every angle. Then, very carefully, he gripped the sides of the secretary, and very gently pulled it slightly away fom the wall. There was, at the rear of the secretary, a very slight noise, as of wood striking the wall. Which was precisely what had happened.

Carlisle got out of his chair, lifted his candle and stepped to the side of the secretary. Yes, there it was, a hidden drawer protruding our from the desk. It was a miracle that the Victorian cabinet maker had not boarded up the rear of the old desk too, but he had not done so, probably because the frontal appearance of the secretary was his main concern, and he didn't want to add the expense of more wood. Carlisle did not think highly of these Victorian cannibals of furniture. They were neither craftsmen nor artistic, come to that. But out of such an odd reworking of the desk, the second hidden drawer still worked. Gingerly, Carlisle slid the secretary by the side farther away from the wall. Now the hidden drawer was fully open, and it contained a parcel. It looked to be wrapped in leather of some sort.

He took it into his hands. This was perhaps the first time in centuries that anyone had seen these documents. The ribbon tieing the leather together fast broke as Carlisle tried with impatience to untie it. He took out what seemed to be several documents, and leafed through the first. Good Lord! It was dated and signed by John Donne. He couldn't begin to speculate as to its value. And then, there was a second memorandum, by Christopher Marlowe!

Carlisle was simply thunderstruck. These were treasures beyond his dreams. And then, glancing through what Donne and Marlowe had written, he saw another sheath of papers, far older, possibly even more valuable. He looked at it, page by page, and putting aside the Latin *Confiteor*, was thankful for his excellent French, for that was the language of Baron Crecy. It seemed to concern the crusaders, the Shroud of Turin, and Saladin himself.

This was the treasure of a lifetime. But not his lifetime.

Carlisle was just aware of others. A small group had gathered unnoticed just behind him. And the lights suddenly came on, and as they did, two men behind him seizing his arms, and then snapped on handcuffs.

"What the hell is going on?"

One of the men was clearly an American, for that was his accent, and his first, instinctual move, was to begin to read Carlisle his Miranda rights. "You are under arrest for the murder of Ambassador Mary McGowan."

"I wasn't even here in this country, you fools!"

Robbie Cutler answered. "Yes, you were. The airlines have confirmed your round trip from Heathrow, where I saw you late that night. You had probably just returned from Dublin, and I was supposed to supply proof that I had seen you there. No wonder you were so pleased to see me. For you had earlier discovered something in that desk. You said so when we were here before. You talked about 'five sparrows,' and Charley Sherburne thought you were referring to birds. But that was the secret emblem on this desk. You just showed us those markings on the rear lid. Clearly Elizabethan. You thought about it, then called Ambassador McGowan before returning from Britain, asking her to dismiss the staff for the day. That set the stage for murder.

"As to the motive, I think that is in your hands right now. To have caused all this, it must be something priceless. You returned to Dublin to have a second look at the desk. But you didn't find it. Ambassador McGowan must have already done so. Here is the missing paper, with the quotation from the Book of Isaiah. She was frightened, or had a premonition, and she left it for me with a note, in her upstairs study.

"When you came back, she must have tried to stop you. She had figured out what you were doing. You murdered her. And having already committed murder, now you wanted to try once again, to find the second hidden drawer that this paper clearly refers to.

"As we've just seen, there are two hidden drawers, not one. You thought you had figured it out, that second mechanism. The problem was to find it. That is, after all, your special field of expertise, antique furniture. That's why the security cameras caught you lingering at this desk earlier today. We thought you might come back for a more thorough search with the cameras turned off. So we made sure they stayed off.

"And clearly, that is just what you did. The second hidden drawer could only be noticed when the secretary was moved away from the wall, and the right lever was pushed. And you have just shown us all how it was done."

"You can't do this! This is American property," Carlisle managed to sputter with what was supposed to be indignation. "And anyway, I have diplomatic imunity from arrest." Over the past few days he had practiced these melodramatic lines to the point of boredom, and they came out now automatically.

The answer came in the measured tones and unmistakable voice of the Secretary of State. "You can't commit murder in this very spot, and then claim that law has no jurisdiction here, only murder. If there is a legal issue on whether this is American territory, I waive it.

"And by the way, you are not accredited to this government, so the question of personal diplomatic immunity does not even arise. Please take him away. He offends us all."

CHAPTER FIFTEEN -
Runnymede and Westminster

JOSUHA RUNNING DEER SPLASHED WARM water on his face, and finished his morning routine. Strictly speaking, daily shaving should not be part of the ritual, but he had once tried pulling his facial hairs out, one by one. It was too much trouble, he told himself. Also, it hurt like blazes. From his mirror above the faucet he could see the wall mirror just opposite. It was always reassuring to see the turtle etched on his upper right back, near the shoulder. It had been colored by the tribal artist who had done the tattoo, and the greens and dark browns still held.

He had been told as a young boy that this was a great honor, and a badge of chieftanship. Not every Seneca could carry on his back the symbol of the great animal who carried the earth. That was only for a future chief. It was not, however, something that he wished to share. And so, he had avoided where possible sports where a top would not be worn. He realized that there was a cost to this reluctance. Swimming, actually several strokes, had been his best sporting events. Well, there were others in which he had competed, and with success. He didn't need more Indian stories in the newspapers.

He finished dressing, drank some cranberry juice, which was fortunately now available at the Embassy commissary, after he had raised a fuss. He doubted that it would be easy to find on the economy. The heated rolls and marmelade were fresh and delicious. He flipped on the television switch as he waited for the water to boil for the coffee. An excited announcement was being made from Dublin. An arrest had been made in the murder investigation of the death of Ambassador Mary McGowan. A police spokesman was shown reading a brief statement. It was Rudolphe Carlisle, American Ambassador to Riga, Latvia, who was being detained. More details would follow as they were available.

Well, that would be an interesting item to raise with the Secretary's party when the arrived this afternoon. Just imagine, one Ambassador killing another. Joshua supposed that it must have been a thwarted romance, something that had gone terribly wrong.

He flipped off the television news and looked out the window. There, right on time, Audrey Turner was pulling up in her car. He wondered whether to offer her coffee or not, and decided that he didn't know her well enough to say how she would understand the gesture. So he quickly pulled on a light topcoat, stepped outside his ground floor apartment, locked the door and, smiling, went to join her.

"Good morning, Joshua. Did you see the news? It looks like their last stop was the exciting one," she began.

"Yes. Dublin. Fancy that. One Ambassador doing in another. Well, we'll see how it develops. Just imagine the hell to pay if the police have made a mistake and arrested the wrong man!"

She pulled away from the curb. "We'll have a nice morning for the drive," she said. "And I've doublechecked. They are expecting us at Runnymede. As a matter of fact, we'll have the place pretty much to ourselves. They are not admitting visitors until the Secretary and his party have finished their visit there."

"What security is being laid on?"

"The full kit. Scotland Yard prowling about, reinforced by my lot, and also, the Army for good measure."

"Which outfit?"

"The Blues and Royals regiment of the Household Cavalry."

"Aren't they armored troops?"

"Yes. In particular, armored reconnaissance."

"Bit clumsy for Runnymede, isn't it?"

"Yes, Joshua, if this were an ordinary sort of threat. But it may not be.

So we are overreacting. The Blues and Royals were in Basra, Iraq. They are very used to IEDs."

"Then, thank God for them. Do I remember something about their officer corps? Not everyone who wanted to go was allowed to go, as it turned out."

"You have that right. Prince Harry was furious, but he didn't resign."

"I wonder if he will be part of this detail."

"So do I. Probably not, but who knows?"

They rode in silence as Audrey drove west from London, and followed the sign to "M4 and the West." It wasn't very long before they pulled off onto a byroad towards Windsor, and then, three miles farther on, found themselves nearing Runnymede. What an immense gift of history within a scant hour's drive: Windsor, Runnymede, Eton, the Thames. Audrey hoped that nothing new and violent would be added to the list.

"Have you been here before?" she asked.

"Yes. Actually, I'm an inveterate tourist. I enjoy seeing the historic places, particularly when there is a sense of calm, like this one. It gives scope for thinking about what took place here. King John and the Barons, of course."

"Yes, the Great Charter, *Magna Carta*. The foundation of English liberties."

"And our own. The writ of *habeas corpus*, where civilized society begins. They really ought to have called our history *1215 And All That!*"

"By the way, why is Secretary Adams coming here? It seems a bit out of the way."

"From what I hear, what has leached out from his trip so far, is that he takes the job seriously. He thinks that it is time for a new start in our country. And he wants to make a visible impression doing so. Here, of course, he'll probably stress the rule of law, after Guantanamo. I wonder how he'll put it. I hope he doesn't pull any punches. It's about time that the United States lived up to its ideals again, despite the terrorist threat - or maybe, because of it."

They pulled up to the entrance of the Runnymede historic site, parked the car and entered the field. Joshua took a deep breath, and paced for a few moments around the site, as Audrey greeted the anxious official guide, accepted two pamphlets with thanks, and dismissed him. No, they wouldn't need his services to show them around, thanks awfully.

Joshua continued his odd survey, his eyes keeping to the ground, then occasionally flashing as his gaze darted from here to there. Ignoring her, he paced one hundred yards, turned, and repeated the pacing in symmetrical patterns back and forth for nearly an hour. Audrey suppressed a giggle, to her acute embarrassment. Here she was with this American Indian, and he was behaving exactly true to form, sniffing about. He could be in a forest in the Adirondack Mountains somewhere, rather than in civilized Surrey!

Nothing was said, and the moment passed. The memorials proved to be tasteful and moving. One building was dedicated to the Allied Air Forces. The memorial had been unveiled by Queen Elizabeth II as a young queen in 1953. It celebrated the contributions of those members of the Allied Air Forces who died during the Second World War. Their names were recorded in a nearby cloister, the 20,456 who died for freedom and had no known grave. They climbed to the top of the tower, and from its summit all of Runnymede was visible, as well as Windsor Castle and the surrounding countryside for many miles.

"That's my favorite memorial," Joshua said. "the John F. Kennedy Memorial. Odd, isn't it. I wasn't even alive during his presidency, but it still seems so vibrant, so alive with possibility. Let's see." He checked a pamphlet that had been available as they entered Runnymede. "It was erected in 1965, again dedicated by Queen Elizabeth II. Look. There on the pathway leading to the memorial is one step for each year of his life. It should have been twice as long."

Then they came to the *Magna Carta* Memorial itself, built and paid for by the American Bar Association, "To commemorate *Magna Carta*, symbol of Freedom Under Law." It was here that Secretary Adams would give his address. There were already seats set up, and a temporary platform, and a place for the press reserved.

"That will still do as a symbol of what we stand for," Joshua said.

"Yes, well, shouldn't we now start on our security survey?"

"I've already done it," Joshua said. "Now, keep an absolutely normal demeanor. And do not raise your voice. We could be discussing Wordsworth, for all anyone watching us might gather. Now, there are two things to be done. Urgently. First, the National Trust, which I believe watches over the site and maintains it, must be contacted. Now. This afternoon. We have to know from them if any film companies have used this site, say in the past six months.

You know your own people, and who has got jurisdiction. That always baffles an outsider. You've got to bring some highpowered people, with the ability to make quick decisions and arrests. Maybe have the National Trust people come to your shop. That will be more intimidating."

She couldn't believe her ears. But he did sound serious. "And the second?"

"I want to meet with the responsible officers of the Blues and Royals. Not here. I don't want anyone pulled off the surveillance here. But near here will do. By the way, there are four of them here now, and they are pretty good. I guess the British Army has made some progress since my people last encountered them in the Canadian border region a couple of centuries ago."

"What on earth are you talking about? I've been here with you, every second, and every inch of the way. You haven't been out of my sight for an instant. I haven't seen anyone or noticed anything out of the ordinary. Is this some kind of joke? What's going on, Joshua?"

"Let's pause for a minute at the memorials and have another good look. That's for show. Then we'll amble back to the car and start driving back to London, the same route that we took coming here. I'll fill you in as we go. And you'll want to start making some arrangements fast, with that cellphone if that suits you. If not, if it isn't secure enough, we'll be back in your office in under an hour, and we can make arrangements from there."

"If that's time enough, I'll alert my bosses from the car."

"Fine. Let's get right on it. We don't have very much time. The Secretary arrives shortly, and the ceremony at Runnymede takes place tomorrow."

— — — — — — — —

They had left the formalities in Dublin pretty much up to the authorities. After all, Ambassador Carlisle had been taken into custody, and nobody was going to speculate on the guilt or innocence of a person who had not yet been tried. There was therefore no separate press conference called, and just the usual departure press opportunity scheduled at Dublin Airport. It gave, of course, the international press a field day of opportunity to raise questions about the murder of Ambassador McGowan, and the arrest of Ambassador Carlisle. But the Secretary and his party kept to the script, expressing confidence that justice would now run its course.

Sylvie was intrigued. Sitting with Robbie a few rows from the Secretary's private compartment, she asked her husband why the presumptive reason for the murder had not even been mentioned.

"Why not?" She insisted. "Won't the press get wind of it, sooner or later?"

"Well, they didn't. They will soon enough."

"But the Secretary didn't say anything, either. For all anyone knows, the killing could have been due to a thwarted love affair. What's going on here, Robbie?

"Well, it will all surely come out at the trial. Meanwhile, I think the Secretary may have plans of his own for breaking the news. Just a feeling. Anyway, it's time to brief him. Be back in a bit."

The mood on Air Force Two as they left Dublin was celebratory. As Robbie passed Charley Sherburne and Sam Jardine, he caught the tag end of their conversation.

"We should have special sweaters made, 'I survived Secretary Adams's first trip to Europe,'" Charley Sherburne said, only half jokingly, while he savored an early bourbon and branch water. "Let's see, there was that Kremlin plot, then the murder in Dublin. Fortunately, only friendly London is next. Town of Shakespeare, Dickens and a friendly government. I can use a bit of calm after what we have all been through!"

"Don't get too relaxed, Charley," Sam Jardine said.

"Coming from the head of security, that sounds ominous."

"I'm just being realistic. I have the feeling that we'll earn our money here too."

"What do you hear from the Embassy?" Robbie wanted to know.

"They are doublechecking everything, for about the fourth time. All public venues are being combed by special squads, military and Scotland Yard. The Embassy is on top of it. They seem confident, but are taking no chances."

"Fine. I'll tell the Secretary."

Robbie got up from his seat and knocked on the door of the Secretary's private compartment. He heard something that sounded like permission to enter, and did so. There was Missy Bronson, inundated with paperwork. She looked quizzically at him, then smiled as she saw that he had no papers to add to her burdens.

Robbie told the Secretary that everything was being checked yet again in London.

"Who is handling it, on our side?"

"Well, aside from Embassy security - a bit understrength since their FBI detachment has spent the past week or so in Dublin - the Political Counselor has been checking everything personally, I hear, in tandem with British security."

"That would be...?"

"Joshua Running Deer, Mr. Secretary."

"Yes. I've heard of him. I suppose everyone has. Quite a resumé. Rhodes and Olympic gold medalist, and I don't know what else. Is he really as good as his reputation would have us believe?"

"Better, sir."

"Better run through the program once again, Robbie. What we're doing, not the substance. I've already been briefed on that by the British desk officer. She knows her stuff."

"Yes, sir. Well, in addition to the Embassy meeting there are the usual two events, reconfigured for daytime hours to fit your preferences. There is the reception they will give this afternoon before the theater, and your return reception tomorrow, at the Embassy residence. You have suggested talking points and remarks, for the toasts, I mean."

"Yes. They really strain for humor. I've cut all of that out of the toasts. Never trust a middleaged desk officer who is trying to be funny!"

"Then the three public events. There will be a performance at the Globe Theater tonight, Shakespeare's *A Midsummer Night's Dream*. Then there is the trip to Runnymede tomorrow morning, and the final public event, using 'public' a bit loosely, your address to the Joint Houses of Parliament. It will be at Westminster."

"I'm rather humbled by that. Did we ask for that privilege?"

"No, sir. You were originally scheduled to give an address at a university setting, as you had requested. We particularly requested Oxford, given your study there. That was granted by the Vice Chancellor. It was within the last week that the Brits themselves came forward with this invitation. Clearly it was the intervention of the Prime Minister."

"Extraordinary. Have other foreigners done this?"

"The only one that comes to mind is Nelson Mandela, about a dozen years ago. They clearly want to give you the most prestigious audience possible. Word has been slipping back to London, surely, of what has been accomplished during this trip."

"Apart from murder and attempted assassinations, you mean."

"Well, that too."

"Well, I'll try to be worthy of the occasion. Where will it be held? Do the Lords come over to the House of Commons, the way we in the Senate went to the House of Representatives for the annual State of the Union messages?"

"I hear it will be in a separate hall, sir, the Royal Chamber. That is reserved for addresses to the Joint Houses of Parliament by visiting dignitaries. Do you want a fresh draft for the speech?"

"No thanks, Robbie, the earlier draft has a good basic outline. But I want to go on from there, and I've been revising it. I'll surely need a fresh, clean draft fifteen minutes before the event, but Missy Bronson is used to that!"

He smiled and removed his reading glasses. What was it that made him such a remarkable presence, Robbie wondered. He wasn't that striking looking, certainly no matinée idol. But there was a combination of cutting edge intelligence, compassion and depth. And he had the good politician's ability to assure that you had his full attention, even for a very short conversation. That was always flattering. But Adams went even farther than that. He actually paid attention to what you had to say, took it in, savored it, and that in several languages. Furthermore, when he saw you again some months later, he would recall the last conversation with precision. No wonder he had been an outstanding and successful Senator.

"Tell me about the manuscript, Robbie. You've had a chance to look at it, or rather, them. I gather you believe that this is why Mary McGowan was killed?"

"Beyond any doubt, yes sir."

"All right, tell me what they are, and where they were located and found. And why did Carlisle want them so very badly."

"It is a series of documents, Mr. Secretary. And they come from two hidden compartments from a desk within a desk. The earlier desk dates back to the time of Queen Elizabeth I. As you know, that was a time of great religious conflict, involving the throne and the legitimacy of the monarchy itself. It was a generation after Henry the Eighth, after all, and the establishment of the Church of England, first perhaps a sort of Catholic national church, as Henry may himself have considered it, then more gradually an established Protestant church. Which church you supported led to which monarch you considered legitimate.

"The first memorandum in Latin, dating the desk and signalling the first hidden drawer, is surely Marlowe's work. The second memorandum was originally in the first hidden drawer. It is two sentences in Church Latin from the Book of Isaiah, and points to something further that is hidden. Carlisle took that, correctly, to refer to a second hidden drawer. That Isaiah document is the one that Mary McGowan had found, and left for me with a note. Carlisle understood that she had taken it, and that probably led to her murder."

"And what was this treasure in the second hidden drawer?"

"There are several different memoranda. The first manuscript is a lengthy one, beautifully written. But then, one would expect that of John Donne."

"John *Donne!*"

"Yes, sir. As you may remember, Donne became Dean of St. Paul's Cathedral. That is when Alleyn gave him the desk and its contents. Donne's memorandum is a lengthy one, giving some more history, and his own view of the importance of the documents hidden within the desk. It's just a magnificent record of the times, from the most famous people. I simply couldn't put a valuation on it. We have John Donne's detailed account that gives us the history of how he acquired the desk, from the actor Edward Alleyn, and Alleyn's story of how the desk had been entrusted to him by Christopher Marlowe. Alleyn was Marlowe's leading actor.

"Marlowe's earlier memorandum follows. He states how he procured the third and oldest document, while on a spying mission in France. It is a sort of confessional. He apparently wrote it just before his fatal appointment in that tavern at Deptford. As far as I can gather, Marlowe himself had the desk made, with secret drawers. That goes back to his time as a Walsingham spy. He wanted and needed some privacy. And the fact that his own family history wasn't reliable as far as the prevailing religion of the time was concerned may have counted against him. He details some of this. But that isn't the main thing."

"You have my full attention. If previously unknown manuscripts by John Donne and Christopher Marlowe aren't the main thing, what on earth could be?"

"It is quite a revelation. It actually concerns the famous Shroud of Turin."

"Yes. I've read about it. Weren't there tests which were supposed to settle the matter of the Shroud's authenticity, but ended up just fueling the flames?"

"That's about it, sir. Well, in his manuscript, Marlowe takes us into the world of the Elizabethan spy, and he obviously is having serious qualms of conscience. He was in France fingering students as Catholic adherents. Not very admirable. One of them was returning to England on a missionary quest, I guess you would call it, an idealistic attempt to bring England back to the Catholic religion. And just before he left, since he trusted Marlowe and considered him to be a true friend, this young man entrusted the poet with a manuscript, an ancient one, that had been in the possession of a French baronial family for centuries. That is the third document in this hidden drawer."

"What was it?"

"According to Marlowe's own estimation, it is a masterpiece of literature. It dates from the early thirteenth century. It is the record of a Baron Crecy of his faith - it even starts with a *Confiteor* - and of his return from the East during the crusades. He was apparently on the one that went all wrong, the Fourth Crusade I think, that ended with the sack of Christian Constantinople.

"This Baron Crecy thought to save one relic from his fellow marauders, and it was the Shroud of Turin! That's how it got to France. This document complements what the Vatican has recently said, about the Shroud's missing years, documenting precisely how the Shroud got to France in the first place. But Baron Crecy goes further than that - he even supplies a chain of evidence of the Shroud's location going back centuries. Some of it is copied from something older, a disintegrating parchment probably, but part of it is that same parchment.

"The most amazing part of all this is his statement that the Shroud was taken back to the Holy Land by the Crusaders. After Saladin won the Battle of Hattin in 1187, as a gesture towards his enemy he allowed the Shroud to be returned to Constantinople, under his protection."

"Good Lord! It staggers the imagination." He thought for a moment, savoring the revelation. "So, you're saying that the enemy of Richard the Lionhearted, their most capable leader, turns out to be chivalrous as well. How did Carlisle find out about this, if he did?"

"You'll recall that he was an authority on period furniture. Especially, it turns out, the late medieval and early Renaissance period. It seems that the Elizabethans constructed furniture built to last. The Victorians, never ones to waste anything, often constructed larger pieces, like secretaries, and put the earlier furniture inside. That is what happened here. Clearly, on our first visit, Carlisle's attention was attracted to the secretary at the foot of the stairwell.

"I saw him there once. He must have returned more than once, for he seems to have found a paper that had been left within - not one of the manuscripts, but a sort of clue. It was the Latin quotation from the Bible, the Book of Isaiah. It seemed to refer to something being hidden, for the people were not worthy to receive it.

"When I went back to Dublin, I saw Carlisle at Heathrow Airport. That was late in the day, actually suspiciously late, for he might have gotten off to Riga on an earlier flight. He was very glad to see me, and I wondered why. Perhaps he thought that established an alibi of some sort. But I never suspected that he had actually made another round trip to Dublin. How he managed to get to the Phoenix Park residence and back must have been sheer luck. Also, he must have paid cash for his ticket. He probaby cashed some extra travellers' checks, not to have it on a credit card, where the trip could be checked. He surely also has an ordinary tourist passport, so that the trip wouldn't show up on his diplomatic passport. But, of course, he was on the passenger manifest both ways, once we thought to have them checked.

"But it was that odd reference to the Book of Isaiah that got my attention. After discovering the body, I did a light search. I looked in Ambassador McGowan's private library and found, half concealed, a note to me. She clearly wrote it after Carlisle had telephoned her from Heathrow, and she was concerned. It said very little, except for enclosing that quotation.

"Well, my Latin isn't up to snuff, so I called Kelly Martin. You remember her, sir. She's the professor whom we met at Ambassador McGowan's dinner for you. We talked a bit, and she said something to the effect that the Book of Isaiah must be topping the charts on the Amazon.com list, so many American diplomats had asked her recently what that same passage meant!"

"And they were...?"

"Ambassador Carlisle, Ambassador McGowan, and myself. That told me that the reference was a link to what had happened. The fact that it referred to important matters being hidden was a contemporary reference as far as Marlowe was concerned. But what it would have told Carlisle was that in some secret place, the desk contained a treasure. And so it did."

"And that is why you suspected Carlisle?"

"Not at first. It was quite a mystery. So we put out some bait, that cock and bull story of the second cause of death, which the police concocted. They agreed with me that the evidence was slim to nonexistent. Certainly there was not enough to make an arrest, much less go to court. Plus the little matter of diplomatic immunity. Now, the way I understand it, a diplomat has no immunity except in his country of assignment. That meant Riga, not Dublin, as far as Carlisle was concerned. If we made him comfortable enough, by raising some doubt as to whether he actually was responsible for her death, he just might be tempted to return to Dublin. And once there, he could then have a second go at rifling through the Elizabethan desk. Because surely he suspected what was there, but he hadn't yet found it all.

"There were two hidden drawers, as it turned out. That's what he puzzled out. He finally showed us that. And the treasures that were found therein are wonderful, full of interest and value."

"And they give some new context to our old friend Saladin. Just think, we have been tracking our enemies with the series NODIS SALADIN! It seems somehow unwarranted now."

"I'll leave that to the terrorism experts, sir. But you are certainly right. There is a larger point here. Thank God we were able to piece it all together."

"It is, indeed, food for thought. Well, that's Heathrow approaching. Please check on the arrangements for London with Joshua Running Deer once we've settled in. And Robbie, many thanks for your fine work."

Robbie flashed a big grin, nodded, and left the compartment.

— — — — — — — —

The meeting began with questions and ended with an action plan. Joshua Running Deer described the tiny signs, visible to himself alone, that seemed to show an intersecting pattern of wires. There was no harmless explanation. And if this was all somehow harmless, it at least must be checked out thoroughly. Audrey was incredulous. She had been where he had been, and had seen precisely nothing. Hearing it through Running Deer's perspective, it all sounded so vivid. Actually, it had been invisible to all but the most highly trained, nuanced observer. The final and convincing touch was when he described the freshly disturbed wires near the area where the ceremony would be held. Clearly, the terrorists had gone back after the chairs and portable stage had been installed, to make sure that their wires were still in place. It was an unnecessary thing to do, and for Joshua Running Deer, it showed that the signs that he had seen were not accidental. They had been too thorough.

Once he described the pattern, combat veterans from the Blues and Royals nodded their heads. Yes, that was the pattern.

Then came the embarrassed report from the National Trust. There had been just two film production companies at Runnymede during the past six months. One was a well known British production firm, doing a television special that had already been shown for the anniversary of Magna Carta. The other, "Friends of Deportees," was stated to be an NGO that agitated for prisoner rights. It would not have been politically appropriate to question the application. Yes, said the nervous National Trust official, here were the contact references, names and addresses.

"That's the trouble," Joshua Running Deer said. "When we start violating civilized rules, it opens the door for the other side. They can then come in in the name of the values that we espouse and they do not. Disgusting. How long was the film crew at Runnymede?"

They had spent four full days at the site. No, they were not supervised. That was not the customary procedure. Yes, now that you mention it, a crew from Friends of Deportees had returned within the past week to film a recent shot, to touch up the production for another viewing. They wanted to be exactly contemporary, they had said, showing the change of seasons.

"Sure," growled Joshua Running Deer, "and at the same time, test out to make sure that their wires were still well in place under the Secretary's party."

"So, they didn't abandon their plans after the Kremlin plot failed," Audrey concluded.

"Worse than that. Far worse. The difference this time is that they had in mind not a single killing, but blowing up the entire American diplomatic élite, plus half the British Government, not to mention whatever Royals might be attending."

"Why are they using wires in the first place? Isn't that fairly low tech?" Joshua Running Deer asked the question that had puzzled more than one civilian.

"It has worked for the terrorists in Iraq well." The speaker was Major Ancil Browne, the senior operational soldier present. We went through this, the various stages, when I trained at your National Training Center in California. At first, IEDs - "improvised explosive devices" - were often set off by radio, or some other form of transmitter. Then, you chaps got onto that, and started jamming. It didn't always work, but it did cut down on the operational IEDs. If you jam the right frequency, of course, you have interrupted the radio signal."

"So the IED can't be detonated."

"Precisely. However, that led to countermeasures from the terrorists. You are quite right, Mr. Running Deer, to suppose that using command wire is lower tech. But it is designed to foil our reliance on jamming."

"And how about contact IEDs?"

"Yes, that is what the world has seen. They can be rigged with very high explosives, old artillery shells, for example, and be covered with some sort of pressure plate. When an armored vehicle rolls over them, the impact explodes the device. They couldn't do that here, of course, for the Secretary will be on foot inside the enclosure. There probably wouldn't be enough pressure for the detonation. But we will now be double-checking anyway for pressure plate devices, in the enclosure as well as on all roads that the Secretary's party might take, for miles.

"What they had in mind took a lot of advance planning. It had to be arranged well in advance, of course. They must have made their plans as soon as the public announcement was made of the Secretary's itinerary here. Why not? It's rather out of the way, full of historic interest, and could be sabotaged well in advance.

"And they used command wires. One of the advantages is that buried wires don't show up very well, if at all, with ground penetrating radar. So the best - no, the only - way to locate the wires is often just by sheer personal observation. The soldier who enjoys hunting, for example, as a civilian pursuit, is much more attuned to minute changes in the terrain than an average person would be. And fortunately Mr. Running Deer is an expert at such detection..."

He paused, his face reddening, not knowing whether he had made the compliment he had intended, or been politically incorrect instead. He was saved by Joshua. "Many thanks, Major Browne. I'm sure that you now will have operational matters to tighten up."

The civilians coordinated plans for shadowing what remained of "Friends of Deportees," and arresting the leaders when the signal was given. A tactical military plan emerged, using black light in a thorough early morning operation at Runnymede. The explosives would be removed. For good measure all command wires would be severed, rendering them inoperative in case any buried explosives were missed. Several picked squads would patrol the perimeter, lying in wait for the arrival of the terrorists who expected to set off the explosives. They had Joshua Running Deer's sketch plan of the site, his account of what he had seen, and what they could surmise from their experiences in Basra.

When they finished, there was just time for a quick cup of tea before the officers moved out to brief their waiting soldiers. "We have something in common, I believe, Mr. Running Deer," said Lieutenant Wales as they finished their tea.

"Yes, Your Royal Highness. In theory. But your prospects for succession are far more secure than are mine. In my nation, though, the honor would be comparable."

"Well, you still have the advantage of me, in any event. Is there a title I should use in addressing you? Of the Iroquois nation, if I understand correctly?"

"How thoughtful. Actually the term 'Iroquois' is French, not Indian. It was their mispronunciation of the way our council speeches used to end. It referred to the six nations, but the term stuck, and is still in common use, even though there was no 'Iroquois' tribe. We all use it as shorthand anyway for the overall group of nations, the confederation over which my father now presides. Actually, we are Seneca. My father is also Lord or *Royaneh* of the Turtle family, one of the fifty or so paramount clans of the confederation. Before I joined the diplomatic service, he invested me as War Chief. It's an odd designation for a diplomat, but as we've just seen, sometimes the two intersect."

"Well, we owe you an enormous debt. As we owed your ancestors in the Seven Years War, or French and Indian War, as I believe you call it."

"Yes, my father still has a rifle with the crest of the House of Hanover. It was presented to his ancestor during that war, in the name of King George the Second. But sir, as to this one, may I offer a suggestion?"

"Yes?"

"For God's sake, don't wear redcoats! It didn't work in Ontario and New York two and a half centuries ago, and it certainly won't work now at Runnymede!"

"You have my word on it."

The general meeting ended with purposeful laughter.

— — — — — — — —

Shakespeare would have been at home here, Robbie thought. This reconstructed Globe Theatre was a great success. It seemed to capture the very mood of Elizabethan theater. And standing as a groundling was tiring, but a dimension was gained in enjoying, even participating in, the spectacle on stage.

It was *A Midsummer Night's Dream*, and the performance was delightful. For a time, it was possible to forget the world of peace and war, diplomacy and, yes, murder. In this setting, even the Shakespearean jokes, that usually left him cold, acquired meaning and relevance. Even the Bard's "rude mechanicals," the carpenter Peter Quince, and Snug, the joiner, had their importance and advanced the play.

All of a sudden, Robbie started. He seemed to peer through a disused window into the past. What did "Quince" mean, anyway? Wasn't it a fruit of some sort? Why give a carpenter that name? Then he remembered, *Petrus Quintus fecit,* and a late sixteenth century date. He looked at his program.

Yes, *A Midsummer Night's Dream* had been in the First Folio, in 1623. But the usual attribution put its composition in the 1595-96 range.

It was tantalizing enough to make Robbie wonder, about Shakespeare's London, friends at the Mermaid Tavern, a custom made desk, and the elusive national playwright, William Shakespeare. He was, after all, the same man who had famously left his wife his "second best bed" in his will. He would always remain an enigma. Perhaps there were still some moments of recognition, clues that had been left for later, safer ages.

— — — — — — — —

Secretary Adams's capacity for singleminded absorption never ceased to amaze Robbie. Here he was, being driven to Parliament, having just been the target of a thwarted mass assassination attempt, calmly lining out references in his speech, and marking in new ones. He could have been returning from a weekend in the country, not a care in the world. Finally he finished, and turned to Robbie.

"This should be quite an occasion. To put it mildly."

'Yes, sir. I gather that you are incorporating some reference to what happened at Runnymede."

"Well, I was going to anyway. But now it will be even more emphatic. The world just has to know about us, what we are really like."

He thought for a moment. "You know, Robbie, we have been through a very bad time. I'm no angel. In the first angry reaction to 9/11, I'm not sure that I would have reacted any differently, or perhaps not even as well. But we've got to have our perspective back."

Robbie nodded. "Some might say, sir, that it's all a matter of politics, reacting to the last Administration."

The Secretary frowned, and looking sharply at his young aide, saw that he had not meant anything personal. "That would be people who are ignorant of politics. It isn't even a party thing, not really. But despite that, I expect to make so many enemies with this speech, that any future political aspirations that I might have at home would become impossible." His tone had started harsh, then mellowed like a mature wine from a newly opened bottle blossoming in the glass.

He thought for a moment longer, and then smiled at Robbie. The moment had passed, and it was back to their roles, Secretary of State and aide. "Too late to get these changes on a teleprompter, I suppose?"

"I'm afraid so, sir."

"So much the better. I hate those teleprompters. They try too hard to make you seem spontaneous, when everyone in the audience knows that is not true. Much better to use a speech, and then take off the reading glasses from time to time. It is more genuine. Now, from the listening you've been doing to your own cell phone, I gather you've heard even more about that picnic at Runnymede?"

"Yes, sir. Last night, Scotland Yard coordinated arrests of the group involved, the 'Friends of Detainees.'"

Secretary Adams winced. "That sounds like a group I might send money to!"

"Yes, sir. They often, I'm told, disguise themselves and hide behind names of causes that sound all right, even praiseworthy."

"Did they get all of them?"

"They picked up eight or ten immediately, right after the action at Runnymede very early in the morning. At Runnymede itself, several squads from the Blues and Royals, Household Cavalry, disabled several sets of command wires that could have detonated huge qualtities of C4 explosives right under the speaker's platform and audience seats where the ceremony was just held. It would have been enough to cause mass casualties.

"After disabling the command wires, and removing what explosives they could locate ahead of time, they remained in wait towards the perimeter where the terrorists would have done the detonations. They nabbed another six men. Two of them, by the way, had detonation devices for command wires that hadn't been located."

"A close run thing, as Wellington said of Waterloo."

"Very much so. Here we are at Victoria Tower."

"Oh, not the usual St. Stephen's Gate? That's the one I'm used to. The Foreign Relations Committee used to come over from time to time for joint meetings with our British counterparts, in both Houses of Parliament."

"No, sir. This is the entrance that is most convenient for the Royal Gallery. The Queen uses it, I'm told, to proceed to the Robing Room just before she enters the Royal Gallery to deliver her annual address."

The Secretary smiled in silent reply. Soon protocol officials arrived to escort him to the Royal Gallery, and it seemed within minutes, he had emerged into that long and glorious hall, over one hundred feet long, and nearly half again as wide, with a soaring high ceiling that added to the grandeur of the setting. He blinked for a moment and took in the sight, parliamentarians and lords in every direction, some he recognized or thought he did as old acquaintances, all applauding and stepping forward to shake his hand as he made his way to the rostrum where he would speak. Nearby were the two grand frescoes, hailing "The Meeting of Wellington and Blucher at Waterloo," and "The Death of Nelson."

An introduction followed, and more applause.

Secretary Adams rose, collecting his thoughts for a moment. Then he put down his prepared remarks and began to speak extemporaneously, or so it seemed. "These grand pictures evoke two of Great Britain's heroic victories, at Waterloo and Trafalgar. But there are some victories that take place not on the battlefield, but when we conquer ourselves, and let our best traditions, many of which were forged on this island, once again inform and guide our actions.

"As you have heard, this trip has been planned to reassure our friends of our dedication to defeat terrorism, our adherence to the rule of law, and our promise to engage fully in international concerns such as the environment. We have also sought new openings to those with whom we disagree. I have seen the reaction of those who wish us well. And I have seen the consternation of our enemies. But I wanted to do something visually understandable, to rededicate our commitment to our best traditions - and yours.

"For it must be made unmistakably clear that the United States will return to its settled practice of adherence to the precepts of international law - much of which we ourselves drafted.

"Let me be quite specific. The obscene practice of 'waterboarding,' a taudry euphemism if ever there was one, will be called by its real name, torture by simulated drowning. If it ever happens again in the United States, or in any place of detention under American control or supervision, it will be the subject of vigorous prosecutions.

"I want to be absolutely clear on this. There will be no secret or extraordinary prisons, courts or interrogators. We will apply the Geneva

Conventions in full where required, in spirit when they are not required. There will be no vocal trickery about torture. There will be no extraordinary rendition. Our Department of Justice will understand this as a bedrock part of their oath of office. In the future, those who violate that oath will be prosecuted to the full extent of the law. That applies in spades to the Attorney General of the United States, to the Office of Counsel in the White House, and to the Director of the Central Intelligence Agency, and all who work for them, directly or by contract.

"As I started this trip, in Dublin a week ago, I saw a sign being held by a woman. It said, 'America is back!' Well my friends, she was absolutely right. And so let me repeat her words for the benefit of all our friends, and the caution of those who are our enemies.

"America Is Back!"

Secretary Adams was startled to be interrupted by loud and sustained applause, as his audience stood. Finally he was able to continue.

"That is why I wanted to go to Runnymede, with its traditions of *Magna Carta* and the rule of law, especially the great writ of *habeas corpus*. I had not realized fully before today just how dangerous that rededication would seem to our enemies. But you see, the very last thing that they want is for a reasonable United States of America, acting in full harmony with our finest traditions, and in concert with our many good friends.

"And so they sought to destroy us. I am told that with cooperation between British security forces and our own Embassy officials, that a mass assassination attempt at the field of Runnymede itself has today been thwarted. Nearly two dozen arrests of terrorists and their ringleaders have been made this very night.

"At their headquarters, leaflets were found. They trumpeted the expected triumph of their Operation Salah al-Din, or Saladin, which was their code name for the mass murder by the use of implanted IEDs at Runnymede, that they had planned. But they failed. As they will always fail.

"Our friends are resolute. Those who disagree with us will find us ready to discuss our differences in full candor. And those who seek to destroy us will find our resolve stronger than ever, because henceforth we will be united by the best in our heritage. We will not be divided by the counsels of fear and expediency."

Long, sustained applause.

"I would also like to say a word to our Muslim audience. What was attempted at Runnymede was said to have been done in the name of the great leader, and adversary of King Richard the Lionhearted, Saladin. But Saladin has always had a high reputation with us, known for his skill and his chivalry. And just within the past few days, there has been newly discovered proof of that stature.

"You will have heard of recent events in Dublin. We must, of course, let events take their course, as a trial will certainly be held. But the discovery that caught my attention was what seems to have been the reason for the murder of Ambassador Mary McGowan. It was a very old desk, with hidden compartments. The desk, now a rich part of Elizabethan history, may actually contain documents from that period, and even far earlier. Tests will of course be held on that point.

"But what a discovered medieval manuscript seems to tell us is something about the history of the Shroud of Turin. The claim is made that the Shroud of Turin was allowed to leave Jerusalem by Saladin himself, respecting the Christian tradition, as the Muslim holy writings always have done.

"And the Saladin that emerges from those pages is not a one dimensional fanatic warrior, but a principled man who attempts according to his own lights to do the right thing. He does not resemble unlettered fanatics that would strew bombs to cause mass murder on the field of Runnymede.

"What is the proof of this manuscript? Tests will be held, of course. But scholars of the period have already given their preliminary assessment that the documents surrounding this ancient manuscript are worthy of credence. These later documents are said to have been written by Christopher Marlowe, and by Dr. John Donne. They validate the medieval manuscript. They are major discoveries. Relating of course to the period of Shakespeare, they even contain references to him. These priceless documents will all be made public shortly.

"In an earlier day, Samuel Sewall stood in the Old South Church in Boston, and the light shone as his confession of error for the hysteria at Salem was read to the congregation. Let us learn from these recent sad events as Sewall's generation did, and go forward together with a spirit of renewal, learning from error, joyful for our discoveries. I hope they will unite all of us, as we should be united."

The audience rose in a standing ovation.

— — — — — — — —

"So this was the result of our careful planning, this *débacle*!"

"They were careful. This time. There will be other opportunities. You'll see."

"What do you mean?"

"Secretary Adams has proved to be a reasonable man. That will be his undoing."

Finis

Printed in the United States
by Baker & Taylor Publisher Services